Schuyler Hall Gilmore is 28 years old and lives in Texas with her two cats, Boo and Spookie. She graduated from Santa Fe University of Art and Design with a BA in creative writing and literature. She loves creating music, watching anime, and reading, but most of all, she enjoys telling stories. She has been creating stories since she started to talk and encourages everyone to follow their dreams no matter what.

To Gamma, for always believing in me and my dream! You will always be my favorite person.

Schuyler Hall Gilmore

SANCTUARY

AUSTIN MACAULEY PUBLISHERS™

LONDON · CAMBRIDGE · NEW YORK · SHARJAH

Ordering Information:
Quantity sales: special discounts are available on quantity purchases by corporations, associations, and others. For details, contact the publisher at the address below.

Publisher's Cataloging-in-Publication data
Gilmore, Schuyler Hall
Sanctuary

ISBN 9781641829861 (Paperback)
ISBN 9781641829878 (Hardback)
ISBN 9781645366607 (ePub e-book)

Library of Congress Control Number: 2019939414

www.austinmacauley.com/us

First Published (2020)
Austin Macauley Publishers LLC
40 Wall Street, 28th Floor
New York, NY 10005
USA

mail-usa@austinmacauley.com
+1 (646) 5125767

First and foremost, I would like to thank my God, who blessed me with a talent and a love for words. I will be grateful all the days of my life.

Thank you so much Mom and Dad for always encouraging me to follow my dreams and for being there for me and never giving up on me, even when I gave up on myself. I love you both more than any words could ever express.

Thank you to my brother, Chase, for always having the best advice and for encouraging me. I love you!

Thank you to my beautiful cat-children, Boo and Spookie, for the countless hours you've spent listening to me ramble on about *Sanctuary* instead of sleeping.

Thank you to Amanda Higgins, not my sister by blood but by choice, for always being there for me and for taking care of me, and most importantly, for listening to all my crazy story ideas since we were 11 years old. You rock and I love you!

A huge thank you to Sharon Forsyth for loving *Sanctuary* when I wasn't sure if I loved *Sanctuary*, and for making me finish the manuscript multiple times. You're awesome. *Sanctuary* and I thank you and love you!

Thank you Melloney Wood, Amelia Wilson, and Miranda Bass, for putting up with me and encouraging me to write *Sanctuary* and all my other stories. I love you guys!

Thank you to Megan Powell for setting up the 'GoFundMe' page and thank you to all the people who have donated to make *Sanctuary* possible!

Thank you, Jacey Ellis, for reading/editing baby *Sanctuary*, and for all your amazing comments and suggestions! You rock!

A special thank you to the editors at Austin Macauley who saw something in *Sanctuary* and were willing to take a chance on me! And thank you so much to my production team who helped my dream come true!

|Part One|

Io

Somewhere

Io shivers.

In this dream, there is no sun. Instead, a murky greenish-gray sky looms overhead. She stands on dirty, cracked pavement, tucked in the shadows of an alley—somewhere. She has seen this place before, in other visions. The once tall, silver buildings that encase her are now nothing more than jagged heaps of broken glass and bent metal. Smoldering skeletons. They are hollowed out, discarded.

Her stomach churns.

It is this place, somewhere far from her home in the valley, a place that has forsaken Paradise that Io dreads to dream of. Biting her bottom lip, she takes a step, the glass cracking beneath her chunky, black, combat boots. She tugs at her army-green coat, wishing for warmth that never comes.

Ash swirls around her like snow.

Before she has the chance to talk herself out of it, Io walks forward. The grass that peeks out from beneath the piling ash at the mouth of the alley is too green, too perfect. It must be fake. Everything in this place must be. How else could it be so full of destruction and despair? She thinks of death; of the Hell she has been told about since she was very young. That's what this place is—a hell on earth.

Her lips tug downward into a frown. How childish of her to be so naïve as to have not thought that there could be a place like this. Io isn't a child anymore—almost eighteen—and even though she has yet to witness the horrors of the world (no doubt because her mother, Chrezabel, has tried to shield her from it), she knows that evil exists.

She sees it every night in her dreams.

That is her curse—to see things. Things that have already happened, things that are to come... she sees all of it, and so does Chrezabel. She knows all too well why the angels were sent from Paradise to live in Spiritus Vallem—she knows why they have to save the earth.

11

"There will be a final ending," God had told them. "One I will not stop."

There are too many souls left to save, and they are running out of time.

Mostly everyone good has already been taken to Paradise. Those who are left in this place are either here to bring others to God, or to be punished. Humans called it 'The Rapture,' and only half-heartedly believed it could happen, until, at last, it did.

Io almost laughs, but the cold burns her throat. Lifting her hand to protect her eyes from the ash, she gasps and takes a swift step back, quickly dropping her hand back to her side. Like in other dreams, the fingers that greet her gaze are metallic, spiderlike spindles stretching out—an imposter's hand. She shakes her head, her black curls falling around her gaunt face. In the glass of the broken building beside her, she catches a flash of color from her lavender gaze.

Everything else here, besides the lawn, is gray and black and white. There is no beauty. Io frowns again and turns her attention to the mouth of the alley, where the lawn is waiting to be stepped on. There is a large, black marbled fountain in the center of the city's square, a brilliant black stallion rearing up, as if to face an unforeseen foe. She and this stallion are a lot alike, in the end, she thinks—both of them must face their fears and survive if they wish to see another day.

Chrezabel has told her many, many times that this is her fate. Her mother has predicted a horrible prophecy: one angel will try to destroy the world, but one angel will save it. She tells Io that Io is the one—that she will save them all in the end. Io shivers, but not from the cold.

A blur of red catches her eye.

A man has sauntered out in front of the fountain. He is wearing a jet-black uniform, decorated with red and silver stars, and a black beret that hides what is left of his short blond hair. He stares at her, his red mechanized eyes looking deep within her, like he can tell all of her secrets just by looking at her. It is a very predatory look—an animal about to strike its prey. This man is half-metal-half-flesh, a cyborg, like she has become in all of these visions; a monster. She shies away, deeper into the alley.

The man takes a step toward her, his metal mouth set in a terrible grin.

Calm down, she tells herself, taking a deep breath. Her heart races. She listens to the thudding sound of blood as it rushes through her body. *Stay calm.*

"Io," he says, his voice flat, too metallic to be real. "How nice it is to see you again. I must say, it is quite the surprise. I thought you were dead."

And somewhere, deep in her conscious, she knows she *was* dead, that this man had killed her, here in this faraway place from her home—yet she is very alive in the visions. Something marvelous has happened.

A knot forms in the pit of her stomach.

She considers his words and her own thoughts, tilting her head.

Something is not right.

"I would say the same," she finally says to the man, "but under these circumstances, this meeting is anything but *nice*."

This must be where it ends, she tells herself. *This must be how I will save them.*

In the valley, she's never had to save anyone. Not yet.

The man chuckles, a startling boom in the ever-quiet city around them. Somehow, his grin turns more sinister. She knows then that he must know. He must know how close to the final end everything is, how close he is to dying. She lets out a slow breath, watching the steam rise up, out of the alley. Neither one of them will make it out of this alive—she's seen it before, in other visions. That is, everything she has done until this point has led her to either a victory here, or an utter failure. Io knows she can't fail. The world is counting on her— both people she has yet to meet in the waking world, and those she will never meet in her lifetime.

She must not let them down.

"I can't let you live," Io finally says, the words heavy on her tongue. She doesn't want to kill anyone, but she has been created for this moment. Io wonders, had things not gone this way, if perhaps the two of them could have been friends. In every dream, he is not very likable. In every dream, he cares only for himself. Perhaps, in a different life, he is not so evil.

Perhaps, in the next life, he will be saved.

"I know," he says—and the dream starts to become hazy.

Io is about to open her eyes. Someone is about to wake her.

She fights to stay in the dream, just a little longer. She wants to know how it ends this time. She wants to *see* it.

"It's a shame that you must go with me," the man says.

You are Chosen, Io, Chrezabel whispers. *You will save the world from this horror.*

This dream world that she always seems to find herself in starts to shake. Glass and metal and paper fly into the air like confetti.

Someone touches her shoulder.

"I love you," a familiar voice says.

She turns to see who has spoken, but—

Io opened her eyes.

"You were having a nightmare," Kale said, his voice soft and gentle. "I'm sorry for waking you, but you were shaking."

She rubbed the sleep from her eyes, staring down at Kale's small six-year-old body, and sat up, pushing her quilt down over her knees. Though she had wanted to see the ending, she couldn't be upset at her little brother.

"Thank you, Kale," she said instead. She crawled from the bed. "You saved me... again."

Kale smiled.

Io let out a slow breath.

She grabbed his tiny hand and led him to her bedroom door. For an instant, her heart hurt—not because of the dream, but because very soon, she knew that Kale would not be able to wake her up. Her nightmares were going to become reality. And, very soon, Kale—along with everyone she knew from this life—would probably be dead.

"Not dead," Kale said. His curse (for every angel had one) was that he could read minds. He tugged on her hand. "We'll be reborn, and will simply be waiting for you, in Paradise."

How someone so young could be so wise, Io would never know. But she smiled anyway, thankful that her brother always knew just what to say to make her feel a little bit better.

David

Imogen Square

Lieutenant David Lancaster lifted the black beret from his head, running a hand through his damp, thick blond hair and looked out over the crowd of angry rioters with certain disdain in his pale blue eyes. He tugged at his black uniform jacket, fighting the cold. He could hardly hear his own thoughts over their unsynchronized shouting, much less the stark commands from his fellow officers as they tried to settle the situation. David let out a sigh. It had already gotten far too out of hand for his liking, but he knew there was nothing that could be done about any of it now. They would have to stand their ground in the square for hours, and continue to shout out pointless pleas for the irritated crowd to stop their rioting and return to their homes; if they had homes to return to.

Most of these people had probably come from the small outer cities where the Wasteland's rebels had begun to take siege. David supposed that some rebels had made their way into Neo Victoria and were among the rioters today—they were just as angry about their situation as the outer city civilians. The Demetrius Core had made enemies out of the rebels long ago when they had started their campaign in the Wastelands. Outside of the city walls— uncivilized humans and demons lived amongst the horrible creatures that the Great War had created with all its dark magic and nuclear warfare.

They had destroyed the world, and now they would do it again.

Like this riot, the war had gotten uncontrollable. It would continue to spiral out of control until some sort of leverage was made between the rebels and the cities. However, the odds of that happening any time soon were slim to none. The rebels were so low on the hierarchal ladder that this war would probably only end when they got what they wanted—the freedom and safety of the cities—or when they were destroyed. The Wastelands were too vast, though. There were far too many of them to kill. Until something good happened, David and his unit would be stuck on the crowded streets, every passing day, trying to stop rioters from hurting themselves or others, with little to no progress.

Rioters did not want to listen, they wanted to be heard. David was hearing them loud and clear, but there was nothing he could do about it.

At least twenty times already, David had tried his best to talk Graggöry out of the war. "Just give them what they want," he had said several times over. "Just give the people what they want."

All the war was doing was getting in his way, but he supposed he could use the war to his advantage. The weaker the Core was, the easier it would be to take it over.

He knew, though, that what he asked of Graggöry was impossible. Neo Victoria was a sanctuary city, and yet its inhabitants had recently shown their true colors. Stragglers from the Wastelands were not welcome—they were dirty and uncivilized. There was no room in the city, or in their hearts, for refugees.

It didn't matter. Every time he'd brought it to Graggöry's attention, it seemed to be more pointless than the last, with Graggöry not listening to a single word he said. That's what they got for electing a demon king.

Graggöry was too caught up in his own daunting problems to be concerned over what the people of Neo Erta, the new Earth, wanted or needed or demanded of him. Graggöry had been power-hungry before, after his father had been assassinated, but recently David had sensed a change in him. Something had shifted.

"I'm hearing voices," Graggöry told him. "I think I'm going insane."

Perhaps he was. That's what the rumors had said, anyway. But Graggöry was in too deep to just step down and walk away from this mess. He would have to finish what they started.

David looked up into the dark sky, holding a hand over his eyes to shield them from the falling ash: the daunting, constant reminder that their ancestors had destroyed the world. Their world was broken, and it had only just begun again. Aside from the Waste-landers, they had not been out from the Underground but for 50 years, and again they shouted for war and peace and were destroying all the progress that the world had made of beginning again.

It disgusted David how people were so quick to throw away their chances at life. The people this new world had birthed were undeserving of the second chance they were given.

Of course, Graggöry didn't think so.

"They're only a little undone," he had said to David one morning. "The world is only a little undone. It can be fixed."

David didn't think it could be fixed. Believing so would be foolish. Graggöry was feeding the Core complete and utter bullshit, and anyone who believed him was just as undeserving as the rioters on the street. He didn't think any of it could be undone in a way that would bring their world any peace, and perhaps giving the people what they wanted was not enough.

If they did that, the people would only grow greedier... always out to obtain something better than what they already had.

David supposed he was guilty of that himself, though he hardly wanted any part of it. He and his brother, Jeremy, would avenge their parents, and take over the Core, if it was the last thing he ever did. He had made a promise to Jeremy to do that much, even if that meant betraying his best friend and taking over a broken world.

David was tired, and ready for something new to happen.

Damn, he thought. *We're all just the same.*

He frowned. He did want more than what he had been getting out of life. He wanted that higher ranking—he would have gotten his higher ranking had it not been for Graggöry's little pet. She had ruined everything, but that hardly mattered.

They would all pay for it soon enough.

If he could, David would take the world from Graggöry, snatch it right out from under his nose—that demon king didn't want it, anyway. Not really. That had proved to be harder than David thought, though, and he was not mentally prepared for that sort of psychological warfare. Though he hated to admit it, he needed help taking Graggöry down. But who would help him? Who could be trusted? If he had learned anything from his friendship (or, what he thought was friendship) with Graggöry, it was that even the closest friend could turn on you. One moment, he was Graggöry's right hand man... and then that woman came along.

There was Jeremy. David suspected his dear brother would never betray him, but when he thought about it, a very uneasy feeling washed over him. Perhaps, Jeremy could not be trusted either.

The world was a muddled mess, but if David had the right tools, he supposed he could fix it. He could restore order amongst the hierarchy, somehow. Those poor, confused fools had an appetite that was easily sated. It would take a lot of time and pretty words, but it could be done.

The shouting in the square grew louder as a group of rioters broke through the unit's poorly made blockade, storming past the dazed soldiers and blossoming into the center of the square like ants after their mound had been kicked; a horde of them branched off, running to the other side where more rioters awaited them from behind the unbroken blockade.

"Damn," David cursed.

Everything was so unnecessarily anarchic.

David sighed and set his beret back onto his head, lifting the megaphone he had been holding at his side up to his lips. "Everyone, please vacate the premises, and return to your homes!"

The rioters were unmoved by this, their shouts growing more frantic.

"Those who do not return to their homes will be arrested," he said, cringing as his booming voice clashed with the loud cries from the horde. "Please, leave the square and go home."

"I have no home to return to!" one angry woman yelled in his face, tearing the megaphone out of his hand and throwing it to the ground. *"You people took my home from me!"*

A Waste-lander, he assumed.

"Get back, rebel," David hissed, pushing her away.

She stumbled back, hissing in return.

David supposed she had every right to be angry. He was angry, too. If his home had been taken from him, surely, he would be out on the dirty streets revolting as well. But it irked him when they became restless like this, when they attacked the people who were there to serve and protect them. The Demetrius Core was their friend, not their foe. Well, he supposed that was untrue where the rebels were concerned. The Wastelands had been forsaken long ago—the bombs that still fell, swept under the rug. President Graggöry urged the cities to turn a blind eye to it all. It was for their safety, he had said. The cities were indebted to the Core.

The woman, angrier now that he had pushed her away, huffed and reached out to push him back, when all of a sudden, a blast of white light cascaded over them, followed by an earsplitting boom. An explosion. Without thinking, David grabbed the rebel rioter and tossed her out of the way behind him.

Stunned, people stood in the square, staring, some bloodied, while others collapsed. Without thinking, David began to grab rioters and push them to safety. He knew that the majority of rioters were demons. That bomb had been made with light to disorient them, if not to kill them right off. His duty was to protect these people. No matter how much he disliked them, he didn't wish them dead. Not really.

He surveyed the square. The windows had all been blasted out from the storefronts—shattered glass was scattered on the sidewalks and on the plaza. The buildings seemed fine. The damage was repairable, but the people…

People were perched over their dead, sobbing and screaming and cursing the attacker. David made his way over to them, called out for them to seek shelter, but before anyone could heed his warning, another smaller blast set off, this time on the other side of the square.

His vision blurred.

People were shrieking.

There was a sharp sting in David's back and another on his side. He was disoriented by the heat and the ringing in his ears. He took a step forward before toppling to the ground. He tried to breathe, but it was too hot and too painful. Smoke plumed up over the fountain in the center of the square and blackened the already darkening sky.

Night was falling, not that it mattered.

He thought of everything he could to keep from thinking about the pain. He thought about how he was not ready to die, about how ironic that the people he lived to serve would be the death of him.

He coughed, blood splattering the pavement. He took a deep, agonizing breath and realized his lung was filling with blood; the shrapnel had gotten him.

Fuck, he thought. *I'm going to die.*

He grabbed his side like he could stop the pain or the blood, like he could heal himself. All around him, people were dead. The ones who were not, crawled across the fake lawn, toward the dirtied water of the fountain—to clean themselves, to check for wounds. Those who could had run away seconds after the blast; the only people left in the square were the ones who were too injured to leave, and the dead.

David coughed again, his mouth filling with blood. He would have laughed had it not been choking him. How pitiful he was. How meek and unfathomably human. He had never thought much on how he would die, but he never pictured it being quite like this. It irked him that this was the way he was to go—not in some heroic battle on the frontlines, but merely in a riot on the square. He spat, thick rich crimson, realizing that it now dripped from his nose as well. He was either going to die a slow, agonizing death or he would choke on his own blood. Neither sounded pleasant to him. He settled himself down onto the ground, a hand still pressed firmly against the open wound on his side. How pathetic he was, how—

David.

The voice was distant, soothing and sweet, like the lullabies his mother used to sing to him. He longed for it, for the comfort it washed over him.

David, my darling, come find me.

David had heard this voice before in his dreams, had memorized the way his name slipped off her tongue. He tried to take a deep breath, but he couldn't anymore. He tried to cough, tried to spit up more blood, but it was of no use. He felt himself starting to fade, and willingly he slipped into darkness—

Darkness so deep, it pains him to think of light. The dampness of the ground beneath him meets his eager curling fingers, and the shadows smell of mildew and musk. The air around him is colder than any cold he has ever felt. He shivers and lets out a slow breath.

He can breathe. He must be dead.

There is no pain. He feels almost… new again.

"Open your eyes," the voice says from beside him. "You're here with me now, my darling, and everything is going to be all right."

His eyelids flicker open. Everything is just as dark, save the woman's round pale face smiling down at him. The tips of her auburn hair graze across his face as she leans in closer, inspecting him. He has never seen anything quite like her before. She stares down at him with large, deep crimson eyes—a striking color he'd not have guessed was even possible.

"That's it, my darling," she coos, and he focuses on her mouth. Her lips are painted the same dark red as her eyes. "I've been waiting a very long time to meet you."

"Waiting?" he asks.

She nods and hurriedly helps him to sit up. Her hands are impossibly hot on his arm and his back. He coughs, but feels no pain.

"Are you an angel?"

She shakes her head.

"I need you to do something for me," she says. "I'm afraid you'll have to go back."

He blinks.

"Go back?" he asks, his voice laced with confusion.

She smiles, an almost unnatural smile.

"Yes, silly," she nearly giggles. "You aren't dying yet, and besides, my perfect darling—you're the only one who can help me now."

It sounds like it could be a lie, but oddly enough David doesn't care.

She drops her hands away from him and leans back, her palms digging into the ground. There is something about her, something strange that David can't put his finger on, something off and very dark that draws him to her. She's quite lovely.

"What are you?" he asks.

She laughs and stands, slowly lifting him along with her.

"My name is Lucie," she tells him.

"Lucie," he repeats.

She nods again, another bright, too wide smile plastered across her face. Her hair gently brushes against her pale shoulders. For the first time, he notices she's wearing an off-white sundress, spotted all over with dark red polka dots. *It suits her nicely*, he thinks. The longer he stares at her, he begins to notice an odd shadow that seems to cascade down her body: an aura that hovers all about her.

"That's right," she says. Her voice is high-pitched and precise.

"I'm glad I'm not dying," he tells her. He can't die yet. No. He is so close now to his goal. There are far too many things left to do. "I wasn't ready yet."

"Oh, nobody ever is," Lucie replies, in a sing-songy voice. "It's tragic, really."

Perhaps, he thinks, *she really is an angel.*

"I've too much to do," David continues, shaking his thoughts.

"I know," she says, and sounds a little annoyed.

"Ah, but you needed my help with something, you said?" David asks.

He smiles at her, his gaze focuses on her serious expression. Her smile has faded; her lips now contort in a lopsided line beneath her perfect nose. She is far too lovely to be real. He wants to reach out and touch her. Her gaze lifts and she stares back at him just as intently as he must be staring at her. He's been told before that he has a charming smile. It is nothing compared to hers, but he wonders if Lucie, his dear angel of death, thinks so, too.

She is truly fascinating. Her face is completely unreadable. He has no idea what she is thinking. That intrigues him.

"Yes," she says. "Are you going to help me?"

"Well," David says, "I suppose that largely depends on what exactly it is I'm supposed to do for you, wouldn't you say?"

"Oh," she sighs. The corners of her beautiful mouth twitch down into a frown. She looks him in the eye, not blinking. "Where's the fun in that? I was rather hoping you'd just say yes, no questions asked. I don't care much for cowards, nor do I care for disappointments."

David thinks this is a little odd, but again, he's not exactly bothered by it. He doesn't want her to frown. It pains him to see her look so distressed, though he hardly knows why. He reaches out to her, gently placing his hand on her arm. Without thinking he says, "Hey, I'll do it, okay? I'll do anything that you ask of me."

A slow, sly smile creeps onto her face as she continues to stare right into his eyes. "Anything? How lovely."

"Anything," he confirms.

"But you don't even know me," Lucie murmurs, looking away. Her smirk only grows. "Why would you ever do such a thing?"

David shakes his head. He doesn't have an answer for it. It just feels natural. He needs to please her.

"I just knew you were perfect, my darling," Lucie says, before he has the chance to change his mind, "but unfortunately, our time here is up for now."

David blinks again, a bit bewildered.

"You've not yet told me what it is you need for me to do," he says. He doesn't want to go away, doesn't want to wake from this dream—because that's what this has to be, just a cruel comatose delusion.

"Next time, my darling," Lucie says. She reaches out and touches his face, the tips of her fingers caressing his jaw. "I promise."

"But when will—" he can't finish. The rich, blissful feeling that overtook him previously is slowly descending once more. He closes his eyes, focusing on her fingers against his skin, before giving back into the darkness—

And when he opened his eyes again, he was in the back of an ambulance, barely conscious, but alive. He tried to speak, but a tube was protruding from his throat.

"Lieutenant Lancaster," a paramedic said, turning to face him. "You're going to be all right now, rest easy."

He wanted to say that he didn't want to rest, but the paramedic clicked a button on his IV and he drifted back into a peaceful slumber.

Crosbie
Imogen Square/The Metal Shop

Crosbie Scott, leaned back against the pale white bricked wall of a shop located on the furthest side of Imogen Square, and watched as people were either saved or discarded. He had made his way into the square moments after the second blast had gone off, and had tried his best to help those that he could and said silent prayers for those—the mortally wounded, and the dead—that he couldn't. Now all that was left to do was watch as people were carted off in the back of ambulances—his best friend's brother, being one of them. He had hoped to gather some information on David, but everything had happened so fast that he hadn't had the time to ask the paramedics anything, and as soon as his thoughts had caught up with him, David had already been whisked away off to St. Mary's. Well, Crosbie hoped it was to St. Mary's. That was the only hospital in Neo Victoria worth a damn. If anyone could save David, it was the doctors there.

It had been night for quite some time now, and surely people were missing him at home, but there was just something about being in the square after such an attack that rejuvenated Crosbie's inner fire. This would only help the resistance, in the end—now the rioters would be getting news coverage… their cause would be plastered all over the city and in the outer cities, as well. He clapped his gloved hands together, applauding the resistance. Those idiots had probably set the bombs off themselves, just for a little attention.

Crosbie shook his head and pushed himself from the wall. He needed to get back home. His father and sister—well, she couldn't really be called his sister—were probably waiting for him. He'd have to come up with a pretty clever excuse to get himself out of trouble, but he didn't mind. For all he knew his father was probably out late, drinking with friends. That's all he had done since Crosbie's real sister had passed. Crosbie guessed the passing of his mother hadn't helped. He frowned and tugged at the messenger bag that hung at his side, dusting it off as best as he could as he ducked under some pallets in an alley. There was a certain thrill in knowing how much trouble he could be in if his father found out where he had been all day.

He could lose the apprenticeship altogether, if he didn't play his cards right. That would disappoint him, but life would go on. If anything, he could still work for Jeremy. Jeremy always needed odd jobs done, and he always picked Crosbie or David to help, because neither of them would ever open their mouths to rat him out. Crosbie wouldn't, at least. He didn't know if he could say the same about David. There was something about the lieutenant that didn't sit right with Crosbie, something he could never quite put his finger on. David made him feel uneasy… but Jeremy was all right. He and Jeremy had been friends for the past four years, but it had seemed like they'd been best mates for ages. Crosbie laughed to himself as he rounded his street's corner. He was probably Jeremy's only friend, but that was okay with him.

Crosbie didn't like sharing, anyway.

Upon reaching his house, he climbed up the fire escape and snuck in through the open kitchen window. Though he was trying his best to not make any noise, he hit a pan in the sink, and it clobbered down to the floor. He flinched and crouched down to pick it up.

"Where have you been?"

He looked up to see his sister's clone, Jynx, sitting at the kitchen table, a book opened in front of her. She ran a hand through her dark hair and closed the book. She snapped her fingers and the kitchen light turned on.

Mischievous shadows danced in her piercing green eyes. She leaned back and crossed her arms in front of her chest, shaking her head but never once looking away from him. He cursed under his breath. There was no escaping her—Jynx knew everything. There was just something about clones, he figured, that made things that way. He smiled at her.

"You look like you've been through hell and back," she said, a little worry in her voice. He looked down at himself and shrugged. He was covered in ash and soot, but he wasn't hurt. It could have been a lot worse.

"I'm fine," he said, flashing another smile. "I was just running an errand for Dad—"

"You went to watch the riot again, didn't you?" Jynx asked, frowning as she scooted the chair back. She stood and walked over to him, inspecting his face and then his arms. "Jesus, Crosbie, you could have been killed today. What were you thinking?"

"I was just having a little fun," Crosbie said, he backed away from her touch and shooed her off with a hand. "I didn't know there would be an explosion."

"Max won't be happy about this," Jynx said, shaking her head. Her eyes sparked to life again as she smirked. "I guess it's a good thing he isn't home."

Relief flooded through Crosbie.

"And you aren't going to tell him, either," Crosbie said, grabbing her shoulders. "This is between you and me. A secret, got that?"

She cocked her head to the side and pursed her lips, thinking. "Well, I guess so."

"Swear you won't tell him," Crosbie said, a little panicked. "If Dad finds out I was in the square, he'll—"

"I'm not going to tell Max," Jynx said. "But in return you have to take me to see the ducks."

Jynx was obsessed with the ducks—probably because they were artificially made, too. Every animal in Neo Victoria was a clone. Most real animals hadn't survived the Great War.

"Can't you go by yourself?" Crosbie finally asked. "You're twenty-two-years-old, you don't need a chaperone *every* time. It's just right down the road—"

"It's no fun when I'm by myself," Jynx interrupted, pouting. "You haven't gone to see the ducks with me in weeks. You know I don't want to walk to the park by myself, especially not with all the riots and—"

"Okay, okay," Crosbie groaned, hoping she'd shut up. "I'll take you to see the stupid ducks. Get your coat."

"Oh, not tonight," Jynx said, going back to the table. "I have to study."

"Then tomorrow," Crosbie said. "I'll take you to see the ducks after I work on my project."

"It's a deal," Jynx said. She opened the book back up and flipped a couple of pages. "You want to see something cool, Crosb?"

Crosbie sat at the opposite end of the table and ran a hand through his hair. He supposed it looked gray instead of black, with all the dust that had been flying around earlier. He would have to take a shower before Max got home.

"Sure," Crosbie said. "Show me."

"Okay," Jynx said. She lifted her hand, palm up, above the table and whispered a small incantation, a purple sphere of fire bursting to life an inch away from her hand.

"Whoa," Crosbie said, trying his best to sound excited. "You know; Jeremy will think that's cool. You should impress him with that, next time."

That broke her concentration and the flame died. She gaped at him from across the table. She clapped her hands together and said, "Do you really think he'd be impressed?"

Crosbie rolled his eyes. Her obsession with his best friend was kind of entertaining but Jynx would never get anywhere with Jeremy, since he was so focused on his work with the Core. That and, Jeremy was oblivious to any special attention females gave him.

"Yeah, totally," Crosbie lied. "You already impress him with your magic all the time."

"I thought he wasn't really into magic," Jynx replied.

"Well, he's skeptical about it, but… I think we've changed his mind, sort of."

"You'd better go clean up before Max gets back," Jynx said, flipping through pages in her book. "You don't want him asking questions."

"Okay," Crosbie said, standing from the table. "I'll see you in a bit. Keep up the good work."

Jynx nodded her head and started chanting again, focusing her attention back to her spells. Crosbie sighed, thankful for that, and walked to the back of the apartment, to gather some clean clothes. He had been avoiding Jynx for a while now, but he supposed she wasn't so bad. She just wasn't his real sister, though she looked identical enough to the real Jynx. He paused in the hallway to watch another flame come to life above Jynx's palm.

"It would be better if you just gave up on Jer," he said, but she didn't hear him.

Jeremy

St. Mary's Hospital

Everything seemed to be completely falling apart; however, maybe a twenty-four-year-old was not supposed to have their life so completely put together, and this was just the universe's way of cruelly putting him back in his place. Whatever it was, Jeremy Lancaster was not having any of it.

He paced the length of the wide, mirrored, sliding glass door in front of the ICU wing of St. Mary's Hospital, deep in the heart of Neo Victoria. This was probably the best hospital there was, in any of the bigger inner cities, and he found some comfort knowing that his brother had been brought here; however, he still felt an urgent sense of anxiousness that had pitted itself deep in his core, because things weren't looking too good for David.

"He's dying, Jeremy," the nurse, Clara, a slender brunette that he knew from his years at the medical academy had told him last night. "It's not usually my place to tell people these things, but the doctor said it might be easier to take from me, since we were good friends, you know?"

Jeremy had wanted to laugh. They were far from 'good friends,' ever since David had broken her heart (and she was mostly mad at Jeremy for introducing them to each other). But he had swallowed his snide remarks and instead asked, "So there's nothing you can do?"

"I'm sorry, Jer, but it's entirely up to him now," Clara confirmed.

Bullshit, he had wanted to say.

There were things they could do. They lived in a world of science and magic, and anything was possible, if you knew the right people. He knew some people. Hell, the hospital knew some people—but most magic had been outlawed a few months back, a play, he figured, to help keep the Demetrius Core in power. Magic scared people. Science could be explained, but magic could not. Even if magic had been outlawed, the scientific field was continuously growing; medical theory, medicine making, the creation of fully functioning artificial organs, were always expanding. Science was doing fantastic things for the world. There was, however, the question of how ethical any of these things were.

When it came down to it, the hospital had plenty of options, ethical or not; they didn't want to have to deal with the backlash of the wealthy Neo Victorians. The only reason the hospital had tried keeping him alive this long, was because David was the highest-ranking lieutenant in the Demetrius Core, and President Graggöry Demetrius II's best friend. People like David were not easily replaced.

Jeremy wasn't so convinced that they were trying their hardest to save his brother. If only Jeremy and David had come from an aristocratic family lineage—if they had had Old Money—then something more would have been done about his brother's life.

Jeremy paused his pacing long enough to stare at his reflection in the mirrored glass. His auburn hair was mussed, his pale face unfamiliarly gaunt. There were dark circles under his hazel eyes. He looked like hell. Running a hand through his hair, he walked to the wall beside the door and propped himself up against it. He stared at the holographic screen, precariously perched in the corner of the waiting area. For a top-notch medical facility, this place certainly didn't look the part. He hoped they had fired their interior decorator.

On the flickering screen, a news story was rolling about the explosion that had happened in the square. The news reporter, a pretty blonde with too-large blue eyes—Jeremy assumed it was horrible lighting that made them look that way—stared at the camera with a practiced, serious expression. He chuckled. It was almost too much. He looked away from the screen, tilting his head back against the wall and closing his eyes.

Everything was so messed up thanks to Graggöry Demetrius II, that insufferable demon who ruled them all like it was just some sort of game.

If Jeremy had believed in a god, he would have prayed for a lot of things. That seemed to work for all the other miserable hospital goers, though he had hardly seen anyone except for Clara, the three days he'd been lodging in the ICU's waiting room. At some point, he figured that he should probably go home, but he didn't want something tragic to happen to David while he was gone. Though he wasn't very sentimental, David was his brother, and the only family he had left in the world—so he would stay here for David, until he was awake or stable or dead.

For the first time in a long time, he thought of his mother, Adalyn. Adalyn Lancaster had probably been the nicest, kindest person Jeremy had ever known. There was probably no one left in Neo Victoria—in Neo Erta, even—who was kind and caring and giving as his mother. Unfortunately, Adalyn had died fourteen years ago when Jeremy was ten, in a tragic accident, out in the

Wastelands. His poor, wonderful mother had been out there, teaching the Waste children how to read (the Bible of all cursed things), on a doomed mission trip with her church, when the Core had dropped a bomb on the village. He liked to think her death was quick, and she had not suffered.

If the loss of their mother had not been enough for them, their father, who was a general in the Core, was killed mere days later, under what Jeremy considered to be suspicious circumstances. David had kept the details from Jeremy, and as he got older, he found that he just didn't care to ask. He assumed the Core killed his father because, after his mother had died, Adler Lancaster had wanted to leave the Core, but he knew too much. Jeremy would probably never know what really happened, but the death of his parents had driven him to where he was today: Head Scientist of the Demetrius Core. He had to admit that he'd had a little help from David—he probably would never have gotten this far on his own.

That didn't matter anymore.

Being discharged was not part of the plan.

He supposed it was up to David now, to take down the Core from the inside. David could probably do it all on his own. Jeremy lived for the day that the Core would crumble, whether it was because of him or not. He frowned, shoving his hand deep into his pocket, crumpling the letter he'd received just hours ago from Graggöry. The sniveling, greasy haired messenger had been almost too scared to give him the letter. The thought of him made Jeremy chuckle despite it all. The Core would be nothing without him, just as the Core would be nothing without David. Hopefully, his brother could pull through, and if he didn't—

Graggöry Demetrius II had something else coming if he thought he could get away with any of this. It was his fault the square had been bombed in the first place. Neo Victorians couldn't very well turn a blind eye to it now that it was in their inner-city walls. Graggöry wouldn't make it much longer. The people already yelled in the streets for a new president, for a new government. Jeremy hated him. Whatever happened to him, he had it coming. That's what he got for acting so regal and above the rest of the lowly peasants of Neo Erta. How demons had ever gotten on top of the hierarchy ladder, Jeremy would never understand. They were awful creatures. They couldn't be trusted. Jeremy would do something about all of this—he would take Graggöry out, somehow.

The door slid open, knocking him out of his thoughts, and Clara stepped through, glancing to him with, what he thought, was a bit of unease. Her green eyes danced in the flickering hospital fluorescents. Their eyes met. She moved a strand of her brunette hair behind her ear. He wondered if she had bad news.

Jeremy let out a sigh and asked, "Can I see him now?"

She locked her fingers together in front of her and looked down, away from him, shaking her head.

"I'm afraid, not yet," she said, her voice just a whisper. It comforted Jeremy, despite the disappointment he felt at not being able to see his brother.

"Well, when can I?" he asked, frowning.

"Tonight," Clara replied. "Tonight, or tomorrow morning."

"So, he's doing better?"

Clara nodded. "He's doing much better now, but still needs his rest. The doctor has him on a strong pain medication."

His shoulders relaxed as relief flooded through him. David would live, that lucky bastard. Jeremy knew his brother had it in him to survive this, all along—after all, David was the resilient one.

Luckily for Jeremy, he was only a Core Scientist—well, he had been a Core Scientist until ten o'clock this morning. He mumbled under his breath and watched Clara for a moment before thanking her.

"It's my job, Jer," she said with a bright, white smile. "Can I get you anything? You've been out here for a while."

"No, thank you. I'm fine," Jeremy replied, not really trusting Clara's overly caring attitude. He always felt she was up to something.

Clara turned around and reentered the wing, the sliding glass doors closing behind her. Jeremy watched her, almost sad to see her go. David would be so disappointed in him for not having made a single move on Clara—David had broken her heart so Jeremy would have a chance, but that plan had swiftly gone south now that she hated both of them. It wasn't really his fault, though. Losing his job and dealing with his dying brother really put a damper on any hopes of having a decent social life. Who was he kidding? He was so dedicated to his work—to the plan—to be social with anyone.

He was probably the loneliest twenty-four-year-old in all of Neo Erta, though he did have David and Crosbie. But Crosbie was like family—so he wasn't sure he could count that.

He glanced at his watch. Nesa would be missing him at home.

Jeremy shrugged and paced in front of the door a few more times before moving to sit down in one of the chairs in the waiting area. He squirmed in the chair, the hard cushion hurting his back. Frowning, he leaned back, tilting his head up so that he could stare at the ceiling. He squinted his eyes at how bright it was. He wondered what he would say to his brother when he finally came to. He wondered what there was to say.

Congratulations, he thought. *You didn't die!*

Io

Somewhere

Io reaches out to turn the rusting, fake-gold knob of a small, chipping, maroon painted door. Tonight, she is not part of the dream, merely a guest, viewing fate from afar. She steps onto the first of many crooked steps that lead down into a damp, dark room—the basement of an old house somewhere far from the valley. In the valley, they have very small outdoor buildings for storage. She's never set foot in a basement before, at least not in the waking world.

She peers down the length of the rickety stairs, to the middle of the room, where a bright light is shining down on a body strapped to a table.

She eases down the stairs, one by one, leaning against the wall for support as she focuses on the body. It's a young woman wearing an oxygen mask, her thick black hair is in brambles and hiding her face, but she looks eerily similar to Io. Io runs a hand through her own hair, watching as the tips shimmer in the flickering Florescent light.

"All right, sweetheart," someone says from across the room, quickly approaching the body on the table. "Let's see if we can't fix you back up."

Io turns her attention to the young man as he steps into the light. He moves his hair out of his face, muttering something about getting a haircut. She smiles. She's seen this young man many times before in different visions. Jeremy, she believes his name is. In the beginning, she didn't much care for him—he wasn't very pleasant, but he had grown on her these many late hours she spent stealing glimpses of borrowed time.

Slowly, the body comes together—all her missing pieces are replaced by newer, better parts. She looks down at her hands made of flesh and shivers. This must be where she changes—where everything in her fate changes.

Jeremy pushes away from the table for a moment, switching the bit on his drill, and mumbling to himself, when the body stirs. He looks over to her and smiles a genuine, full smile unlike anything Io has ever seen.

"You're awake," he says, still switching the bit. "I'm glad. I lost you several times until the serum took. David thought I would never have you stable."

Stable.

Io looks back to her hands, flexing her fingers. In a few short weeks, she is sure nothing in her life will ever be stable again. Change is coming. Her mother says so, and her dreams only confirm it.

The dream begins to fade.

She is about to wake up.

Very soon, she knows, she will lose her family and her beliefs and even herself, but there is always a flickering hope in the dream world. A voice, deep within her, whispers: *You will find yourself again, and you will save them.*

David

St. Mary's Hospital

David felt completely disparaged, being so weak and so fragile, so unfathomably mortal. It pained him to think he'd almost died in such an unnecessary way. However, he was still alive, and that was all that really mattered, he supposed. His whole body hurt, though, especially his side and what he could only assume was his punctured lung. His head had not stopped throbbing for days, probably, he figured, due to the morphine they had tried giving him on that first night. That had had little effect on the excruciating pain he'd been feeling. The only comfort he had found in any of this was that he would soon see Lucie again.

He closed his eyes, thankful for the brief darkness that flooded over him. Hospital lights were too bright—almost as bright as the explosion had been. It was impossible for him to get any real sleep around here, between the lights and the incessant comings and goings of the staff, but a nurse would be here soon, and she would administer his new pain medicine, and perhaps he would sleep then, and when he did sleep, he hoped to see Lucie. He had to know what she needed from him—he didn't care if she was just a figment of his imagination, because she felt so real that maybe she was. She had to be.

And if she was real, he would find her.

His thoughts were interrupted by Clara, his ex-girlfriend, who happened to be his nurse. He had been pleasantly surprised when she hadn't tried to kill him—he probably deserved it after what he'd done to her. She quietly-but-not-so-quietly walked up to his bedside and began to mess with his IV drip. He kept his eyes closed. It was best to maintain that he was sleeping, as to not have to start small talk with her, even if she was very pretty and even if he—sort of—regretted letting her go. If there was one thing David hated more than rioters, or the war, or even almost dying, it was forced small talk. He liked to get straight to the point, wanted deeper, more meaningful conversation, when he bothered to talk to others. Clara would give him an earful, probably—he didn't want that either. Clara ran a thermometer across his forehead and wrote his temperature down on his chart. She stepped away from the bed and flipped off the lights, closing the door as she left. He was left in total darkness—

And then Lucie is here. She watches him from where she is perched—on an almost too-wide wooden swing, under a giant tree. Her pale hands clutch the fraying tan rope as she leans back in the swing, watching him. He walks toward her, shielding his eyes from the ash. They are in the countryside; a place he has only been to once or twice before. Here, the land has not been diced up and developed; everything is wild and open, though they are still safe inside of the outer city walls. He remembers this tree, he finds, as he looks up at it—his mother had brought them and Jeremy to it, once when Jeremy was very small. This is a place he holds very dear to his heart. Of course, his angel knows this place. It is the setting of his fondest memory of his mother.

"Lucie," he says in greeting, when he finally makes it up to the swing.

He looks her over. She is wearing a white blouse, with the same red polka-dots as her dress, and tight black jeans. Her overcoat is blood red, and so long that it is almost dragging the ground.

"I've been waiting," he finishes.

"As have I, my darling," Lucie says. She leans back a little further and kicks out her feet, slowly lurching the swing forward and back again. "I've a lot to tell you."

He leans back against the tree, crossing his arms in front of his chest as he watches her swing. He's somehow traded his hospital gown for his Core Uniform, and he's thankful for that because the countryside is cold, so far from the warmth of the bustling city. Lucie looks so innocent in this dream, though there is still something dark about her.

"Yes," David says. "You've still not told me what it is you need me to do."

"I'm afraid that when I tell you, you won't like me anymore," Lucie says, halting briefly. She looks to him, with her large crimson gaze, her lips puckered in a frown.

"Oh," David says, with a chuckle. "I don't think I could ever not like you."

This revelation stuns him. What has gotten into him lately? Why is he so smitten with her when she is only a dream?

"Well, if that's the case, there are a few things you should know."

"Such as?"

"First, your friend—the president, that demon king, Graggöry—" she pauses for a moment, her face contorting like she is trying to figure out how to explain something. "I don't know if I should tell you this or not."

"Tell me," David pleads.

"I don't know if you've noticed, or heard the rumors, but he's going a little bit insane. Believe it or not… that's my doing. I don't want to go into all the details, but that's all you really need to know about that."

He cocks his head to the side, intrigued. "Go on."

"Well, I'm working on him as best as I can, but things are going a bit more slowly than I would like, and I'm hoping that by getting your help, I can move things along a bit more quickly."

Lucie pauses again and scrunches her nose.

David considers what she's saying. This is his best friend they're talking about—but it's not like he's not conspired against Graggöry before. Graggöry had abandoned him for that wretched street-trash. He supposed they weren't really friends anymore.

"What you, and the rest of the Core, don't know, is that the unrest in the Wastelands is about to hit its high point. They're angry—they have every right to be—and they're going to show Graggöry and the rest of you very soon how angry they are. A lot of people are going to die, my darling," she continues when he doesn't say anything.

This doesn't surprise him.

"There needs to be a balance, but it's far too late for that, and Graggöry is too prideful to give in to them now. If a demon is to be in control of your world, he should be fair and just—he should listen to what all the people want. Graggöry is too busy following his own personal agenda."

David nods his head in agreement.

How far his friend had fallen.

"However," Lucie says, that sly smile creeping back onto her face. "I know that you desire the position of ruler, and I know how to get you there, if you'd like."

"I'm listening," David says.

"Well, you see… if you help me get rid of Graggöry, I'll give you the whole world," Lucie says, her voice barely a whisper, as if she is a little unsure of herself.

He thinks for a moment. This truly is complete mutiny. Graggöry is—was—his friend, before the war and that girl had formed a rift between them. It wasn't a question of whether or not he was capable of doing something like this—he was definitely capable of doing it, he had been thinking about doing it on his own before Lucie had ever mentioned it—but was he really ready for that kind of power? He pushed his fear aside. This was for Lucie. He wanted the world, and he wanted Lucie (though he hardly knew why). He could do this. He was ready.

"I told you before," David says. "I'll do anything you say. I meant it."

"Good," Lucie says. "Then next time. Next time I'll tell you more. However, your brother is waiting for you. He's been waiting a long time. I think you should probably go."

He wants to tell her that his brother can keep waiting, but she is already fading from his vision.

"Until next time, my darling," she says, and then she is gone—

David opened his eyes, squinting against the glare of the lights. He turned his head to the side and lifted a hand to shield his eyes. Jeremy was sitting in the chair by his bedside, his head tilted back, his hand over his eyes as well. David coughed to get his attention. He flinched, a pain rushed through his chest. Damn punctured lung. Jeremy jerked in the chair, moving his hand away from his eyes and smiling down at David, with what David thought, seemed like genuine happiness.

"David—thank God," Jeremy said.

The irony of Jeremy thanking God was not lost on David. He smirked at his brother. He was thankful that the annoying tube had finally been removed from his throat.

"You didn't think I would be killed off that easily, did you?" David asked, but his voice sounded soft and scratchy, so foreign to him.

"No, of course not," Jeremy laughed, but it sounded like a lie.

David chuckled, though it was slightly painful. If truth be told, he had thought he was gone as well. He didn't blame Jeremy for thinking this was the end.

"Well, what have I missed?" David asked. He must have been out for days, or even weeks—all the days had blended together until he had no way of knowing how many days he'd really been in the hospital. Jeremy looked like a mess. His hair was rumpled and a little greasy. He had bags under his usually striking hazel eyes. They were a dull brownish color today. He supposed Jeremy must be really tired. "Anything interesting?"

"Nothing much," Jeremy said. "They caught the guy who detonated those bombs in the square, and after interrogating him, Graggöry had him executed—that was pretty exciting, I guess. Looks like Graggöry is finally tired of those rioters, too."

"Well, I'm glad they caught the bastard, and I'm glad he's dead," David said, nodding his head. "I would have killed him myself, but I've been a little preoccupied. I'm glad Graggöry finally did something right, though. *Good for him.*"

Jeremy laughed, probably at the sarcasm, but then he frowned. His aura had shifted; a dark halo seemed to hover about him in the bright hospital lights. "Oh, and there's something else."

David's brows furrowed together as he watched his brother. He thought for a moment that maybe he was really dying, and Jeremy was going to have to break the news to him.

"What is it?" David asked, almost dreading whatever the answer was.

"Well," Jeremy started, sighing. He ran a hand through his unkempt hair before shoving it into his pocket. He pulled out a couple crumbled papers and handed them to David. "Just—read this."

David took the papers and smoothed them out. He read it:

To Whom It May Concern:

On this, the 23rd day of October, in the 57th year of Our Glorious Neo Erta. I, President Graggöry Demetrius II, of the Royal Descent, hereby proclaim the dishonorable discharge of Dr. Jeremy A. Lancaster, from his position as Head Researcher of the Demetrius Core Scientific Guard, until further investigation, for the following reasons:

A.) Dr. Lancaster has been deemed Mentally Unsound, a level 4, by Core psychiatrists, due to his psychopathic tendencies, including lack of emotion toward failed experiments (which in all cases have ended in the death of the subject). He has lost sight of reality. He is a danger to himself and those around him—a leading reason for most discharges made by the Demetrius Core (though the character of this particular case deems it dishonorable).

B.) In this particular case (though the test subjects were all convicted criminals sentenced to death) a murder trial has been set to examine Dr. Lancaster's innocence. An investigation has been opened to examine whether or not the acts of Dr. Lancaster can be defined as treason, and thus used against him in trial. Until further notice, Dr. Jeremy A. Lancaster is heron dismissed of his scientific duties, and is no longer permitted to preform experimentations of any kind.

With best regards,
President Graggöry Demetrius II

David set the letter down on the bed beside him and ran a hand through his hair. He glanced at his brother, who was sitting in the chair, his head now in his hands, shoulders slumped, clearly bothered by the whole situation. David thought of what he could say.

"Graggöry can't do this," David said, evenly. It was completely wrong. Graggöry had known all along what could happen to those convicts—and they were just convicts, they were going to die anyway. He let out a slow breath. "He was the one who gave you permission to use those convicts—he didn't care what happened to them before."

"People were really angry when they caught wind of the situation," Jeremy said, sighing into his hands. "They said it was more humane to execute them properly, or some bullshit. I don't know. I knew it was only a matter of time before this happened."

"We will fix this," David said, matter-of-factly. He had done it before. Hell, he had been the one who had gotten Jeremy the position in the Core in the first place—Graggöry would listen to him. Maybe their friendship wasn't completely void—yet. And in the end, if taking to Graggöry did him no good, he would find another way to get his brother back into the Core. This was only a small bump in the road. They could still continue with their plan.

The Core would fall, and Jeremy would have just as much of a part in its demise as David would. They were in this together, for now. Besides, he needed Jeremy's help. He needed that experiment to work.

"I will fix this," David said again, confidently. "I promise, Jeremy."

Jeremy looked up at his brother, a little hope restored in his red-rimmed eyes.

"Okay," Jeremy said. "Thank you."

David nodded and leaned back against the hospital pillow, sinking into them, they were so soft. He had a lot of planning to do, but first, he needed more rest. He would be no good to Lucie or even to Jeremy if he was not well. He closed his eyes, only intending to keep them that way for a moment, but before he could stop it, he felt himself drifting back to sleep.

Lucie
Hell

Lucifer peeled out of *her* skin the way people shed their clothes. Her careful, gorgeous façade melted away to reveal the true, disfigured being underneath it. God had taken her beauty from her long ago, when he had cursed her to live for eternity in these fiery chambers of Hell. She was damned to live life this way, horribly scarred, her beautiful wings ripped from her back, never again to see the light of Paradise. She chortled and flexed her fake, bat-like wings—this was as good as the lingering magic she still obtained could do. They were nothing like her wings before, so bright and lovely and perfect. Everything about her had been perfect, and that was why God had done this—because he was frightened of her, because she was everything he was not. She smiled, her too-wide-lips stretching her contorted face. The remnants of David's 'Lucie' puddled at her feet, before fading from her entirely. The only likeness they shared were their eyes: burning, bright crimson spheres, the only eyes of their kind.

Oh, she was indeed a sly one; God had not taken her perfect wit, when he had taken everything else. That was probably a mistake, on his part—one he would someday come to realize, but by then, it would be too late for him to save himself. She couldn't help but to cackle at that—God on his knees, begging her for forgiveness. Just thinking of it brought her such great joy, joy she had thought long ago that she would never feel again.

This entire antic with David was just too fun. She thought so, at least. She had picked David, out of a large group of Core members for two reasons: because he was Graggöry's right hand man, and because he had long ago forsaken the idea of God. People who believed in any higher power were harder to break. Lucky for her, this had all worked out. She had David right where she wanted him, eating out of the palm of her hand. The poor, handsome fool. She sometimes felt a little bit awful about what she was going to do with David. After watching him for several months, she had sort of taken a liking to him.

When she had first decided to show herself to David, she was afraid the plan wouldn't take, that David would see through her glamour and know that he was being deceived into doing something utterly unthinkable—but he had taken to the glamour very well, and he had agreed, gloriously, to help her with no questions asked. She hadn't really had to glamour him much at all, only enough to push him in the right direction. He had agreed to everything mostly of his own free will—she had hardly had to do anything at all. All it had taken was a little deceptive beauty.

She had only cheated a little bit. She had never been one for rules anyway.

Now all she needed to worry about was Graggöry. Hopefully, David could get that taken care of, but if not, she was pretty sure Graggöry was also right where she needed him to be—going a little bit insane, and perhaps, at any moment, prepared to end it all for her. But, she couldn't kill him just yet. There were still a few things she needed him to do.

After that, she would let David end him.

All she needed was a little time, but it was time she feared she did not have.

Feeling a bit tired, she climbed up the black marble stairs that led to her throne of iron and bones, before falling back into it and lounging, as she often did when she was bored. She looked up at the endless black ceiling and smiled again. This was too easy. She wondered if God knew anything of her plan. After all, the mortals believed he was All Knowing, and sometimes it seemed so—but Lucifer knew the truth. He did not know everything. He only pretended to.

"Oh God... you poor, righteous fool," she laughed, staring up into what she could only imagine was the infinite space between Hell and Paradise. "Whatever will you do now?"

She laughed with joy, a mad cackle that echoed in the vast darkness beyond the fire. All of her suffering would soon be over. If everything went as planned—and it would go as planned—she would finally have what she always wanted: Hell and Heaven and the whole world bowing at her feet.

Very soon.

She glanced to the fire that burned around her throne and smiled.

"Finally," she whispered to the fire. "Finally, my time has come."

Jeremy
Lydia District

Discharged—dishonorable at that.

Jeremy sneered and tried to hold back a baleful laugh as he walked down the filthy, crowded streets of the Capitol, headed toward his little townhouse in the Lydia District of Neo Victoria. He'd been at the hospital for four days straight, waiting for David to wake up, and then waiting some more to make sure David was going to be all right. He was sure that Nesa probably missed him. He pulled his scarf up more securely around the lower half of his face, the fabric sticking to the stubble on his chin, as the ash continued its fifty-seven-year (but probably longer) constant descent from the darkening sky. A dreary reminder to the Neo Erteans to not be like those before—the starters of the Great War. They called the phenomenon, The Falling. No one knew when or if it would ever stop. The ash caught onto Jeremy's sleeve and he watched as it melted into the dark grey fabric like snow.

He hated it.

He hated everything about this world, save its incredible scientific expansion. New things were being discovered constantly, almost every day, and every new finding thrilled him immensely. It was a glorious age for the scientific mind, for him. Only—

He sighed and reached into his pocket, pulling out the crumpled letter from Graggöry and scoffing a bit at how pretentious the bastard really was. At the hearing, Jeremy had found the contents of the letter to be quite humorous. He had laughed, even. However, the cold and the ash had a way of changing things, and made it all a little less laughable, leaving a sort of rage he hadn't felt in ages growing in his gut.

But David had said he would do something about it, and Jeremy believed him. David had a way of being able to fix all of Jeremy's mess-ups, in a way only an older brother could. David was also the reason Jeremy had gotten that position in the Core in the first place, so maybe he could pull off a miracle and get Jeremy reinstated.

David was good friends with Graggöry, after all.

Jeremy crumpled the letter back up, shoving the damned thing deep into his pocket. He cursed the entire Core as he rounded the corner of his block. Neo Erta's whole governing faction had a way of ruining everything, it seemed. The war was really mucking things up for them, and Jeremy certainly did not feel sorry for their suffering. In fact, if the rebels took everything, it would be almost a little satisfying.

With the tip of his boots, Jeremy kicked at the piles of ashen snow that had clumped onto the sidewalk's edge, avoiding the eyes of a street-rat beggar who stuck his long, bony fingers out, searching for an offering. Jeremy didn't have anything to give, and even if he had had something, he probably wouldn't give it away to the beggar anyway.

The beggar continued following him all the way to his front steps, a feeble arm still outstretched and beckoning. Jeremy tried shooing him away. The world wasn't so giving anymore, but much colder and crueler, like the man it had created in him.

"Just a bite to eat," the beggar said, but Jeremy shook his head. Kindness got you either nowhere or killed. His mother was proof of that, rest her soul. The beggar kept on down the sidewalk, muttering curses under his alcohol-laced breath. *Good riddance.*

Jeremy took his ID card from his other pocket and held it up to the scanner on the door. The scanner's red light worked its way down the card before a cheerful voice welcome him.

"Welcome back, Jeremy," his Neo Erta Security Assistant said in its bubbly, electronic, girly voice. "Security code, please, sir."

"Ah, Nesa, vigilant as ever," Jeremy chuckled before entering his code onto the dial beside the scanner.

The door clicked open and Jeremy made his way into the house.

"Did you have a good day, sir?" Nesa asked, turning the lights on in the main hall. "Has David awakened yet?"

"Finally, yesterday," Jeremy said. "But he was asleep again when I left him. That's been the only good part about the last couple of days, I'm afraid. Everything else has been completely horrible."

"Still upset about your discharge, then," Nesa said, matter-of-factly. "That's good about David, though, sir. I'm glad he's going to be okay."

"Me too," Jeremy said, locking the door. He turned back to face the foyer.

"I'm heating water for your shower," Nesa said.

Jeremy threw his coat onto a hook of the white antique hall tree his mother had left him with, which helped—he had to admit—decorate the rather plain wall, opposite the staircase. He supposed it had been pretty once with its bright pink lilies that had faded now into nothing. Any beauty had long ago disappeared from the townhouse.

"You must be the best NESA system in all of Neo Victoria, Nesa," Jeremy said.

"Thank you, sir," Nesa replied.

Jeremy made his way up the stairs. "I'll take that shower now."

"Of course, sir," Nesa said, turning on the lights along the stairs. "It's ready now."

Jeremy made his way up the stairs.

"Let me just put this in the study," he said, reaching into his pocket and pulling out the letter. He glanced over it once more as he walked into the room, before tossing it down on the desk amongst other various papers.

He left the study and went to his room, undressing in the dark. He could hear the water in the shower already running, before he opened the door to the bathroom. Light flooded out into the dark room from the doorway. He stepped into the bathroom and looked at himself in the mirror, frowning in disgust.

That insufferable bastard, he thought. *I was so close, at the prime of my experimentation, and he—*

He shook his head and stepped into the shower.

It was obvious to Jeremy that President Demetrius had no idea what he was talking about. How could a dimwitted demon say such things when he knew nothing of science? Everything for the non-humans was enchanting and morbidly magical. Yet, in a certain light, magic was nothing more than an unexplained science. Jeremy jeered and slammed a fist down onto his desk. Everything that he had done in those Core labs was for the better good of all humanity—of every intelligent creature that walked the planet—so what if a few convicts had died along the way? It was bound to happen with any experiment. Besides, they were just convicts, nothing more than good-for-nothing criminals—he was doing the world a service by wiping them from existence.

Graggöry knew that, and still, here Jeremy was: furious and jobless and exhausted.

"I'll show him," Jeremy said to no one, pounding his fist against the slick tiled wall. "I'll create the greatest weapon his petty Core has ever seen."

Graggöry would see the error of his ways, and in a fit of desperation, he would beg for Jeremy to come back. That's when Jeremy would get him. He would take the whole Core. He could take the world from Graggöry's grasp.

It was David's new plan, actually, not Jeremy's, but he liked it just fine. It could work, too, if he did it right. All he needed to do was tweak a few of his outlines, and he could have it finished in no time—well, there was one thing that he didn't have, and that was a test subject. He supposed he would be able to find one with David's help, though, so he wasn't too concerned about it.

Jeremy smiled. It was brilliant. He would be back in the Core in the blink of an eye. He needed to be a little more patient; that was all.

He turned the water off and stood in the shower a moment longer, water dripping from his hair. He reached for his towel and dried his face.

"Nesa," he said as he stepped out of the shower. "I think I'll have some food now."

"Right away, sir," Nesa said from the speaker in the bedroom. "Come down when you're ready."

He dried himself and dressed in comfortable clothes before making his way back down the stairs, toward the kitchen.

Jynx
The Metal Shop

Jynx Scott closed the book she was reading and carried it back to the bookshelf, tucking it away amongst the other books she had finished reading. She sighed and made her way back to the kitchen, sitting down at the old, wobbly table. Max had said many times now that he would make them a new table, but he never had—probably because he was too busy with orders from customers, which of course took priority over the kitchen table. Max hardly ever did what he said he would, so it didn't really surprise Jynx much at all.

She didn't really care about the table anyway. Crosbie had left an hour ago with a delivery and had not come back yet. It made Jynx feel uneasy when he took so long. She was sure he had gone to see the riots again, even though she had begged him not to go anymore. Crosbie hardly listened to a word Jynx said. In fact, he spent most of his time going out of his way to ignore her. This hurt her feelings some, but she understood where he was coming from. She was an imposter. She could never be his real sister, even though she felt that he was her real brother. She felt closest to Crosbie… since Max hardly had time for either one them anymore.

Sometimes Jynx wondered what it would have been like if Molly, Crosbie's mother, hadn't of died. Jynx was alive thanks to Molly. Max and Crosbie hadn't really wanted a clone of the real Jynx. She was just a replacement that couldn't really replace what they had lost.

But Jynx would not stop trying. If she tried hard enough, Crosbie would learn to love her. She knew he was really struggling with his emotions lately. Maybe she was growing on him. She smiled and leaned back in the chair, crossing her arms in front of her chest.

Downstairs metal clashed together as something fell to the floor. Jynx cringed and considered going down there to help Max out—it would give her an opportunity to spend time with him, at least. However, she was waiting on Crosbie to come back and take her to see the ducks.

45

She loved the ducks. They were like her—they lived in a world where they didn't really belong. They were copies, just like she was. They were beautiful.

The door rattled and popped open and Crosbie made his way inside, dusting himself off.

"Welcome back, little brother," Jynx said in a singer's voice. "Did you get Max's project delivered?"

"Yeah," Crosbie said, walking over to the table. "It took me a little longer because I walked by the park, to make sure it was safe so we could go see the ducks."

You were at the riots, Jynx thought, but smiled.

"How thoughtful of you," she said. "I was starting to get worried about you… I figured you'd gotten caught up in another riot."

Crosbie shook his head, smirking. "Not this time."

"Good," Jynx said. "It's dangerous."

"You think everything is dangerous," Crosbie laughed.

Jynx rolled her eyes. It was conversations like this that made her think she was finally making a connection with Crosbie. She only had to wait a little longer now, and soon they would be the best of friends.

She hoped so, anyway.

"Well," she said, standing and grabbing her coat from the chair. She slid her arms through the sleeves. "I suppose we ought to go before it gets dark."

Crosbie stood from the chair and flipped the hood of his coat up over his head. "Yeah, and maybe we can stop and get some food, 'cause I'm starving."

Jynx smiled even wider.

"Sounds like a plan," Jynx said. "Should we tell Max where we're going?"

"Nah," Crosbie said, glancing toward the basement door. "He'll be fine."

"You sure?" Jynx asked, scrunching her nose. "We should at least bring him something to eat."

"Okay," Crosbie said, rolling his eyes. "Come on, let's go. Got to beat the crowds."

Jynx skipped around the table and joined him at the door.

"Thanks for taking me," she said as they walked out the door and down the back stairs. "It means a lot to me."

"I know, sister," Crosbie said. He reached out and took her hand in his. Jynx blinked but didn't say anything as Crosbie led her down the street. "I've been unreasonable lately. I'm sorry."

"Oh," Jynx said. "It's okay. I understand."

"Okay. Thanks," Crosbie said, and tugged her along all the way to the park.

Graggöry

The Palace

Graggöry flinches.

Lysithea ignores him as she continues to pour a capful of hydrogen peroxide over the infected cut on his right wrist. As the chemicals slowly mix with the infection in his blood, the wound begins to bubble. The fingers of his other hand curl into a tight ball, making a squeaking noise against the mahogany desk. He concentrates on the feel of the towel beneath his arm, watches the bubbles dissipate and then the faint red liquid that's left behind slip down his arm toward his bent elbow. Lysithea brings his wrist back down to the towel and begins to smother the cut with some sort of thick, odorless cream she's found somewhere, which to his great displeasure, stings worse than the hydrogen peroxide.

"Stop flinching," Lysithea says, her blonde bangs falling over her eyes.

He tries not to move, cursing under his breath. Lysithea looks up from his wrist and sighs, her haunting gray eyes meeting his. She quickly looks away, screwing the lid back onto the ointment before setting the container down onto the desk next to the towel.

"It wouldn't have gotten this bad if you weren't so stubborn," she continues, shaking her head. She picks up a small bundle of gauze next to the ointment, unrolls a bit and places it over the cut, carefully smothering and wrapping it. This way the wound wouldn't get more dust or ash inside of it. "Honestly, Graggöry, *what were you thinking?* You've seen what an infection can do to a person nowadays. For instance—David. They kept him in the hospital two extra days just because of that rusty shrapnel. He could have died. You could have died."

He only nods and watches her. His charcoal eyes concentrate on her pale thin fingers as she continues to wrap his wrist. She's right, he admits to himself. Even though after the Great War, the world had become much more advanced in medicine, an infection could kill you almost quicker than a bullet ever would. Graggöry hopes to continue to be lucky. The cut isn't deep enough to do any real damage. Lysithea is just being dramatic out of worry for him. If he keeps the ash and dust and filth out of it for a few days, it will soon be as good as new.

"Being a demon doesn't make you indestructible, you know," Lysithea says when he keeps silent. Her voice holds a kind of sadness he's never heard from her before. "Nothing in this world is safe anymore. Not during this war. Not after…"

She's referring to his father now. He shakes his head.

"I know," he whispers, taking her hand in his. He runs his thumb over her knuckles and smiles as best he can. Pushing his chair away from the desk, he pulls her into his lap, nuzzling into her neck as she falls against him. "You don't have to worry so much, silly girl. I promise, Lys, *I'll be okay.*"

"I know you will," she says, "but—"

All of it seemed like a distant dream now.

Graggöry watched Lysithea as she slept, took in all the details of her fragile body. Her arms were wrapped around her legs. Her mouth was slightly opened so that the tips of her teeth were showing beneath her plump lips. She was probably the most beautiful woman he'd ever seen, small boned and delicate on the outside, but so strong and courageous within. Something about her moved him in a way he had never been moved before.

She was sleeping in her usual chair, the large faded leather masterpiece left over from the First World. It had been a gift from him to her when they'd first started their atypical courtship. Graggöry wasn't so sure what it could be called now.

It was *parasitic.*

Graggöry sighed and pulled a cigarette out of the pack in the pocket of his vest, bringing it up to his lips. The cigarettes contained a neo-magical herb used to repress demonic nature, and had been used by the demons in his father's 'rebellion' for years, to keep their humanoid forms and minds functioning properly, and to keep Lucifer's influences at bay. He snapped his fingers and the tip lit up with a green flame. He couldn't help but to smirk. A little magic never hurt anyone, even if it was against most of the new laws to use. He took a long drag before pulling the thing away from his lips. His tongue slowly moved over his teeth as he closed his eyes.

Nothing seemed to be going the way he'd planned.

Though the infection on his wrist had gotten better (a little more slowly than he'd hoped), the one in his mind grew worse by the minute. When the war had first started, he had become plagued by strange voices. At first, they only spoke to him while he slept; however, they were getting louder now, more frantic—and to his dismay, they were much more frequent. Graggöry was losing himself and everything he'd worked so hard to gain, all in one fell swoop. The war was going to claim everything. Either he would be assassinated, like his father, or he would have to leave Neo Victoria and go into hiding because his people—the rebels were his people, too, whether they liked it or not—were ready to rip him to shreds. It wouldn't be long now.

Do not worry, a voice whispered to him. *We will show you the way.*

Graggöry almost laughed, but kept himself quiet as to not wake Lysithea. He would have to tell her today, about the worsening voices. It wasn't like him to keep secrets. Not from her, at least. He would not allow this *thing*—whatever it was—to change him completely. He would hold onto what little sanity he had for as long as he could.

Oh, but we will change you, the voice told him, in a sickeningly reassuring sort of way.

"Silence," he said, a little too loud.

But it's true, another voice cackled. *We will change you, and you will lead us all into a new era.*

Graggöry had no idea what any of it meant. He wasn't capable of leading the world into a new era. After all, he wasn't even capable of leading the world out of its old ways. The war was proof of that. There needed to be change, but for the better. The world had fallen back into its old conundrum. It had become undone. They were once more on the brink of disaster.

He thought of his father and what he would do in this situation. It was his fault this was happening, in the first place—the start had not been entirely Graggöry's doing. It was Graggöry Demetrius I who had begun to drop those bombs on the Wastelands. He had closed Neo Victoria's doors to those seeking refuge. Neo Victoria was, after all, a sanctuary city. It welcomed all—or it was supposed to. Once the out cities had fallen victim to the rebels, his father had decided enough was enough—open doors meant more room for failure. Open doors meant undesirables could enter the city.

Unfortunately for his father, some undesirable had already come in and had just been biding time until the perfect opportunity showed itself.

Graggöry had tried so hard to change the mistakes his father had made—to change the world, but he was failing.

When we're through, you'll see. Nothing will be the same.

"Silence," he pleaded.

"Graggöry?"

He opened his eyes and brought the cigarette back to his lips. His gaze fell onto the picture of an angel he had found in an old book from around the 19th century—centuries ago now. First World. Old World. A world that was gone.

The book's pages were beginning to deteriorate into nothing more than dust, but the angel was still brightly plastered onto the page, triumphantly holding a trumpet in one hand. Its halo shown illustrated light that seemed to cascade down its body.

Angels, the voices hissed in unison.

He studied its form, the serene look on its face, and wondered whether his father—who had so wished to regain his place in the lost, promised Paradise—had gotten his wish upon leaving this troublesome world, a place more like Hell than home. He shook his head. Probably not; not after all the atrocities his father had committed, yet he could still hope. His father had been very brave. He had rebelled against Lucifer, in the end. Graggöry had a feeling that wasn't enough to save him. Graggöry Demetrius I had left him, his only child, with too big of shoes to fill and a world that was rapidly falling apart. Perhaps, there was no hope at all.

"Graggöry?"

He closed the book and took another long drag of the cigarette, trying his best to push the voices away. He turned his attention to Lysithea. She was watching him with the same worried stare she'd been wearing for days. Her fingertips curled into her knees as she squirmed a bit in the chair. As she tilted her head to the side, her ashen curls fell over her face; the colors all clashed together, bringing out an odd shade of gray in her eyes.

"Is it the voices again?" she asked, her voice barely audible.

Graggöry nodded and shifted his gaze beyond her, out the window.

"They're getting worse—more persuasive. I think they won't go away until I do exactly what they tell me," he said. He looked back to her, afraid of how she might be looking back at him.

Lysithea shivered and crawled out of the chair, standing and stretching her arms over her head before taking a few steps toward him. She ran her hands over her jumbled blouse a few times, her fingers nervously gliding over each button in a failed attempt to straighten it out.

Graggöry knew the voices scared her, but he also knew that Lysithea was probably the only person he could trust.

Io

Spiritus Vallem

Spiritus Vallem, the 'valley' of the spirit, was nestled between two large areas of devastated forest that was burnt and blackened by the dark-magic infused bombs that had ended the way things had been before the Great War. For centuries, the valley had been a place untouched by the magic that had ruined the rest of the world, and had—in more recent years—become the home of the Angels of Terra, the protectors of the land. These angels had been specifically chosen by God to start healing the earth and to try to guide its wary people away from the Final Ending, the ending where no one had a chance to survive. The Great War had brought about what people in the Old World had referred to as the Second Coming, a rapture of sorts—those who had inherited this horrible version of Earth had been desolate inside, but they had been given a second chance to prove themselves to God, and most of them were failing. At least, that's what Io had heard. She hadn't been allowed to leave the valley. Her parents were trying to shield her from the horrors of the world—though it had been her mission, just as well as their own, to save the world from the final ending. She sighed and wished her parents would stop treating her like a child. She was almost a mature angel now. She deserved to be treated as such.

She supposed the talk in the village was all true, though, even if she hadn't seen it with her own eyes. Things in the outside world were not going so well, but that was all hearsay—the village was full of gossipmongers, after all. They had nothing better to do than to talk about the depleted world and its sorry inhabitants. And in two weeks, Io would get to go to the cities with Abraxos, her father. It was probably the most exciting thing to happen to her since she'd come to live in the valley. She would finally get to help. She'd been waiting for a long time, but Chrezabel hadn't let her go until she finished all the training.

It didn't matter, though. The little victory of finishing her training was probably going to be short lived. The end was probably very near. She had seen it all in her dreams.

Io sighed, sitting, perched on the sturdy branch of an ancient pine tree, looking down over Spiritus Vallem in all its unscathed glory. She shifted her weight, her tall and lanky body wobbling unsteadily for just a moment before her wings moved, balancing her. Her wings were folded, so that they draped over her like a shield of sorts, though they didn't really do much good protecting her from the sun's vibrant rays. Unlike the angelic wings she had seen in the book her parents owned, made of gorgeous white feathers that sprawled and fluttered, her wings were made up of light and energy; the only similarity between the two was how they were both shaped. She turned her attention to the way the sun's light reflected on the tips of her wings, slightly enthralled by the rainbow of colors it was creating.

This was the furthest that she had ever been from the cluster of houses or the fields that surrounded them, and she felt a little rebellious. She had come so far because she needed to get away. Her visions were worsening. It nauseated her to think about them, especially the one she had had just this morning. The village stood solid and peaceful before her now, but in her dreams, it was burnt and blackened like the trees that surrounded the valley. In her dreams, everyone was dead—her friends, her family, the only people she had known for her entire life.

Io shuddered and stood on the branch, turning so she could look out over the 'forbidden' forest—the place where the trees had withered and charred and died. She supposed the forest had been beautiful once, long, long ago, before war had ruined it. Io didn't know much about the Great War, or the world beyond the valley, but what she did know was that there was nowhere left on Earth, beyond Spiritus Vallem, where ash didn't fall so heavily that the sun couldn't shine through. That world seemed terribly drab, a desolate wasteland, a place not survivable. She couldn't understand why anyone would want to leave the valley to live there, in that world, and yet, the person closest and dearest to her had.

She wondered briefly about her sister, but shook the thought from her mind. She gave one last look out over the charred forest. She supposed what her mother always said was true: beauty can never last.

She turned back to the valley and frowned. She thought of all the things that made the valley beautiful and it saddened her. It could be in months, or it could be tomorrow—the valley was going to be destroyed, lives would be ended, nightmares would come to life.

She stretched her wings and fell from the branch, her wings catching her in midair. She needed to head home before her parents became too worried about her. She didn't want them to think she had run away, too.

Io loved to fly. The wind blew her long, curly black hair every-which-way, smoothed and caressed her pale skin. The air was pure and crisp, it's piney taste strong on her tongue. She spread her arms out, feeling the force of it. She loved the feeling, the rush and free-fall, the soaring; this was what she lived for. Flying cleared her mind, made her less troubled about the things she had no control over. Up in the sky, she could forget about her visions, if only temporary, and she desperately wanted to forget them. Some things were too much to bear.

Landing in the front lawn of her family's cottage, her wings flickered and went out. She reached for the door, which was already slightly ajar, but paused when she heard her mother's hushed voice.

"It's happening," Chrezabel whispered, her strained voice drifting through the crack in the door. "It wouldn't be long now, Abraxos. I knew it wouldn't be long after—"

"Chreza," her father cooed, his voice ever steady. "Listen to yourself. This is madness."

"You keep saying that," Chrezabel said, "but you do not *see* as Io and I see. I have seen what is to happen next, and it is exactly as I told you before. Please believe me before it's too late. We should leave. We should take our children and go."

Io smiled. Her mother loved them all very dearly, but that love would not be enough to save them.

Chrezabel and Io both shared the gift her mother was referring to—the curse of Sight. Her mother had always said that it was a burden. Io hardly knew anything of it, only that sometimes it gave her horrible nightmares while she slept, and more times than not—those things came true while she was awake. She pushed the door open a smidgen more so that she could look in on her parents. She felt bad, like always, for eavesdropping, but they hardly ever told her anything anymore. Once she had asked her mother about the dreams she'd been having of—what she thought was—the Great War, but her mother told her she would learn in time. She knew better now. Some of them had probably been the Great War—she often saw things that had happened long ago, but most of her visions were of what was coming—the end of the valley. The end of their lives, though it was not the end of everything.

She had completed her training. She wished her parents would treat her more like an adult and less like a frightened child.

"Please, calm down, Chreza," Abraxos said, leaning forward and placing his hand affectionately onto her mother's upper arm. "Please, don't think on it anymore."

"It hurts," Chrezabel whispered. "It hurts to see these things and to *know*."

"I know," Abraxos said. "Just try not to think of it for now. You know we can't leave. You know we have to stay—"

Io pushed the door open the rest of the way, plastering a smile on her face as she walked in, giving her father a way out of the conversation she knew he did not want to have. She grabbed a shiny green apple from the fruit basket on the counter by the door. Giving her father a knowing look, she leaned back against the counter and took a bite out of the apple.

"What are you two talking about?" she asked.

"We're just talking about boring things, sweetie," Chrezabel said, trying very hard to hide how distraught she was. Io saw through her. She knew her mother better than anyone else. "Nothing you would be interested in, I'm afraid."

Try me, she wanted to say as she raised the apple back up to her lips. She'd seen enough of her own visions—had heard enough of her parents' conversations to know what her mother was so worried about. It was almost time. The end was coming soon. Chrezabel knew it.

Io knew it.

"If only your sister hadn't—"

"Chrezabel," Abraxos said through his teeth.

He *did not* like to talk about his other daughter. He *did not* want to be reminded.

Chrezabel shook her head, her blonde curls falling in front of her face, and pushed the chair away from the table, standing and walking out of the room in a huff.

Io watched her go.

"Your mother is just worried, Io," Abraxos said, leaning back in his chair. He ran a hand through his graying black hair, looking at the doorway Chrezabel had disappeared through. He looked back to her with a glint in his eye that told her he knew she had been listening. He always knew. Io looked away, down at her apple.

"I know," she finally said, frowning a bit as she looked back off, after her mother. She looked back to her father, at his gentle face and dark, knowing lavender eyes. Her father who loved his family fiercely, though he had been cursed with a lunatic for a bride, and had been betrayed by his careless, eldest chosen daughter. How could Io tell him that she was worried, too? How could she possibly explain to him that the darkness in her dreams was coming for them, would be upon them any day now? She shook her head and turned her gaze to the window on the other side of the room, just above the kitchen sink.

"It's going to snow," she said instead, and quietly walked after her mother.

David

The Palace

A bitter cold had found its way deep inside of David. A cold loathing incomparable to the arctic chill that had followed him in through the extravagantly ornate oaken front doors of the governor's manor, known affectionately to everyone in Neo Victoria as 'The Palace.' Since Neo Victoria was indeed the capital of Neo Erta in all its chaotic glory—it was only fit for them to have a palace, he supposed. After all, they did have their demon king. David frowned and took a moment to peel his gloves off. The Palace was always either too warm or too cool, and never seemed to have a comfortable in-between. He shrugged his coat off, finding that today it was the latter today.

At the start of the war, Graggöry had offered up rooms in his glorious mansion to all of his top officers, to use as offices, he said, while they planned their triumphant victories against the Wasteland rebel forces. David hadn't been in his office in weeks, having been a little preoccupied with the entire goings on of hospital life; he had thought for a long while, that perhaps he was never going to be re-released out into the world, that he would live in the hospital until the end of his pitiful life. Thankfully, that had not been the case at all. They had finally discharged him mere hours ago, and after going back to his flat to freshen up a bit, he'd walked the three blocks to The Palace in hopes of speaking to Graggöry about Jeremy's ridiculous discharge from the Demetrius Core.

Something had to be done about it, he kept telling himself, over and over until the mantra was imbedded in that deep cold place. He would do something about it. He had promised.

He stood at the end of the long, slick marble staircase, his hand resting on the elegant banister as he looked up them, on to the darkness that led to Graggöry's dowdy office and thought of what exactly he would say to him. What reasonable thing could be said to a man who was said to have been losing his mind? David would say anything of only to get his brother back where he belonged, working long hours in those Core laboratories, using that brilliant mind of his to create a weapon great enough to win the war. Jeremy was wasting away back at the townhouse, where he had nothing to do but tinker in his basement and mourn the loss of his budding career. David *had* to do something about it.

He couldn't possibly take the Core down all by himself, anyway. He needed Jeremy's intelligence. He needed that weapon—and Jeremy would build it, after all, he had been so close before Graggöry had sent him away.

David would change Graggöry's mind. He had to.

With that thought, he finally began his ascent up the stairs, chewing on the inside of his cheek as he continued to think of what he was going to say. What could he say? What could he do but go in there and demand that Graggöry change his mind? If he knew anything about Graggöry—and they had been friends for many years now, so he was sure he knew everything about him—it was that he was stubborn and set in his ways, and that didn't bode well for David or Jeremy. Not at all.

But Graggöry was losing his mind. Perhaps, David could use that knowledge to his advantage. Those sorts of pre-guerilla warfare tactics were not beneath him. David sighed through his teeth and continued down the long hallway that led to the office, focusing on the dim light that was flooding out through a gap in the door, which must have been slightly ajar. David found that odd. Graggöry never kept his door open. He was a creature of secrets.

David took a moment to give himself a little pep-talk. He had gotten Jeremy into the Core to begin with, and surely, he could persuade Graggöry to let him back in again. It would be easy. He started down the hall again.

Voices—just whispers—flooded into the hallway, as David approached the door and paused again. It was Graggöry, playfully bantering with Lysithea—his pretty five-star-general-plaything. David hated that woman for what she had done, for what she had taken from him. He cleared his throat and knocked on the door. The voices hushed. Through the crack in the door, David watched as Lysithea peeled herself away from Graggöry, frowning at the door. David almost laughed. Lysithea hated him, too.

She had ruined countless things.

"Excuse me," David said, tugging the door open a little wider. "I've come to talk to you, Graggöry. It's important."

"I'll leave you two be then," Lysithea said in her too-light feathery voice, like she had thought for a single second that David would ask her to stay. She slinked around the desk and made her way to the door, passing by David without looking him in the eye. She reminded him of a beaten dog, sometimes. He brushed off her sickening submissiveness and turned his attention to Graggöry, who was looking at him like he'd just seen a ghost.

"I suppose you know why I'm here," David said, walking up to the desk.

"Well, it's certainly not to catch up," Graggöry tried to joke, but when David did not as much as smile, he frowned and shook his head. "David, there's nothing I can do about it. You know that. My hands are tied."

"That's bullshit," David said, the corners of his lips tugging into a slight frown. "You gave him permission to do those experiments—on *convicts*, might I add, and you didn't have a problem with it before."

"People found out," Graggöry said, no remorse in his voice. "Important people, and they were angry. I can't afford to let people—"

"What? Throw a little tantrum? Fuck those people, Graggöry. They're all already rioting in the streets."

"I can't afford to make more people angry," Graggöry finished with a sigh.

He didn't want to end up like his father; that's what it was.

"People will always be angry," David said.

"That may be so—"

"But you don't want to end up like your father."

David supposed he couldn't blame him. Nobody wanted to die.

"I would like to live to see the end of this, yes," Graggöry said, a bit bitterly.

"Reinstate Jeremy, and we can win this thing," David said, resting his hands atop a comfortable looking chair that was placed in front of Graggöry's mahogany desk. "Nobody else has to die."

"Except for all the people your brother experiments on," Graggöry said. He sighed. "I'm sorry about your brother, David, but I can't do anything about it. He will be okay, and we can win this war another way. You know it as well as I."

"There has to be something you can do. You did something before..."

"And look where that got me."

David fell silent for a long time.

"Okay," David said, at last.

Graggöry tilted his head; a gesture that David assumed meant he was confused. To not argue a point was very much unlike David, and he supposed that Graggöry must have known that. He shrugged his shoulders and peered into the mirror that hung on the wall behind Graggöry's head. David's lips were set in a dismissive line across his gaunt, phantom-like face, but his eyes were bright with a newfound fire that burned within him.

"You're right," David continued. "We shouldn't anger anyone else."

Graggöry leaned back in his chair and visibly relaxed, as if for the whole conversation he had been tense and uncomfortable.

"I'm glad you agree," Graggöry told him. "Perhaps, after we win the war—
"

"Jeremy will be all right," David said, already thinking of the next plan. He smiled at Graggöry, but there was nothing familiar or friendly about it. This conversation only confirmed David's suspicion that their friendship was over. He had known for a long time that there was no way that he could put those pieces back together—their friendship would not be saved.

Perhaps now he could do what Lucie had asked of him.

"I'm sorry," Graggöry said, like he too knew the friendship had come to its demise. His voice was heavy, laden by sorrow.

"Don't worry about it," David said, as he turned to leave. "I'll be back at my post first thing in the morning."

"Take as much time as you need," was all Graggöry could say before David was out of the room and making his way back down the hallway. He would think of something, he was sure. He always thought of something. Jeremy would be okay, and he would get that weapon—very soon, Graggöry would pay for all of it. David smiled and walked back out into the cold.

Graggöry
The Palace

Graggöry tapped the hologram above his desk until the war plans were on the screen in front of him. There was so much going on, and it made him tired. It was a sort of exhaustion that he had never felt before: a tiredness that had settled in his bones. He flipped through the plans and sighed—not really impressed by any of them.

The war had gotten so out of control, and it escalated more and more with each passing moment. Somehow the rebel forces had gotten their hands on bigger bombs... and they made no secret of it. They were going to use them on Neo Victoria, and if Graggöry didn't do anything about it, countless people would die—Neo Victorians and rebels alike.

Graggöry thought their bloodshed was useless. There were other ways to resolve conflict. When he had taken over his father's position, he had had dreams of a world not like this. He had dreamed of a world that could be at peace. Unfortunately, that kind of world just could not exist.

Sometimes Graggöry wished he hadn't dropped those bombs on the Wastelands, but there were monsters out there—phantom things that sucked the soul right out of you. Someone had to kill them. The inner cities had walls to keep them out, but the people in the Wastelands had no protection. But phantoms were just an excuse. He knew they really dropped those bombs out there to test them, to prepare for if the world wanted to end again. People died at their hands, and the Demetrius Core didn't care so long as their weapons were working.

If truth be told, the Core was full of monsters. Some of them meant good, but most of them lived off of the destruction and death. There were people like David's brother—people who meant well but went about doing good by doing bad.

Graggöry was just so tired of it all. He wanted out, but he was in too deep. There were plenty of other people better suited for this job. David could do it. Lysithea could do it. He wished he could give it to one of them.

He tapped on a picture of enemy propaganda:

We're coming for you. Your king is corrupt. Free yourselves.

He laughed.

The door clicked open and Lysithea sauntered in.

"I just came from a briefing," Lysithea said, making her way to her chair. "It's just getting worse out there."

"I know," Graggöry said.

"It's a mess," Lysithea said, and then after glancing his way, "I know you're tired."

"I'll be okay," Graggöry said, "but I don't think I can say the same about the world."

Lysithea nodded and looked out the window.

"We'll figure something out," Lysithea said. "We always do."

Jeremy

The Townhouse

Jeremy walked through the back door, throwing his coat onto the back of one of the chairs around the little yellow table in his kitchen. He had figured that a stroll around the Lydia District would clear his mind and bring him out of his despair. Unfortunately, it had been bitterly cold, like always, and having time to think only made things worse.

"I've got an idea," he said to Nesa, whom he assumed was listening, as he closed the door and stepped up to the kitchen sink. Turning it on, he squeezed some soap onto his palm and watched as it bubbled around the edges before scrubbing his hands clean of the ash from outside.

"What's that, sir?" she asked, her electronic voice giving no sign of true curiosity.

"We're going to have a guest for dinner," he said, watching the last of the soap bubbles drift down the drain. "Prepare something nice."

"Who are we expecting?" Nesa asked, the mechanical hands hanging from the ceiling bursting to life as Nesa opened the refrigerator to find something suitable for a guest. "Is it David? Or Crosbie, perhaps?"

"No," Jeremy said, biting his bottom lip as he thought of what to say. "David will be by after dinner with his friends."

Jeremy couldn't say he had many friends to have dinner with. There was only Crosbie, and he had been equally as busy his own project, so Jeremy had only seen him once or twice in the last month. He was so preoccupied with his work that he didn't have time to hang out, let alone make new friends. He had had plenty of friends when he had been at school, but now he hardly saw any use for them—being social got in the way, he had decided long ago. All he needed was Nesa and David and Crosbie, and he supposed he could count Jynx. They were enough.

"Well, who is it, then?" Nesa asked. The refrigerator door shut and the hand, holding something leafy and green, moved over to the counter, where the chopping board was.

"The key to my success," Jeremy said, after a long moment. In a little more chipper voice he added, "I'm going to try just one more time."

"Oh, Jeremy," Nesa said, and he supposed it was supposed to be a disappointed sigh.

"I know what you want to say," Jeremy said, "but this is important to me."

"I know," Nesa said. She chopped the vegetable in silence and then asked, "When can we be expecting our guest?"

"Shortly. I invited him over during my walk. I did have good intentions—at first," Jeremy said. He walked back over to the table. "Oh, and Nesa? Slip it in the wine this time. I think that puts them out better."

"As you wish," Nesa said.

Silence followed as Jeremy moved his coat from the chair, taking it out and placing it onto a hook on the hall tree. He walked up the stairs to clean himself up a little before dinner. Upon entering his bathroom, he stood in front of the mirror and watched his reflection for a moment, pondering what his mother would think of him now.

She would not be pleased, but this was the only way he had to avenge her.

"I'm sorry," he said to her, wherever she might be. He didn't particularly believe in heaven, but he supposed that was where he would want her to be, if she were anywhere now. It sounded nice, anyway. Maybe she would forgive him, if they did cross paths again one day.

That was doubtful.

He splashed his face with some cold water, wanting to be as awake as he possibly could be—the next few hours were crucial to his experiment. He didn't have the luxury to mess up—not now that he wasn't being given test subjects whenever he wanted them. That was one thing he missed about his job with the Core.

Oh well, he thought, walking back down the stairs. He would make his weapon and he would either get back into the Core with it, or he would destroy the Core with it. Either way, Graggöry would be sorry. All he really wanted was an apology, he supposed. An apology and a reinstatement.

The doorbell rang.

Jeremy hopped off the last step and chimed, "I'll get it," to Nes, who was finishing up dinner in the kitchen.

He opened the door.

Edgar, the homeless beggar who frequented his street, stood on the doorstep, and smiled kindly at Jeremy, who smiled back at him as friendly as he could. Edgar looked frail, which worried Jeremy some—he needed someone in much better condition, but desperate times called for desperate measures. He was also a little older than Jeremy, but those convicts had been older, too. Jeremy would take what he could get.

Edgar probably just needed to be fed properly, and he would be good as new in no time.

"Well, Edgar, I'm glad you could make it," Jeremy said, stepping out of the way and gesturing him in. "Nesa almost has dinner ready."

"Your NESA cooks?" Edgar asked, walking into the foyer. He looked around, his eyes wide as a child's. Jeremy felt a pang of guilt but shook it off.

"Yes, my NESA does a lot of things," Jeremy replied. "I can tell you over some wine. Come this way. We'll be eating in the kitchen."

Edgar followed him into the kitchen, still wide-eyed and looking every which way, though Jeremy hardly knew why. The townhouse was nothing fancy, and was a little outdated. It was nothing compared to the flat that David owned, where everything was silver, and the floors were polished marble. Jeremy had been offered one when he had started work for the Core, but he was adamant to keep the townhouse. It reminded him of his childhood.

Jeremy pulled out a chair for Edgar and gestured for him to sit. Nesa placed a sparkling wine glass down on the table before him.

"Enjoy your wine, sir," Nesa said, in greeting. "I opened a special batch, this time."

"Thank you," Edgar said, politely.

Jeremy felt another pang of guilt, watching him. If this didn't work, it wouldn't end very well for Edgar, and if it did work, he would be a slave to the Core for the rest of his life. It was easy to feel a little guilt, he supposed. Jeremy was human, too.

Edgar lifted the glass to his lips and drank the wine.

Jeremy drank his wine and told Edgar about the townhouse until the pill set in, and Edgar began talking gibberish as his mind shut down. When at last Edgar slumped over the table, still in his chair, Jeremy stood and walked around to where Edgar sat.

"That worked quicker than the last time," Jeremy said to Nesa, who was still cooking dinner. "You'll have to save dinner and reheat it for me. I've got work to do."

"Yes, sir," Nesa said, and Jeremy thought for a moment that he heard a bit of annoyance in her monotone drawl.

Jeremy hunched down and pulled Edgar's arm around his shoulders, picking him up and half-carrying-half-dragging him down to the basement workshop. He laid the body down onto the table and began to tinker with his tools. He had a bionic arm that he'd gotten from his metal smith just days earlier, and he was itching to get it attached to Edgar—he was ready for his experiment to work in general, but there was something exciting about testing a new subject.

Jeremy hooked Edgar up to the IV and placed the oxygen mast firmly onto Edgar's face before he turned away and pulled out his saw. It wasn't too dangerous—just cutting off an arm. He had tried to do too many things at once, the first few times. He would take this one step at a time. If Edgar could survive the arm extraction, Jeremy would plan to do the other arm, or a leg, or all his limbs at a later date.

He wished he had all the luxuries of his lab back at The Palace. Doing the experiment in his basement was risky—he hardly had anything to work with at the townhouse. It was dirty, in the basement lab—if it could be called a lab— and his equipment was deplorable at best. It was going to take a miracle for this to work. He knew that much.

He injected the anesthetic into the IV drip.

Sighing, he began to saw off the arm, not in the least bit phased by the blood that squirted and oozed out from the wound he was creating. He concentrated on the little beeps the heart monitor made, catching his breath as the heart faltered and fluttered—this had to be done, he reminded himself. It was for his mother and his father, both murdered by the Core.

"It has to be done," he told Edgar, as he continued to saw away at the arm. "It's for the better good of the world. You'll be a hero. I'll be a hero."

That was what he told himself, at least. In the end, after all the horrible things he had done to these people, he would be a hero. People would applaud him. They would look up to him with awe and admiration. That was what he wanted more than just peace for the world.

Once the arm was off, Jeremy lifted the other arm from the table beside them. Edgar's heart began to falter again, just as Jeremy had feared. Edgar was too weak. He was so malnourished that this had been a failed attempt from the very beginning. Jeremy tried to give him the Vicificantem serum, but he didn't take it.

Jeremy sighed as he stared down at the corpse on his operating table. Failed again. Edgar hadn't even made it to the hardest part of the surgery. Disappointment flooded over Jeremy as he walked back up the stairs and into the kitchen to wash the blood from his hands.

"Send a message to David," he said to Nesa, who did not question whether or not the experiment was going well. "I'll need him here sooner than I thought."

"Right away, sir," Nesa said.

"I'll be down in the basement," Jeremy said. "When David gets here, send him down."

"As you wish," Nesa replied.

"We'll eat when we're done," Jeremy said, noticing that Nesa had already put the food away. "I wouldn't want your good cooking to go to waste."

"Thank you," Nesa said. "I will send for David."

Jeremy nodded as he made his way back into the foyer, pausing at the basement door. How many times would he fail before the experiment became a success? He wondered if he should give up. This must be fate telling him it could not be so. Maybe it was just too great of a feat for a mortal man. He made his way back down the stairs of the basement, contemplating how he and David would hide a body. David could get away with killing a man, but he couldn't. Graggöry would sentence him to death if he ever found out about this.

"Well, Edgar," he said to the corpse as he began dismembering it. "I'm sorry about this, really I am."

He knew that Edgar knew that he was lying. He didn't feel that sorry, in all actuality.

Edgar's pale green eyes watched Jeremy as he worked.

Nesa
The Townhouse

Nesa watched through the camera in the basement's lens, as Jeremy and David placed what was left of the poor beggar into large, shiny black trash bags, and pondered on whether she really was the greatest NESA system in Neo Victoria or not. Certainly, she was, for being able to keep such a secret from the Capitol—but certainly, she wasn't, because of the secrets she kept. She had seen many things take place that any normal NESA would report. Faithfully, she had kept her speakers—she did not have a mouth—shut about it.

She would have told the Capitol, if the culprit hadn't been Jeremy. Nesa was very protective of him, for various reasons, and had sworn long ago to keep him safe, which was getting increasingly harder to do with each passing day. She could tell that Jeremy was plotting to do this again—he would do it over and over until it finally worked.

She wasn't so sure it ever would.

Jeremy was not a quitter, and the Capitol had made a rather impressive enemy out of him when President Graggöry had dismissed him.

"Where are we going to put this?" Jeremy asked, giving a sideways glance to the camera—his gaze all knowing. She was not a very good spy, and anyway, the red blinking light on the camera always gave her away. "We can't very well get out of the city to leave it somewhere out there in the Waste."

"I'll take care of it," David said, hoisting the bag up over his shoulder. "You don't worry about a thing."

That was easy for David to say. Nesa knew that Jeremy worried about everything. It was just part of who he was, she had learned long ago. David, however, never seemed to have a care in the world—everything always seemed to be going exactly his way. That was, until he tried to get Jeremy back into the Core.

"Okay," Jeremy said, as he followed David back up the stairs and into the foyer.

Nesa clicked on the camera over the front door.

The both of them stood in the foyer for a moment, not talking, but giving each other a sort of knowing look.

"Go out the back," Jeremy finally said, starting for the kitchen. "Nobody will see you."

Nesa clicked on the camera above the kitchen door.

"If I hear any news about you-know-what, I'll come back first thing in the morning," David said with a nod, and Nesa watched as he left out the back door, quick on his feet, light on his feet and hardly struggling to carry the bag over his shoulder.

"Shall I fix anything for you?" Nesa asked after a moment, having cooked ham and potatoes and cabbage earlier. "I can reheat dinner, if you're hungry."

"I would like that," Jeremy said, as he went to the sink. He stood there, washing the blood from his hands, for a few minutes before turning to the table. "Thank you for the food."

He gave her another glance, and she knew he knew that she would never tell of what she witnessed in the basement, or the conversation she overheard in his office. He knew where her loyalty was, how faithful she had been.

Things had been a little hectic lately, but she would not waver.

"It's never a problem," Nesa said, placing his plate onto the table. "I enjoy cooking."

Jeremy lifted his fork. "And I enjoy eating."

Nesa laughed and for a moment, things seemed back to normal again.

Lysithea and Graggöry
The Palace

Rain pours down over Lysithea's body. Her clothes are heavy with water and sticking to her skin. She stands in the middle of a meadow, looking up at the clouds as they push east. Her fingers are clinched into tight firsts at her sides. Lately, she doesn't understand anything. She wipes the water from her face, shielding her dark lavender eyes from the rain. Like her clothes, her blonde hair sticks to the curve of her face, and her neck, and her shoulders.

Find me.

His voice is clear in her mind. It's a passionate plea, but she doesn't know whose voice it is. She's only heard it a few times in her dreams.

Please find me.

Suddenly, the once vibrant green valley before her, turns dark.

"I will," she calls out to the darkness and the rain. She takes a step forward and blinks back the tears that have suddenly sprung to her eyes.

She needs to find him.

She has to.

Not saying a word, she waits for his reply, her heart breaking a little at the silence.

Lysithea could not tell him that she knew how it felt.

"What do they tell you?" she asked instead.

"A lot of things," Graggöry said. His voice fell to a whisper. He looked back up at her face, his own shadowed by his ever-growing fear. "They tell me gruesome things."

"Tell me," she said, slinking around the desk. She leaned against the cold wood and watched him, her grey eyes dancing with both sadness and curiosity. "Tell me what they say. Tell me what we have to do to make you better. I'd do anything."

"I know," was all he said, but she wasn't convinced.

"So just tell me. Tell me everything."

"I couldn't possibly subject you to this horror," he said. "It's not something I could easily ask you to do for me, Lys. What they want—I just couldn't ask you."

"Yes, you could, and you will," Lysithea said. Her palms nervously pressed into the desk. "You can ask me anything, always."

Graggöry tried to come up with a lie, contemplated an alternative task or another way around all of it. The voices hissed inside of his head.

Perfect, a voice whispered. *This is the perfect way to get exactly what we want!*

Kill the angels, another voice said. *Kill them and we'll go away.*

Graggöry shuddered and closed his eyes. It didn't have to be like this. Things could be better, could be different without having to end the world as it was, without having to start over again.

"Just tell me," she said again, leaning forward a bit. "Please."

"There are angels," Graggöry started, "that God sent down to guard the world after the Fallout. Most people have never heard of them, but they do exist. They live outside of the main cities, in a place known as—"

"Spiritus Vallem," Lysithea said, her mouth going dry. Her body stiffened at the words, and she slid from the desk to stand next to him. She hoped he hadn't noticed her shaking, but he always saw everything. "Yes, I do actually know something about that, but what about them?"

He noticed she was shaking. Did it scare her to see this side of him? He kept his mouth shut about it and continued, "If they were to be eradicated from the valley... from Earth, then perhaps the voices would disappear."

"You can't actually mean the voices are telling you to..."

That would be genocide.

She tried to steady her breathing. There was no way she could ever consider—*but he can't find out.* She swallowed back the bile that rose in her throat. She had promised when she had first been given her position in the Demetrius Core, to always, *always*, do what was best, what was for the better good for Neo Erta as a whole—but really all she wanted to do was what was best for Graggöry. To kill the angel—*those innocent fools*—would make her a traitor, in more ways than one. What had they done to warrant this attack on them? Why would these voices want to kill every angel, angels that had only been sent to protect the earth and keep the peace?

Unless it had something to do with the prophecy.

She shuddered and looked up at the veiling. She'd always been corrupted. Her head and heart had never once been in the right place... until now. She had finally made peace with her demons, but what Graggöry was suggesting would only bring them back.

"I told you I could never ask you to do it," Graggöry said. He sounded so miserable. He looked away from her, wishing he could lie to her, but it was too late for that now. "I am a murderer, but you are too gentle, much too kind."

Lysithea bit her bottom lip and looked everywhere but at Graggöry. She was neither of those things. Her heart and mind raced, and it took all of her strength not to crumble at his feet.

Traitor.

She swallowed again and gained some composure before looking back to him. She would leave her past where it belonged and do whatever she needed to do to save him, even if that made her a traitor. After all, Graggöry had saved her even though he didn't know it.

"I told you before that I would do anything if it were to make you better," she said. She took a shaky breath and reached out to steady herself on his arm.

She tried to smile but it felt forced and fake. "Do you truly believe that this will make you better? That if—if we do this one thing, the voices will go away and you will only be you again?"

"Lys, you don't have to…"

"Well, will the voices go away?"

Yes.

"Yes," he said. "I think so."

She closed her eyes and took a deep breath, thinking. There was no way for her to know if it was Graggöry or the voices telling her this. Lysithea could not tell one from the other anymore. It pained her to know he was keeping secrets, but she was hiding things from him, as well. Important things. Things that could get her killed now. She knew deep in her heart that it wasn't going to work, but she had to try. For Graggöry—for his love—she would do anything. She just wanted her Graggöry back, but she knew that he was probably long gone. The voices had hushed him, permanently.

"Then give me your order," she whispered, "and it shall be done."

David

Somewhere

Somehow, he has found his way back into the familiar darkness, where Lucie seems to be always waiting for him, however, this time David finds himself in a room with a throne made of iron and bone. A throne, he decides, that is fit for Lucie. He ponders for a moment about what this means. Surely, he has not been speaking all this time with a devil that he does not believe in.

Lucie must be short for Lucifer.

"Your Highness," David says as he steps around the back of the throne. Lucie is lounging, her legs hanging over the side as she stares at him, an almost bored expression plastered on her lovely face. "I had no idea I was always in the presence of someone so important."

"This is merely just a little detail I felt was unnecessary at the time," Lucie says. "I came to you as you wished to see me—an angel of death."

"I suppose you still are an angel of death," David replies, cocking his head to the side as he watches her. "You are an angel of everything."

"Except for Paradise," Lucie says, frowning.

"So that's what you need help with," David says, putting tow and two together. "You want Paradise."

"I want it all," Lucie says, exasperated.

David laughs.

"Just seconds ago, you didn't even believe in a Paradise," Lucie says, swinging her legs around to the front of the throne. She leans forward a bit, her arms resting on its long, boney arms. "Tell me. What do you believe now?"

"I believe I'm just dreaming," David says. He looks around the room. A new, dim light cascades around them from the fires in the distance. Hell doesn't seem very pleasant, but then again, Hell wasn't supposed to be. "I've made you up in my head."

"I'm very real," Lucie retorts, laughing a bit. "Someday soon, I will come to you in person. You'll believe me then, but for now, this will have to do."

David stays silent, thinking.

"So, my darling," Lucie continues. "Have you decided to help me? You were very much on the fence about it last we spoke."

"I will help you," David says. "In return, you must give me what you promised."

"The whole world will put you on a pedestal," Lucie says. "You will take Graggöry's place, and rule it all. I will give it to you, if you will do as I say."

David smiles, already calculating in his head how he will get rid of that damned demon president. He will deal with Lucie when the time comes. He likes her enough—once could say he is in love with her—to keep her around, after it is all said and done.

"How is your part of the plan coming along?" he finally asks her.

"The angels will be taken care of," Lucie says, leaning back in the throne. "Graggöry's lover is going to execute the poor fools for me."

"And all the angels on earth must die?" David asks.

"Yes," Lucie says.

"Why?"

Lucie's plump red lips tug down into a frown. "An angel on earth could stop me."

And there it is, David thought. *There is my loophole.*

If he keeps an angel alive—if Jeremy uses an angel to create his weapon—David will have a way to control Lucie. That is what he wants. Complete control.

"Well, we certainly don't want that," David says, his smile never faltering.

"All you need to worry about is how to eliminate Graggöry," Lucie says, watching him very carefully. He wonders for a moment if her deep crimson eyes can see right through him and his plan. If she is really the devil, she probably knows ever dark thought in his head. If she knows, she plays the part of the unknowing very well.

"I've got that part taken care of," David says. "I just need time."

"We have some time, my darling," Lucie says, her face contorting as she thinks. "Take as long as you need, for now."

"When will I see you again?" David asks.

"Soon," Lucie says. "I'll come to see you next time."

"All right," David says. "I look forward to it."

"As do I, my darling," Lucie replies.

She smiles at him in a warm, adoring way that makes David feel a little uneasy.

"Until next time," Lucie says—

David opened his eyes and stared up at his dark ceiling. Everything was going to fall into place exactly how he wanted it to. He had Lucie eating out of the palm of his hand. It wouldn't be much longer now, he knew. Soon, he would have what he wanted.

Jeremy

The Townhouse

Almost a month had passed since Jeremy had been discharged from the Demetrius Core. One very long, almost uneventful moth that bored Jeremy entirely. He was wasting away here at the townhouse, where there was nothing very exciting to do, and only weak, homeless beings to experiment with—it was all very drab and not to his liking.

Jeremy sat at his desk, flipping through piles of papers, trying to find some sort of answer as to why his project kept failing. There had to be a flaw, somewhere—or it was as simple as the fact that humans were too meek.

David was leaning against the wall on the far side of Jeremy's office, his cold blue eyes set on Jeremy as he rocked back and forth in his chair. David ran a hand through his hair and sighed.

"The attack on Spiritus Vallem starts in twenty minutes," David said, keeping his voice down. "It's the perfect opportunity for you, Jeremy. You always say the human mind is prone to error, that the mortal body is too weak—that's why every time you've tried this experiment of yours, it hasn't worked—but those *things* in the valley aren't human!"

"What are you going on about?" Jeremy was only half paying attention. His mind was clouded by the most recent failure with Edgar.

He had hoped before that he would be back in the Core by now, but things were looking pretty grim.

"Those things living outside of the city are apparently in some kind of new-age Eden or something, and—you won't believe it, but they aren't human! They aren't even demons. They're angels! I mean, who knew, huh? First we get ourselves a demon king—"

"President, now," Jeremy corrected him.

"Oh, sorry. A demon *president*, and now there are angels in the valley," David continued, lowering his voice down a bit more. "Anyway, the attack I was telling you about starts in—" he glanced down at his watch, "less than twenty minutes now."

"Graggöry wouldn't let me test on anything non-human," Jeremy said. "He said it was too—"

"You knew he wouldn't let you test on any of those demons," David chided. "They are his *brethren*, after all. Up until a month ago, the brute hardly cared how many humans failed making it through your experimentation—the moment you suggested using a stronger prototype, however… but anyway, he's not making the rules now. We are."

"I don't know," Jeremy said, leaning back in the chair and folding his arms in front of his chest. "Seventeen tries and not a one of them made it. The outcome would have probably remained the same even if he had given me permission to work on a demon body."

"But, perhaps, it would be different with an angel," David said. "They're much stronger than a human, and much more powerful than any demon. Don't you see? This is what you've been waiting for. You could get back into the Core if you pulled it off."

"We wouldn't even need the Core if I pulled it off."

David nodded, waiting for his answer.

Jeremy bit his lip and thought for a moment. His hazel eyes seemed to darken in the flickering fluorescent light as he focused on the blue prints in front of him. He sighed, running a hand through his thick brown hair now, and looked back up at David.

"You're right," Jeremy said, standing from the chair. "Grab your parka, David. We're going."

A sly smile spread across David's face as he reached for his parka, which was strewn across the back of the armchair in front of Jeremy's desk. "Ah, now that's the Jeremy I know and love. How exciting!"

Jeremy pulled on his own parka and both of them made their way out of the office and down the stairs.

"I'm going out for a while, Nesa," Jeremy called when they made it to the bottom of the stairs. "Have the water heated for when I return."

"Of course," Nesa replied as the men slammed the front door behind them.

Io

Spiritus Vallem

The snow cradled Io's mangled body.

Heat seeped out, as the cold crept in. Her thoughts were jumbled and fleeting. She could not remember what had happened aside from the sound of her bones snapping as she'd been tossed through the air like a ragdoll, over and over until there wasn't strength enough to stand and fight, or run.

She could smell the dead around her. Their blood and urine mixed into the snow and covered the scent of smoke and pine. The fires were close. She could hear the flames crackling over the treetops, toward the village. Opening her eyes, Io turned her head to the side. The smoke burned her eyes and choked her lungs. Io groaned as the pain began to overtake the numbness. It was all becoming so real, but she was suspended in a state similar to that of waking after a dream.

A dream.

Was this a dream? No. Though she desperately wished that this was just another dream, just another dark and daunting vision that plagued her, she knew it was not. The visions had never felt so *real* before. In her heart, she knew this was real—but why was it happening?

Her vision drifted in and out of blurriness. She was staring into the lifeless dull lavender eyes of a nameless soldier. His face was covered in blood, locked in a grimace. His arm was outstretched toward her, his palm facing upward, fingers pointed to the sky. His skin was pale and pasty looking. Death had taken him quickly. She imagined that rigor mortis had already set in.

Io held her breath.

The memory of the battle came to her in pieces. Glimpses of fire and magic filled her mind. She could remember the sound of the soldiers' boots and peoples' screams. Her people had fled but not fast enough. Io had watched them die, even the soldier lying beside her. They met their end here. This was where everything ended—they were in the meadow near the village, the place where everything came to die.

77

But her memories were fading. One by one things began to disappear. It felt as if she were slowly forgetting important things—things she needed to hold onto, things she needed to remember. She was stuck in the here and now, though, and what had been her past suddenly was a bleak spot in her mind.

Her lungs burned.

Io reached out, her hand shaking, to the soldier and took his hand. Her boney fingers wrapped around his. Io thought about the other corpses scattered in the meadow, the bodies that nobody would find in the village. They would all be forgotten.

Io shivered.

Closing her eyes, she gripped the soldier's hand tighter. She focused on his fingers. They were cold and stiff. She tried to think of a reason to live, but couldn't seem to find one. She looked to the soldier again. Calmness settled over her. She would much rather die in the company of someone, even if the man was dead, than all alone.

"There. Someone's still alive," a male voice said.

Io went rigid. How long had there been anyone other than the dead and herself in the meadow? How had she not heard them? The snow crunched under their heavy boots as they walked toward her.

"It's only a girl," the same voice said, sounding disappointed.

"She isn't just a girl," the other said, his voice dripping with sarcasm. "Remember?"

"Yes," the first chortled. "Just look at her wings. Beautiful."

Wings? Yes, wings, she thought. She held her breath and tried to remember for sure. Something was blocked. Io knew it must be important. Why were they talking about wings? She thought harder and for a second she remembered.

She felt something prodding at her side, and then her right shoulder blade. She gasped as pain surged through her arm and up her neck.

"She's barely breathing," the second voice said.

One of them knelt down beside her. Io could feel the heat coming from his body.

"Does it matter? Jeremy, don't you think we should look for someone a bit more... suited for your little project?"

Jeremy. That sounded familiar.

Yes, she thought. *I've seen him in many dreams.*

It brought her slight comfort to know she knew this man—and yet, there was something about him that she wasn't remembering. Something dark, something feral. She let the memory of him fade. It didn't matter, because she was dying.

The other man was obviously very annoyed. Io trembled as the second man, Jeremy, touched her twisted arm with a gloved hand. He pulled it away from her, turned it slowly and examined it. She gulped and waited a moment before breathing in slow jagged breaths. It hurt to breathe. He caressed her cheek and asked if she could open her eyes, and she wanted to say, 'No, I can't open my eyes. I'm dying. Just leave me here. Let me die.'

The words would not come out.

Lysithea

Spiritus Vallem

Lysithea watched as the flames overtook the village, listened to their demonic cackle as they devoured everything in sight. The last of the cries had died down many moments before she'd come to stand at the edge of the forest. Everyone was dead, and what once had been clear blue sky was gray and spreading the same dirty, ashen snow that fell in the cities and the Wastes. All the color and beauty had fled. Spiritus Vallem was dying, becoming the same as the rest of the horrid, ruined earth. She couldn't bear to look anymore. Her home was destroyed, and it was all her doing. She turned away from the valley and started through the dying forest, back to where her men were patiently waiting.

She had killed them, every last one that had stayed in the valley. Her parents, her sister, her brother…

She shivered and pressed on through the trees.

She shook those thoughts from her mind and instead thought of Graggöry, wondered if he was a bit better now. She had a sinking feeling down in her gut that gave her the answer. It was impossible for the voices to go away. She knew it. There was no way of knowing how many angels had fled before the onslaught began. Not everyone stayed in Spiritus Vallem.

Some people wanted more than what they were destined to be.

Lysithea knew that best.

Jeremy
Spiritus Vallem

There was something about this girl that Jeremy couldn't shake. He felt almost… drawn to her, though he hardly knew why. He knelt beside her and took her all in. Her twisted body looked so fragile, sprawled there in the snow. He set her arm down beside her and let out a sigh. Something so fragile would never make it through the surgery. Something so pure couldn't be made into a weapon of mass destruction. He wasn't sure what David was thinking—bringing him here—but he certainly couldn't stand by and let this girl die.

He had to try.

"I can make it work," he told David, who had crossed his arms in front of his chest and frowned down at him.

"I hardly think so," David said. He laughed. "Look at her."

Jeremy rolled his eyes and took the glove off his left hand to check for her pulse. It was barely there—but he could work with this, he'd worked with much worse before.

But they would have to leave the meadow soon. Time was not on their side. He glanced at the burning trees, then to the burning homes in what must have been a quaint little village. He wondered if she would survive out in the horrid world, or if he could do this to her. It would be more humane to end her right now—before he had the chance to change her, or worse, before she had the chance to change him.

He couldn't deny the pull he felt. He was compelled to help—somehow.

Something told him he had to save her, no matter what David said, no matter what the future would hold for her. For the first time in his life, he felt he had to do something—and not just because of his experiment or the plan to out the Core, but because this girl in front of him meant something even if he had no idea what that something was.

If he had believed in the notion of fate—this would fit the description.

"I can save her," Jeremy said, and put his glove back on. "She's the one."

David laughed.

Jeremy shook his head, and turned his attention back to the girl. "Are you with us?" he asked, nudging her. "Can you hear me?"

Io

Spiritus Vallem

"Can you open your eyes? Can you do *something*?" the one standing asked. His voice was low and his words were short and snappy. He shifted his weight, the snow groaning beneath him. "She's a lost cause, Jeremy. We should leave her. Let's find someone else."

"She's not a lost cause," Jeremy said. He continued to caress her cheek. "Won't you open your eyes for me, sweetheart?"

Sweetheart... it sounded nice. He had called her that before many times, in her dreams. Io almost laughed. Here she was, dying in the snow and blood and corpse covered meadow, and she felt *wanted*. Io wanted to open her eyes again. Her eyelids fluttered but failed to stay open. Jeremy ran his thumb over her bloodied forehead.

"Poor thing," he cooed. "It's all right now."

Finally, her eyes stayed open long enough for her to gaze up into his face. Jeremy was wearing a parka and goggles that made it impossible to see his eyes, but she already knew what they looked like. He looked cold and warm all at once. She envied his heat—her whole body felt like ice. Steam rose from her lips and mixed with the steam that left his.

"Welcome back," Jeremy said, smiling down at her. It was a warm, familiar thing—his smile. She almost wanted to smile back.

Instead, she watched the way his chest rose and fell slowly, noted that both men's parkas were red and covered with frost on the hoods and shoulders. Ice was hanging from the fur around Jeremy's face, and the other man—

She had seen his cold empty blue eyes before in her nightmares. She shivered and turned her attention back to Jeremy. She tried to speak but couldn't muster the courage or the breath to. He tried to sit her up, and she felt a scream stick in her throat as the pain rushed down her back. She tried to push him away, but her arms stayed limp at her sides.

"Y-you're not an angel, are you?" she asked Jeremy at last. She knew the answer before the words had even left her lips—she had never seen these men before, aside from the visions—not in Paradise, never in the valley.

Jeremy shook his head. A frown played across his face. He ran his hand back down her arm and said, "Far from it."

"Are you—" she tried to think of the words in their correct order, tried to steady her breathing long enough to finish her sentence, even if she was terrified to know the truth, "going to kill me?"

She supposed that if the visions she vaguely recalled were right, one of them would, in the end—but that had happened far away from the meadows of Spiritus Vallem. The way Jeremy was handling her arm was too tender. He wasn't going to kill her.

He didn't answer.

Io studied him a bit closer. On the parka, over his heart, was a patch, something scientific. His name was sewn above it in thick black letters. The other man stepped closer. He was holding a white bucket with an orange sticker plastered on the side. It was full of something, but she couldn't see well enough to tell what. Her eyesight had begun to blur again.

She coughed and her body jerked. He gently rubbed her shoulder.

"You're a—" she searched for the word, struggling to find it, "scientist, aren't you?"

"What's your name, sweetheart?" Jeremy asked, ignoring her question. He turned to the other man. "David, look at her eyes."

"Her eyes?"

"Io," she said.

Her memories began flooding back to her. She flinched at the pain they caused inside her.

"Yes, her eyes," Jeremy said, and then, "What a lovely name. Io, like Jupiter's moon."

She trembled. In all her life, she had never heard her name said quite that perfectly. The man, this scientist, had to be an angel from somewhere beyond Spiritus Vallem. He had come to save her.

"What about her eyes?" David asked, sighing.

He leaned over Jeremy. He glanced at the watch on his left wrist and rolled his eyes, moving the goggles back over his face. He pulled the edges of the parka hood closer.

"They're lavender."

Io wasn't sure why they were talking about her eyes. She tried to keep focusing on Jeremy's face, on the sound of their voices, but it was all starting to mix together again. Her body tingled and went numb once more.

"We're losing her," David said.

Maybe she was still going to die. She'd almost forgotten. The future could change; her mother had once told her. Nothing was ever set in stone, not even her visions. Io knew it would be any moment now. At any given second her heart would give and she would be free to drift into the dark oblivion that waited for her. There would be no more worries. There would be no more suffering where she was going.

"I'm going to die," she said to no one.

She didn't sound frantic, or sad, but instead she sounded a little relieved. Living was such a heavy burden to bear all alone. She was trying to convince herself that dying would be all right, that everything would be okay if she just accepted it, if she welcomed it. She couldn't, though. Io felt in some way that she had failed someone, something. There was something she had been meant to do that she hadn't. She remembered then, her mother talking about the end— the prophecy that loomed over her head—and she knew. It was her fault that everything had turned out this way. She had not done anything to save them.

She had failed herself.

"Jeremy? We're running out of time," David's voice drifted over the lonely white snow.

Io pictured the face of the solider, her fingers had frozen against his. The loneliness hit her then. She felt so empty, she couldn't even cry.

"You're going to be okay now," Jeremy said, and she wanted to believe him—but there was something she just was not remembering. Something she needed to remember about him.

She felt his arm scooping underneath her, and the pressure against her shoulders and back as he lifted her from the snow. Io wanted to scream and tell him not to touch her, but the confusion swept back over her until she couldn't decipher the real from her dreams. She was barely breathing. She was so tired. Io just wanted to die there in the snow.

"You'll be okay now, Io," he said again. The warmth of his breath pressed against her ear. "I promise."

It sounded like a lie. She closed her eyes, welcoming the darkness.

"Wait," David said, peering over Jeremy's shoulder. "Her wings are gone."

She couldn't really understand what they were talking about anymore, but didn't care. Io leaned her head against Jeremy's shoulder. He smelled like chemicals.

"We'll have to hurry," Jeremy said, and then there was nothing.

Jeremy
The Townhouse

Jeremy and David had somehow made it back to the townhouse without being seen—by some miracle, or just because it was cold and raining and nobody in their right mind would ever want to be out in that mess. Whatever it was, Jeremy was thankful for it. He carried Io in through the kitchen door and headed for the basement. He had to get an IV in her and fast—she needed a dose of the Vivificantem serum, because somewhere along the way they had lost her. He was sure, however, that he would get her back. She wasn't too far gone—not yet. If he could get her stable, he could start the procedure.

"Nesa," Jeremy said. He carried Io down the narrow staircase that led to his make-shift laboratory.

"Yes, sir?" Nesa replied, the basement camera blinking red in the dim light.

"Send word to Max. I need those parts tonight."

"Right away, sir," Nesa answered. "Shall I ask him to have Crosbie bring them?"

"Yes," Jeremy said. "David has to go back to work and I—"

"I know," Nesa interrupted. "I'm on it."

Jeremy nodded with appreciation and laid Io's lifeless body onto his homemade operating table. He strapped down her good arm and her good leg and set to work hooking up her IV.

"Well, I'll be on my way now," David said, giving Io a suspicious glance. "If you're sure this is going to work…"

"I'm sure," Jeremy said. "I've got a good feeling about this one."

David shook his head, unmoved and not thrilled. Jeremy tried not to feel too discouraged by it. He stuck the IV drip into her arm, and got the Vivificantem shot out of a nearby drawer. He stuck the needle down into Io's heart, and prayed the serum would take. He took a step back to survey his new test subject. David gave him one last small smile, in what Jeremy thought was an almost sarcastic-yet-reassuring gesture, and turned to leave.

"Send word when it's over," David said. "I'm counting on you."

Jeremy was counting on Io. She seemed strong, though she was only a girl, not but seventeen or eighteen years old. He wasn't sure. All he knew was that she had to be strong to survive what happened to her in that meadow for as long as she had. Anyone weak would have given up, but for some reason, Io was still clinging on to life. He was almost rooting for her—not entirely because he needed this to work.

There was that something inside of him that urged him to help her.

"You can do it, Io," he said to her as the serum took. "Come back to me."

Io gasped on the table, but did not open her eyes. He checked her pulse— barely there, but something. He could work with that.

He dug around his tool drawer until he found his saw and set to work on her severely twisted arm. He supposed it had to have hurt a great deal—another way he knew she was strong. She hadn't given in to the unbearable pain she must have been feeling.

"I spoke to Crosbie," Nesa said. "He's bringing you your parts right now."

"Perfect," Jeremy said as he cauterized the wound.

He set to work on her leg, pausing to check her pulse once more. She definitely was a fighter. That was good for him, but that might make things a little difficult for the Core. He shrugged and kept working until his doorbell rang.

He stepped away from the table and made his way back up the stairs.

"I'll be right there," he called to the door.

He hurried to the kitchen sink and washed his hands, before walking back to the door, and peering through the peephole. Crosbie was standing in the rain, hauling two packages wrapped in plastic. Jeremy opened the door.

"Hey, Crosbie," Jeremy said as he stepped out of the way, letting Crosbie in from the cold. "Long time no see. Bring those in."

"Nice to see you, too," Crosbie laughed as he carried the first of the packages into the foyer. He set them down and tugged on the sleeve of his drenched coat. "I'm sorry it took a little longer than it should've. Jynx wanted to make sure the mag—er—that it stuck."

"You don't have to worry about saying magic," Jeremy laughed, unwrapping the first package. "Nesa won't tell a soul, will you Nesa?"

"Of course not, sir."

"Anyway, it's not a problem," Jeremy said. He closed the door behind Crosbie and went to where hung. "I have your money right here. You'll have to forgive me for being in a rush… my patient is… not doing so well."

Crosbie took the crisp bills from Jeremy's hand and counted them silently before stuffing them deep into his coat pocket. "Thanks."

"No, thank you. I'm sorry you had to make a trip in this horrible weather," Jeremy said, "but it was urgent that I get these parts tonight."

"You're my pal, so it's no problem," Crosbie said, tugging on the hood of his jacket. "I've been out in worse. Besides, I had to get away from Jynx."

They both laughed. Jeremy smiled and stuck out his hand for Crosbie to shake.

"It's always a pleasure doing business with you," Jeremy said. "Your father does excellent work—oh, and good luck with getting your apprenticeship!"

Crosbie took his hand and shook it, his bright green eyes shimmering in the foyer's dim light. "Thank you, Jer. We're always glad to help you out."

Jeremy opened the door for him and wished him well. As soon as Crosbie was out of sight, he picked up the first package and carried it down the stairs, before coming back for the other. Once they were down in the basement, he turned his attention back to Io. She was barely breathing again, so he put her on some oxygen and slipped one more dose of the Vivificantem into her IV line.

"You'll be good as new in a couple of hours," he said, almost unable to conceal his excitement. He supposed he shouldn't be too excited yet; after all, several of his other test subjects made it further than this. He just had a feeling that this time, everything was going to work out.

He set to work un-wrapping the second package, growing even giddier by the moment. He placed the arm beside Io on the table and smiled when the magic shrank it down to the perfect size. It was truly fascinating to watch Jynx's magic. It never ceased to amaze him, though he was still rather skeptical about the whole thing. For what he needed, it would serve its purpose well. He did the same thing with the leg, turning from her and back to his tools. He dug around in the drawer for a little while, mumbling under his breath, before turning back to the body. He started for the table.

"Okay, sweetheart," he said. "Let's see if we can't fix you back up."

Father Baxley

Cathedral of Our Lady Victory

Something had shifted deep within the spiritual realm.

Something vital had disappeared from the earth, but Father Baxley could not quite think of what that could possibly be. Whatever ethereal thing it had been, was important, and now it was gone. Father Baxley crossed his arms and looked closely at his rejection in the window he was standing in front of. He had been doing this for many years, had seen many things, and had watched the world go through many changes, but never had he ever felt this hollow feeling inside. Something was terribly wrong. He sighed and looked beyond his reflection at the forever-darkening clouds in a sky that would never be blue again.

Lately, the world had been very broken. When he had been born, the Underground people were thriving and faith was strong—there had been great peace. The world was falling back into its old ways. Yet, loyally he kept the faith—whether it was because of duty, or because he truly believed.

He did not know.

Father Baxley supposed that he still believed, or eyes, like most of the others, he would have fled. The war had grown larger, the tragic onslaught growing impedingly closer. Still, here he was at the Cathedral, and he supposed he would stay with the Cathedral until the very end. If the others did not persuade him to flee—like a good captain, he would go down with his ship. There were many days when he did want to leave, however. He prayed for hours for answers that his God had not yet given to him.

They were answers, he supposed, that could only be given to the dead.

And somewhere, something important had finally died, something that had held the world together—at least, that's what Father Baxley felt in his heart. He said a quick prayer and turned from the window, deciding to seek solitude elsewhere. He had to think—had to really think—about what it could be that was gone. Such a large spiritual presence should not have just disappeared. What could it have been, and in how much trouble was the earth? He sighed and paced down the hall, pondering. The nuns were starting to settle in for the night, but he would not be able to sleep. He had to know. He had to put his finger on what it was that was gone.

If he was lucky enough, by the morning, he would have it figured out.

|Part Two|

Lysithea
The Palace

Lysithea stood outside of Graggöry's office. Her grey eyes focused on the slender gold dragon-shaped handles that twisted their way along the center of the polished oaken doors. She took a breath, fluffing her ashen curls before pinching her cheeks to give them a slight flush. She crouched down in front of the door, so that she could see herself in the wood's polished sheen. To her disappointment, she could tell by the reflection of her face in the door that all her makeup had faded and smeared. Great. If anything, she was only semi-presentable, but Graggöry wouldn't hold that against her.

Maybe I should use some magic. She frowned. There were new, stricter laws against that. She had seen Graggöry use magic on a number of occasions—but he was the president, and she was not. Her magic was unique to angels, anyway—if she used it and someone found out about it, everyone would know the truth. If she wasn't careful, she would wind up dead. Lysithea certainly did not want that, not after the monstrous, traitorous thing she had done to those unknowing angels in the valley. She feared the punishment that awaited her in her afterlife almost as much as she feared Graggöry finding out the truth.

She sighed and stood back up, smoothing her hands over her jet-black uniform skirt. She hoped that Graggöry was—at least—a little bit better. After all, the massacre in Spiritus Vallem had, for the most part, been an overall success and one of the greatest military feats of their time. However, there was still that one little thing—

She shook her head.

It worked, she told herself, because after what she had done, she had to believe that it had. If she thought of it long and hard, she could will it to life, somehow. *Don't worry, Lys. You'll see. He'll finally be the man you fell in love with again. You'll have your Graggöry back. You've saved him.*

It was probably hopeless.

93

Her lips twitched and she furrowed her brows, making a soft, hesitant noise in her throat.

What if he's not...?

She shook her head again and reached for the dragon handle.

"Well, you look like shit," someone said from behind her.

Lysithea pulled her arm back and hesitantly turned toward the voice. She groaned and gritted her teeth.

"David," she said.

He smirked and took a step toward her. She stood a bit straighter and bit her bottom lip. He held out a file he was holding, nodding his head toward it as he said, "Nice job with Spiritus Vallem. Graggöry must be so proud."

She shuddered and snatched the file from him. She was still trying to convince herself that she was doing the right thing, but her conscience was starting to get the best of her.

"Well, are you going to look?" David asked, with his permanently annoyed tone. "It's the final archive. You have to approve it."

Lysithea opened the file, slowly looking through it. Her eyes fell to the pictures; burned bodies of angels and animals, burned cabins, snow and blood and corpse covered fields. She paused on a page, her fingers pressed tightly into the corners as her eyes focused on the face of one body in particular. It was a girl, mangled in the snow, lavender eyes looking up but not really seeing.

Her breathing stopped—

Night has fallen over Spiritus Vallem.

A cold wind rushes through the cracks in the cottage walls, howling and reaching for any life it can hold onto. Death. This kind of wind tastes different, feels different.

"It's going to snow," Io says.

She is sitting in front of the window, watching as the large black clouds smother the stars. Her fingertips curl into the splintered wood as she focuses on Lysithea's reflection, but to Lysithea's disappointment, she won't turn to face her sister.

"You should stay," Io says.

"I can't. You know I have my reasons for leaving."

"Leaving won't change who you are. What you really are," Io says.

"You're wrong," Lysithea whispers. How could Io not know? How could she really not know of the darkness that grows in Lysithea's heart, Io is supposed to know everything. Lysithea's chest aches. She must go. She *must* find him.

"What if you don't find him?" Io asks, like she can read Lysithea's mind. Just like Kale. She pushes away from the window and turns to face Lysithea. "What if you never find him?"

"I know you know about the voices and the dreams," Lysithea snaps. "And you pretend, but I know you know about the darkness, about the prophecy. You're just like mother. How could I forget? I *will* find him. You know I will!"

"Please stay," Io pleads. "It doesn't have to be this way."

Lysithea remains silent. It does have to be this way. She knows this is the only way. This is the only way to escape what she is, the only way to save them all.

"Do what you want, then," Io says, her voice dripping with disappointment. She turns back to the window.

"Io—"

"I'm certainly not going to stop you," Io whispers, her voice every bit as cold as the wind outside. "If this is the only way, then go."

Lysithea turns to the door, grabbing her coat and clutching it tightly in her arms. She glances back up the stairs. Her mother and father probably know that she is leaving, but she hasn't told them or her little brother, Kale. It's better this way. It's better to silently slip into the night. Perhaps, that won't hurt so badly. She'll miss them, but she knows that this is for the best. She doesn't belong here—there's too much darkness inside of her.

"Goodbye," she whispers to the darkness at the top of the staircase. She turns back to Io, watches her for a brief second before speaking. "I'm leaving now. I'm sorry, Io."

Io shrugs.

"You won't even say goodbye?"

"Goodbye, Lysithea," Io murmurs.

"Goodbye, Io," she says and shivers as she steps out into the cold—

Io.

Lysithea trembled and closed the file, shoving it back into David's hands as quickly as she'd snatched it from him. "Yeah, it's fine. Archive it."

He eyed her. "Is something wrong?"

"No."

"You aren't really going in there like *that*, are you?" he asked, tucking the file under his arm.

She growled and took a step back toward the door. "Yes."

"Let me help you out," he said, taking a step toward her. "I know a few tricks."

"Tricks?" Lysithea asked, sighing. She turned back to him. "A human who knows a few tricks sounds very… illegal."

Ignoring her, David continued, "We both know what Graggöry likes, you know. You aren't wearing enough eye shadow, not enough mascara."

"Like you would really know!"

"Who do you think found his *prey* before you came along *and ruined everything*?" David asked, chuckling lightly. "Oh hey. You have horrible bags under your eyes, haven't—"

"I haven't slept very well," she spat.

"Oh, well, I'm sorry, *Your Grace*," he remarked, a sarcastic grin spreading across his face. "Forgive me. Shall I grovel at your feet? I mean you are practically our queen, playing house with Graggöry like that."

She really hated him.

Lysithea was about to make a snide remark when the door on the left clicked open enough so that the light from the room stretched out in a thin line onto the bottom of her knee-length skirt.

"Well, that's my cue," she said to David and turned toward the door, before muttering under her breath, "Now carry on, asshole."

She could hear David laughing as she closed the door behind her. It infuriated her that he was such a jerk, and not just to her, but to everyone. If Graggöry hadn't been so fond of the bastard, she would have put an end to it a long time ago. She had tried hard to contain her hatred, but her angelic qualities were few and far between now. She was a Grade A demon—had fallen so far from God's grace, for sure this time, with the things she had done.

"Graggöry," she said. "You've got to do something about that fucking prick. Really. Who does he think he is? I swear, one day I'm going to—"

Graggöry looked up from the papers he was holding. The long sleeves of his burgundy shirt were rolled up to his elbows, the first three buttons undone, his tie tossed across the corner of his desk. He ran a hand through his prematurely graying hair. Even his eyes were darker, more troubled.

Oh no...

"Lys," he said, and sighed.

Lysithea sat down in her chair. The blinds were closed and the curtains were drawn in all but one window, which made the room look gloomy despite its canary yellow wallpaper. She ran her fingers over the arms of the chair and sat back, looking at the rest of the Old Victorian styled furniture in the room. Graggöry always had a taste for older things, preferably styles and antiques from way before the Fallout. She tried to smile, but it quickly faded as she glanced back to him.

"I'm out of cigarettes," he mumbled, setting the papers back down and shuffling through them again.

"What's really the matter, love?" she asked. "Aren't you happy?"

"I should be," he responded. The fingers of his right hand balled into a fist atop the pile of papers. "After all, you did so well with what I asked."

She frowned a bit and closed her eyes, bringing her hand up to massage her forehead. It was just as she had feared. The Graggöry she had known was still gone. It hadn't worked. She had killed all those innocents for nothing.

"They're all dead, aren't they, Lys?" he asked. His voice cracked.

There was a pang in her heart that Lysithea had never felt before, so powerful that she almost couldn't breathe.

"Yes," she whispered, lying to him. She placed her head in her hands, her elbows digging into her knees.

It was all for nothing, she miserably thought. *He's not coming back.*

They were silent for a moment. He pushed his chair away from the desk. She opened her eyes and watched him. His eyes had lightened a bit and he was smiling. She felt a little relieved.

"Come here, love," he said.

Lysithea stood from the chair and went to him. He pulled her down into his lap and she smiled, resting her arms on his broad shoulders. She had missed being this way with him. The voices had made Graggöry so distant, had made their relationship seem almost void. He pulled her closer, running his hand up her neck, his palm coming to rest on her cheek.

His eyes seemed to dim again.

"What is it?" she asked, tilting her head toward his touch.

She wanted him to fill the emptiness she suddenly felt. He was right in front of her, but she was utterly alone.

He stiffened and shook his head. "Nothing."

Lysithea pulled away from him. She dreaded asking him what was wrong, dreaded hearing his answers. "You seem… frightened. Please tell me. Are things really not better?"

He said nothing.

"Please tell me," she pleaded.

"You did everything I asked—" his voice broke, was barely even audible. "You did more than you needed to, to heal me."

"Are you not healed?" she asked. Her voice sounded high-pitched and shaky with fear, a pitiful whimper.

He watched her, his arm tightening around her waist. Lysithea already knew the answer. She could see it in his eyes. She could taste the panic on his breath.

"Well, aren't you?" she tried again.

"Lys, I—" he took a breath and sighed. "I wish I could tell you yes, that it worked, that everything is okay now. I had hoped for you that it would be, but the voices aren't gone."

"Aren't gone," she echoed.

"They're worse," he whispered.

She stared at him, horrified, and felt tears beginning to swell in her eyes. She couldn't cry or the magic she'd been using to conceal her true eye color would fade, and he would know the truth. She tried blinking back the tears. She wished that it could be a lie. He was just kidding with her. He had to be. She knew, however, that he was telling the truth. It was almost as though the voices were taunting her from behind his hollow stare.

"They told me that all the angels aren't dead," he tried to explain. "They told me—"

Lysithea covered his mouth with her lips, pressing her body closer to him in a desperate attempt to make it all go away.

"Hush," she begged and pulled away. "No more, love. No more about the voices right now. *Please.*"

"It frightens you," he said, and stroked her hair. He curled a strand of it around his finger.

"No more," she whispered. "Just—let's be how we were before. Let me comfort you."

He let the strand of hair slip free from his finger and dropped his hand down to her blouse, unbuttoning the first button, his fingers grazing her collarbone.

"I think I'm beyond comforting now," he murmured, but she wasn't listening.

Lucie
Hell

"Dammit," Lucifer hissed, slamming a fist down onto the arm of her throne. She stared off into the distant glow of hellfire, leaning all the way back until she was uncomfortably pressed against the bones and iron.

Something was not right.

Though her plan had worked—for the most part—there was still a glimmer of goodness left somewhere in the vastness of the earth. Goodness that should have been slain earlier, along with the angels in the valley.

An angel was still alive.

Lucifer cringed and closed her eyes, tilting her head back in an attempt to control her anger. The insatiable feeling only continued to grow. Not a single angel should have walked away from that valley, and yet one had—it was the only explanation she could think of.

"How can this be?" she asked the darkness.

Everything had been going just as she had planned. The valley had been attacked, the angels had been slain, and still the nagging goodness shimmered through, taunting her, though it was barely there. Someone was hanging on by a thread. Someone had left the valley. But who could that be? She searched the minds of countless, nameless people, trying to find the little bit of pureness that remained, but every mind she encountered was just as corrupted as the last—except for one.

Graggöry's mate.

Her claws scraped against the arms of the throne as she searched for Lysithea in what seemed like a sea of people. Her spirit was tainted now that she had killed all those poor angels, but still there was something there—something innately good that Lucifer could not easily dismiss. She would have to do something about it before the prophecy could ruin her plan. It very easily could be said that Lysithea was the angel who would help destroy the world. She had done the unthinkable by slaughtering the rest of the angels. There was a chance, slim as it may be, that she could be the angel to save it.

That poor girl had long ago given in to the darkness—her soul was so corrupt that the goodness barely shown through. But just to be sure, Lucifer would end her. It wouldn't be hard to do. Graggöry would eventually snap and when he did—

Lucifer chuckled. She would make a game out of this. David would soon take care of Graggöry, but in the meantime, she would have her fun. Now that Graggöry had finally run out of those damned cigarettes, her influence on him would not waiver. She would have Graggöry do her dirty work for her before he died.

It was a simple enough plan. It would work.

She flicked her wrist and snapped her fingers as a mirror-like portal shimmered to life before her. She watched her reflection before the image changed to Graggöry and Lysithea, tangled together in his office. He was already questioning her—he could also sense the goodness—so tipping him over the edge wouldn't be that hard.

She smiled, her too-wide mouth stretching across her scarred face. It was a lovely thing to cause someone so much pain. It would be even lovelier when he finally broke.

"She's an angel," Lucifer whispered to his mind. "She's the last one. Slay her."

She watched as Graggöry's face contorted at the thought. She leaned forward and cackled as she wisped the portal away. Lysithea had to be the last one left—try as she might, she could not find another soul that seeped goodness like an angel's. She would kill Lysithea, and if the goodness still prevailed, she would move on to her next plan—time was running out.

She needed to hurry or all would be lost. She had come so far and she had conquered so much that victory was on the tip of her tongue. There was no room for failure this time—the last time she had failed, she had been cast out of Paradise... left here, Queen of Hell. Though that did not displease her, she still longed for more. Paradise and the mortal realm would be lost to her forever if she failed again. She could not afford to let that happen. Not now.

Lucifer bit her lip, her fangs digging into her skin. She leaned back again and thought about David. She would go speak with him. He would reassure her. It was about time she made an appearance to him in person—before he lost faith in her.

"My darling," she said, as she stood from the throne, "I'm coming."

She took a step forward into the darkness and let it consume her.

Io

Somewhere

Io woke to the distinct sound of a tool whirring. Beneath her was a cold, hard metal surface—a table? She tried to sit up but found that her arms were restrained. With a glance to her side, she tugged a wrist up against the thick crimson stained straps that held her firmly down. Her eyes concentrated on the straps. Her mind slipped out of its in-between state. She shuddered and turned her head. Her eyes widened with horror. Instead of her wrist, a long, slender, silver, almost cylindrical piece of metal extended from her shoulder to where her elbow had been. Another piece extended down from that, ending with a horrifying spider-like robotic hand. Io had only seen something like this before in her visions—but this was too real to be a vision.

Everything had been real.

Her heart sank. She thought briefly about her family, about how they were all dead now—left to decay in the fields in a ruined Spiritus Vallem. Everyone she had known lay dead in their houses and in the fields and in the forest—there was no way anyone had escaped. How had she? How was she alive? Why was she alive?

Panic coursed through her body.

She focused her attention back to the almost cylindrical pieces of metal that were now her arm. She tried to move the fingers and shivered at the sound the fingertips made as they lightly tapped at the table beneath her. Io let out a frightened squeak and adverted her eyes from the left side of her body to the man who was now staring back up at her. He stopped the drill. She felt nothing.

"You're awake," he said. He sounded relieved. He reached down to switch the drill bit. He said something under his breath and closed the drawer beside him, tending to the drill before glancing back up at her again. "I'm glad. I lost you several times until the serum took. David thought I would never have you stable."

Jeremy. This is Jeremy. Slight relief flooded through her. This was just as her vision had been, and yet—she struggled to remember exactly how it had gone. She had thought for sure that the future had been changed. She had thought that she was going to die in the valley along with her family and friends, but fate was a fickle thing and here she was—reliving her nightmares.

"M-my arm," she said, finally finding her voice. Shock had settled in. Though she had seen this all before, she couldn't believe it was actually happening. There had to be some sort of explanation as to why she was alive and why she was missing her arm. Jeremy could give her answers, but maybe he wouldn't. She couldn't tell.

Jeremy took the goggles he was wearing off, wiping a hand across his forehead before his gaze fell to her left side.

"Oh yes," he said, frowning a bit. "Yes."

His deep hazel eyes focused on her face again. "About that, sweetheart. I'm very sorry. Your left arm and right leg were just too damaged for me to consider saving."

She had not even looked down at her leg until now. "But this—"

"It was all I could do," he interrupted.

He patted her leg and it made a sort of hollow metallic clank. She still felt nothing. It frightened her. Io bit her bottom lip almost all the way through, stopping herself from screaming as she continued to stare down at him. She could taste her blood, warm and sweet as it filled her mouth. Trying to calm down, she thought to focus on anything but the fear. Her body shook.

She noticed a different scent than the chemicals—rotting flesh.

Panic enveloped her. She struggled against the binds. How could this be happening? Why wasn't she dead? She would have much rather have been dead. Those visions, the nightmares, everything that awaited her—she didn't want any of it.

"But my body!" she screamed as she continued to try to free herself, yanking hard on the straps around her wrists. To her dismay, her new metal arm proved to be completely useless.

Jeremy sighed and set the drill down, rolling his stool up until he was right beside her. He reached down into another drawer and pulled out a syringe full of a light-yellow liquid, and grabbed the IV line that was protruding from her remaining arm.

"You need to stay calm, Io, or you'll hurt yourself. I'm going to give you this—" here he paused to give her a better glimpse of whatever was inside of the syringe, "and you will fall back to sleep, okay?"

She eyed the syringe and shook her head. "No! I don't want it!"

"You need it. Trust me, sweetheart. I'll be done before you know it and then we'll discuss what happens next when you wake up," he said as he stuck the needle in. "I'm so sorry for all of this. I really am."

It sounded like a lie. Jeremy's voice was monotone and cold, not as gentle and laced with concern as it had been when he'd found her. This was the Jeremy of her early visions, the cruel version. The uncaring man she had watched change night after night. She knew he wasn't sorry. Not yet, anyway.

Her arm stung only for a moment and then she groggily watched him rolling back down to her leg. He picked the drill back up.

"Wait," she said. He didn't answer so she tried again as everything was beginning to cloud over. Her mind felt foggy. She tried to cling onto this moment, but it was hard to keep her eyes open. She took a deep breath and felt herself falling asleep. No matter how many times Io tried to get his attention, Jeremy ignored her and continued to work on her new leg. Io felt tears swelling in her eyes and slipping down her cheeks as she drifted back out of consciousness.

From the fields, men are shouting.

Io can hear the low drone of something that must be big and mechanical as it crashes through the timber of the forest behind their house. The voices from the fields become more frantic, louder, and then nothing at all. Kale is trying to climb up onto the windowsill to see what's going on.

"Sissy," he says and turns to her, his lavender eyes spark in the dim morning light. He reaches up to her, "Sissy, what's going on? Can you see?"

She reaches down and picks him up, setting him onto her shoulders as they both look out the window and to the east, where the shouting has stopped. A loud boom rattles the house. The glass in the window sucks in before shattering. Io steps away. Her brother jumps down from her and she catches him, turning his face to her chest and holding him against her.

"It's happening," Io says.

"What's happening?" Kale cries, clinging to her now.

"It's war," she says, before he can read her mind.

She's seen this in her dreams. Knowing all too well how it's all going to end, she desperately tries to think of a plan anyway. Her mother has always told her that the future isn't set in stone. All things can be changed.

Kale asks a question that she doesn't quite catch. She doesn't answer.

Io looks out the broken window. Smoke is rising from the field where their father works.

"Where's Momma?" he asks, pulling his body away from hers, his little fingers digging into her collarbone, cutting her skin. "I want Momma."

Io flinches. She doesn't know what to do or what to say.

"Io!" Kale calls. "Where's Momma?"

"Hush," she says, a little too sternly. Her voice is low and harsh, stiff with terror. "Momma went to the fields to find Daddy. We have to go find them there."

"We can't," he says, and his eyes are watering from tears. "It's scary in the fields, that's where those noises are coming from, Io."

"I know," she says, but they have to find a way to escape. If they stay in the house, they'll die for sure.

"I can hear their thoughts," Kale whispers. "Io, I can hear their thoughts."

"Shh," Io coos.

Women are rushing their children through the streets. Io steps out of the house and follows them, pulling Kale along with her. He's tugging on her hand, trying to make her go back into the house.

A soldier from their village has arrived from the south field.

"Come with me," he tells them, leading the group of women and children through the forest and to the east field. "We must be quick."

"We shouldn't go this way," an older woman says. Her two small children are pulling on her skirt. She grabs their hands and starts to turn back.

"We don't have a choice," the soldier says, reaching out to stop her. "Going back is suicide. This is the only way out."

Io shivers. It's exactly as it was in her visions. She looks down at Kale, who's now clinging to her leg, sobbing. She frowns. As a six-year-old, his life on earth has just begun… he shouldn't be running for his life—he should be playing in the fields. He chose this life, so he could be a child again—not so he could be slaughtered in cold blood.

She reaches down to pry his tiny fingers from her leg, tightening her fingers around his.

"I'm afraid this is the end," Io whispers.

The woman tugs her children closer and lets out a sob.

This is the end. There's absolutely nothing they can do. Io knows it.

She looks back to Kale and pulls him closer, running her hand lightly over his raven curls. She's always been so fond of the way they resemble each other. Neither of them looks like their mother. If only he had the chance to, Kale would grow up to look just like Abraxos. Her heart hurts.

"I love you," she says to Kale. "No matter what happens. I want you to be strong and know that I love you."

He nods his little head, looking up at her with wide, teary eyes. "I love Io more. Promise."

They arrive at the clearing and halt. They're walking into death. The meadow is already sprawled with massacred bodies. She lifts Kale into her arms, squeezing his fragile frame against her, and kisses his forehead. The soldier looks down at them and tries to smile. No one is brave enough to step into the open land alone.

"Listen to me, Kale," Io says, looking straight into his eyes. "You run. No matter what happens to me, you run until you can't run anymore."

Kale says nothing, only nods.

The girl to their left goes first.

"Hurry!" the soldier yells, but his command is drowned out by the shouting and gunfire.

"Io!" Kale shrieks, his arms wrapping tightly around her neck. He's shaking. "Io—"

Io stands frozen at the entrance of the clearing and looks around. People are falling to the ground as soon as they step out. She looks down at Kale as he buries his head into her neck. His fingers dig into her shoulders. She frowns. She knows they are going to die.

"I'll wait for you in Paradise," Kale whispers. "This isn't the end."

She nods, stepping out into the field. She springs for the other side. It's all she can do. She knows of nothing else now, her mind has gone blank with fear.

"Run, sissy, run faster!" Kale screams. She can feel his heart pounding against her chest. He's trembling so fiercely, it's almost too hard to hold him.

"I'm trying," she says, but as she thinks of what to do next, her side begins to burn. Kale cries out one last time and then becomes limp in her arms. She can't feel his heart beating anymore.

Io falls to her knees and clings to him, a sob racking her body.

"I love you," she whispers, but he doesn't answer this time.

She buries her face into his neck now, unable to control her weeping. Another intense sting rips through her shoulder and she starts to go numb. She sets Kale's little body into the snow and stands. It isn't Kale anymore. She knows that, but she can't take her eyes from him.

Someone knocks into her, desperately trying to make it to the other side, but they only make it two or three more steps passed her before they're shot down. They stumble forward and crawl until some enemy soldier puts them out of their misery.

She looks back down to Kale's body for the last time. There's a part of her who wants to die with him, but there's another part that's screaming for her to run, to survive. She looks up at the falling snow. Suddenly, she's yanked out of her thoughts.

"They're using dark magic!" the soldier shouts, catching up with her. He tugs on her arm. "Hurry! You must flee!"

Before they can run, she's suddenly in the air. She's thrown a few yards from where she left her brother, over and over until she can't breathe, and then she's left in the snow. She can't focus enough to see what's doing it, but the next thing she knows, she's in the air once more. The field of massacred bodies lies below her, their bloodied hands reaching up as their voices beckon for her to save them. They call her name. They beg her, but she can't help. She doesn't know how to go back down, because she doesn't know what's controlling her. She's continuously pulled further and away from them, pulled so far that now she can see the entire meadow below her.

Beneath her, their voices scream for her to come back down. They call her a traitor. Their faces contort until they aren't even faces at all.

They scream out, "Traitor—"

Io gasped and opened her eyes.

Jeremy

The Townhouse

Jeremy leaned back in his chair, tapping his fingers on the edge of his desk, his almost-vacant stare fixated on the wall on the other side of the room. Everything went much better than he had expected. Io was the first to ever make it through the experiment, but now he was faced with a much greater problem—Io had a strong-willed mind of her own. That wouldn't bode well, not with the Core. It put a little kink in the plan, that was for sure. He frowned. He had never really thought much farther ahead than the actual experiment before, knowing good and well that his subject would not make it through the first phase. Now he had a living subject and a lot of work to do. He already knew she was not likely to jump on board with the plans he had for her, though. She would especially be against it when she realized that the Core had been responsible for the death of her whole clan.

Jeremy sighed. What could he do, but lie to her?

Dim light stretched across the floor from the small window behind him. It was almost nighttime—the sun was setting. He wondered if he should go check on her. She hadn't emerged from the guest room yet, and he was getting concerned that he'd given her too much Somnium to make her sleep.

"Nesa," he called out to the room.

Nesa's bubbly voice crackled through the speaker by the door. "Yes, sir?"

"Check on Io for me, would you?"

There was a moment of silence and then Nesa said, "She's awake now, sir."

He thought for a moment. He had to try something. He at least needed to feel her out—maybe she would go along with it, though the chances of that actually happening were few and far between. There was no way—and he knew it—that she would want to become a murder machine. The Core would make her into a monster. He sighed and shook the slight feelings of guilt from his conscience. It didn't matter what she thought or what they did to her as long as it got him back where he needed to be.

He couldn't very well take the Core down when he was stuck in the townhouse. He needed Io. He needed her, to get back into the Core, so he could continue with his and David's plan. His parents' deaths needed avenging. He wouldn't let his good-hearted conscience get the best of him now. He had saved her so she could save him. That's all this was.

"Send her to me," he said to Nesa.

"Right away, sir."

He tapped his finger on the desk three times, a holographic screen flickering to life before him. He had to get word to David. If he had believed in miracles, maybe this would be one. It was a rather impossible feat.

He would soon get what he wanted.

Lysithea and Graggöry
The Palace

Lysithea looked down at the scratches on her pale wrists. There were teeth marks that trailed up her arms to her neck. She looked at her face in the mirror. Her eyes were dull, the light drained from them. She cringed and ran her fingers up and down her arms. She knew better than to wonder about where it had gone. Of course, it was Graggöry. He drank those things away from her— he needed those things.

"I'm sorry," Graggöry said, but he didn't sound like himself. "I'm so sorry, Lys. I didn't mean—"

"It's okay," she said a little too quickly. "I know you didn't mean to take so much."

He pushed himself off the desk and watched her. She looked back at the mirror. Her hair looked lighter in the evenings. She turned to him and smiled, a soft smile that she hoped would reassure him. He was changed, but she would not be like the others and accuse him or blame him or even hate him. She could never hate him.

Graggöry watched her, a knot forming in the pit of his stomach. She was so lovely and so kind and so undeserving. What kind of monster was he to be doing this to her?

Take more, a voice snickered. *Take as much as you want.*

He must have made a face because she frowned and stepped away from the mirror. She turned back to him. "As long as you're feeling better now."

"I am," he told her, running a hand through his hair.

Take more, the voice urged.

Graggöry growled and slammed his fist down onto the desk.

Lysithea jumped. She walked back to the desk and wrapped her arms around him, pressing her body lightly against his. "Don't worry, my love."

He stroked her hair and caressed her cheek to keep himself from looking into her eyes. Lysithea shivered. She could feel the change in him, the horrible aura that had claimed everything familiar to her. It made her chest burn, her fingers feel repulsed, but she stayed there with her arms wrapped tightly around him.

"I won't let you down," she said and kissed his cheek. She knew it was a lie. She would always let him down, now that he was not her Graggöry anymore. Her very being was keeping him from getting better.

Graggöry watched as the bruises on Lysithea's arms healed. It was too fast to be the work of a normal demon body. She ran her hands over the fading bite marks on her arms and frowned. He noted that she tasted different from the rest, too. She tasted sweeter. He stood and took his tie from the corner of the desk, rolling it up and stuffing it into his pocket. Lysithea had told him a long time ago that she wasn't a human. "A demon,' she had said, "just like you."

But she couldn't be a demon. Not with that taste. Not with how quickly she healed.

What was she?

He frowned. He should let it go. He should believe her. Her fingers intertwined with his. She smiled up at him. He knew the truth, though he didn't want to admit it. It was obvious what she really was.

In the back of his mind, a much more sinister voice whispered, *Angel.*

He thought of asking her.

"I need to get some more cigarettes," he said instead.

Io and Jeremy
The Townhouse

They watched each other, neither one saying anything for a long time. Io stood beside the chair that sat in front of his desk, her mechanized hand resting on the arm. She looked a little pitiful—still dirty and scuffed up from the battle in Spiritus Vallem, and standing there in an oversized tee shirt. It had been the only thing Jeremy had in the townhouse for her to wear.

"I would like something else to wear, please," Io said, after a long moment.

"I don't have anything else for you," Jeremy said and frowned.

She could be a little more grateful to him. He had just saved her life.

"I'm sorry," he said. "I'll get more clothes for you, soon."

She frowned.

"Would you like to take a bath?" he asked her.

"I would like something to eat, please," she told him. "I haven't eaten anything since—"

How long had it been? How long had she been sleeping? Had it only been just this morning that her whole world had crumbled, or had it been days? She looked up at Jeremy, panicked. She didn't want to think about what had happened in Spiritus Vallem. She didn't want to remember that her family was dead—that everyone she knew and loved was dead. All she could think about was her brother's little lifeless body in her arms. She came around to the front of the chair and sat down, leaning back and closing her eyes. Unstoppable tears spilled out and slipped down her cheeks. The chair groaned under her.

"I'll have Nesa make you something," Jeremy said, trying to ignore her tears, though he was having difficulty doing so. She looked frail and fragile. How was he supposed to make something so innocent into the greatest weapon the Core had ever seen? How would he ever get her to agree to it?

He bit his lip. She would never have whatever life she had led back in the valley. Those days were over for her. The sooner she came to realize this, the better off she would be. Jeremy felt something stir inside of him as he watched

111

her. Something gentle and foreign that caused his stomach to ache. He looked back down at his papers.

Her tears continued to fall.

"I'm sorry, Io," he said, because, for the first time, he *was* sorry—if only just a little.

"They're all dead," she whispered. She buried her face into the palms of her hands and let out a sob. "Jeremy, they're all dead."

He looked up when she said his name, but didn't know what to say. He had never been good at comforting people, but he wanted to comfort her.

She looked back up at him, tears still spilling from her large lavender eyes. "And what happens now? What happens to me?"

A part of her didn't want to hear his answer. She knew whatever it was couldn't be good—her visions had shown her that much. At the end of all of this, there really would be nothing left of her. She could only recall a few more visions of Jeremy, visions where she had forgiven him for whatever he was about to do to her. Visions where, maybe, she loved him. She shook her head. She had no way of knowing what was to be and what were only dreams.

Jeremy couldn't possibly tell her the truth. He tapped his finger on the desk, thinking... but nothing that would help him came to mind. He didn't say anything to her for a long while as he struggled to think of what to say. Maybe it was best not to tell her anything about the plan. It would be easier, if he won her trust first. If she knew the truth, she would never cooperate with him. She would fight. He could have told her, to get it out of the way, but something in his gut told him to wait. *Tell her what she wants to hear.*

She didn't need to know how desperately he wanted back into the Core. That could wait. The whole thing could wait. She needed time to heal. She needed time to come to grips with what had happened. He didn't know her, but he could tell that she was very broken. Who was he to break her even more? He frowned. Breaking her more was inevitable. As soon as he told her the truth—that she was a weapon of mass destruction—she would break again.

He was at a loss. Maybe he really should get it over with. Jeremy would lose either way. Shaking his head, he leaned back in his chair and watched her closely. No. The truth *could* wait.

"You'll stay here with me," he told her. "Until you're doing better, you'll stay here with me."

Io watched him, replaying his words in her mind. That didn't sound too terribly bad, she supposed. It wasn't like she had anywhere else to go now that the valley was gone and her family was—

She shook her head and chewed on her bottom lip. Not quite knowing what to say, she stayed like that. She listened to the clock on the wall tick each second by. Could she trust Jeremy? She didn't know. He had been kind and gentle in her dreams. Life in the townhouse could be as normal as it had been before.

"Thank you, Jeremy," she finally said. "Thank you."

He nodded in reply, a little torn. She seemed genuinely nice, so sweet and pure, and he was going to change her—corrupt her in an irrevocable way. She shouldn't be thanking him. She should be figuring out a way to get away. He frowned and tapped his fingers on the desk. He wondered for the first time since he'd brought the girl home if this was really such a great idea. Surely it would work and he would get back into the Core, but at what cost?

Jeremy shook his head. It didn't matter. All that mattered was that he continued on with the plan, and that the Core crumbled. He could use her to get what he wanted. That had been the plan, and he needed to stick with it. He shoved the little voice in his conscience away.

"I'll have Nesa prepare your food," he told her. "I'll have her call you when it's ready. Why don't you go get cleaned up?"

Io nodded and took that as her cue to leave. She stood from the chair and hesitantly walked toward the door. She turned once more to look back at him. Something wasn't right. He was hiding something. She sensed it deep in her bones, but she knew not what it was—and there was virtually nothing she could do about it even if she figured it out.

"Thank you," she said again, and left for her room.

Lysithea
The Palace

"Should we drop the bomb, General Noctisvolo?"

Lysithea looked up from the war plans, a frown plastered on her face.

"Is there no other way?" Lysithea asked.

"I'm afraid not, ma'am," Rogers said. "We're backed into a corner... they've left us no choice. Winters has the bomb prepared, we just need your permission to fire, ma'am."

She listened to the clicking of the equipment surrounding them.

"I guess we drop them," Lysithea said. "Tell Winters to go ahead."

Rogers nodded and walked out of the room, leaving Lysithea to the war plans. She'd been messed up ever since the attack on Spiritus Vallem. For as long as she could remember, her mother had told her she would kill many—and after killing countless people, it had stopped messing with her conscience, but after Spiritus Vallem, it was like a wound had been reopened. She felt remorseful, but there was nothing she could do about it now.

The people of the Wastelands were going to have to die until they understood that the new world was not going to stand down. Though it seemed unlikely, she hoped Neo Victoria would be just that—a new victory.

The rebel forces were closer now—much closer than she liked. She wasn't about to lose her new home to filth. She frowned at the thought—it was that kind of thinking that had gotten them into this mess. Waste-landers were people, too.

They were people, and they were angry.

"We're so fucked," Lysithea said to herself, and walked out of the room.

David

The Palace

She was sitting in his chair, wearing a blood red dress and white fur coat, swinging from side to side out of what looked like boredom. When she saw him, she stopped and leaned forward over the desk, her elbows pressing against the dark wood.

"I told you I was real," was all she said, a too wide smile plastered onto her face.

David stepped into the room and closed the door, locking it out of habit before turning off the NESA system. He didn't want their conversation to be reported to Graggöry. That would ruin his plans, and he couldn't have that. Not now that he was so close. He turned his attention back to Lucie. He wondered how she had gotten in, and hoped that however it was, that she had remained unseen by the guards. The last thing he needed was Graggöry hearing about her. Though it was perfectly okay for Graggöry to play house all day, he didn't like for his officers to—especially with someone who wasn't in the Core.

"Lucie," he said in greeting, walking toward the desk. He came to a halt and rested his hands on the back of the chair that sat directly in front of the desk, still watching her with slight curiosity. "I haven't had the pleasure of meeting you in—person."

"How rude of me, I know," Lucie drawled. "But do you believe me now, my darling?"

David only nodded, quite amazed to find that she *was* real. He wondered why she had come to see him so urgently. She looked a little distressed.

"Well, why don't you come give me a kiss?" Lucie asked in a singing voice. Perhaps she wasn't that distressed after all. "It's been so long, and I've been so lonely without you."

He stepped around the desk and leaned down to kiss her chastely on the cheek. Lucie giggled and leaned back in the chair, looking up at him.

"It's only been a couple of days," David said, but smiled none-the-less. He supposed it was nice to be missed, though he knew if she found out about his plans, she probably wouldn't miss him anymore. It was probably dangerous to play games with the devil.

"I've come to talk to you about something really important, actually," Lucie said, suddenly very serious. "However, first, you must tell me how your plans are coming along, my darling. Have you figured out what to do about Graggöry? I will help you, but I can only do so much—you see, there are some rules that even I can't break."

David wondered what those were.

"Do tell me everything," Lucie pushed.

"Well," David started. "I haven't quite figured it all out yet, but I'm working on it. I promise."

He hoped that she couldn't see through his lie.

Lucie frowned, but shook her head and smiled once more. "Well, as long as you're working on it. I suppose it will be fine."

"What about you?" David asked. "Lysithea did what you wanted—are things going well on your side of the plan?"

"They aren't going so well," Lucie admitted, "but they can be fixed."

David reached out to stroke her hair, wrapping a strand of it around his finger. "Is there anything I can do to help?"

He didn't quite like to see her down.

Lucie's lips curved into a lopsided smile. She was cute when she was thinking, but he couldn't allow himself to be blinded by a foolish love—there was too much else he needed to do. Perhaps, when things fell into place they could be more than this—whatever this was. He supposed it would be nice.

"I need you to hold off on killing the demon king," Lucie said, after a moment. "Just for a little while."

"Why is that?" David asked.

"I need him to take care of a problem for me," she replied.

"I can take care of your problem," David suggested.

"I know you're more than capable of doing so, but it's more fun this way," Lucie replied. She ran her fingers through her hair and smiled again. "You know what they say… about all work and no play."

David felt exasperated. "Yes, I know."

"I think I've gotten it taken care of," Lucie quipped. "If I need you, you know I'll come to find you."

"Do you want to talk about it?" David tried.

"Maybe next time," Lucie said. She stood from the chair and reached out to gently caress his cheek. "I feel a lot better, just being able to see you like this, but I've got to go now. I'm a very busy girl, you know."

David smiled.

"Yes, I know," he said, and in the blink of an eye, she was gone.

He stood and stared at the space where she had been standing for a moment before turning his attention to the blinking light on the edge of his desk: a message. He tapped the desk three times, a screen shimmering to life above the desktop. It was a message from Jeremy. He tapped it open.

David, she made it! Come when you can.

He closed the message and turned the screen off, sitting down in his chair. Against all odds, that girl had actually survived. He couldn't believe it, for a number of reasons, but he knew that Jeremy wouldn't lie about something as important as this. He supposed he would have to go visit the townhouse, but first he needed to finish a few things. The night was young.

He picked up a pile of papers on the desk and shuffled through them, pondering on how long it would take for his plan to fall into place, and praying that Lucie stayed in the dark about it.

"Well," he said aloud to himself, jotting down a note on the paper in front of him. "I can't very well accomplish this if I make her an enemy…"

Jeremy and David
The Townhouse

David stepped into Jeremy's office and shook the ash from his hat and shoulders. He frowned and made his way over to the chair in front of Jeremy's desk. Jeremy was sitting, shuffling through a pile of papers and blueprints, mumbling under his breath, as usual—only he seemed a little peppier about it today. The room was small, with barely enough space to fit the desk and chairs, much less two people. David eyed the space and shook his head. The townhouse was definitely no place to be doing experiments. It would do Jeremy some good to be back in the Core laboratories, with ample room and ample supplies. Hopefully he would be back there soon. If everything went as planned with Io, he would need the space to further investigate the success of the experiment. He would need to find a way to clone the girl—they would need to make more weapons like her if they planned on having the perfect army. And David planned on having the perfect army, even if in the end, he supposed, it would make Lucie his enemy. Love was not as important as power—and if he could have power over the devil herself, what a victory that would be.

His gaze fell on the small circular window behind the desk, above the makeshift bookshelf Jeremy had hung on the wall. He wondered how they would do it. How could they pull that off? The girl was the start. Everything was resting on the girl and Jeremy's ability to create the perfect weapon—one David could use to rid them of Graggöry and any other power-hungry demon, once and for all. He let out a sigh and smacked his hand against the desk, loud enough to bring Jeremy out of his train of thought.

"Nesa let me in," David said. "I hope you don't mind."

David sat down and leaned back in the chair in front of Jeremy's desk. He watched Jeremy with cold, observant eyes, glancing down to briefly look over the plans that Jeremy held in his hand. He put his hat on the arm of the chair and ran his hand through his messy hair. When Jeremy remained silent, David continued, "You'd think that after fifty years, it would stop snowing ash."

"That you would," Jeremy agreed. He set the paper down and leaned forward, resting his elbows on the desk. He put his head in his hands and looked back down at the blueprint. "It's probably been snowing ash for hundreds of years—there's no telling what happened up top while we were all living in the Underground."

Jeremy shoved the blueprint across the desk. "I just drew this one up."

"I came as soon as I saw your message."

"Was it too much trouble?" Jeremy asked. He leaned back again, pressing into the back of his chair and crossing his arms.

"You mean to tell me that she actually survived all of that?" David asked, ignoring his brother's question. He had to know about Io. He gave Jeremy a skeptical look and set the coffee thermos he'd been holding down onto the desk. They both watched as a bead of murky liquid dripped from the rim and puddled around the bottom, slowly inking the corner of one of the many blueprints brown.

Jeremy snatched the paper away and put it on a pile of prints on the floor beside him. He eyed his brother as he tried to think of a way to describe it all without having to take David down to see the girl. He'd barely just come up with a plan for telling Io the truth about her situation. He didn't need to frighten her mere hours after she'd woken up. She was hurting, and scared, and David would only make it worse—he wasn't the sensitive kind.

"Yes," Jeremy finally said. "I lost her two or three times, but lucky for me, I still had some Vivificantem left over from the research lab."

"I thought it was all destroyed," David said. "The Core Scientists said it didn't work."

"If the Core Scientists still had me on their staff, maybe they'd know how to use it properly," Jeremy replied and handed David the document with the wiring instructions for Io's mechanical arm. "But I'll be back soon enough after they see Io. She's going to be brilliant. I'll probably get some sort of metal, maybe even a nice letter of apology from that bastard president for getting rid of me in the first place. That is—if he hasn't really lost his mind like everyone says."

David looked down at the instructions.

"Look over those, would you?" Jeremy asked, shuffling through papers again.

"I've always admired your spirit," David said. He leaned back further in the chair and looked out the window for a moment. Through the dust covered glass, he could tell that it was still snowing. It even looked colder. A neon light reflected on the window from the pub across the street. "When we were kids, everything was always so damned hard, but you never gave up. Hell, you didn't give up when the Core said you were insane."

"Am I insane?" Jeremy asked.

David only laughed. "Of course not. Only bloody genius."

Jeremy smiled.

They were both very quiet for a while before David handed the paper back to Jeremy. "These are good. I'm really impressed. You've come such a long way from your original prototype."

"Well," Jeremy said, looking down at his hands. "I had to, since all the other models never made it out of the first surgery."

David laughed again and leaned forward, tapping his fingers on the desk. He looked over the papers on Jeremy's desk again, memorized the mechanical numbers and formulas. He memorized how to construct new brain matter, and how to attach a metal limb fully to a body. These things could be useful later.

"So, can I see her now?" David asked.

"Unfortunately, she's still recovering. As you could imagine, it's a slow process. She's had a rough last couple of hours."

David frowned. "What do you plan to do with her?"

"I already told you. She's my ticket back into the Core. You'll tell them about her when she's ready. She's going to be a very valuable, powerful weapon," Jeremy replied. "If they are interested, I'll hand her over to them— but only if they give me my position back, and if they refuse, I'll end them with her. It's very simple."

"How sly," David chortled, wondering if his brother could really go through with that threat. He supposed that he could—after all, Jeremy had a big grudge against the Core since the Core killed their mother. David had made sure to plant a seed of hatred deep inside his brother's heart after their father's death as well. Jeremy didn't need to know the truth about it. The truth really didn't matter now, anyway. All that did matter was getting back at the Core. David was in business to take over the world, not to sit around with Jeremy and cry about the past.

"Well, I have to try something," Jeremy said. "What good is it to be an inventor and not be able to invent anything useful anymore? If they don't want Io, I'll get what I want another way. That's what you would do, right?"

David nodded.

Jeremy looked up at the ceiling. The florescent light he'd installed above the desk flickered and buzzed as it continued clinging to life. The paint was beginning to peel, revealing all the old Victorian wallpaper he'd tried to cover up. Everything about this place brought back memories of his childhood, when he had lived in this house with his family.

They were all gone now—all he had left was David, but even David seemed to be drifting away. That's really why he'd called him here. Not to show him the girl, but to see him face to face. Besides, he couldn't have a conversation like this with David over the phone, and sending such things in an email would be too risky. He looked at his brother and frowned.

David stood from the chair and put his hat back on. "I should really be going now. Send for me when I can properly see the girl."

Jeremy nodded, looking back through the papers on front of him as David left.

Io

The Townhouse

A week had passed since she had been brought to the townhouse. Io took a sip of milk from the glass that Jeremy had set in front of her on the table, watching him as he fumbled around the kitchen, trying—to her amusement—to gather some biscuits for, as he put it, 'a midnight snack.' She had spent most of her days down in the basement being worked on. Hour after hour, the minutes slowly dragged on as Jeremy worked without talking. She had come to realize quickly that the townhouse was rather boring, and that made her more homesick than anything for the valley she could never go back to. She frowned at the thought. She had been trying to keep her mind preoccupied with other things—thinking about home only made everything worse. Never again would she feel the warmth of the sun on her pale skin. She would never feel the rush of air as she soared through the sky. Her life was here now—here in the townhouse, more of a prisoner than Jeremy's guest.

"I was thinking," Io said, mustering the courage to engage in conversation with him. "I was thinking that maybe tonight we could talk about... about what's going to happen now? You've hardly told me anything, and... are you even listening?"

Jeremy looked up from the box of biscuits he'd found, frowning slightly.

"I'm listening," he said, digging out two biscuits and setting them on a napkin in front of her. His hazel eyes were more brown than green tonight, and she had figured out days ago that he had brown eyes when he lied.

"You just don't want to tell me."

She had grown accustomed to Jeremy's secret keeping over the last two days or so. She had thought to ask if she could go outside, but she already knew the answer to that—apparently, no one could know she was here. At first, she had told herself it was because someone was out to kill her—someone had killed all the angels, after all—but it seemed less likely that this was the reason, the more secretive Jeremy became.

"That's not entirely the truth," Jeremy said.

Io picked a biscuit up, lifting it to her lips. How long did Jeremy think he could keep this up? How long was she supposed to stay his prisoner, trapped with nothing to do in the townhouse but to think about all the things she had lost? She sighed, growing more annoyed by the second. She was tired of his avoidance of the subject. She already knew enough from her visions, to know that whatever was about to happen to her was not good. In her visions, they talked about something called the Core, and deep down, she knew that they were responsible for everything that had happened—but that something darker was upon them—something she would ultimately have to destroy. But the visions came to her in pieces and were hazy now. She thought that maybe she was blocking them out because they scared her. Maybe the massacre in the valley had been the last straw. She wasn't sure.

"Well," Io said, taking a bite of the biscuit. "What is the truth?"

She tried giving him the benefit of the doubt, thought that maybe he was really doing this for her own good—but she knew he was selfish. Whatever he was up to, it was only for himself, not her. She sighed again and eyed him, wary of whatever answer he was about to give.

Jeremy sat down in the chair opposite of her, setting his napkin full of biscuits down on the placemat before him. He brought one up to his mouth, biting into it and chewing it slowly.

She listened to the clock in the foyer tick-tock until she found herself squirming from Jeremy's silence.

"I just want to help you," Jeremy finally said.

Io wanted to believe that, but her gut told her that it was not entirely the truth. She smiled anyway and nodded her head, finishing her biscuits.

There was another pause before Io finally whispered, "I'm trying to understand."

She understood that nothing that had happened in the last week had made any sense to her at all. She wanted Jeremy to tell her something—*anything*. He continued eating his biscuits.

She tugged on the edge of the oversized tee shirt she'd been using as a nightgown. There had to be some explanation for everything, and surely this— this being prisoner in the townhouse—was not all that was left. She moved a cluster of bangs from in front of her eyes and watched him as he ate. Io wanted to understand him. She knew, from the visions, that he wasn't really a bad man. Maybe he really did just want to help her, but Io could not shake the uneasy feeling that had settled in her gut. Something wasn't right.

Maybe things will never be right again.

She fought away the emptiness that lingered inside of her.

"Look," Jeremy said, his hazel eyes darkening a shade as a frown sprawled across his face. "I saved you. You were dying in that field, and I… I brought you back. I fixed your broken body. I'm just trying to help you. Know that, but also, know that there are some things that I can't explain to you right now. I'll tell you everything when the time is right."

Io considered this. When would the time be right? How long would she have to stay here, tormented by her past and terrified of her future?

"Okay," Io said, standing from the chair. He was annoyed with her, she could tell, but she was annoyed with him, too. She wouldn't force him to talk with her any longer. "Goodnight, Jeremy, and thank you for the biscuits."

She strode out of the room and back up the stairs.

She tried to make sense of her visions. This was not the Jeremy she had come to love. Not yet. He would change, if the visions were right, but she was impatient and frightened and wanted answers. The future was ever changing, as Chrezabel had once told her.

There was still time to stop the darkness that would come for them, she just needed to push Jeremy a little harder.

Tomorrow, she thought as she climbed the stairs. *I'll try again tomorrow.*

Jeremy

The Townhouse

The clock on the wall read 2 A.M., and Jeremy fought sleep as he swiveled in his chair, down in the basement. There was still so much left to do before he could even think about presenting Io to David, and still more before she could be given to the Demetrius Core. Everything he was doing here had to be absolutely perfect—his invention was going to change the future. This was his one and only chance to prove to everything that he wasn't crazy. He could help Neo Victoria and the other Inner Cities win the war.

Everything was resting on Io.

Jeremy tapped the hologram screen that sprawled out in front of him, exposing the blueprint for his newest and greatest invention—the arm and leg he had installed on Io. He had gone against his better judgment with these, using both science and magic. The blueprint spread out before him and he studied it. It had to be perfect, thus tomorrow he would test it for flaws.

"All right, Nesa," he said, swiveling back to the table. There, he looked over the model arm one more time, prodding and tightening screws before tapping the table with his palm. "I want to try the system again. If I can get it to work on this prototype, I can get it to work on Io, in theory…"

"We'll try it again from the top, then," Nesa said.

The computer to his left buzzed to life, the screen flashing large white numbers as they counted down from ten. Jeremy scooted away from the table, standing from the stool. He told himself that it would work this time.

"Third time's the charm," he said more to himself than to Nesa.

"Right, sir," Nesa chimed in, her singsong voice cackling through the speaker.

When the computer reached one, the screen switched to a picture: a hunting rifle. Jeremy looked at the .270 rifle on the screen, tilting his head. It was simple enough. He turned his gaze from the computer screen back to the table where the arm was beginning to move. It burst apart into a billion tiny pieces, refiguring itself into the shape of the rifle. Each little piece clicked into place, forming a perfect mirror of the rifle on the screen.

"So far so good," Jeremy yawned. "Next."

The computer screen blinked, an image of a shield replacing that of the rifle. Without a second's delay, the rifle on the table burst into pieces before forming a solid shield. Jeremy smiled. His hard work was paying off.

"That's good for now, Nesa," he said, and the computer screen went black. Jeremy scribbled a note onto the holographic blueprints before turning back to the arm. The shield somewhat disintegrated back into a solid plate around the metal bones.

"Anything else, sir?" Nesa asked.

"I think that's all for the night, Nesa," he said. "I'll be heading back to my room shortly."

"Goodnight, Jeremy," Nesa said, and the speaker clicked off.

Jeremy stood by the table, looking down at the arm. He ran a hand through his hair before rubbing his forehead. Io would have a lot of questions in the morning. Io seemed to have a lot of questions, lately. Of course, she had a lot of questions—he wasn't being very cooperative. He was keeping her prisoner here. She was probably scared and confused and angry. *Maybe*, he thought, *she would have been better off dead.*

He shook that thought from his mind, scolding himself. Surely a life serving the Core was better than no life at all. He was doing her a favor. He let out a sigh and started for the stairs.

A life serving the Core was better than no life at all. He would keep telling himself that until it was over and she was no longer here with him. It was best to not get attached. Io did not belong to him. The moment he'd brought her home; she had belonged to the Core.

Lysithea
The Palace

Lysithea watched Graggöry while he worked. She inhaled, breathing in the sweet vanilla scent of the room. She smiled when he glanced her way.

"Say, love," she said, moving her blond bangs out of her eyes, "don't you think there has to be another way? You know, to make the voices go away? Surely we could—"

"Stop it," Graggöry said. He frowned and looked back down at the papers on his desk. He reached into his vest pocket for a cigarette. "You know there isn't."

She grimaced. What was he so angry about? She leaned back in the chair and thought about what she could possibly say next. Lifting her gaze to the ceiling, she let out a soft sigh and bit her bottom lip. He wasn't going to talk to her about it anymore. It was her own fault, telling him not to in the first place. However, she was still desperate for some cure that didn't involve her own death.

He's never coming back, she told herself. *Get used to this.*

She found no comfort from the silence, so she turned her attention back to him.

"What are you working on?" she asked, hoping he would perk up with a change of subject. He lifted a piece of paper up and rolled his eyes.

"David's been acting rather strange lately," Graggöry said. "I'm reading through the NESA transcripts from his room log to see if I can figure out what's gotten into him."

"You don't say," Lysithea said. "How interesting."

"I know you don't like him," Graggöry said, setting the paper back down and glancing over to her, "but he is my friend."

"I know," she said, rolling her eyes. "I just wish you had *better* friends."

Graggöry let out a chuckle, some light returning to his eyes. "If it makes you feel better, you're my *best* friend."

She leaned forward, wanting to go to him, but paused.
Instead, she smiled and whispered, "I know."

Lucie

Hell

Some people were hard to break. No one knew this better than Lucifer, but she was starting to lose her patience. This girl—Lysithea—needed to die. And soon. She was getting in the way, always by Graggöry's side, always calculating how to save his sorry soul. Lucie had been sending Graggöry the same message constantly for the last week, and still he fought her—and he would continue to do so.

"Kill her," she growled to Graggöry as she watched him through the portal me=mirror she'd summoned moments before. He was laughing with Lysithea. It repulsed her. "Kill her and be done with it, already."

But Graggöry would not. Lucifer hadn't broken him enough. She sighed and turned her attention to Lysithea, who was lying on the bed beside him. She snarled and whisked the portal away. She cursed love, for always getting in the way.

Love complicated everything.

Lucifer knew that.

She hissed to the darkness. All that meant was that she would have to try a little harder.

She's an angel, she sent him. *Kill her now and we'll go away.*

It wouldn't be long now. Either Graggöry would snap, or David would just have to kill both of them. Either way she would get what she wanted.

All she had to do was wait.

Father Baxley
Spiritus Vallem

The hike up to Spiritus Vallem was rigorous—with so many fallen trees, and rocks, and debris scattered along what was left of the worn path. The valley had not been meant to be entered by foot. The angels that came to the cities from the valley, teleported themselves there with their magic. It was a treacherous idea to climb through the devastated forest, on foot, and though he had magic of his own, he needed to keep it in check—just in case he had to use it later. Somewhere, far off, a howl started and echoed its way through the trees. The devastated forest was full of ungodly creatures—monsters who had been created for The Great War. Father Baxley paused momentarily before he hurried on his way.

Light was fading by the time he had made it to the forest's edge. When he stepped out of the forest and into the far meadow, he was not greeted by the warm rays of the sun. He shivered. The valley had died—just as he had suspected. He shielded his eyes from the ash.

This was why Abraxos hadn't come.

In the meadow, sprawled out and carelessly left to rot, lay countless bodies. Their arms and legs were bent and twisted in such a grotesque manner that Father Baxley looked away.

Several moments passed before he snapped his fingers. The ground shook as the earth peeled away from itself. Father Baxley inspected the hole.

"This will have to do, my friends," he said, and set out to collect the bodies.

He didn't have time, or the magic to bury them all separately. He did, however, have the magic to locate their bodies. He checked each body as they came to him, looking for any signs of life. Frustrated tears slipped down his face. This was cruel, and they were undeserving.

Finally, as the sun set, he came to a boy, about five or six years old. He was badly wounded. Father Baxley snapped his finger. The boy's body floated to the mass grave.

"Wait... please..."

Father Baxley paused.

"Wait..."

Father Baxley motioned for his magic to bring the boy closer.

"It can't be..." Father Baxley gasped. "You're still alive."

"Yes," the boy whispered. "Still alive."

Father Baxley set the boy down in the snow and rushed to his side. He peeled out of his coat and tucked it around the boy's fragile little body. "Thank goodness."

"My sister..." the boy said. "Have you found my sister?"

Of course, Father Baxley had no idea who his sister was. He merely shook his head.

"I'm sorry," Father Baxley said. "Everyone else was dead."

"I'm very weak," the boy said. "I don't have much time."

Father Baxley placed two fingers onto the boy's forehead. A light formed at the tip of his fingers as he fed the boy some of his life-force.

"You'll be all right now—"

"Kale," the boy said.

This was Abraxos' boy.

"You'll be all right now, Kale."

"The prophecy came true," Kale whispered. "Lysithea..."

"Hush," Father Baxley said. "Rest now."

He lifted Kale into his arms and said a quick prayer for those he was about to bury. With the snap of his fingers, the hole in the earth recovered itself, burying the angels, and all the hope for the world.

Well—maybe not all of the hope. There was this boy.

From what he knew of the prophecy... one angel would destroy the world, but one angel would save it. Father Baxley tightened his arms around Kale and hurried back out into the forest. He had to get the boy help, and quickly. There wasn't much time.

Io

The Townhouse

Another dream.

Io sits at the small, round kitchen table. She's staring at it intently, taking in each chip of yellow paint as if she will never see it again. She supposes that it doesn't matter—this is not her home, merely a place she has been kept prisoner, and yet there is something somber about leaving here, something that doesn't bode well within her. Upstairs, David and Jeremy are talking. She can hear their voices drifting down through the ceiling, low, muffled, heated discussion. She knows what they're talking about.

Her heart hurts.

This is the part where Jeremy hands her over to David.

A part of her wishes she had died that day in the valley. In all fairness, she *should* be dead. She glances to the door. There's still enough time left to run. She ponders this as she hears Jeremy's chair roll across the floor. They're about to come down, and David will take her. Like before, she'll go willingly, because that's what Jeremy wants her to do.

She goes rigid with fear and wishes that Nesa could save her, though she knows that Nesa desperately hates her—she will be glad to see Io go. Misery begins to fester in the hollow place inside of her that only grows more hollowed by the day.

"Well, if that's all, I'll be taking her now," David says, from the top of the stairs.

"All right," Jeremy says, a little dismissively. Maybe he doesn't want her to go.

David steps into the kitchen. She wonders briefly if this is what will happen. If this is the true future, the one that can't be changed. If it is, then the other visions, the one where David is not really David anymore will probably not happen. If this happens, she will become the angel who destroys the world.

She shivers—

Io opened her eyes, safe in her room in the townhouse. Dim morning light was peaking in through the gaps in the blinds. She let out a slow breath. Of all her visions, she dreaded that one the most—the uncertainty of it made her feel uneasy.

"Io," Nesa said, her voice barking from the speaker above the door. "Are you all right?"

"I'm all right," Io said, testing the words. Is she all right? Will she be all right again?

"Breakfast is ready," Nesa told her. "Jeremy is waiting for you."

"I'll be down in a moment," Io said, slowly crawling from the bed. "Thank you."

Nesa said nothing else.

Io reveled in the silence.

Graggöry
The Palace

Graggöry stared at his reflection, noting the bags that had started to form under his sleepless eyes. His irises were slowly lightening, turning more crimson now than their usual coal color.

He needed blood, and soon. Reaching into his vest pocket for the last of his cigarettes, he frowned. When he'd sent Lysithea out for more, she'd come back empty handed with a story about the closed magic shop. The poor old warlock who'd been making the cigarettes for him had passed away under some mysterious circumstances. That was not good.

Upon hearing that story, he had vowed to save this last once. Graggöry gazed down at the small stick between his fingers, his brows furrowing. His lips twisted into a lopsided frown. He'd been suppressing his true self with these damned magical cigarettes for the past ten years and was scared of what the outcome would be now that he would have to go without them.

Good riddance, the voice cackled.

He growled.

Just ask Lysithea for a drink, the voice continued. *She won't mind.*

He had thought about asking her, but it was much too soon after his last feeding, and he had taken so much from her then that he was too concerned to try and take anymore. Though the voices had been persistent about it, he certainly did not want to kill her.

She recovers so remarkably fast, the voice chided. *Her blood supply has replenished itself.*

Graggöry knew it was true. She recovered much too quickly every time. He looked back up at his reflection, his lips set in a straight line across his gaunt face.

You know why that is, the voice said.

He had thought about it before. She had been lying to him. He knew from the beginning that she was different, but it hadn't really mattered—before. He had decided to trust her. There were many reasons why she wouldn't come

134

right out and tell him the truth, and he couldn't very well blame her for that. She would tell him in time, whenever she was ready to. If she said she was a demon, then he would play along and pretend she was. It was as simple as that, and if the voices thought otherwise, he would just have to ignore them.

She's the last one. The angel who got away.

A part of him didn't want to believe that truth. Why would she slaughter her whole family for him, knowing that it wouldn't work? He knew why. She was delusional with love. There was no hiding the truth from him—he had caught a glimpse of her lavender eyes one night before bed.

So—kill her, the voice hissed.

He would not. Maybe before, he could have killed Lysithea. There had been a time when she had meant absolutely nothing to him. She had been just a play thing… something to pass the time with. That was back before he had even thought it was possible for him to love someone. Things were different. Lysithea was all he had left in this horrid world. He could hardly imagine a life without her. He let out a sigh and lifted the unlit cigarette to his lips. He shuddered to think of what might happen.

The world is still new and so is the power lying in Graggöry's grasp. At a young and foolish twenty-one, he's taken over his father's post as President of the United Nations of Neo Erta, after winning the popular vote—just days after his father had been assassinated. His father has left him with a mess.

A war has started. There are angry Wasteland rebels who are tired of the Core's military campaign and of the bombs that are dropped on their home day in and day out. The rebels want protection, want the same rights as those living in the inner and outer cities, but they are less civilized, they are less than the others. He can't give them what they want and win. He will have to destroy them.

Of course, his father would leave him in the middle of a war, but he can't really blame a man who died against his will. He sighs and leans back in his chair, closing his eyes. He's put a lot of faith in his father's best young general, and his very best friend, David Lancaster. He tries to rest easy with David in charge. However, with the state of the world, he often finds that he can't. He closes his eyes and lets out another sigh.

There are three knocks at his door. He drags his attention away from his thoughts and, taking a slow breath, opens his eyes. He leans forward in the chair and rests his arms on the desk. He stares somberly at the door before saying, "Come in."

David marches in, dragging someone along behind him. Graggöry notices the extreme annoyance shimmering in David's piercing blue eyes. David shoves the person forward, frowning, and Graggöry's gaze lands on the wide-eyed stare of a panicked girl. She stumbles as she takes a step forward, trying to steady herself. She lets out a shaky breath, rubbing her arm where David had grabbed her.

"I'm sorry for disturbing you," David says, "but this girl was lurking around on the grounds looking for you. Street trash, if you ask me. Probably a rebel."

The girl does look a little like street trash. She moves her muddy blonde bangs out of her face. Now Graggöry can see that what he mistook for fear was actually wonder. She smiles, a small timid thing, and takes a step forward before David reaches out and grabs her arm again, stopping her.

She flinches and lets out a small yelp, but she doesn't struggle. She stands there in David's grasp, watching Graggöry with large, timid grey eyes. There is something about her that strikes Graggöry odd. He very much wants to get to the bottom of this. She could be a number of things: the timid girl, a rebel spy, a blood thirsty monster. The possibilities are endless, and it excites Graggöry to think about it. He averts his attention to David, who is staring at him with the same look of annoyance he's always wearing. Graggöry wonders if David is ever anything but annoyed.

"What should I do with her, sir?" David asks. His voice is edgy, but slightly amused. He looks the girl up and down again, frowning a bit more. The girl obviously does nothing for him. "She's been asked to leave several times but continues to insist that we let her talk to you."

Talk to her, he tells himself.

Graggöry straightens and watches the girl. Perhaps her parents were killed in the war, and she's come to exact her revenge. But there is no way this girl is any match for him—unless she is much better versed in the ways of magic. Even then, he has her beat. He isn't too worried about her.

"Leave the girl," Graggöry says, eyeing her with careful consideration. What will she do when they're left alone?

This could be fun, he thinks. He hasn't had fun in years.

"But President Graggöry, sir, if I mi—"

"It's all right," Graggöry interrupts. "I'll get to the bottom of this. Right now, I need you to go debrief your men. They've had a long day."

David mumbles under his breath and nods, a look of defeat etching across his face. He lets go of the girl, turning to the door and hesitates for a moment before shaking his head and leaving.

The girl jumps as the door slams behind them.

"He has a temper sometimes," Graggöry says to the girl. "I apologize on his behalf."

She rubs her arm, flinching slightly. She eyes it and frowns. He can tell a bruise is already forming.

"Please, have a seat," he tries, gesturing to the chair in front of his desk. He feels a little bad about David manhandling her; after all, she does look to be just a girl—he isn't quite certain, but he doesn't think she's come to kill him. "Tell me why you were lurking around The Palace's grounds? I'm sure you've got a good reason."

"I was looking for you," she says softly, as she sits down in the chair. He likes the sound of her voice. She looks up at him and smiles. Her eyes are an odd shade of grey. He wonders why.

"Why were you looking for me?"

She is certainly an interesting girl, and if she were to be cleaned up, she wouldn't be half bad to look at, either. He smiles and her smile stretches even further across her dirty face.

"This might sound strange," she stars, and then she shakes her head. "Well, actually, it is pretty strange."

"Go on," he encourages her.

"I um... well," she starts, nervously squirming in the chair before continuing, "You see, I think I can help you."

He tenses. Does she know? She couldn't possibly know. He's not told anyone about the voices. No one knows. No one could. His eyes narrow. Outside, a horn honks in the street. The girl tenses and glances toward the window, where the curtains are drawn.

"Help me how?" he asks, a bit curious. How could something so feeble be of any help? He leans back in his chair and folds his fingers together, his hand resting on the pile of papers stacked on the desk in front of him. "What could you possibly do to help?"

"Well..."

She lets out a soft, frustrated sigh, and bites her bottom lip, her face contorting. He waits.

"With the war, with your loneliness, with anything you need, really," she says. "I can help."

He can tell that's not what she really wants to say, but lets it slide.

"Why do you think I need help?" he asks.

The girl tilts her head. "That's the strange part."

"Well?"

"I just had a feeling," she says. She touches her chest, above her heart. "In here."

"Hmm," he murmurs, considering. "I don't know."

She looks even more helpless now, her muddy hair clinging to her perfect face. Her grey eyes burn with less wonder and more fear. She gives off a glow, almost. He's never seen anything quite like it before. Graggöry realizes he's already a bit taken by her. Perhaps he will let her stay. He has not quite decided yet.

"Please," she says. She scoots to the very edge of the chair. "Don't make me leave. I have nowhere else to go."

Maybe. Maybe he can let her stay. It could be fun. A distraction is certainly welcomed.

"What's your name?" he asks.

She blinks and swallows, steadying herself.

"Lysithea," she says.

She's glowing again. Graggöry tilts his head, watching her. There is something about her that he can't quite put his finger on. Something strange and new and wonderful.

"What are you?" he asks her, genuinely curious.

"A demon," she tells him. She smiles. "A demon like you."

"Come," he says, standing. "We should get you out of those dirty clothes."

Graggöry frowned, flicking off the lights. He stood in the dark for a long time, thinking. They had come a long way since the day David had dragged her into the office. It had been five years now, and Lysithea had really grown on him. He cared for her deeply. Perhaps, he even could go as far as saying he did love her.

But she's a liar, the voice hissed.

He opened the bathroom door and fumbled forward in the dark, making his way to the edge of the bed where he sat down, putting his head in his hands. Maybe she had lied, but it didn't change how he felt about her.

You have to kill her.

He let out a frustrated sigh. The voices were getting worse. He needed more cigarettes. Somehow, he would have to find someone else to make them. There was probably no one left—no one who would openly admit to having that much power. Graggöry had brought this on himself with all those magic laws he had passed in recent months. He cursed himself.

What was he going to do?

Behind him, the bed shifted, the sheets rustling as Lysithea sat up.

"Graggöry?" she asked.

He didn't reply.

How would he ever get better now?

138

"Graggöry, are you okay?"

You have to kill her.

"No."

Io

The Townhouse

Io stood by the window, looking out over the ash covered street. She missed the valley. What she wouldn't give to feel the warmth of the sun on her skin just one more time. But it had been months since that fateful day in the valley—and she was sure that she would never feel the sun again, not like before. The sun hardly shown through the clouds. There was just too much ash. Io stepped away from the window, closing the curtain as she turned to face the bed. Nesa had laid out an outfit for her. Jeremy had been kind enough to bring her more clothes so that she wouldn't have to wear the oversized tee shirt all the time. She supposed she was thankful for it but not even new clothes could fill the massive hole she felt inside of herself.

Io wasn't much of herself these days. There was no way of knowing if she could ever be herself again. That Io *had* died that day, and they had left her strewn in the snow as they carried this body back to the townhouse.

"Hurry and change," Nessa snapped.

Nesa did not like her. Ever since she had come to the townhouse, Nesa had been nothing but cold to her. She snapped at her any chance she got. She hardly did anything nice for her, and if it hadn't been for Jeremy, she probably wouldn't have taken care of her, either. It was the same in her visions, too. Io decided it was because she was taking all of Jeremy's time away from Nesa. Nesa did not like the idea of another female getting close to him. However, Io was anything but competition. Io didn't ask for his attention, and most days Jeremy didn't pay her any. She didn't know how that could possibly make Nesa upset.

It wouldn't matter if I could just go back to the valley.

A pang gripped Io's heart and she brought her hand up to her chest, clutching the top of the tee shirt she was wearing as she tried to steady her breathing. She wanted more than anything to just go home. She missed her parents and her brother. They were gone, though, she told herself. They would never be back. Hopefully, she would see them again when she went back to

Paradise. If Io ever made it back, that was. Life didn't seem too promising. In her visions, she had had to do terrible, un-angelic things.

But she knew not what any of those things were—the visions were always so vague, and Jeremy never told her anything. In fact, Jeremy seemed to be avoiding telling her, even when she made the point that it was her life and she had the right to know what was going to happen to her. In the visions, very bad things happened. Io had hoped that she could convince Jeremy to change his mind, but that didn't seem very likely.

"David will be here any minute, Io," Nesa hissed through the speaker. "Stop sulking and change."

"Right away, Nesa," Io sighed, picking the dress up from the flowered, purple and teal comforter on her bed. She held it out in front of her, eyeing it in the bored manner she used to observe most things in the townhouse. It looked cute enough, she supposed, but Io had come to dislike anything that showed her metal extremities. She was very self-conscious about them. Io did not like feeling different. Once she had asked Jeremy if he could make her prosthetics that looked more humanlike. *Maybe you could cover them with some fake flesh,* she had tried, but Jeremy had only told her things like that would get in the way.

Get in the way of what? she wanted to say, but she already knew the answer. She knew what she was—a weapon. She just desperately wanted Jeremy to tell her this, and to not treat her like a fragile child. She deserved to know what she was being turned into.

Jeremy hardly ever told her anything, but she had had enough visions to put two and two together. She was not dumb, though she continued to play it where Jeremy was concerned.

She peeled out of the tee shirt and tossed it to the floor before tugging the lavender dress down over her head and the rest of her body. A pair of leggings lay stretched out on the bed. She took them and silently thanked Nesa. The leggings would cover up her metal monstrosity of a leg. She was thankful for that. Maybe Nesa wasn't all that bad, after all. Io slipped the leggings on and stepped into the black flats that had been strewn on the floor by the edge of the bed. Walking to the mirror, Io ran a hand through her curly raven hair, carefully avoiding the small wires that protruded from her neck. She looked into the mirror, which was hanging on the back of her bedroom door, and smiled. At least, even with her new arm and leg, she was slowly starting to look like herself again—no longer just a shell of a girl with a sorrowful, hallow gaze. There was some life behind her eyes.

"That's good," she told herself, straightening the folds in the dress.

It wouldn't be so long now until she was finally completely herself again.

Io frowned. There were parts of her that were gone forever. Parts of her that had died that day in the meadow. More than likely, she would never be able to fill those parts of her with anything other than the immense sorrow she felt when she thought about that day, or her family, or her friends. Jeremy told her it took a long time to heal, but that she would, eventually. That was all that mattered. Io wanted to believe Jeremy, but always there seemed to be a part of him that was still untrustworthy—a part of him that he would never show her. How could she expect him to show her any side of him other than what he already had? Jeremy owed her nothing. In fact, it was Io who owed him everything.

Often times she wished that she could feel closer to him. He was all she had. But he was always so distant, so far out of reach. She had tried everything to get him to open up to her, but he avoided all her advances. After these weeks that she had spent in the townhouse, they were at the very least—friends. That couldn't be too much to ask for. But he didn't seem to want friendship. Jeremy was too caught up in whatever it was he was trying to achieve by improving the monstrosity that had become her body. Io had asked Jeremy about that, too, but he had only said, "You'll learn in time."

When was that going to be?

Io had already learned so much through her visions. She already knew what was about to happen to her—but she wanted to hear it from him. Io was growing tired of his silence.

She shook her head and gave herself a once over in the mirror, straightening her back.

"Ask him today," she told her reflection.

Her reflection smiled back at her, but she noted the uneasy gleam in her dark lavender eyes. Maybe not hearing it from Jeremy was better… it could be best to just pretend to stay in the dark. She took a deep breath and let it out slowly before reaching out for the door handle.

"Okay, Nesa," she said, her voice a little too soft for her own liking. "I think I'm ready."

She kept her fingers curled around the door handle, but didn't move to open the door. Was she actually ready to see David again? He hadn't been too thrilled about her that day Jeremy took her from the meadow. David had wanted to leave her to die. Io swallowed back the bile that rose in her throat. Maybe things would be different. They had to be. *Things can't really get much worse, right?* she thought, nodding her head in slight reassurance—but she knew the truth. Things could get much worse, and things waiting for her in the near future, definitely were.

"Jeremy is waiting for you in his study," Nesa replied.

"Okay," Io answered, opening the door.

She made her way into the hallway and closed the door behind her, standing in front of it for a moment as she gathered up the courage to actually see David. Why had he asked to see her anyway? He didn't seem like the type of person who actually cared about anything other than himself. It made Io uneasy. She shook her thoughts and took a deep breath, starting off down the hall. Once she made it to Jeremy's study, she knocked on the door.

"Come in," came Jeremy's voice through the door. "It's unlocked."

She pushed the handle down and waited for the door to click open. When it did she kept still for a moment, considering telling Jeremy that she didn't want to see David after all. She shook her head. She couldn't possibly tell him she'd changed her mind. Io would be brave, like Jeremy wanted.

"Hello, Jeremy," she said, stepping into the office. She closed the door behind her and made her way to the chair in front of his desk. Jeremy glanced up from his work.

"You look lovely today, sweetheart," Jeremy said, sliding a paper across his desk.

Heat rose to her cheeks. What was wrong with her? She smiled politely and hoped he was too preoccupied with his work to fully notice. "Thank you."

"Of course," Jeremy said, and looked back down at his papers. "I suppose David will be here any moment."

"Yes, that's what Nesa said," Io said. She held her breath for a second. It wasn't too late. She could back out. Surely Jeremy would not force her to do this. Something was not right about any of this. She bit her bottom lip, her fingers digging into the arms of the chair.

"Jeremy, maybe we could—"

"David's here, sir," Nesa interrupted.

Jeremy tapped his papers into a pile and set them down on the corner of his desk. He pushed his chair back and stood up. "What was that, Io?"

"No, it was nothing," Io lied. She would be brave and she would figure out just exactly what was going on. "Don't worry about it."

"All right," he said, and stepped around the desk. He reached out for her hand. "Let's go, sweetheart."

She swallowed and set her hand in his. *Here goes nothing,* she told herself, and followed Jeremy out of the room.

David
The Townhouse

David tapped his fingers on the table, waiting for Jeremy to finally bring the girl to meet him. How he'd managed to keep Io a secret from Lucie, he wasn't quite sure. So far, she didn't know a thing about Io, and David planned to keep it that way. It pleased him to play these games. David hoped to keep Io a secret, for just a little while longer, because he had his own agenda and he couldn't let Lucie get in his way—no matter how smitten he was with her.

"May I get you something?" Nesa asked from the speaker in the corner of the kitchen. The original NESA systems had been pretty nifty, but after Jeremy had tampered with his and sold the updates to the Core, they had become like fully operational robots, able to take care of most household chose with ease. Everyone wanted one. He sighed and glanced up at the two 'arms' that dangled from the pipes on the ceiling.

"No, Nesa. I'm fine," David said. He turned his attention to the kitchen door.

Jeremy stepped into the kitchen. Stepping to the side of the door, he gestured toward the opening and said, "Well, come on, Io. He doesn't have all day."

David tried not to laugh at his brother's annoyance. He would have gladly given up his entire schedule just to come see the girl. David had a lot riding on her. His intentions were anything but pure, however, he needed the girl to get rid of Graggöry, whether or not his brother got back into the Demetrius Core.

"It's all right if she's shy," David chuckled, eyeing the doorway.

Jeremy sighed with more annoyance and tapped on the peeling wallpaper beside the door.

The girl timidly stepped through the door, her hands at her sides, fingers clutched into little nervous fists.

"Well," he said. "Let me get a look at you."

She stepped further into the room and watched him with those large lavender eyes. Her lips were stretched into a nervous smile. He wanted to laugh. This girl was supposed to be the greatest weapon ever created, and yet she was as scared as a small child—there was nothing brave about her at all. It was kind of disappointing.

"Hello," she said, at last. "It's nice to see you again."

Could she be any more frightened? He nodded in reply and reached out to grab her mechanical arm, lifting it for inspection. His brother had done a superb job, just as he had expected him to. Jeremy would put out all the stops to get back into the Core. David need only to sit back and wait. He turned the arm over and Io flinched.

"This is the newest one?" David asked, looking up at Jeremy.

Jeremy nodded and leaned back against the kitchen wall. "I think this one will be the final."

David ran his fingers over it. "It works, then?"

"Yes," Jeremy replied.

David looked to Io. "Can you show me?"

"She doesn't know how to use it yet," Jeremy said, pushing away from the wall and putting a hand on Io's shoulder. "I haven't taught her."

"That's a shame," he said. He frowned. How long had he been waiting to see this? How much longer could he bide his time? He looked up at his brother and his frown deepened. "You know, Jeremy, the Core can't wait forever. I've already put in a proposal for Io, and—"

"The Core?" Io asked, a pure look of confusion washing over her slender face. She looked from David to Jeremy, taking a step back out of the kitchen. "What is he talking about?"

"You know," David said, a little confused himself. "You'll be going to the Core as soon as Jeremy is done with you."

Jeremy made a face and looked everywhere but at David or Io. "I haven't told her about that yet."

"You mean; she doesn't know she's going to be a—"

"What is he talking about, Jeremy?" Io asked. Her voice was so soft, that David almost didn't catch what she said.

"Does she even know what she is?" David asked. He leaned back in the chair, watching his brother, a bit amused at the situation unfolding before him.

"What am I?" Io asked, her lavender eyes sparkling with rage. "Jeremy…"

"Well, you're a weapon, of course," David said, matter-of-factly. "How could you not tell her, Jeremy?"

Jeremy swallowed and moved his hand from Io's shoulder. "Well, you see, I…"

"A weapon?" Io asked. He turned to Jeremy. "I knew you weren't up to any good. When were you going to tell me?"

145

"I was going to tell you soon, I was just waiting for the right time," Jeremy said.

"Oops," David chuckled. He stood from the chair. As comical as this was, he had other things to be doing. If the girl wasn't ready for the Core, she was of no use to him. "I suppose I ought to let the two of you talk. You should let me know when she's ready for the Core. They'll want to see her soon."

"Right," Jeremy said. "I'll let you know."

Io was standing in front of them, gaping at Jeremy, her once calm lavender eyes dark and seeping with rage. David let out another chuckle. "I'm sorry for, uh, blowing your cover, Jer. If I had known, I certainly wouldn't have brought it up."

"Yes, well," Jeremy snapped. "I suppose I was going to have to tell her eventually."

"There's no better time than the present," David said. He patted his brother on the shoulder as he stepped out of the room. "I'll show myself out. Good luck."

"Thanks, I guess," Jeremy said behind him.

The whole episode had cured him of his annoyance at Jeremy for not having the girl one hundred percent done. He could wait a little longer. He still had a little time.

"I'll stop by again soon," David called behind him, as he reached for the door. "Later."

The door clanged shut behind him as he walked out into the ashen snow. He looked down the street. What was his brother thinking, just playing house with the girl for all these weeks? He should have been training her. She should already be ready for the Core.

"Patience," he told himself, watching the steam escape his lips. "You've got to be patient, David. These things take time."

But he was going to run out of time.

He would need Io soon.

Lysithea
The Palace

There had only been one cigarette left, and Graggöry had refused to light it for weeks. Instead, he moped around the office, going through stacks of paperwork with the damn thing sticking out of his mouth—like that was going to help anything.

"What are you looking at now?" she asked him, leaning back in the chair. Lysithea draped her arms over her knees, watching Graggöry. She tapped her forefinger and thumb together, sighing.

"A weapon proposal," Graggöry said. "Believe it or not, David thinks he knows how we can win and end the war with the Wastelands."

"You've got to be kidding me," Lysithea said, her voice laced with bored sarcasm. She shifted her weight, turning her body in the chair so that she could better watch Graggöry. "What kind of weapon is he proposing?"

"It's very vague," Graggöry said, a frown tugging at his lips. "More details to come, it says."

He placed the paper back down on his desk and glanced her way with a shrug and continued, "I have no idea what that means."

Lysithea thought for a moment, wondering if David really had anything of importance to propose to the Core. Whatever it was, it was probably highly illegal, and he'd probably talked his poor, awkward brother into helping him out with it. Jeremy Lancaster was not supposed to be doing anything, banned from experimenting until his trial. Lysithea frowned.

"It's probably David being typical David," she said after a moment, laughing. "It's probably not anything impressive, love. Don't get your hopes up."

Graggöry leaned back in his chair, still watching her. "I suppose I'll just ask him about it when I see him. Surely, he'll be around here sometime. He can't hide from me forever."

Lysithea nodded, but frowned with unease. Something was definitely up with David, she just wasn't quite sure what that was. And now that she had

Graggöry to worry over, she didn't have the proper time to snoop and find out. She hoped however, for Graggöry's sake, that whatever David was doing was not completely horrible and that perhaps it would actually help them win the war, after all. It seemed very unlikely.

"Well… one thing is for damn sure," Lysithea said, tilting her head to gaze out the window at all the people busy going places on the street. "It's going to take a real miracle to end this war… and win."

Graggöry sighed, but did not answer.

Io and Jeremy
The Townhouse

Io watched as David left, feeling, for the first time since she'd come to live with Jeremy in the townhouse, a sort of rage building up in her heart. She knew, of course, that all of this was going to happen, but there was something so final about hearing it all said out loud and not in a dream. For days now, she had been giving Jeremy the benefit of the doubt, thinking that maybe he really was a good person that meant well, that she could even trust him. The future could be changed, after all. At least, that's what her mother had said. Now she realized that she had been terribly wrong to think any of it. Io felt foolish for believing that Jeremy had done everything out of the kindness of his heart, but she had not wanted to be right about the off-ness and the awkwardness she felt in the moments they spent together, during meals or whenever she was down in his workshop. She had not wanted to believe her visions would come true.

Io sighed and glanced to Jeremy, who ran a hand through his hair and leaned back against the wall. Neither of them spoke, they only stared at each other until Io finally looked away, her anger and sadness threatening to escape her in the form of frustrated tears. Io had not cried since that first night, when all hope had been lost and she had come to the horrible realization that she was alone and that she would never see her family again for as long as she lived on earth. Biting her bottom lip, Io took a deep breath. She would not cry in front of Jeremy again. He did not deserve to see her tears. Not now.

"I was going to tell you," Jeremy finally said, after what seemed to be an ion of silence. "I was just waiting for the right time, that's all."

"When would it ever be the right time to tell me any of *that*?" Io asked.

Jeremy shrugged and shook his head, his fluffy brown hair bouncing and falling in front of his eyes. "I understand you're upset, but I had my reasons for doing this and—" he paused and frowned as he considered what to say, "I didn't want to risk your recovery by stressing you out over something so unnecessary. You really ought to be thanking me…"

Io took a deep breath, trying desperately to fight the anger boiling inside of her. She let it out slowly. Had she just heard him wrong?

"Something so *unnecessary*?" Io whispered. "This is my life you're talking about. This is about my future, and you're deeming it unnecessary—really, Jeremy?"

"I didn't mean—"

"Don't you think I deserve to know what's going to happen to me?"

Jeremy didn't reply.

"What is going to happen to me, Jeremy?" she asked, leaning back against the table. She crossed her arms in front of her chest. There was a hollowness inside of her that she'd never felt before, a dark and bitter feeling that festered in her thoughts. "You are going to tell me, aren't you? I thought we were friends."

Jeremy stayed silent.

"Or should I just wait until the next time David comes to find out?"

Jeremy pushed away from the wall and marched across the room to the table, pulling out a chair and sitting down. Io kept her back to him, staring off into the foyer at the front door. If she were so powerful, it wouldn't be too hard to just leave. She could march out of the house right now, and Jeremy probably couldn't stop her' however, she knew nothing of the world outside, nor did she know anything about her own stupid, useless, mechanical limbs. Leaving now would be a disaster, as much as she disliked the idea of staying. She closed her eyes. Behind her, Jeremy tapped on the table, pondering what to say.

"I'll tell you," he said, leaning back. The chair groaned under him. He glanced over to her. "I'll tell you everything you want to know—just sit down."

"I don't want to sit down," Io replied, feeling slightly like a stubborn child. She didn't want Jeremy to see the fear in her eyes. Her face would give every insipid emotion away, and she could not risk being that open with someone so closed-off like him. If she stayed like this, she would be safe if a tear accidently spilled out. "I'd much rather stay like this."

"Have it your way, then," Jeremy sighed.

"Thank you," Io said.

"Well," Jeremy started. "What would you like to know first?"

"Did you have anything to do with the death of my people?" Io asked. "You were there—you were wearing Core coats—when it happened. You found me. So, did you have anything to do with it?"

"No," Jeremy said. "I didn't."

"Then why were you there?"

"I knew about the attack because David told me," Jeremy said. "I needed a stronger body to… to do my experiment on, so I could get back into the Core—"

"So," Io interrupted. "You took me from the valley to experiment on me?"

She dropped her arms, flexing her mechanical fingers. "You took me from my home to do this?"

"I saved your life," Jeremy responded. "I—"

"You did *this* to me!" she shouted, turning around and slamming her metal fist down onto the table. "You turned me into a monster!"

"I had to," Jeremy said. He pushed the chair away from the table, the legs scraping against the tiles on the floor, as he tried to contain his own anger. "You have no idea what I've gone through to get this far! You were a miracle, Io. You are my salvation."

"I couldn't even save my own people," Io said, her voice so low, Jeremy strained to hear it. "I'm not anyone's salvation."

"You're wrong," Jeremy said.

Io shook her head.

"Because of you, I'll get my life back," Jeremy said.

"A life for a life, then," Io spat.

She glanced at him, a confusing sort of feeling tugging at her heart. Part of her wanted to run away, to get as far away from Jeremy and the townhouse and the Core as she possibly could, but another part of her, a darker part, wanted to stay and see this through—for herself, for Jeremy. After all, he did save her, even if it was for his own selfish reasons. She owed him her life, but right now she hated him. Io had not hated someone in a long time, not since her sister had left the valley. He was going to give her to the people who had murdered her family—and it wasn't even going to faze him. Maybe she shouldn't let it faze her, either.

"Why did the Core want my people dead?" Io asked.

"I don't know," Jeremy said.

"What are they going to do with me?"

Jeremy sucked in a breath of air and held it for a moment. He wanted to tell her that she was no monster—that he was—but the things the Core would have her do…

"Awful things," Jeremy finally answered. He felt sick to his stomach, his conscience finally getting the better of him. "You're a weapon now, Io. They're going to make you do horrible things."

"…and you're going to let them."

Jeremy looked away from her, saying nothing.

"I thought I could trust you," Io said.

"Your mistake," Jeremy answered.

Io blinked back her tears, all of the pain and rage and sadness finally reaching a breaking point inside of her. She stepped away from the table, her mechanical arm falling to her side, her real hand clutching at her dress, above her heart.

"Excuse me," Io whispered, turning from the table. She paused for a moment, wondering if she should say anymore, before shaking her head and marching out of the kitchen. Io hurried up the stairs and down the hall, to her room, slamming her door behind her like some sort of spoiled teenager. Fitting, she thought, since she had only just turned eighteen at some point during her stay in the townhouse. She stood in the dark for a long time, letting the tears fall freely down her cheeks. After a while, she made her way to the bed to lie down, her face buried into her pillow. When she had almost cried herself to sleep, the speaker clicked to life, Nesa's all too happy, singing voice interrupting the silence.

"May I get you anything, dear?"

Io cringed at how smug she sounded.

"No," Io answered. "I'm fine."

"If you say so, dear," Nesa chirped. "Goodnight."

"Goodnight," Io groaned, and drifted into turbulent sleep.

Nesa

The Townhouse

On nights like these, Nesa wished, more than anything, for a body of her own. Before Io had come into their lives, Nesa had thought to ask Jeremy to make one for her. However, by the time she had finally mustered enough courage to ask him, he had brought the girl, bleeding and broken, through the back door of the townhouse, and any time he had had before that moment was gone—every second was dedicated to Io.

Nesa hated the girl, though she supposed it wasn't wholly her fault. Perhaps it was merely because she had what Nesa did not: a body, and to Nesa's great displeasure, (most of the time) Jeremy. True, all of this had started out only as a simple obsession to somehow get himself back into the Demetrius Core, but now Nesa could see a transformation in her master. He was becoming someone she was not truly accustomed to, someone *changed.* Nesa didn't like Io's Jeremy. It could be that she was simply jealous. After all, Jeremy had programmed her to feel those insipid human emotions. Before, when Jeremy didn't have the girl to look after, he spent house of his time talking to Nesa. Jeremy had encoded her to be his companion. Nesa had been someone for him to come home to. They were friends, she thought, but he scarcely spoke to her now, if only to ask her to cook something for the girl, or set out some clothes for her, or to heat water for her bath. Io was slowly taking the townhouse over.

She was also starting to ruin everything.

In the study, Jeremy was sitting in the dark, brooding over the fight with Io, probably. Nesa wondered if she should reach out to him, as she often had before. It could not hurt to ask him if he needed anything—Nesa was his friend, wasn't she? She wanted to know what he was thinking, how he was feeling. If Nesa were human, if she only had a body, she could comfort him somehow. *A simple hug would be nice,* she thought. There wasn't much she could do as just a voice over a speaker system.

It pained her.

Nesa wanted to help, though she hardly knew how. For once, her intelligence did her no good. She was completely stumped on how to fix this problem. Unless—

She could get rid of Io.

Nesa pushed that thought aside momentarily, focusing on the matter at hand: Jeremy. She considered speaking to him. It would do him some good to talk to somebody about it, even if whatever he had to say would only hurt Nesa more in the end. It was Nesa's duty to be there for Jeremy. That was what a friend was for, wasn't it?

"May I get you anything, sir?" she finally asked him, her voice almost too loud for the silence that seemed to echo throughout the townhouse.

Jeremy inclined his head, glancing toward the little camera that had become Nesa's eyes. She focused on the sullen look upon his face.

That stupid, insignificant girl.

Nesa felt livid. How dare Io come into Nesa's home and ruin her master? She didn't deserve anything Jeremy did for her. It just wasn't fair.

Jeremy said nothing for a long time, only watched 'her' watching him, his eyes narrowing as they focused on the camera in the dim glow cast by the lamp on his desk. He looked away and poured himself another glass of Scotch, tilting the glass atop the scattered papers on the desktop.

She waited.

"No need," was all Jeremy said.

If Nesa had had a real heart, she supposed it would have ached for him. She had no idea what to say to help. For once, she felt completely useless. Who was she kidding—this was absolutely all Io's fault. Nesa wished that David had just taken Io earlier, when he'd come to visit. If there happened to be no more Io, there would be no more of these ridiculous problems.

Perhaps, she could make the girl leave of her own free will.

Nesa pondered this.

It wouldn't be so hard after tonight's events. The girl did not seem to be too pleased with her current situation. She certainly did not want to have anything more to do with Jeremy.

That was a step in the right direction.

She felt a bit pleased, even.

Jeremy remained silent.

"If you need anything, Jeremy, please don't hesitate to ask," Nesa said to him.

Without waiting for a reply, she clicked the camera in Io's room on. Io was sleeping, her body sprawled out on top of the comforter. She hadn't changed out of her dress, so Nesa supposed she had fallen asleep crying sometime after Nesa had last checked on her.

Good, Nesa thought. *It serves you right.*

It did serve her right to be so sad for all the trouble she was causing Jeremy and Nesa and everyone involved; however, everything would be changing soon, if Nesa could help it at all.

Nesa would convince Io to leave, if it was the last thing she ever did. It was the only way to right all of the wrongs the girl had caused just by being in their lives.

Clicking the camera off, she surrounded herself in darkness. There was a lot to do now. She would need to think of a plan. With Io gone, they would need another way to get Jeremy back into the Core, but they could figure something out, she was certain.

Surely, it wouldn't be so hard to get rid of Io. She supposed it wouldn't take much convincing her at all. Nesa pictured herself grinning ear to ear.

She would start tomorrow.

Jeremy would be good as new in not time.

Crosbie
The Metal Shop

"Jeremy's been busy for such a long time," Jynx pouted, crossing her arms and leaning back against the kitchen door. "He's got no time for us anymore."

"He'll have time for us again soon, sister, don't worry," Crosbie said, not looking away from the handheld game he was playing. "He's busy with work."

"He's always busy with work," Jynx sighed. "We haven't hung out in ages."

"We'll hang out soon," Crosbie said.

"He's been acting very suspicious lately, too," Jynx pointed out. "Asking for all those things for work, and never explaining what or who they're for."

"It's not really any of our business," Crosbie replied. He switched the game off and set it down on the table. "He'll tell us if he wants to."

"Yeah, well... I don't like it," Jynx said. "He's always keeping secrets."

"That's what happens when you work for the Core," Crosbie countered. "You have to keep secrets from everyone—even your closest friends."

"I don't know how close we are anymore," Jynx snapped. "We haven't seen him in two months."

"Oh, come off it," Crosbie sighed. "Two months isn't going to ruin a friendship."

"I don't know," Jynx replied.

Crosbie watched her, a smirk stretching across his lips. "You sound like a jealous girlfriend."

"I'm not his girlfriend, and I'm not jealous of anything," Jynx said, eyeing him. "Don't be so ridiculous."

Crosbie supposed he couldn't blame Jynx for being so upset. They really hadn't seen Jeremy in a long time, and he didn't tell them anything anymore. He knew Jynx was growing bored, sitting in the apartment all day just practicing magic and doing odd jobs for Max. There wasn't really much else to do, and Crosbie was so busy with his project that he hardly had time for Jynx either. Jynx was probably just very lonely.

"How about we go see the ducks?" Crosbie asked.

He couldn't help but feel sorry for Jynx. She hadn't asked for this life. It wasn't her fault that she wasn't his real sister—or that Max had abandoned his children in their time of need because he was selfish and grieving. Crosbie needed to be more understanding. She was kind of growing on him, he hated to admit.

"You never want to go see the ducks," Jynx replied.

"I want to today," Crosbie said.

"All right," Jynx said. She gave him a weird look. "We better hurry before it gets dark. There is the curfew to worry about now."

Crosbie nodded. The curfew was ridiculous, but he guessed Graggöry had placed it to keep the denizens of Neo Victoria safe. The enemy was close to the wall now—it wouldn't be much longer before they broke through and the warfront would be at their front doors.

"Yeah, let's go right now," Crosbie said, standing from the chair and grabbing his jacket. "I'm sure the ducks will be happy to see you."

"Only because I feed them," Jynx laughed.

She grabbed the bag of bread crumbs she kept for the ducks from the kitchen counter and turned toward the door. Crosbie followed her out into the street, glancing at their surroundings out of habit. Too many bad things were happening nowadays, and it was Crosbie's duty to keep Jynx safe at all costs— even though she was the older sibling. Crosbie had an unrealistic fear of the people he cared about dying—that was why he had tried so hard not to be close to Jynx all these years. If he wasn't attached, it wouldn't hurt so badly in the end.

"It is rather gloomy out here today," Jynx said, as they sauntered along the sidewalk toward the park. "Sometimes I wish we could see the sun."

"I know what you mean," Crosbie said. He stepped closer to Jynx as someone made their way down the opposite side of the street. The person never looked up. Crosbie sighed with relief. "It would be nice to see a blue sky."

"Maybe someday the ash will stop falling, and we will get to see it," Jynx offered. She glanced over to him and smiled.

Crosbie smiled back at her.

David
Imogen Square

"It's not going so well," Lucie sighed, tugging the hood of her crimson coat up over her chocolate curls. She frowned and huffed steam into the air, looking up at David. He had not been back in the square since the accident, and found it only fitting, if not slightly ironic, that Lucie had chosen to meet here of all places. He sat down next to her on the park bench, leaning back and watching his own breath as it wisped up into the starless night sky.

Sometimes David wished that he could see the stars. He often wondered if they were even still up there, or if, after all this time, the stars had given up on the world, too. Lucie hooked her arm up around his, leaning into him, to keep warm, he supposed. He peered over at her. She was looking straight ahead at the lights inside of a shop window, watching them as they twinkled. It was almost romantic. *Almost.*

Those lights were probably the closest they were ever going to get to seeing stars.

"Care to talk about it?" David asked, supposing he should try to be a little more intimate. After all, he was interested—just preoccupied.

Lucie had told him hardly anything about her plan. The not talking seemed to be going both ways, at this point.

"I'm not much of a talker, my darling," she replied.

Neither am I, he thought.

"I supposed you had something you wanted to tell me," David pressed on. "Why else would you call me out so early in the morning?"

"I came to check on your progress," Lucie said, and then added, a little more defensively, "I also came because I *missed* you."

David wondered if that was true. Lucie hadn't come around in a couple of days, and only ever sent for him when something was not going right with her own plans. He was starting to wonder just what she was interested in— certainly it was not just him. It would be completely absurd for *Lucifer* to have a crush on a mere mortal man.

"I think I've found a way to accomplish what you've asked," David told her, hoping he wouldn't have to go into much detail. The less Lucie knew, the better off the whole thing was. However, he felt that she was catching on and doing so rather quickly. She was the devil, he supposed—she was bound to catch on eventually.

"That's wonderful, my darling!" Lucie purred. She frowned a little and unhooked her arm from around his. "Though, there is one minor detail I must speak with you about."

And there it was—the true reason she had called him out to the square in the wee hours of the morning.

"That is?"

Lucie sighed, a little too dramatically, and glanced around the square as though to make sure they were truly the only two souls daring enough to be out in the frigid cold.

"One of them is still alive," Lucie whispered.

David's breath caught in his throat. Did she know about Io? Surely, not.

When David didn't answer, Lucie continued. "I'm not completely sure of it, but I suspect that it's Graggöry's little playmate, Lysithea."

David felt relief wash over him. She didn't know about Io! His plans were still safe.

"Oh?" David asked.

He reached out and tugged her a little closer.

"Yes," Lucie said. She let out a slow breath. "So, I need you to wait a smidgen longer."

"To do what?"

"To kill Graggöry, silly," Lucie giggled. She rested her hand on his shoulder and let out another sigh. "I need him to kill her."

"I could kill her for you," David suggested. He already wished Lysithea was dead—killing her would bring him great pleasurable joy.

"No, my precious darling," Lucie said. She licked her lips. "I don't want too much blood on your hands. Besides, it's a little bit of torture, don't you think? It's fun for me. Let him do the dirty work."

She sounded genuine enough. He smiled. She was just as sadistic as he was. Maybe the both of them were truly meant for each other.

David nodded his head. "If that's what you want."

Lucie nodded and peeled away from him.

"It is what I want," Lucie told him.

He supposed he could give this one thing to her. She had given him so much just by keeping him alive that day. Though he had his own plans, he did kind of want her to be happy. If she was pleased, he was pleased, too.

"I've got to go," Lucie said, standing from the bench.

David followed, standing and looking down at her.

"Are you happy, Lucie?" he asked her, the question startling him a little.

"Oh, I will be, soon," Lucie replied. She smiled up at him, her crimson eyes glistening in the lamplight. "Thanks to you."

David leaned down to kiss her cheek.

"Goodnight, my darling," Lucie said. "Until next time."

"No," David replied, as he watched her go. "Good morning."

Lysithea
Spiritus Vallem

This is only a dream. It has to be.

Lysithea walks through the upstairs hallway of her family's cottage, her bare feet pressing against the slick, cold wood floor. It's been so long since she's been here—it's been so long since she's left, that everything about this feels wrong. Spiritus Vallem has been destroyed, and yet here she is, standing at the edge of the staircase in her childhood home... a home that, in the waking world, has been taken by dark magic and flames.

She makes her way down the staircase, clutching the bannister to keep herself from toppling over. Why is she here? Where are the others?

"They're all dead," a voice says from the kitchen. The voice sounds so familiar, so comforting, though its words are not. "The others are dead, dear."

That's right, she tells herself. *You've murdered them.*

She exits the staircase, pausing at the bottom to look around the foyer. Everything is as it was the night she left. Nothing has changed. She sees a shadow stalk by out of the corner of her eye, and turns her head to the kitchen. Chrezabel stands in the doorway, staring contently at her.

"Momma," Lysithea whispers. She can hardly believe her eyes.

Her beautiful, tormented mother smiles and opens her arms. "Come Lysithea. Give your mother a hug."

She hurries to her mother, wrapping her arms around the woman's neck and clinging to her like a small child. "Momma, I thought you were dead."

"I am dead," Chrezabel whispers into her hair. "You're only dreaming."

Lysithea frowns. That's right. This is only a dream. *Everyone I've known is dead now.* She clutches her mother tighter, burying her face into her neck. Lysithea takes in her mother's scent, rosemary and lavender. It's very comforting.

"I forgive you, you know," her mother says, all of the sudden. "For leaving. For... for what you've done. You need not carry this burden any longer."

But how can Lysithea not? She's murdered them all. *All my family is dead because of me.*

"I'm sorry," Lysithea whimpers. "I'm so sorry, Momma."

"I know," Chrezabel coos, stroking Lysithea's pale hair.

"The prophecy was right," Lysithea says. She pulls away from her mother's embrace and looks away. She can't bear to look her mother in the eye. "I destroyed the valley. I've doomed the world."

"There is still good in you," Chrezabel says after a moment. "There is still hope."

"I can't save him," Lysithea says, her hopelessness looming over her like a cloak.

"My beautiful, foolish, little girl," Chrezabel answers, tilting Lysithea's head up so that their eyes meet. "All is not lost. You must believe."

"But I can't," Lysithea murmurs, shaking her head. "I don't know how to anymore."

Her mother smiles. It is the most comforting thing Lysithea has ever seen.

"Soon," Chrezabel says. "You will see, soon."

Lysithea tries to ask when, but everything is starting to fade. Her mother dissipates. The cottage dissipates. She clings to the dream, but it's of no use.

Soon, a voice says.

Lysithea gasped and opened her eyes.

Jeremy
Lydia District

When the sun had finally begun to ascend the miserable, ash-filled sky, Jeremy had stumbled out of his office and down the stairs, grabbing his coat from the hall tree as he decided to go out for a walk to clear his head. Without saying a word to Nesa, he slipped out the front door and staggered down the front steps. He was probably too drunk to be walking around town so early in the morning, but he really did not care. He had found, earlier on in the night, that he had stopped caring about most things entirely over the last couple of weeks, most things, that was, except for Io. What had started out as a brilliant plan to get back into the Core had turned out to be the one thing that would drive him into a quarter-life crisis. He scoffed, kicking at the piles of ashen snow that had piled up on the sidewalk overnight.

He shouldn't care about the girl.

Every bit of logic in his head told him it was a bad idea. He was getting more attached to her day by day. In fact, he had realized, right after she had fled to her room, that he actually was bothered by how sad she had been. *These things shouldn't matter*, he reminded himself. She was just his ticket back into the Core—she would help him destroy it. Io was nothing more than that, and he ought to be quick to remind himself of that the next time he found himself feeling weird feelings.

Jeremy rounded the corner at the end of his block and headed down a stretch of road lined with quaint Victorian-styled homes that he had never bothered to walk down before. It was amazing how unfamiliar he was with the Lydia District, when he had lived there almost all of his life. He had never had the time to explore, always busy with the Core or coming straight home to plan and eat and sleep. Things were better then, when he had had nothing to worry about.

Now he worried about everything.

He let out a sigh and paused his walking, leaning back against a lamp post on the corner of the sidewalk. What was he going to do? Io couldn't possibly want to help him get back into the Core, not when it meant giving herself up to the people responsible for the death of her entire clan. But she was his only hope. All he had to live for was the Core, and his plan to destroy it. Without it, he was nothing, just a shell of a man whose existence was moot. How could he persuade her to help him? What could he give her in return?

He had given her life, but what did that matter when she would just be treated as an object in the Core, and not as a person? Io would be completely miserable. Io was already completely miserable, cooped up in the townhouse day after day, never allowed to go outside and never allowed to interact with anyone besides himself or Nesa. It was not the greatest quality of life, Jeremy had realized. He could not blame her for wanting more.

And she must be terribly lonely, he thought. He was not the best of company, and he knew that Io could sense the distaste Nesa had for her.

What a mess he had created.

Jeremy shook his head and pushed off the lamppost, turning around to walk back home. The air was frigid and had sobered him up a little. He needed some rest. Yet Jeremy could not stop worrying about what to do with Io. He couldn't just let her go—not after all the time and effort he had put into making her what she was now. He *had* to rejoin the Core at all costs. David needed his help, taking it down. He needed those things to feel useful, to feel like his life had a purpose.

He would have to see this through to the very end. There was no other way. It did not matter how attached he was getting, or how wrong all of it felt now, or that, somehow, he wanted her to be happy—all that mattered was that he got what he wanted. In this world, it was every man for himself; he certainly could not continue babysitting Io all day. He was a scientist, not an entertainer, and hardly one for keeping good company with others. Io would be sold to the Core and he would move on with his life. He would follow through with the plan. He had to.

Upon arriving back at the townhouse, Jeremy pulled his ID card from his coat pocket and shoved it up against the scanner. Nesa scanned the ID.

"Welcome back, sir," she said. "Security code, please."

He dialed his security code and ran a hand through his hair, waiting for Nesa to unlock the door and let him in. The door clicked open. He pushed his way inside and slipped out of his coat, tossing it over a hook on the hall tree, before making his way up the stairs.

He would have to tell Io that he hadn't changed his mind, and he would have to stick with that, no matter how horrible it was beginning to make him feel.

"Nesa, heat the water for my shower," he said as he topped the staircase.

"Right away, sir," Nesa replied.

Jeremy started down the upstairs hallway, toward Io's room. He paused in front of her door and rasped his knuckles against it lightly. She did not answer. His breath caught for a moment—was she asleep, or had she slipped out while he was away? Slightly panicked by the thought, he cracked the door open, peering inside the dark room.

Io was asleep on the bed, the covers all strewn about as if she'd had a nightmare and tossed and turned in her sleep. Io looked so peaceful now, though, so pretty and fragile all at once. Jeremy's stomach churned. He couldn't let himself think those things.

Closing the door, he sauntered back down the hall to his study. He stood in the doorway for a long time, just looking at the blinking neon light outside the little window. This was bad. This was very bad. He had never felt so torn about anything in his life; however, getting back at the Core was important, a priority, and like before, he told himself that he absolutely had to see this through until the end. It did not matter if Io was just a young, sweet, innocent thing. It did not matter if he cared for her. *It cannot matter*, he told himself. This was how it had to be.

Jeremy turned from the door and made his way to his room. Hopefully, he would get some rest before he had to face her again. It would be no good if he snapped at her out of tiredness. He yawned and walked into his room, closing the door behind him.

This is for the best, he told himself. *You'll see.*

He hoped, for his sake, that it was.

Io

The Townhouse

When Io awakened, dim light was cascading into the room from the window. She continued to lie in her bed for several minutes, staring up at the ceiling as she wondered what exactly she was going to do about everything that had happened the night before. Though she was not at all okay with the knowledge that she was going to be sold, like an object, to the very organization that had brought on the onslaught against the angels in Spiritus Vallem, there was hardly anything she could do about it. Jeremy would do whatever Jeremy felt he needed to, and Io knew that. To have thought this whole time that perhaps the both of them could be friends had been a foolish venture, she realized, but it was entirely too late for her. She was his friend, whether he was hers or not. It bothered her that he seemed to care so little about anyone but himself, but she would not let that stop her from trying to understand what was going on in his head.

Somewhere inside him was the Jeremy that she had fallen for in all of those stolen visions of borrowed time. Somewhere, that man did exist. Io just had to be patient and find him.

She turned onto her side and stared at the closed door. What could she do but continue on as if nothing had transpired between them? Jeremy was probably not at all bothered by any of it, so why should she worry herself over something that, as Jeremy would put it, was completely unnecessary? It wasn't like she would get an apology from him. He owed her nothing, after all. And though she felt like she was the one who had carelessly intruded upon his life, she knew in her heart that he had brought all of it on himself.

Io frowned and closed her eyes, trying to think about the valley.

Those had been simpler, better days—days she had taken for granted. What she wouldn't give to just be home again, to see her mother and father and Kale. What she wouldn't give just to see even Lysithea again, as well, though she still harbored a slight anger at her sister for leaving the valley. Leaving the valley had probably saved her sister's life, however, so perhaps Io shouldn't be too angry. Io wondered if Lysithea had found what she was looking for. Maybe she was finally happy somewhere, finally able to be herself—

Io frowned.

In her dream last night, Lysithea had stood over the burning valley, watching as her people died. There had been no remorse in her now gray eyes, nothing shone in them but the wild gleam of desperation. Perhaps, the prophecy had been right after all; an angel would destroy the world; however, there was still a chance for an angle to save it. Io wondered who else might have escaped the valley that day; who had left the village in previous months, like Lysithea had? Someone had to save the world, and that someone was certainly not Io. Io could not save anyone. Not her parents, not her people, not Kale.

But there was still Jeremy. Io could do this one thing for him, and perhaps his life would be saved, returned to how it had been before Io had come to know him. If she could save him, perhaps, it would be enough to heal the part of her soul that had withered when she had been so helpless to stop everything from happening in the meadow that day. Io let out a slow sigh, stretching her arms above her head. She knew that that part of her would never be healed again, especially if she went to work for the Core as a weapon.

A weapon. That was what she was now. Io would be used to destroy things, to destroy people. Her stomach churned at the thought of it. Perhaps, she was the angel the prophecy spoke of, the angel who would destroy the world—it may never have been Lysithea at all. All those years of Chrezabel speaking of it behind closed doors, all those visions… there had never been an explanation, there had never even been a definitive answer. Her mother had never told her *who* she saw in her dreams; only that it had started with Lysithea. Io wondered if her mother had known the truth before she had died. Had she kept it from them all? The only other person who knew the truth was probably Abraxos, and now he was dead, too. If it was true, and if she was the angel who destroyed the world, who would save them?

Her heart sank. How was she ever going to be able to go through with any of this? She was no monster, though she looked like one now, she supposed. She did not want to hurt people. Yet, the Core would make her do unthinkable things—Io knew that much. If only she weren't indebted to Jeremy for saving her life, however selfish his reasons had been. If only she could think of another way.

There was no other way. If she left, she would not be able to make it out on the streets. She knew nothing of this world, nothing of how it worked. Perhaps, she could learn, though. If Jeremy would let her leave the townhouse for the day, she could go out and observe. Leaving the townhouse, however, seemed like an unlikely possibility.

Tired of moping, Io sat up and ran a hand through her hair, careful not to hit the chords that were protruding from her neck. She took a long breath and let it out slowly before pushing herself up off the bed. She opened the door and peered out into the hallway. Light streamed through the front windows, flooding the foyer; however, the hallway remained dark, untouched by the light. Making her way into the hallway, she started for the stairs, pausing in front of Jeremy's study door. She pressed her ear against the cold wood, listening for any sign of life.

"He isn't in there," Nesa said from the speaker by the door.

Io jumped back, a little startled. "Oh. Where is he?"

"I suppose he's still sleeping. He was up very late," Nesa said.

Io frowned and walked to the banister, looking down over the foyer. She wondered what he was doing so late at night. "I see."

"Come downstairs," Nesa chirped. "I'll make you some breakfast."

Io perked up. She wasn't very used to Nesa doing things of her own free will, especially when it came to her. It was no big secret that Nesa hated her.

"Thank you," Io said, making her way down stairs. At the foot of the staircase, she stopped and stared at the front door. How easy it would be to just leave—Nesa wouldn't stop her. In fact, the AI would probably rather she be gone anyway. But Io couldn't bring herself to leave—not yet. She cared too much about what would happen to Jeremy, as ironic as that was. Though he didn't seem to care much about her own wellbeing, Io was not the kind of person who could easily not care about others—even complete strangers.

I'm a good person, she told herself. She looked down at her robotic hand. The slender metal fingers flexed and curled into a fist. *I am not a monster.*

"Are you coming, dear?" Nesa asked from the kitchen.

Io nodded and descended the last step, slowly making her way into the kitchen.

"What would you like to eat?" Nesa asked.

Io wondered why she was being so nice. Surely, there was some ulterior motive behind it.

"An egg would suffice," Io replied, sitting down at the kitchen table. "Fried, please."

"One fried egg, right away!" Nesa sang.

Io rested her head in her hands. Behind her, Nesa clanked pots and pans together as she tried to find the frying pan. Io wondered if she could confide in Nesa. She had no one to talk to, and it was getting very lonely.

"Say, Nesa," Io said. "Could I ask you something?"

"Of course," Nesa replied.

"What was Jeremy like? Before he was exiled from the Core?"

Io heard the refrigerator open and close, and then the clank of an egg cracking against the counter. She wondered if Nesa would answer. Perhaps, that was a side of Jeremy that belonged purely to Nesa and would never be shown to her. Perhaps, that Jeremy was gone forever. Or he would be back, as soon as Io was out of his life, and he was back in the Core. Still, she would never be able to witness it. She assumed that she would still see Jeremy; after all, he was her creator, he would be needed when she broke, or... or worse.

"Don't mind Jeremy," Nesa said. The egg sizzled in the pan. "He gets this way when he's stressing over something. Don't take it personally."

But how could Io not take it personally? He was just going to sell her away to monsters, to be turned into a monster herself—and she was just supposed to be okay with it?

"He's just been so cold all of the sudden," Io said. "Did I do something wrong?"

A faint laugh escaped the speaker, followed by silence.

"I'm sure it wasn't you," Nesa finally said. "I would assume its David again."

"Oh," Io said.

Nesa slipped a plate onto the table in front of her.

"There you go, dear," Nesa said. "Eat up."

Io picked up the fork that Nesa had laid upon the table. She took a bite of the egg and chewed it slowly, thinking. What could she do? She was entirely torn.

"Could you kindly bring me some juice?" Io asked, curious as to how far Nesa's act of kindness would go.

"Of course," Nesa said. In a short moment, a glass of juice was set onto the table. "Can I get you anything else, dear?"

"No, thank you," Io said. "Thank you for breakfast."

"Any time, dear," Nesa said.

Io finished her breakfast in silence, deciding it was best to not talk to Nesa after all. When she was finished she carried her dishes to the sink, and looked longingly out the kitchen window. Many months before the attack on Spiritus Vallem, her mother had made her feel like she had such a great purpose in life. Big things had been waiting for her, but now there was nothing waiting but the cold, loveless Core.

I'm not a monster, she told herself again.

"I've heated water, if you'd like to take a shower, Io," Nesa said, breaking the silence.

Io slipped back out of her thoughts and turned for the kitchen door.

"I've also left your clothes for the day on the bed," Nesa continued.

"Thank you, Nesa," Io said, making her way back up the stairs.

Io's chest hurt. She had to decide what she would do, and quickly. She didn't have much time left. It was only a matter of days now before Jeremy sent her away with David.

Graggöry
The Palace

Graggöry sat in his office. The curtains were drawn and the lights were off, cocooning him in total darkness. He was glad to be completely alone for once—the voices in his head had gone quiet ever since Lysithea had left earlier that morning. It was easier to think when Lysithea was not around, but he did miss her presence while she was away. Though, she wasn't safe with him now that he had run out of cigarettes. Her blood was so addicting and she would give it all up to him freely. He rubbed his eyes with a trembling hand. He needed those cigarettes, but it was of no use. He had called the several people he would have hoped could make the damn things, and all of them politely declined, saying they either didn't know how to make them, or reminding him that the magic used to make them was illegal to use now.

Graggöry groaned.

Why had he made those stupid laws to begin with? What good had any of it brought upon Neo Erta? Regardless of what he had tried to do to help the world, he felt like a failure now. How was he supposed to protect anyone like this? He couldn't.

"Excuse me, sir," the NESA system chirped, jolting him.

He glanced up at the speaker, waiting.

"David is here to see you."

He sat back in his chair and let out a sigh. "Send him in."

The lock on the door clicked and one of the double doors squeaked as it opened just a crack. Light from the hallway seeped inside, painting a line across the floor and up and over his desk. He shielded his eyes from it and pushed the chair away from the desk, standing.

"You can come in, you know," he called to David, his words a little too staccato for his liking. "I don't bite."

How could it be that the whole time he had wanted to talk to him, David had been nowhere in sight, but now that he wanted to be left alone, David suddenly felt the need to come and talk to him? Whatever it was, it better be important.

"Why are the lights off?" David asked, slipping in through the crack in the door. He shut the door behind him and blinked, adjusting his eyesight to the darkness. "Were you napping?"

"No," Graggöry said. He walked around the desk and stretched his hand out to David, who in turn, took it. They shook hands like they were strangers. Graggöry frowned. At one point in time, David had been his only friend. "I wasn't napping."

Graggöry sat back down in his chair and leaned on the desk. He snapped his fingers, light bursting throughout the room from the light fixtures above their heads. David blinked again, cringing slightly as if the light had blinded him.

"So—what brings you to my office?" Graggöry asked. *You could have just sent a message on the NESA.*

"Does a man need a reason to come see his best friend?" David asked. He sat down in the chair in front of Graggöry's desk. "I've been so busy with this war that I've hardly had the time to come and see you."

"I was starting to wonder if I'd ever see you again, actually," Graggöry laughed. He moved some papers into a small pile on the corner of his desk.

David glanced around the room. "Lysithea's not here?"

"No," Graggöry replied. He followed David's gaze to the window. "I sent her away for the day."

"Why?"

"Even I need some time to be alone," Graggöry said. He watched David. Why had he come? There had to be some reason. His head throbbed with agitation. He sighed. "So, tell me why you've really come? It must be important."

David cleared his throat and looked down at his hands. "We thought we were taking the war out to the Wastelands and the unclaimed territories, but my men have reported that the war has been brought right to us, instead."

Graggöry let out a groan.

"It would seem that Neo Victoria is under attack, Graggöry," David continued. "I've sent a unit to the outskirts of the city, but I'm afraid we aren't prepared and they're going to take us under siege."

"We'll start evacuating," Graggöry said. He exhaled through his teeth. "I'll have a message sent to the NESA systems shortly. I suppose now I'll have to think of a good battle plan."

"I can help you," David said. "Put me in charge, and—"

"It is my job to keep these people safe," Graggöry interrupted. "I'll think of something."

"You're so busy with everything else," David said, gesturing to the papers sprawled on his desk. "Let me help you. I already have some ideas."

If truth be told, Graggöry didn't want anything to do with the war anymore. He dreaded having to make plans, having to execute them. He glanced at David, who was eager to help in any way he could. Of course, David lived for this—he was the person who should have been in charge, but Graggöry had chosen Lysithea every other time before.

"I suppose it wouldn't hurt. I'll leave you in charge of making the battle plans. You actually know more about all of this war mess than I do, I'm ashamed to admit."

"I'll do my best, sir," David said as he stood from his chair. "But you should also fill Lysithea in on this. She did such a good job with the attack at Spiritus Vallem, that I might need her help with this one."

Graggöry knew it must have pained David to say those words, as much as he hated Lysithea. He nodded his head in response and tapped a button on his desk, a large holographic screen appearing above the slickened wood surface.

"I will send for Lys immediately," Graggöry said. "As for you, go and get your men briefed. It's going to be a long day."

"Right away, sir," David said, and turned to leave the room. He paused half way and turned back around. "Despite it all, I think your father would be proud, Graggöry."

Graggöry looked up from the screen, taken aback by the comment.

"I just thought you ought to know that," David said, before turning to leave the room.

Graggöry watched him go and wondered if those words were really true, or if David knew just what to say to really hurt him.

"I thought we were friends," Graggöry said as the door clicked shut.

Lysithea
Imogen Square

Lysithea paced back and forth in front of the fountain in the middle of the square, chewing on her bottom lip as she mumbled to herself. Four attempts to get Graggöry those stupid cigarettes had failed for one reason or another, and she was running out of people to ask. Though she hardly knew anyone in the city, she'd met a few sorcerers over the five years that she had been living in Neo Victoria—all of whom had helped her learn the right spells to make her eyes grey instead of lavender, and how to suppress her spiritual aura. She had learned many things from them, that all seemed pointless now. The end was coming for them. Of course, none of her sorcerer friends could help her now.

Lysithea supposed she understood, but it was still frustrating nonetheless.

Sitting down on a bench that overlooked the entire square, Lysithea leaned back, lifting a hand to her eyes to block out the ash as she looked up to the sky. It had been a long time since she had flown, so long of a time that she wondered if her wings even still knew how to work. When Graggöry had told her to go out for the day, she had thought about going to the forest to fly, but she was too afraid of being caught.

She let out a slow breath, watching the steam drift out into the square. Any day now she would have to tell Graggöry the truth. It was only a matter of time. She felt that she had kept it a secret for long enough—if she loved him, she shouldn't continue to lie to him. She had no way of knowing what he would do when she told him, though. Telling Graggöry the truth seemed scarier than leaving the valley all those years ago. There was something final about that truth, like she knew in her heart that everything would change.

He could have me executed, she thought, but she was equally as sure that he loved her. Maybe he wouldn't do anything, because maybe he already knew. Maybe they had both been playing the lying game—a game that neither one of them would win. Maybe Graggöry was just waiting for the perfect time to throw her out. Maybe he didn't love her after all.

"Don't be silly," she told herself. *Of course, he's in love with you.*

But the darkest part of heart thought differently.

She shivered and ran her hands up and down her arms. She could always run away again—but where would she go? There was a war going on out there—nowhere outside of the city walls was safe. She shook her head. She couldn't keep running away from things. Eventually, she would just have to face her demons like everyone else. She had friends here now. There were people she could turn to. Before when she had first come to Neo Victoria, hardly anyone had paid her any attention. She had been like a ghost.

There was only a slight chance that Graggöry would turn her away. He had a heart—he was a good man, regardless of the recent choices he'd made. If she told him the truth, maybe he would understand. She would never know until she mustered the courage to actually go through with it. Regardless of being brave enough, she would have to do it soon—she was running out of time. He had to know the truth before something could happen. She owed it to him. He had given her a life she had never imagined she could have.

"Oh, Graggöry," she whispered to the sky. "Please don't hate me."

Surely, he would not. He would be upset, but if she gave him time, he would probably calm down enough to where she could talk to him about why she had lied. There was a chance, however, that he would see this as a total betrayal. Lysithea's heart hurt as she thought of him turning her away. He was all she had left.

Wrapping her scarf back around her neck, she pushed herself off of the bench and walked to the fountain again. Lysithea looked down at her reflection in the murky water. Io had been right all those years ago. She couldn't escape what she was. She let out a slow breath. She would tell Graggöry. She looked away from the water and started down the sidewalk, when the watch on her left wrist began to buzz. She paused and lifted it up so she could see the screen. A message from Graggöry. She wondered what it could possibly be about. Clicking on the screen, the hologram formed above the watch, with the message: *Come home, Lys. This is urgent.*

Lysithea clicked the button on the side of the watch, the hologram disappearing. She supposed she had better get back to him. Anyway, perhaps he had already figured her out. She hurried down the sidewalk, headed back toward The Palace. Whatever it was, she was ready for it. She was sure of it.

Io

The Townhouse

Today was the day she would ask to go outside again. The first time she had asked, Jeremy had said no, but only because the filth would cause her wounds to get infected. It had been a believable excuse, but now Io was restless and ready to get out of the townhouse. If she went outside, perhaps she could determine whether or not she could survive out on the streets until she found her way to somewhere safe and far away from Jeremy and David and the Core. She wondered what it would be like, out there in Neo Victoria. Certainly, it would be much different than anything she had known in the valley, but she was ready for whatever the city would throw at her.

She opened the door to her room and hurried out into the hallway, wondering where Jeremy might be. She walked past his study. The door was wide open and the lights were off. She figured he must be down in his workshop. She glided down the stairs two at a time and slipped into the kitchen.

"I'm going to make some tea, Nesa," Io said. She filled her tea kettle up with water and set it down on the stove. "Where do you keep the mugs?"

"Top right cabinet," Nesa said, "but let me make it for you, dear."

"No... I'd really like to do this for myself, but thank you," Io said.

"Are you sure? I'm here to help—"

"I know, but I just miss doing things for myself sometimes," Io interjected. She set the mugs she'd gotten down on the counter and glanced around. "And where are the tea bags?"

"I'll get them for you," Nesa said, her robotic hands reached into a cabinet above Io's head, and pulled down two boxes of tea bags. "Take your pick."

Io decided to make one of each, not knowing what kind Jeremy favored.

She waited for the water to heat, and when the kettle went off, she poured the water into the mugs, each already containing a tea bag. She stirred in some lemon and honey, the way her mother used to do it when she'd make tea for Io and Lysithea and Kale.

"Thank you for your help," Io said to Nesa as she carried the mugs out of the kitchen and down to the basement door.

"Let me get that for you," Nesa said, opening the door. "But you do know he doesn't like to be disturbed—"

"I know," Io said. "What I need to ask won't take up much of his time."

"If you say so," Nesa said.

Io made her way down the stairs. The basement was definitely not her favorite place in the townhouse, though it seemed to be the place to always find Jeremy. Before her arm had been finished, the basement was where Io had spent most of her time; though, it hadn't been so bad since Jeremy was there to keep her company. She paused at the bottom step and glanced around the room. The holographic screens were all up, running data on whatever it was Jeremy was working on. Jeremy was in the middle of the screens, scratching his head as he worked.

He probably wouldn't be too happy about being interrupted. Io considered going back up the stairs and waiting until a better time. She started to turn when Jeremy stopped her.

"You can come in, you know," Jeremy called to her.

That was a first.

Io turned back around and walked the rest of the way into the room.

"I brought you some tea," Io said. "I thought maybe you could use a bit of a break."

"Thank you," Jeremy said, he glanced from Io to the mugs of tea.

Io lifted the mug in her left hand. "Green tea."

"I'll take that one," Jeremy said, reaching out to take the tea from her hand.

Io looked down into her own mug. The florescent lights reflected on the surface of the dark liquid. She pondered about what to say first, not wanting to anger Jeremy. It was nice when they were getting along, and though she had felt somewhat betrayed by him the night before, she was hoping to salvage whatever bit of their friendship that she could—even if their friendship was, in a way, a little false. He was all she had. Without Jeremy, Io would be completely alone.

"So, what are you working on?" Io asked, looking around at the screens Jeremy had pulled up all over the room.

"Oh, it's nothing really. I'm just messing around with the metal I used for your upgraded arm," Jeremy said. "I was trying to see how hard I could push it before the program crashed."

"I see," Io said. She really didn't care much for anything that had to do with her new arm and leg. In fact, she'd rather not think about them at all. "How is that going?"

"Rather well," Jeremy replied. He took a sip of the tea and set the mug down on the table as he started to mess with the holographic keyboard that sat in front of him. "Did you need something?"

"I just had a question, whenever you're available to talk," Io said. She watched him. He was biting the inside of his cheek as he worked. It made her feel happy to know these little things about him—they were probably things no one else had noticed before. It made her feel closer to him, connected to him.

"Ask away," Jeremy said. He pushed the keyboard away and turned on the stool he was sitting on, now facing Io. They made eye contact, but Io quickly turned her gaze away. She already knew her question would annoy him. In fact, she wondered if she should just think of another question to ask—perhaps she could say she had changed her mind.

"Well?" Jeremy asked. "What is it, sweetheart?"

There it was again, that feeling she got every time he called her some sweet something other than her given name—no, even when he said her name, her heart fluttered. It was wrong, she supposed, to feel this way. He was, after all, her captor. He cared nothing for her, at all.

"Well," she said, faltering with her thoughts. "I was wondering if perhaps I could go outside. Just for a walk, really. If it isn't too much trouble, that is."

Jeremy frowned. His eyes darkened. Io knew she had made a mistake.

"You can't go outside," Jeremy said. "You know that."

She frowned. Of course, she knew, but she had hoped that perhaps he would've changed his mind. She let out a sigh and took another sip of her tea.

"I just thought that maybe…"

"It's too dangerous to go out there," Jeremy said. "I don't know if you've heard, but the war has made its way into the inner city and—"

"I won't go far," Io interrupted. "I'll just go for a walk around the block, or I'll just go sit on the front steps, or—"

"Io, you cannot go outside," Jeremy said. "And that's the end of this discussion."

"But why?" Io asked. She clutched the mug with her metal fingers. "Why can't I go outside? You go outside."

"Yes, well I'm not a—"

"Monster," Io finished for him.

"Weapon," Jeremy corrected her.

Io absolutely hated that term. She hated being called a weapon. She looked everywhere but at Jeremy, who was staring at her now, quite intently.

"I am not a weapon," Io finally said. "I'm only a girl."

"Io, if you went outside and someone saw you…"

"What, Jeremy?"

"They would be frightened," Jeremy replied. "They would call on the Core—and the Core cannot know of your existence just yet. It's… it's very important that they know as little as possible until the time is right."

"Or what?" Io asked, rolling her eyes. "They'll kill me?"

"Us," Jeremy corrected her. "They'll kill us."

Io focused her gaze back on Jeremy. His face had gone very pale, and his eyes had lost some of their color. He chewed on his bottom lip and then took a deep breath.

"No matter what you may think of me," Jeremy said, "I don't wish for you to die."

Io wondered if he was only afraid for himself.

"Everyone will always think I am a monster," Io said. "That's no way to live."

Jeremy looked absolutely panicked. He set his mug down on the table beside him with a loud thump and looked back to Io. "Io, you don't want to die, believe me—"

"Of course, I don't want to die."

"Being this way doesn't make you a monster," Jeremy tried.

"Doesn't it, though?" Io asked.

The core wanted a monster, not a cowardly little girl.

They both stayed silent for a long time.

"I have a lot of work to do," Jeremy finally said. "Perhaps, you should go. I'll see you at dinner. Thank you for the tea."

"Of course," Io said. She took Jeremy's empty mug and turned to go. "I'm sorry for interrupting you. Good luck with your work."

She walked back up the stairs, watching her feet to keep herself from tumbling back down them. Of course this had happened. She had known better than to ask Jeremy. He did not want his ticket back into the Core to just waltz out the door and never come back. Definitely not. For her to think that he had any interest in her actual wellbeing was a lie. Jeremy obviously did not care whether she was miserable, here in the townhouse or not. He did not care that she would be miserable in the Core.

He only cared about himself.

But in the visions, he had been different. He had been kinder. There had been hope, where now there seemed only miles and miles of ruin. The Jeremy of her dreams was not real—her mind had made him up to cope with what was going to happen to her. She thought for a fleeting moment, as she paused by the kitchen door, that maybe she could change him, that if she did, he would

179

become that Jeremy, and everything would be righted. She shook her head and walked into the kitchen.

Io deposited the mugs in the sink and sat down at the kitchen table. She supposed she could just leave. The door was right there. No one would stop her—Jeremy was busy in his workshop, and Nesa... Nesa wanted her gone anyway. It pained her to think that Jeremy didn't care. After their talks, after she had confided in him about how she felt, about how she missed the valley and how she missed flying. About how she missed everything.

To think that he really didn't care broke her heart in a way it had never been broken before. They had spent weeks down there in that workshop, talking and getting to know each other—or so she thought. Now she wasn't quite sure who was down in the workshop. It was most certainly not the Jeremy from her visions, and it was not the Jeremy she had gotten to know. She rested her head in her hands and glanced to the door.

Why had God forsaken her? Why was he putting her through this? She had just wanted to die in the valley with her parents and her brother.

If God wouldn't help her, she would help herself.

She would forsake God, too.

"Nesa," she said, after a long while.

"You rang?" Nesa asked, her voice crackling with slight annoyance.

"I need your help."

She had to leave. It was the only way to save herself.

"How may I help you?" Nesa asked.

"I need you to keep the front door unlocked tonight," Io said, "and leave the chimer off."

"Are you trying to leave us?" Nesa asked.

"Yes," Io said.

"I don't think t hat's such a good idea," Nesa said. "As much as—"

"Please, Nesa. I'm miserable," Io whispered.

"Jeremy will kill me," Nesa said.

"Please. I know you want me gone," Io begged.

Io listened to the hum of the lights.

"Okay," Nesa finally said.

"Okay," Io repeated. "Please don't tell Jeremy."

"Certainly not," Nesa replied.

Nesa

The Townhouse

Nesa felt giddy with unbound joy. Finally, Io would be gone, and the best part was that Nesa had not had to do a single thing to persuade her to leave. Jeremy would belong to Nesa, alone, again. He would have ample time to spend with her, just like before. Maybe she would even get a body. Even though Jeremy would be really upset with her—he would eventually get over it, and they could find a new way to get him back in the Core. Yes, she would gladly help Io escape as long as Io promised to stay far away from the townhouse and Jeremy. After tonight, Io would not be Nesa's problem anymore.

There's no way she can make it out there on her own, though, Nesa's artificial conscience urged her. *She'll die out there, or worse—*

Nesa shook those thoughts from her mind. It did not matter what would happen to Io. This was about Jeremy. Jeremy would be better off without that insipid girl. Jeremy would thank Nesa when this was all said and done.

But how will he get back into the Core without her?

Nesa would think of something when the time was right. For now, however, she would just rejoice in the fact that Jeremy would soon be wholly hers again.

"Io," Nesa said, making her voice sound extra harmonious as she buzzed into the girl's room. "Could I prepare anything for your journey?"

It was the least she could do, after all. Io was doing her a great favor by leaving.

Io was staring out of the window. She turned to look up at the camera and smiled a faint, almost-not-there smile.

"No, thank you," she said.

That certainly makes things easier on me, Nesa thought.

"All right," Nesa said, "but if you change your mind, just buzz for me."

Nesa clicked Io's camera off, not waiting for a reply, and turned on the camera down in Jeremy's workshop.

Jeremy was busy at work, like always. Nesa always felt such longing when she watched him work—a longing that she had no real way of explaining. She wanted to have a body, so she could be there for him, in the way that only someone with a body could. He was so handsome, always, but especially when he was deep in thought. His lips were pursed in a slanted line across his perfect face, and his hazel eyes, more green than brown today, sparkled as they focused on one of the screens before him.

"Can I get you anything, sir?" she chimed into the silence. "Something to eat, maybe?"

Jeremy stopped what he was doing and wiped his hand on his forehead and then the bottom of his flannel shirt. He glanced up at the camera and half smiled.

"No, thank you, Nesa," he said. "I'm almost done here."

If Nesa had had a face, she would have frowned.

"Are you sure I can't get you anything?" she asked. She wanted to feel useful. She wanted him to need her.

"Yes, Nesa, I'm positive, but thank you."

"All right," Nesa sighed. She watched him a moment longer. "If you do need something, anything at all, you just call."

"Will do," Jeremy replied and started back in on what he was working on.

Nesa clicked the camera off.

Graggöry and Lysithea
The Palace

"This is bad," Lysithea said, her voice so low that Graggöry could barely hear her. "This is really bad."

"I know," Graggöry said. He ran a hand through his shaggy hair and leaned back in his chair, glancing over to Lysithea who was leaned against the side of his desk. Her arms were crossed in front of her chest as she stared out the window. Everything about her was tense. He wondered if she was afraid. She probably had every reason to be.

"What are we going to do?" she asked. She turned her gaze back to Graggöry, a desperate look in her eyes. "People are going to die."

"People were already dying," Graggöry said. "Before."

"Yes," Lysithea said, "but Neo Victoria was supposed to be a sanctuary. Now what are we going to tell them? Evacuate from here? They have nowhere else to go, Graggöry. The city is all they have."

"*I know*," Graggöry said through his teeth, "but this is all we can do for them."

"Did you send somebody?" Lysithea asked. She pushed away from the desk and paced over to the window. Moving the curtain out of the way, she peered down into the busy street at the people quickly walking by. What would they do? How would they protect these people?

"I've sent David," Graggöry said. "He's taking care of it as best as he can, Lys. I promise."

"We have to do more."

Graggöry sighed and looked up at her. He hated that he couldn't do anything to calm her.

"We can't do anything more than this," Graggöry replied.

"David is too reckless," Lysithea said, gritting her teeth. "He'll get innocent people killed."

"He's the best I could do until we figure out a game plan," Graggöry said. He stood from the desk and walked over to her, reaching out to pull her to him.

He stroked her hair, pressing her head against his shoulder. They should have been doing something about this all along, but he had been putting it off—he had been trying to forget that they were in the middle of a war. "It's going to be all right, love. David and his men will keep the rebels at bay until we can figure something solid out."

"Innocent people are going to *die*, Graggöry," Lysithea whispered. "I can't let that happen again."

Graggöry supposed that she was referring to the massacre at Spiritus Vallem. Those angels had been entirely innocent—maybe it was beginning to eat away at her. It would eat away at anyone who had a heart. Even Graggöry was bothered by it sometimes. However, he had done what he thought needed to be done, and he would continue to do what he thought was best for himself and for Lysithea, even if it meant innocent people had to die.

"I'll see what I can do, okay?" he told her. She was clinging to him like a child. He had never seen her this way before.

She bit her bottom lip to keep from crying.

"Lys, really, what's the matter?" he asked. He had no idea how to comfort her.

"I killed them," she said. "I killed them, Graggöry, and this is my punishment."

"You can't be serious," Graggöry said. "Listen to yourself."

"It's true!" Lysithea said, pushing him away. "I killed those innocent angels for you, and now my city is going to pay the price!"

Graggöry watched her, taken aback by her sudden fit. He had no idea what to do, how to calm her down. She would believe whatever she believed, regardless of what he had to say to her. He scratched the back of his head, trying to think of something to do, of something to say to her. He felt guilty for having put her through any of it in the first place.

"What if I put you in charge?" Graggöry asked. "All of what happens will be completely up to you. Would you like that?"

"It doesn't matter who's in charge," Lysithea said. "Those people will still die."

"This is a war, Lys. People are going to die regardless of what we do."

She swayed a little on her feet, feeling faint. Graggöry reached out to steady her, but she pulled away from him.

"Maybe you should sit down," Graggöry suggested. She was starting to worry him. She swayed once more, reaching out for the window to steady herself, before allowing herself to fall down onto her chair. She leaned back and turned her gaze back to the window.

"I'll brief my men," Lysithea said after a long moment. "I'll send them to go help David at the frontlines."

"Whatever you want to do, Lys," Graggöry said. He let out a slow breath and looked back out the window. For five years he had kept this city safe and untouched by the rebel forces that destroyed the outer cities and the wastelands. After his father had been assassinated, he had promised to protect these people at all costs—now he was just out to protect himself. He was not a good leader, he realized. The people deserved someone like Lysithea, someone who truly cared for their wellbeing.

If they survived the war, perhaps, he could give it all to her—Neo Victoria, the UNNE, and the whole world if she wanted it. If they survived the war, he would give her everything.

"I'll send my men," Lysithea said again. She ran her hand through her curling blond hair. "I'll go out there tomorrow, to check on things."

Graggöry watched her, pursing his lips together. She was so determined to save these people, so haunted by what had happened to the angels in Spiritus Vallem.

It's because she is one, a voice whispered. *She's the last one.*

Graggöry shook his head.

"Okay," Graggöry answered her.

"Okay," Lysithea echoed back.

Crosbie
The Metal Shop

Crosbie slid the mask of his welding hood up, so that he could get a better look at the metal contraption that lay on the table before him. He frowned as he tinkered with it, pressing and prodding and bending it to and fro. This was nothing like his father's creation. He frowned and pushed it to the side, tapping the table with his gloved fingers as he thought of what to do next. He only had about twelve hours left before his father came to see if he'd mastered creating the duplicate. It wasn't going very well.

"Crud," he murmured, turning from the table to get another strip of metal from the shelf behind him. He had a lot riding on this—he needed this apprenticeship. What else was he supposed to do, if he could not take over his father's shop? He would be a failure. He could not let that happen.

Flipping the welding hood back over his eyes, he picked up the stinger and started welding once more. Trying to fix what he'd already started was probably futile, but he had to try. His father would wake up soon and come check on his progress. If he weren't such a perfectionist, his creation was probably not half bad, but Crosbie wanted it to be absolutely perfect—he wanted his father to be highly impressed. Pausing, he switched off the welder and looked back to the hologram of the prototype. His creation was pretty close to the original that Max had made. He slid the helmet off and ran a hand through his damp black hair. Maybe he could take a short break. He'd been at this all morning and hadn't had any breakfast.

"What is *that?*" came a voice from behind him. He jumped and turned around to face Jynx, who was staring at his creation with faux disgust.

"What have I told you about coming in here?" he asked, giving her a sideways glance. "It's dangerous, especially if you're not wearing the right protective glasses and gloves and—"

"Oh, calm down," Jynx said. "You sound like Jeremy. Don't be such a downer. It's not like anything in here can hurt *me*."

That was true. She was pretty indestructible—all clones were.

"Still," he said, setting the helmet down on the table. "I don't need you meddling around, annoying me."

"I only came to ask you if you were hungry," Jynx said, feigning hurt. "You needn't be so mean to me."

"I'm not being mean," Crosbie sighed. He looked over to the metal contraption on the table one more time.

"It's not bad," Jynx said, peering over Crosbie's shoulder.

He shrugged her off. "It could use a little improvement."

"Don't be so hard on yourself, Crosbie," Jynx said. "Dad—I mean—Max, will like it."

"You can call him 'dad,' you know. He *is* your dad, too." Crosbie rolled his eyes, turning away from the table. He reached out to grab Jynx by the arm and tugged her along with him to the stairs. "Come on, you goof. Let's go get some grub."

Jynx laughed and followed him out of the workshop. "But really, Crosbie, it's nice. I think *Dad* will be so proud!"

"Thanks, sister," Crosbie said. "I know you're just being nice."

Jynx ran a hand through her long, curly black hair. She watched him, but he tried to ignore her. Something about a clone's eyes freaked him out. Even though they were the green of his sister's eyes, something just was not right about them. He closed the door to the shop behind them and made his way to the kitchen.

"Is there even anything to eat?" he asked Jynx, who walked to the cupboard and opened the door, frowning.

"I thought it was your turn to go do the shopping," Jynx said.

"I've been busy with my project," Crosbie snapped. "I haven't had the time to go to the store."

"Well, then, how about we go tougher?" Jynx asked. "It will be a nice break for you, and it will do you some good to get some sunshine."

"If you can call that sunshine," Crosbie replied. He grabbed his coat from the back of a chair around the kitchen table and shrugged it on. "I guess I could use a break, but the stores might all be closed. We did get that evacuation notice."

"We certainly won't know unless we go find out," Jynx said, hopping out of the room and swiftly returning wearing her coat. "And while we're at it, let's stop by the park! I want to see the duck again—just in case."

"Okay, okay," Crosbie said, rolling his eyes. "We'll go see the stupid ducks."

For a moment, Crosbie had an old thought he hadn't thought of in a long time—that this wasn't right. He should be doing this with the real Jynx, not her clone. Before he had gotten so used to her, he had often wished their mother hadn't spent all of her money on a clone in the first place. He shook that thought from his mind. He did like Jynx. He didn't mind taking her to see the ducks.

"Come on," he called to her as he headed out the door. "Let's go."

He waited for her on the steps and took her hand as they made their way down them.

They steeped out into the weary ash-filled street and stood in front of their door for a long moment. Crosbie hated this world with all its filth. He wanted to live in the worlds his mother had told him about—worlds that could not exist anymore. In another world, perhaps his sister wouldn't have died. In another world, he would still have his mother. All that was left for him in this world was his father and the fake Jynx.

"Can we go see the ducks first?" Jynx asked.

"Yeah, we can go see 'em first," Crosbie said. He kicked a pile of ash that had piled up on the curb.

He wondered if his mother and sister were in a better world now. It had been almost a year since his mother had left them, destroyed by the same disease that had killed his sister. They hadn't thought to make a clone of her. Sometimes, Crosbie was glad for it. He didn't want to baby sit two clones all day, not when he had the shop and his father to worry about. But if they had cloned his mother, perhaps his father would've stuck around more than he did. He would have had a reason to come home, or to leave the confines of his shop.

Crosbie hated that his father had given up.

"Look!" Jynx shouted, throwing him out of his thoughts. "The ducks! They're still here!"

Crosbie followed Jynx's arm until he reached her outstretched hand. There were the ducks, floating carefree on the murky pond. He envied the ducks. He envied Jynx.

They had nothing to worry over. They were free.

Father Baxley

Cathedral of Our Lady Victory

Someone was sobbing, hunched over before the alter, as Father Baxley made his way into the sanctuary. Upon hearing his footfall, the sobbing woman turned her head to glance back at him, tears streaming from her lavender eyes.

"What have I done?" she asked, to him or to no one, he wasn't particularly sure. He paced down the aisle and motioned for her to come join him on a pew. She stood, straightening her Core uniform. Upon getting a better look at her face, Father Baxley knew who she was.

"It's very dangerous for you to have those eyes," Father Baxley said, after a moment. The woman blinked and when her eyelids shot back up, her eyes were a dull gray, like the last time he had seen her. "I think I know what it is you've been coming in here for," Father Baxley continued, "but you are not wholly to blame, Lysithea."

She stiffened when she heard her name, glancing back up at him. After a moment, recognition flashed in her eyes. She became less tense and leaned back, covering her face with her hands.

"Father Baxley, I've killed them all," she whispered. "My family, my friends…"

"I know," he said. "I went to the valley when I had heard nothing from your father. I buried them, Lysithea. They're resting peacefully now."

"I'm being punished for my sin," Lysithea said. "The rebels have breached Neo Victoria's wall. They're going to kill so many innocent people because of me."

Father Baxley reached out to stroke a strand of her hair, letting it fall behind her ear. "My child, this and that have nothing to do with one another. You are not being punished. Do not let these things distract you from the cause—Neo Victoria needs someone strong like you, fighting on its side."

He wondered if he should tell her—that her brother was here, that she hadn't killed everyone—but he wasn't so sure she could be trusted to know. She had killed the others for a reason, and now it seemed she struggled with her own existence as well… perhaps this was not the right time. Soon, they could have their reunion.

If the war did not destroy them all.

Lysithea dropped her hands into her lap and stared up at the endless stained-glass ceiling that stretched the entire length of the sanctuary.

"I'm going to protect Neo Victoria," she said. "If it's the last thing I do here, I will protect my city."

Father Baxley smiled.

"You are not being punished," he told her again. "This is only supposed to make you stronger—you're to learn from it. As you said the first time you came here—your heart knows what it wants to protect. Keep the fire burning in here—" he tapped her chest, above her heart, "and you will make the right choices during these dark days."

"Thank you," Lysithea said, wiping the last of her tears from her face. "I think I know what I need to do now."

"Of course," Father Baxley said as he helped her up.

He watched as she walked out of the sanctuary, a different person than when she had come. She had become someone, in the last five years, that his dear friend would have been proud of. He wondered if she would ever know that, too.

Lucie

The Palace

Lucifer leaned her head back against the far wall of David's office, momentarily letting her guise as Lucie slip. She grimaced as the scars along her arms burned just as badly as they had the day she had received them. It was hard, sometimes, to keep up the façade, but she would do it to get what she wanted—and she would get what she wanted, this time, for damn sure. She'd wasted too much time playing around, but now was the time for everything to fall into place. Soon she would get what she had wanted, what she had started out claiming those thousands of years before she had fallen from Paradise. Before she had been cursed with these scars.

God had another thing coming.

Things had been a little boring with the war, lately, so she had decided to spice them up. Now her minions were within the city's limits. Smiled at the thought. The only bad thing about any of it, was that her precious David had been sent out to the frontlines. If anything were to happen to him—oh, who was she kidding? It didn't matter if anything happened to him or not, he was merely only a tool she was using to get what she wanted. At least, that's what she was telling herself. Though, she had become rather attached to him, she supposed.

But David had been acting very suspiciously lately, like he was hiding something from her. She pushed away from the wall and went to his desk, digging through his paperwork. *What could he be hiding?* she wondered. *Why would he keep something from me?*

She had thought it very strange the last time she had spoken to him, that he would be so closed off toward her. He was supposed to be madly in love with her by now, but she wasn't so sure he was. In the beginning, it hadn't really mattered, as long as she got what she wanted, but now she wasn't so sure of what she wanted—perhaps, she wanted David.

She fingered through a pile of hand-written notes, skimming them for any information. Nothing caught her eye. She frowned. Something was definitely up with him, she just could not put her finger on exactly what it was. She supposed she would go to see him tonight.

She needed a little encouragement.

"Well, my darling," she said, snapping her fingers. A portal opened up on the wall. She stepped through it, back to Hell. "I'll be seeing you real soon."

Lysithea
The Palace

Maybe Father Baxley was right about the angels, and about me.

Lysithea stared at her reflection in the mirror, in the hallway just outside of Graggöry's office. He could have been right about that, but there was still the fact that she was an angel, and she had to tell Graggöry the truth and soon. She was running out of time—and if, God forbid, something happened to her or to him, she wanted him to know. She hadn't meant to keep the lie going for so long, she had really thought before that she'd have told him by now. Life had gotten in the way. His voices had gotten in the way.

She let out a sigh.

Now, there was hardly any time to do anything but worry. The rebel forces were closing in on her precious city—and it was probably, entirely her fault. If she hadn't of killed those poor, innocent angels in Spiritus Vallem, perhaps none of this would be happening. The angels were there to protect the cities, after all, and now they were gone. There was no one left but the Core to protect them, and the Core had fallen astray so long ago, that now she wasn't so sure it was capable of protecting anything.

"What have I done?" she asked her refection. It stared back at her with pale lavender eyes. "Oh, God, what have I done?"

She clutched at her stomach. It made her sick to think about the valley. It made her absolutely sick. She was a monster, a traitor. She did not deserve the peace and comfort that Neo Victoria brought to all who came to her to seek shelter. Now that Lysithea had killed the angels, she deserved a fate much worse than death.

But maybe, maybe Father Baxley really was right.

You have to tell him, she told herself, pushing those thoughts from her mind. *You have to tell him the truth.*

Perhaps, he would understand, but there was a chance, slim as it might be, that he would not. Her heart twisted inside of her chest, and she bit her bottom lip to keep from crying out. If he could not understand why she lied, what would she do? What more could she do but to throw herself at his feet and beg for forgiveness? Would he even listen to her apology?

"Do it now," she told her reflection. "Do it before it's too late."

She took a deep breath and let it out slowly through her nose. Now was as good a time as ever. She turned away from the mirror and waltzed back to Graggöry's office. The door was slightly ajar; the lights were off. Graggöry was sitting in the dark.

"Graggöry?" she asked.

He didn't look up.

"Graggöry?" she asked again.

"What is it?" he finally asked. The shadow of his head bobbed up in the darkness as he glanced up at her. She stayed by the door, clutching the dragon door handle tightly.

"I… I need to talk to you about something," she said.

He was quiet for a moment, considering, and then shook his head.

"Later," he said to her. "Not now."

"It's kind of important," Lysithea said, opening the door a little wider.

"I said later," Graggöry growled. "Leave me be for now."

Time was running out. Lysithea sighed and nodded, stepping back and closing the door to leave him alone in the darkness.

He was not doing so well without those cigarettes. She needed to find someone to make them, desperately.

She was afraid for him.

"Later, then," she said to the door. She turned to walk down the hallway.

She would tell him later, when he was feeling better—if he would ever be feeling better. She wondered if he would be like this forever, brooding, sitting alone in the dark for hours on end, not telling anyone what was going on with him. Not even telling her.

She probably deserved it—the whole him not telling his secrets thing. She had brought this on herself by lying to him all this time.

"Well," she sighed, making her way to her office. "I suppose next time is better than never, right?"

She was answered by a knot in the pit of her stomach.

Next time might be too late.

Next time might never come at all.

Io

The Townhouse

Io watched the digital red blinking numbers on the alarm clock by her beside as they changed slowly, minute by dragging minute. She sighed. Dinner had been rather lonely, earlier in the evening, as Jeremy hadn't come up from his workshop for most of the meal, and had practically refused to talk to her at all the four minutes he had shone himself in the kitchen. He had come up from the basement, his hair disheveled, his face smudged with black streaks of who knew what, had gotten a plate of food from Nesa, thanked her, and then disappeared back down into his workshop again—with not even a fleeting glance Io's way.

Either he was really feeling guilty, or he had decided it was just best to not acknowledge her until he was able to ship her off to the Core. Whichever it was didn't really matter; either way, it left a hollow ache in her chest similar to the feeling she got when she thought of her family and the valley.

Now she supposed leaving was for the best.

She would slip away in the early hours of morning, when she was absolutely sure that Jeremy was asleep, and leave him and the townhouse behind her. *But where will I go?* she wondered, turning her gaze up to the ceiling. Her stomach churned with her uncertainty. Io brought her metal hand up to rest on top of it, the fingers curling into the fabric of her shirt as she clutched at it. She just needed to remind herself that this was what was best for her. Though Io wanted Jeremy to be happy, she wanted to be happy, too. She deserved it.

She would not be happy in the Core. She would be completely miserable.

Still, she felt a little frightened.

Io hardly knew anything of the city, and there was the issue of her metal extremities—people would probably be afraid of her, though she was completely harmless. Well… perhaps she was not completely harmless; after all, her arm had been constructed to be a weapon—she just did not know how to use it as such. She supposed that did not make her any less dangerous. The

195

people of Neo Victoria did not know any of that, however. They would just see her as something different and strange and probably a little frightening.

Io turned her gaze back to the clock, keeping watch as the minutes continued to tick on, waiting. She had heard the basement door open and close a few hours ago, and it had not opened again since. Maybe Jeremy was already asleep. Io wondered how Jeremy found the peace of mind to sleep at night, knowing that he was freely handing her over to a group of real monsters, a group that, for some unexplained reason, he wanted to go back to more than anything. It was unfortunate, really. She didn't think Jeremy was a bad guy, not necessarily; somewhere inside of him there was still goodness—but he had not found it yet. She hoped he would find it soon.

Io closed her eyes and let out a slow breath. It was almost time to go. She would savor the warmth of the townhouse for just a few moments longer. She didn't even have a coat. Out in the streets of Neo Victoria, she would probably freeze to death.

Oh well, she thought. It did not really matter. Any fate was better than the one that awaited her in the Core.

Always choose life.

She opened her eyes again. Someone had told her that once, long ago when she had been very small, and the valley had been bursting with life. Now there was no one left from that life, the valley had died along with them, and being a weapon in the Core was hardly a life worth living. She shook her head. She would be okay out in the world—she would adapt and find a way to survive, somehow.

"Nesa," she quietly said, turning over on the bed. She let out a slow sigh and moved her hair out of her face. "It's almost time."

"Everything is ready," Nesa replied. "Are you sure you can't stay?"

Io wanted to laugh but fought the urge and kept quiet. She knew that Nesa wanted her out of the townhouse and out of Jeremy's life, more than anything. Her faux concern was almost a bit insulting.

"Oh, I'm sure," Io said. "This is for the best, really."

She had to convince herself of that.

"All right, then," Nesa said. "The door is unlocked, and it appears that Jeremy has fallen asleep in his study. Have a safe journey."

A safe journey, she thought. *I don't even know where I'm going.*

She pushed herself from the bed and stretched. She supposed she would figure it all out as she went. She would have to do that, there really wasn't much of a choice.

"All right," she said to no one in particular. "I'm leaving now."

She opened the door and stepped out into the hall.

Jeremy

The Townhouse

Jeremy sat in his office, surrounded by darkness. He hadn't bothered to turn on the light when he'd stumbled into the study about an hour and a half ago. He brought the glass of Scotch he was holding up to his lips, taking another swing. It looked like he was in for yet another sleepless night. It was all Io's fault. No—it was his fault, entirely. If he had never brought Io back to the townhouse, if he had just left her to die in that field, content with the fact that he would probably never be in the Demetrius Core again, none of this guilt would be eating away at him, as it was now. It was like this, every night.

There was absolutely no way he could give Io up to the Core in good conscience now, but he was in too deep. David would come for her any day now, and Jeremy would have to hand her over to him, no matter how unwilling he was to do so now. He took another drink.

This was bad. This was really bad. He cursed himself; he was slightly disgusted that he had ever thought any of this was actually a good idea in the first place. He hadn't just been meddling with life; he had been meddling with *someone's* life. Choosing her fate for her seemed terribly wrong now that he'd had time to think it over. But what could he do?

He set the glass down and folded his arms atop the desk, resting his chin on the tops of his hands. He would have to think of something and soon. If David had already put in a weapon's proposal, it was probably much too late. The Core would want to look into it—they would want to know, and when they found out what Jeremy had been doing all these weeks that he'd been kicked out of the Core, he would probably be tried for treason.

What had he been thinking? He should have never allowed David to talk him into any of this. This was a complete mess. He lifted his head up and reached for his glass, taking yet another drink. It probably was not best to think of a plan when he was like this, but he didn't have much time left to do any thinking at all. Time for Io was running out.

Perhaps, he would tell her tomorrow. He had to. She had a right to know. They could come up with a plan together. *Yes, that would be best*, he thought. Everything was blurring together. He'd had way too much to drink this time. He would know what to do in the morning. Leaning back in his chair, he looked out at the dim-lit hallway, listening to the house creak and groan. A storm was brewing outside, as violent as the storm that had been born in his heart.

He liked Io a lot, he had realized. She was so many things that he was not, and it drew him to her. He did not deserve to love her, did not really have the right to, even.

What a fucking mess, he thought, and poured himself another glass.

Graggöry
The Palace

Stumbling through the darkness, Graggöry made his way to the bedroom, pausing at the door. Lysithea was sleeping on top of the covers, still dressed in her Core uniform. She had probably been waiting up for him. He sighed.

It would be so easy to end it now, a voice whispered.

He shook his head. The voices were much worse now that he'd been days without a single suppressant cigarette. They hardly left him alone.

You could be saved if you'd just end it, it said.

He would rather be damned.

How weak, another voice sighed. *How pathetic.*

Pathetic was definitely a way to describe him. He made his way to the bed. A life without Lysithea was not a life worth living, he had realized.

She's a liar! She's the last one.

So what if she was the last angel? It didn't matter anymore. He crawled into bed, arranging the comforter so that it covered Lysithea from the cold. Lying back, he stared up at the ceiling.

"Graggöry?" Lysithea mumbled.

He turned and wrapped his arms around her, pulling her to him. "I'm here."

Kill her. Kill her now.

He stroked her hair until she fell back to sleep. He would find a way to stop the voices once and for all; a way that did not involve killing his mate. He had to.

Io and Jeremy

The Townhouse

Io tiptoed down the hall, quietly passing by Jeremy's open bedroom door. Thankfully he was not in there, but she paused in front of it for a moment anyway, silently taking it all in. It was so ordinary, so plain. It reminded her of an old lady's home. It didn't really match him at all. Turning away from the open doorway, she took a deep breath and told herself she could do it; she could go out on her own, she would be okay. It would be okay. There was no going back to how life was before she had come to be at the townhouse, but things could be better than the future Jeremy was forcing on her.

I'm sorry, she silently told him. If he were determined enough, and she definitely believed he was, he would find another way to get back into the Core. He did not need her, not really. She started back down the hallway and neared the study. The door was open, but the light was off. She swayed, conjuring the courage to walk passed the doorway. Jeremy was in there— though he was definitely asleep. There was no noise coming from the darkness. Perhaps, she was safe. She took a silent step passed the doorway.

"And where do you think you're going?" Jeremy asked from somewhere in the dark.

Io halted in her tracks. She grew rigid. This was not part of the plan. She turned her head and peered into the darkness, finding his faint outline. He was sitting at his desk, watching her.

"I was thirsty," Io said. "I was just going to get a glass of water."

"You were leaving," Jeremy said. His speech was slurred.

He had been drinking again.

"No," Io said, the word drawn out. "I really was just going to get some water."

"You shouldn't lie, Io," Jeremy slurred. "It's very unbecoming."

He stood and slowly made his way around the desk.

"I'm not lying," Io replied, wearily watching him. "Now if you'll excuse m—"

"I think not," Jeremy interrupted, standing in the doorway now. They watched each other in a stagnant silence, and then Jeremy reached out and grabbed her arm.

Her arm stung as his fingers dug into it.

"Ouch, Jeremy. What are you doing? *That hurts*," Io yelped. She tried to yank her arm away, but he was beginning to drag her toward the stairs.

"Good," Jeremy spat, dragging her along behind him. "Serves you right."

"What did I do?" Io asked as she continued to pull free from his grip on her arm.

"I haven't slept in days. I drank all the alcohol," Jeremy listed. "You've ruined my life."

So there it was. Weeks ago, she had been his savior, and now she was the villain.

"I certainly didn't ask for this!" Io shouted. She tugged harder as he pulled her down the stairs, two at a time. "Now let me go."

"No," Jeremy said. "You want to leave so badly? Do you hate it here?"

"I don't hate it, but—"

"You *should* leave," Jeremy said, shoving her toward the front door.

"You're very drunk," Io said, steadying herself. "Perhaps, you *should* go to sleep."

"Perhaps, you should really leave," Jeremy retorted. "The door is right there. What are you waiting for?"

"I'm scared," Io whispered. She pressed her body against the door, distancing herself from him.

"Scared of what?" Jeremy asked. "Scared of me?"

"Scared of everything!" Io exclaimed.

Jeremy blinked. "Everything?"

"You and David and your stupid Core," Io explained. "But I'm scared to leave."

"I'm only trying to help you, Io," Jeremy said after a moment.

"So that's what you call this?" Io asked.

She watched him, swallowing back the bile that rose into her throat. She had never encountered Jeremy like this before, and this night was definitely not going as planned. She took a deep breath and let it out slowly.

"You don't understand," Jeremy said.

"I want to," Io replied.

"You're scared of me," Jeremy said again.

"Of this you."

Jeremy's mind and heart were racing. He took a shaky breath. What had he done? Why had he gotten so angry? If he were her, he'd want to leave, too. It wasn't her fault. It was his, again.

"I'm sorry," he said. He took a step toward her. "I didn't mean to... scare you."

"I just don't understand why you're so angry."

"I was scared," Jeremy replied.

"You were scared?" Io asked. She took another breath, trying to calm her heart. "Why?"

Jeremy bit his bottom lip and thought about how to answer that, though he couldn't really think straight at all. Everything was blurred.

"I was scared because I don't want to lose you," he said at last.

"Because of the Core," Io said.

"No," Jeremy said. "Not because of that."

Io wasn't sure she understood. All this time Jeremy had wanted nothing but to be back in the Core—that had been the whole reason for any of this. Jeremy wasn't making sense.

"I don't understand," Io said.

"I don't know how to tell you," Jeremy whispered, looking everywhere but at her.

She watched him for a moment and something inside of her ached. She realized that he was incredibly broken, and perhaps she had been wrong about him. All of it seemed to bother him a great deal. He finally lifted his gaze to look at her. They stood that way, looking at each other until Jeremy finally looked away again.

"It's late. If you aren't leaving, you should get some rest," he said.

He was still going to let her go, but how could she now? She took a step forward and pulled him to her, hugging him tightly. "Tell me why I should stay."

He went rigid for a moment before relaxing and wrapping an arm loosely around her waist in an attempt to hug her back. "Let's go sit down... I have a lot to say."

Maybe everything could be righted. Maybe Jeremy had finally found that goodness that had been tucked away somewhere inside of him. Io let him lead her up the stairs and to his study. He flipped on the light switch and offered her the chair in front of his desk. She sat down and watched as he made his way to his chair, running a hand through his hair.

She listened to the clock ticking, to the buzz from the neon sign across the street, as she waited for his words.

202

"The Demetrius Core killed my mother," Jeremy said, "and when my father wanted out, they killed him, too."

Her breath caught in her throat, and all she could do was nod her head.

"David and I made a pact, right after my father died," Jeremy continued. "We swore we would do anything we could to take down the Core and avenge our parents. The plan got messed up when I got kicked out, though… and I was desperate to get back in. I was desperate to create the weapon that David needed to dismantle the Core. I only wanted to avenge my parents, but now I'm not really sure what's gotten into David's head, and… I'm going to need your help, Io. I can't… I can't destroy the Core by myself."

Io leaned back in her chair and closed her eyes. She exhaled through her teeth. "Help you how?"

"I don't know yet," Jeremy said. "I have to come up with a better plan, just—"

"Just?"

"I know I am an awful person, and I can't really take back anything I have done to you. I don't think I can save you from the Core, either, but—if you're with me, we have a better chance to, and… I guess what I'm trying to say is, please stay until I figure this out. If you don't want to help me take down the Core, I understand, but let me at least teach you—"

"I'll stay," Io said. She opened her eyes and looked at him. His eyes were red-rimmed, and his hair was disheveled. He really hadn't been sleeping well, she supposed. "I'll stay, and I'll help you take down the Core, but Jeremy?"

"Yes?"

"No more lies," Io whispered.

"No more lies," Jeremy answered.

She smiled.

"It's going to be okay," Io said, more to herself than to him.

"I'll think of something," Jeremy replied. "Tomorrow."

Io stood from the chair. "Goodnight, Jeremy."

"My friends call me 'Jer,'" he said with a smile.

"Goodnight… Jer," she said. "I'll see you in the morning."

"Goodnight, Io," he said as he watched her go.

He closed his eyes and thought of what to do next. David was not going to be very happy with him. In fact, he was a little scared of what his brother might do. Jeremy couldn't deny that he had mucked things up, but maybe his brother could be persuaded. There was no way of knowing until he tried. He would send for him tomorrow, when he had a plan.

He stood from his chair and let out a sigh as he fumbled down the hall to his bedroom. There would be plenty of time to think about it in the morning.

Nesa

The Townhouse

Nesa was absolutely fuming. Anger, unlike anything she had ever known, coursed through her circuits. It was safe to say that things had not gone exactly as she had planned, to her utter displeasure, and the outcome was definitely not in her favor. She calculated everything that could happen next, and all those conclusions were not so great for her, either. If she had had a face, she imagined it would be permanently set in a scowl. *Well, this certainly could end badly for me*, she thought, clicking the camera in Jeremy's room on.

He was definitely asleep now. If only she had paid better attention earlier. If she had known Jeremy was awake in the study, she would have never sent Io on her way. But more importantly than that, why had Io chosen to stay? He had given her the choice to leave. She could have been free. Nesa could have been free from the shadow of Io always, always looming over her.

There is still a way. She pondered this. It was true that there was still a way to rid herself of Io once and for all, but she wasn't quite sure she could do something so diabolical; she wasn't so sure she could break Jeremy's heart. Even though she truly felt that it would be best for Jeremy if Io was no longer in the picture, she knew how attached he was to the girl now.

You have to do it, she told herself. *It's the only way.*

With Io out of the way, she could focus on getting Jeremy to make her body—and once she had a body, she could show Jeremy just how much she loved him. It was of no use, though, if Io stayed. She would never have a body. She would never have Jeremy.

She clicked the camera in Jeremy's room off.

Accessing the computer in Jeremy's study, she opened up the NESA message board, opening a blank text. She had to do this, there was absolutely no other way to save Jeremy. She determined that he would have his heart broken either way—Io would leave one way or another, since Jeremy had made a deal with David and David had probably already proposed Io to the Core. She would just speed the process up a little; that was all this was.

David, she typed, *Io is ready.*

She paused to think about the message before she deleted it. Although she hated Io, she didn't really wish misery on her, and if Nesa knew anything about Io, it was that she would be completely miserable being a slave to the Core. *Perhaps, I can give it one more day*, she thought. One more day would not hurt her. Things would be so awkward between Io and Jeremy in the morning, that maybe Io would leave of her own free will—she would give Io one last chance before resorting to messaging David.

She turned off the computer and surrounded herself in complete darkness. *One more day will not hurt me*, she told herself again. She could endure it a little longer for Jeremy.

Nesa turned on her sleep mode, deciding it was best to plan later when she wasn't so angry, and drifted into oblivion.

Lysithea
The Outskirts

Lysithea had awakened with the sun, crawling out of bed and leaving Graggöry to sleep, as she straightened her uniform in front of the mirror. She stood in the cold morning air, a scarf loosely tied around her neck, her beret hardly warming her head. She had brought a few of her men along with her, but now that she was in the ruined outskirts of Neo Victoria, she wondered if perhaps she should have brought more. It appeared that David's men needed a lot more help than she had previously thought. She'd had no way of knowing it was *this bad*. She cupped her gloved hands over her mouth and let out a slow breath, clinging to its warmth. This was a disaster, and she really had no idea how to go about fixing it. Of course, the only logical thing to do in this situation was to drive them from the inner city, but standing at the frontlines, she wasn't quite sure that was even possible.

"You made it," David said, walking up behind her. He followed her gaze to the already destroyed buildings, the destruction leaving a pathway toward the heart of Neo Victoria. He frowned and turned his attention back to her. "It's horrible, I know."

"How many are in the city?" she asked, her voice so soft, she wondered if David could even hear her over the roar of the battle drones that were landing mere feet away from them.

"It's hard to say," David replied. "There could be tens or hundreds of them, I don't know."

"Where are all our citizens going to go, David?" she asked. "This was their home. Neo Victoria is supposed to be a sanctuary."

"This is a war, Lys," David said, almost too casually for her liking. "There are no sanctuaries."

Lysithea felt her lips twitch downward into a frown. He was only telling her the truth; she knew it better than anyone, after what she had done to Spiritus Vallem. Nowhere was safe. People would die. Graggöry had tried to tell her that, but she hadn't wanted to listen. Seeing it for herself, there was no way to

206

deny any of it—she would have to accept those facts, and the sooner she did so, the easier things would be.

"What is your plan?" she asked David, who was now looking at the hologram of battle plans being projected from his watch. "What are we going to do?"

"We're going to have to bomb them out," David said. He tilted his wrist so that the hologram became more visible. "We'll start with the ones out there—" he paused and nodded toward the broken wall, "and work our way toward the middle of the city."

"This is a mess," Lysithea said. She eyed the plans and bit her bottom lip. She supposed there was no way to save her precious city, other than to destroy some of it in the process. "All right, David. We'll go with these plans. I think we're going to need more men, though. Call them in."

"Yes, ma'am," David said, nodding toward the radio. "I'll get right on that."

"We'll have to brief them here, there's no time to do it at the base," Lysithea continued, looking back out over the destroyed wall. On the other side, more rebels were still coming—a whole brigade of them marched toward the city. Lysithea wondered what their weapon situation was like—this was by no means a fair war, not from what she had seen before. Perhaps, bombing them was a little too much. She shook her head. It didn't matter how well equipped they were; she could not afford to let any one of them into the city so long as they had the intent to steal it from Graggöry and the Core.

Still she felt a little saddened by it. Before, she had sworn an oath to keep the entirety of Neo Erta safe. She had promised to protect its denizens. But these rebels wanted to destroy everything they had worked so hard for. There was no way that she could let that happen. If they would not stop fighting, neither would she. Someday she hoped the world would be peaceful again; however, now that she had killed all the angels, she wasn't quite sure that was possible anymore.

"It's been radioed in," David said, walking back over to her. "I hope you're ready for this, Lys. It's not going to be pretty."

"Don't forget who you're talking to," Lysithea replied. "After what I did to those angels in Spiritus Vallem, I think I can handle this—besides, half the city has been evacuated. Our citizens will be all right."

"If you say so," David said, rolling his eyes. "You've been nothing but a wreck since Spiritus Vallem happened, and I know that for a fact."

"How would you know?" Lysithea asked, snidely. She flicked some ash from her shoulder and glanced at him. "You've not been around much since then."

"I had a talk with Graggöry the other day," David said.

She highly doubted Graggöry had said anything about her to David. He was just saying it to get on her nerves.

"Watch it, David," Lysithea said. "You *are* forgetting who you're speaking to."

"Oh, forgive me, your highness," David said. "I never meant to offend you."

"Screw you," Lysithea said, turning away from him. She started toward the drones. "I'm going back to The Palace now. I have things to discuss with Graggöry. Look out for Neo Victoria while I'm away, David. People are counting on you."

"Yeah, yeah," David said, rolling his eyes. "I've got it."

We're doomed, Lysithea thought as she climbed up into her Jeep. She looked back at David once she was seated, and bit her bottom lip, wondering if David cared for Neo Victoria at all, or if, maybe, this was all just a game to him—because that's what it seemed like. She turned the key in the ignition and closed the door, resting her arm out the open window.

"I'm going," she called to David, who was busy scrolling through battle plans again. "I'll be back shortly."

"Don't worry," David said. "I'm sure the city will still be here when you get back."

If that comment was meant to make her feel better, it certainly didn't work. She tried to ignore the knot in her stomach as she drove away from the wall, and back toward the inner city. She paid extra special attention to the structures that lined the roadway. This time tomorrow, half of them would no longer be here—almost everything would be destroyed by those bombs. It made her a little sad to think about it.

For the first time in a long time, Lysithea wished she had never left the valley. If she had stayed, perhaps none of this would be happening. Her family might even still be alive. She frowned and rolled the window back up to keep the cold out. She had no time to think about what-ifs, all she needed to focus on was this war, and how she could stop it from destroying everything she held dear.

"There's got to be a way," she told herself, but things were definitely looking grim. Somehow they would fix this, because they had to. She just had to accept that things, even people, would have to be destroyed in order for that to happen.

It started to snow harder. Lysithea sighed and slowed the jeep to a stop, not quite back at the palace yet. This was going to be more difficult than she had previously thought, but she could get through it. She had before, so she would do so again. That was how things had to be.

Chrezabel
Spiritus Vallem

[Before]

A cold wind creeps through the cracks in the cottage walls. Chrezabel stands behind a chair at the kitchen table, gazing down at the flickering flame of the lit candle at its center. For the tenth night in a row, she has had the same daunting dream. It had shaken her at first, but she has come to accept it for what it truly is—it is what is to come, and though the future is never set in stone, some things, she knows, cannot be changed.

"I have seen it, Abraxos," she says to her husband. "The prophecy is true."

"You have put these things into our daughters' heads, Chrezabel," Abraxos says. He leans back in his chair and looks up at his tormented wife. "You're willing it to life."

"No," Chrezabel says. "I'm only telling you what is—what will be. I have seen it, Abraxos. There is no changing this future."

"You don't need to put these ideas into their heads," Abraxos tells her. He crosses his arms in front of his chest, tilting his head back as if to look at the shadows dancing on the ceiling. "They're only children."

"It's better that they know," Chrezabel answers.

"You're making Lysithea believe she's some sort of monster."

"She will redeem herself, my love," Chrezabel whispers. "I have seen it, so it must be."

She looks down at her husband and pities him. It was not his fault that he fell in love with a madwoman. She glances toward the dark foyer, where she knows her daughters are hiding, listening to everything she and her husband say. She has never wanted to keep things a secret from them. Though her husband would rather they not know, she feels it is important for them to understand their future, to either accept it or try to change the outcome. This time, however, what she has seen is permanent—there is nothing about it that can be changed.

"I only hope our children are strong enough to endure the things life is going to put them through," Chrezabel says, and pushes away from the back of the chair. "Come, my love, we should get some sleep."

Abraxos doesn't move for a while. He turns his gaze back to her, and in a small voice asks, "Is she really going to leave? Is she really going to?"

"Yes," Chrezabel says. "Io has seen it, too. I'm sorry."

She knows he is bothered by her visions, by Io's visions. He cannot understand it, because he was not born with the gift of Sight. It is a terrible, terrible thing—hardly a gift at all. She walks to him and rests her arms on his shoulders.

"It will be okay, though," Chrezabel whispers. "When we go, we will go together. Paradise is waiting."

"I'm not scared for myself," Abraxos says. "I'm scared for our children."

"I know," Chrezabel says. She leans over his shoulder and blows out the candle before tugging on him. "I know you're scared for them, but I believe they are strong."

"...and my boy," Abraxos says. "My poor, darling boy."

Chrezabel's heart breaks a little. She hurts for her son, for the future he will never have.

"It's late, my love," she coos. "Let's go to bed."

He stands from the chair and takes her hand. She smiles and leads him up the stairs. Outside the window thousands of stars shimmer up in the clear sky. She looks at them for a moment, taking them in. Very soon she will never see the stars from earth again.

Crosbie and Jynx
The Metal Shop

Crosbie set the shimmery metal arm down on the wooden kitchen table, where Jynx was sitting, with her face hidden behind one of her many books of magic. He rolled his eyes just as Jynx attentively looked up over the book's spine. Rolling her eyes in return, Jynx set the book page-down onto the table and pushed her glasses up the ridge of her nose.

She glanced over the arm.

"Is it ready, then?" Jynx asked, looking up at Crosbie, quizzically.

"Yeah," Crosbie said, taking a step back from the table to admire his work. He glanced over the creation with a small smile on his face. For once, he was actually proud of something he'd done in the metal shop. In fact, he felt he had really outdone himself with this wonderful contraption. It looked exactly like his father's, only beefier—he liked to think that it looked more battle ready. "All it needs now is a little bit of your magic, Jynx, and it'll be good to go."

"Are you going to show Max?" Jynx asked, referring to their father. She scarcely ever referred to their father by anything other than his name, which Crosbie tried not to think much of—after all, though he was their father, he had only supplied her with his DNA, and for the first fourteen years of her life, she had grown up in a lab far away from Max and Crosbie and Laura, their now deceased mother. "Like, are you going to show him tonight?"

"Well, yeah," Crosbie said, tilting his head to the side. His green eyes narrowed as he focused on her face. He leaned forward and patted the metal arm, listening to the hollow clank it made. "That was the deal. Finish it in five days. Today is day five."

"Okay," Jynx said with a sigh. "So, I'm guessing you want me to do the magic thing right now?" She kind of motioned to the book on the table before her and then looked back at Crosbie with a sort of mad twinkle in her eyes. "As you can see, I'm kind of busy."

"Your book can wait," Crosbie said, rolling his eyes again. He tapped his finger on the table. "I'm kind of on a deadline here. Time is of the essence."

"Yeah, yeah," Jynx said. She leaned over the table, getting a closer look at the arm. "Five days. I get it. I'm on it, *right now*."

"Yeah," Crosbie sighed. "Before we grow old and die, would be nice."

"If you're going to be rude, I won't help you," Jynx replied. She reached out to run a hand along the length of the smooth metal. Pulling her hand away, she lifted it up to her face, snapping her fingers. A bright red flame appeared just at the tips of her fingers and flickered there as Jynx let out a soft laugh. She turned her attention back to Crosbie. "When I use the magic, how are we going to know that it worked, anyway?"

"We'll test it, obviously," Crosbie said.

Jynx scrunched her nose.

"We don't have the equipment to do that," she told him.

"Yeah, but we have *magic*," Crosbie laughed. "Don't worry. It's going to work."

"All right," Jynx said. She looked back down at the flame and smiled. "I suppose we can give it a try."

Crosbie gestured toward the arm. "It's all yours, sister."

"No pressure, or anything," Jynx mumbled, touching her finger to the metal.

"Just do it," Crosbie sighed. "Stop messing around."

"Right away, oh Great One," Jynx joked.

Crosbie groaned and took another step away from the table, crossing his arms in front of his chest as he watched the red flame seep down into the metal. Although Jynx was only kidding around with him, she had unknowingly opened up an old, festering wound. He frowned and turned his attention to the kitchen window.

It was raining again.

He did not quite care for Jynx's joke, and he definitely did not care much for the rain, either.

It's been raining for days now, which is only fitting, Crosbie thinks. He is sitting at his sister's bedside, memorizing her sleeping face. When she is gone, there will be an imposter in her place, and though she will look and sound like his sister, the real Jynx will be gone forever and all he will have left are these memories of her. Outside, a rumble of thunder shakes the windowpane.

Jynx opens her jade eyes and turns her head so she can get a better look at Crosbie, without the glare from the florescent lights blinding her.

"It's raining," she says, sleepily, because she does not quite know what else to say to him. She imagines it must be hard, losing someone so close to

213

you. She's never lost anyone before now to know. "Have you been here very long?"

"All night," Crosbie says. "I didn't want you to be alone, just in case—"

"I know," she says. Just in case she slips out of her body and into the infinite, great beyond. *My poor, sweet and wonderful little brother*, she sadly thinks, looking up at him. His face is pale; his emerald eyes seem to be sunken in and dull. His lips are set in an almost-permanent frown. She smiles. "Thank you."

Crosbie nods. He gives her a small smile in return.

She turns her head so that she can gaze up at the ceiling. Everything hurts—even with the pain medication they have given her, so it must almost be time.

"I had a dream, just now," she says to him, all of the sudden. Her groggy mind clings to the last little bit of the dream.

"Was it a nice dream?"

"Yeah," she says. She thinks about the dream, trying to remember every last detail. It was a beautiful thing, the dream. It gave her a fleeting glace of hope in all of her despair. She turns her head toward the window and coughs, wincing at the pain. "I think… I think you're meant for something really great, Crosbie. Something really, really great."

He shakes his head. "I doubt it."

"No—really. I saw it all in my dream," Jynx says, fighting a yawn. She certainly has been sleeping a lot lately. Perhaps, that's' what happens when you're dying; you sleep more and more until you sleep forever. "You'll probably save the world someday. Trust me."

"If you say so, sister," he says. He turns his gaze from her to the heart monitor above the bed, watching the lines her heartbeat makes. "I trust you."

"Good," she says, feeling a little weaker than usual. She stares out the window at the rain for a moment longer before turning her head to face him once more. "And Crosbie?"

"Yeah?"

"Be nice to her," she says. She really looks at him, just one more time—just in case it's the last. "I know she won't be me, but…"

"I know," Crosbie says. "I'll be nice, don't worry about that."

"And Crosbie?"

"Hmm?"

"It's okay to love her," she says. "Just like you love me. That's okay."

He nods, his shaggy chocolate bangs falling over his eyes. He doesn't say anything for a long time. How can he love something that isn't real? How could he love anything like he loves his sister, ever again? He takes her hand, their fingers entwining. He holds it tightly. Her hand is so cold.

He frowns.

"I'll try," he finally says. "For you, I'll try."

"Good," she says. "She'll help you."

Before he can ask how, she's fallen asleep again. Watching the monitor, he keeps her hand in his. It probably won't be much longer now. He lets out a slow breath and lowers his gaze to her sleeping face, once more. Maybe she's right. Maybe he'll do something great, and the new Jynx won't be so bad.

"Maybe," he says, more to himself than to Jynx, who groans in her sleep. He puts his head down on the bed, looking at their fingers as he drifts to sleep.

"Do you even know what you're doing?" Crosbie asked, shaking the memory from his mind. He watched Jynx, as she appeared to be struggling with the magic for his creation. He tilted his head, a smirk twitching at the corner of his lips. "You look like you're really struggling there."

"Shut up," Jynx snapped. "I did it for Max, didn't I? I can do it for you, too."

Crosbie shrugged. "It could have been a fluke the first time. Who knows?"

"It *was not* a fluke, okay?" Jynx groaned. "I know what I'm doing."

"I'm just giving you a hard time, because you make it absolutely too easy to do," Crosbie laughed. "I know you've got this."

Jynx slowly moved her hand down the length of the arm, one more time. The magic bled down from her fingertips, fusing with the metal. Crosbie watched until she was done. She dropped her hand back down at her side and took a step away from the table, sitting back down in her chair. She tried to catch her breath.

"Okay," she said, after a moment. "Want to test it out?"

Crosbie gave it a skeptical look. "Well, we probably should, right?"

"Ye of little faith," Jynx laughed.

"Hurry up."

"Okay, okay," Jynx said, a little annoyed. "What do you want it to make?"

"A katana," Crosbie said, and when Jynx gave him a sideways glance, he shook his head and told her, "just something simple."

"All right," Jynx said, flexing her fingers. She tilted her head. "One katana, coming right up!"

She lifted her hand again and let it hover above the arm. Her magic flickered to life at the tip of her fingers again, and dripped down into the arm, which shook on the table before bursting into a billion tiny pieces.

"Well, that can't be good," Crosbie said, frowning.

"Hush," Jynx hissed. "I'm trying to concentrate."

The pieces began to reconfigure into the slender form of a katana. Jynx smiled and looked from the sword to Crosbie, who was grinning from ear to ear.

"It works!" he exclaimed. "I can't believe it, Jynx. You're absolutely amazing!"

"Thank you, thank you," Jynx said. She set her hand back down onto the table, the katana breaking apart and reshaping back into an arm once more.

"All right," Crosbie said, lifting it up into his arms. "We should go show *our* dad now, don't you think? I think he'll be really impressed. With both of us."

"We should show Jeremy, too!"

Jynx smiled even wider and jumped up out of the chair. She followed him out of the kitchen and through the living room, down the stairs, and to the workshop, where their father was busy at work on a new order.

"Max!" Jynx called, coming around Crosbie with her hands up in the air. She nearly knocked Crosbie over, but he sidestepped out of the way just in time. "Look! Crosbie finished the arm, and it's absolutely perfect!"

Max stopped hammering the piece of metal he was working on, setting the hammer down on the counter space beside it before wiping his hands on his apron and turning around to face his children. "Perfect, you say?"

"I don't know if it's *perfect*," Crosbie said. "But I think you'll like it."

"Well, let's see it then," Max said with a smile. "Impress me."

Crosbie set it down on the worktable for Max to inspect.

Max gave it a thorough inspection before turning to Jynx.

"Does it work?" he asked her.

"Well, of course it works," Jynx replied. "My magic never fails."

Max laughed. "All right. Well, show me."

"Okay," Jynx said, stepping up to the challenge. "What would you like for it to become?"

Max thought for a moment. "Hmm… how about a rifle?"

"Got it," Jynx said. "Stand back and prepare to be amazed."

She touched her finger to the arm and once again it burst into tiny pieces before refiguring into a rifle. Max ran his hand over the barrel, a smile tugging at his lips. "Nicely done, Jynx."

Crosbie huffed. "Of course, Jynx gets all the praise."

Max chuckled. "You did an excellent job as well, Crosbie. I'm very proud. I think you'll make an amazing apprentice. We start tomorrow."

Crosbie blinked. He pinched himself just to make sure he wasn't dreaming. He turned to Jynx and scooped her up into a big hug.

"You're amazing, Jynx!" he cheered. "Thank you, thank you, thank you!"

"You're crushing me," Jynx said, trying to push him off her. "Stop being so weird."

He let her go, laughing. "I'm sorry. I just am so happy, I got carried away."

"Congratulations," Max said, ruffling Crosbie's hair. "You worked very hard for this, you should be very proud of yourself."

"Thanks, Dad. I am," Crosbie said. He smiled. "We should all go out and celebrate this joyous occasion, don't you think, Jynx?"

Jynx clapped her hands excitedly and nodded her head, her chocolate curls bouncing on her shoulders. "Yes! Let's go out! Can we?"

They turned to Max.

"I suppose that would be all right," Max told them. He took his apron off and set it on the table. "This can wait. Let's go celebrate, shall we?"

"Let's go!" Jynx cheered, leaping back up the stairs.

Crosbie gave one last look at his creation before he turned to follow her. Max followed closely behind him. When the real Jynx had passed away, Crosbie had decided that things might never turn out the way he wanted in life. He thought he would never love someone as much as he had loved his sister, but now he could see that all those things were not true. Maybe things could turn out all right for him after all.

Io

Spiritus Vallem/The Townhouse

Io stands in the front room of her family's cottage. The windows are open, but outside, everything is impossibly still. *How strange*, she thinks, walking to the window. This is the valley of the wind, and yet now it appears to be windless.

It is also the valley of the spirit, she reminds herself. This must be why she is here, when everyone else is dead and gone—this is the place her soul yearns for. She places her palm against the cool glass of the window, peering out over the fields, to where they meet with the forest. It dawns on her that she will never see anything as beautiful as this, again—the valley has died, there is nothing left there but skeleton homes and ash that falls and falls and never stops. She frowns.

Suddenly, the vibrant colors disappear, one by one, until everything has become black and white and gray. *How strange*, she thinks again, continuing to stare out the window. She watches the gray sky, the white puffy clouds resting above the trees, and wonders why all the color has fled.

"Io," someone says from behind her. She turns to face the room, catching her breath as her gaze falls upon her mother, standing before her in the most effervescent yellow dress. Her mother, full of life, her cheeks pink from the cold, her long blonde hair falling over her shoulders, smiles. "I've been waiting for you."

Io tries to speak but cannot find her voice. She cannot even begin to fathom the words she wishes to say. It has been a long time since she has seen her mother. She was beginning to wonder if she would ever hear her mother's voice again. But now Chrezabel is standing before her, smiling so warmly, that comfort washes over Io.

"I've come to warn you," Chrezabel says.

"To warn me of what?" Io says, finally finding her voice. She leans back, her palms pressing into the slick wooden windowsill. "I already know what happens next."

Chrezabel shakes her head. "I'm afraid you don't."

"I've had a dream," Io says. "In my dream, I am running through the streets of Neo Victoria, alone, lost—there is no future for me."

"Io—"

"I know you've seen it, Mother. I know there's absolutely no—"

"You are the future," Chrezabel whispers. "What happens next is entirely up to you, Io. The world could end, or—"

"I don't want to hear about the prophecy," Io tells her. "All my life I will never be able to escape it."

"I was wrong before," Chrezabel tries to explain. "What I said before about—"

"I don't want to hear it, Mother, really."

Chrezabel frowns. It doesn't suit her lovely face.

"If you will listen to nothing else I say, please listen to this," Chrezabel starts. "You must leave that townhouse, and quickly. Your future is not set in stone—it can still be changed, but you must go from that place if you wish to find your way in this world."

Io watches her mother. A sadness she has never known grows in the pit of her stomach. How does her mother know she is so lost? Why has she come to her now, when for days, she prayed and prayed for Chrezabel to come to her, yet Chrezabel had never come?

"Why?" Io asks.

"I was wrong," Chrezabel says. Her voice sounds sad and heavy. This is the Chrezabel Io knows well—the tormented angel cursed with the gift of Sight. She realizes that seeing her mother now will only break her heart more in the end.

"I can't leave," Io says.

"You have to," Chrezabel warns. "Be brave and go."

"I am a lot of things," Io says, "but brave is not one of them."

"Then you certainly do not know yourself," Chrezabel says.

"I know enough," Io says.

"If you leave now, there is a chance. There is a chance that this can be reversed, that you will not be the prophesized bringer of—"

"No more," Io interrupts. "I don't want to hear another word about it."

"I'm just trying to save you!" Chrezabel cries.

"It scares me," Io says. "It honestly scares me."

"Yes, the future is a scary thing," Chrezabel replies. "But yours doesn't have to be. My time here is up, darling, and I have to go, but please be brave and leave. He means well now, but that boy cannot save you. Only you can do that."

"Mother, don't go," Io says, suddenly panicked. "Please stay."

"You know I cannot," Chrezabel says, sadly. "I love you."

"Mother, please…"

Chrezabel gives her another warm smile, before turning to leave.

"I love you, too," Io whimpers. "I'm sorry."

Io opened her eyes.

The sheets stuck to her warm, sticky skin as she turned in the bed to face the window, where dim light was beginning to shine through the thin, flabby curtain. It was morning. She glanced to the clock, squinting her eyes to read the bright red numbers that flashed on its face. It was much too early to be awake, but Io felt so shaken she might never sleep again.

Mother, I'm sorry. She could not leave. Not now, when it seemed that perhaps Jeremy wanted her to stay. He was the only friend she had in the world, if you could call any of their encounters an attempt at friendship. He would show her the ways of this new, broken world, and he would keep her safe. Safe. Had she felt that way about any place before? Perhaps, once, a long time ago, before the dreams, she had felt safe in the valley. But visions of fire and destruction and death changed her, in ways she could not possibly return from. There was no going back to the valley; the innocent little girl she had been long ago was gone forever now. She had seen too much. She knew too much of the filth that ruled the world now.

But her mother's words were stuck in her head. The look on her mother's face, the panic she had seen in her mother's beautiful lavender eyes—it made Io wonder if staying was, in fact, a bad idea. *What was she wrong about?* Io wondered now. Perhaps, she should have listened to Chrezabel, but Io had been scared—the prophecy had always scared her. For as long as she could remember, it had been a shadow looming over her and Lysithea. It was the whole reason why Lysithea left the valley.

But Io had seen what Lysithea would do—what Lysithea had done now— in her dreams: the massacre in Spiritus Vallem. She knew in the marrow of her bones that Lysithea was to blame; the visions had come true. Her heart broke for her sister, and though she felt anger smoldering beneath her skin, she could not help but still love her. She could not entirely blame Lysithea for what had happened. In truth, Chrezabel was also to blame, because Chrezabel had put it in their heads first, yet, if Chrezabel was wrong about something, perhaps, she had been wrong about Lysithea.

Io closed her eyes and let out a slow breath. It could be that Lysithea had nothing to do with the onslaught that took place in the valley. Her visions weren't always set in stone. If there were a chance that she could be wrong, that Chrezabel had been wrong about Lysithea being the destroyer, Io would

220

hold onto that ember of belief for as long as she could. She did not want to believe that her sister was a monster.

One of them had to be the monster, though. If it wasn't Lysithea, it was Io. Io shuddered.

Outside, a horn honked. Io thought about getting up and going down to the kitchen for a glass of water. Her throat was dry, and her head was pounding, but still she could not seem to summon up the courage to face Jeremy. Not quite yet.

What would they say to each other?

Io supposed she really was a coward. She listened to see if Jeremy was already up and moving around, but she could hear nothing, not even the mechanical clinking of Nesa's robotic arms. She would wait just a little bit longer before she dared to leave the comfort and safety of her room.

Still, she could not shake her mother's words: *be brave and leave. He means well now, but that boy cannot save you. Only you can do that.* She had not saved the angels of Spiritus Vallem, so she certainly could not save herself. It seemed her mother was wrong about a lot of things.

Jeremy
The Townhouse

Jeremy shuffled through the mismatched papers on his desk in a failing attempt to distract himself from the annoying constant throbbing in his head. Setting the papers in his hand back down on the desk, he tapped his finger against the glass of water he'd brought with him, watching as beads of condensation slipped down the glass. He wondered if Io was awake yet, and whether or not he would be able to face her after his drunken escapade the night before. It was silly that he was so concerned about her opinion of him—she wasn't even supposed to matter. Yet, in the days that had passed, she had somehow managed to slip under his skin. If he let her, she would have him completely wrapped around her little finger. How any of this had happened, he had absolutely no idea. All he did know was that now he could no longer afford to give Io to the Core anymore; his conscience would not allow it.

What could he do about it, though? If he knew anything about his brother, it was that he would not take no for an answer. Not this time, anyway. They had put too much planning into this. David would make it a point to say that Io was too dangerous to be left unsupervised in the general public. Technically, that was only partly true. Io had no idea how to use the arm, so it made it useless as a weapon. However, that also made her dangerous, still. She could accidentally hurt someone, if she wasn't careful. All he had to do was teach her. She could live an almost normal life. Things would never be like they were when she lived in the valley, but he could at least attempt to make her life better than how it would be if he had given her to the Core.

How ironic it was that he would feel this way about the plan now, when for weeks, all he could think about was how he would get reinstated as Head Scientist, and how determined he had been to prove Graggöry wrong. Now he could not care less about what Graggöry thought about him. If Graggöry did find out about Io, Jeremy knew he would be in a world of trouble—it had been treasonous to perform that experiment. David would probably bring that up as well. It seemed that Jeremy had dug a hole too deep to get back out of.

Maybe David could keep a secret. Jeremy highly doubted it. David would want to do what he felt was the right thing, and that would be to give Io to the Core as they had originally planned. He would definitely not be happy. Jeremy leaned back in his chair and looked up at the flickering light on the ceiling. Was Io even worth all of this trouble? He cursed himself for being too soft hearted. He would not be in this position if he had just stuck to the plan in the first place and if he had kept himself from getting attached.

"Dammit," he hissed through his teeth. If he had just left her to die in that field, there would be no problem now; however, he had been moved, that day in the meadow, by some power greater than himself to take her and fix her. This was the price he would pay for it.

"Are you all right, sir?" came Nesa's voice from the speaker above the door. Of course, Nesa was spying on him again. He glanced up at the camera and gave a little shrug. He wasn't quite sure how to feel about any of it. Feelings hadn't even mattered just days ago, and now they seemed to be mucking up his life.

"Can I get you anything?" Nesa asked.

"I'm quite all right, Nesa, thank you," Jeremy said, leaning back in his chair. He ran his hand through his hair, tugging at the tangles he had not yet brushed out. He opened the top desk drawer to his left and dug around its contents until he found a comb. His hangover had him feeling a bit disheveled, but there was no reason why he should also look the part.

He closed his eyes, fighting off his nausea.

"Are you sure, sir? Would you like to talk about it?" Nesa tried. He had to give her credit for trying. Nesa was probably the only one who had not given up on him.

"What would you do?" Jeremy asked. "If you were me, I mean?"

"What would I do about what, sir?"

"Io, obviously," Jeremy replied, sighing.

"Are you very bothered by it, then?" Nesa asked.

"Yes," Jeremy groaned. "More so than you could imagine."

"Though I don't really care much for the girl, as you probably know, I think giving her to the Core is a cruel thing to do."

"I don't want to send her to the Core anymore, but what can be done about it? David will certainly not like this. He'll probably take her by force if he feels he has to."

"Then you should send her away," Nesa said. "The Core will break her."

Io was strong, though, he had noticed; she was not easily broken.

"I thought about it," Jeremy said. "Sending her away is an option, but..."

"What will you say to David?" Nesa asked. "You know he'll—"

223

"I know," Jeremy said, "but I've got to try."

It was all he could do for Io.

"Would you like for me to send for David?" Nesa asked.

"I suppose now is as good of a time as any," Jeremy replied. "Go ahead, Nesa."

"Right away, sir," Nesa said. The red blinking light on the camera above the door stopped blinking—Nesa had turned the camera off.

"Thank you," Jeremy said.

He pushed the chair back, standing up. It was still early, but perhaps Io was up now. He supposed he had to face her eventually. He picked up the glass of water, taking a sip of it as he stepped around the desk and started toward the door. He would have to think of what to say to David, and fast. Knowing his brother, he would be here as quickly as he could.

He had a lot of things to figure out.

"Well, you've really done it this time," he said to himself, reaching for the doorknob.

He stepped out into the hallway and looked toward Io's room. The door was still closed—she was probably avoiding him. He probably deserved that. Sighing, he made his way down the stairs, and into the kitchen to find something to make for breakfast. Opening up the refrigerator, he squinted at the bright light that flooded into the dim kitchen.

He probably should eat something, because this was going to be a long day. He grabbed the carton of eggs, and a stack of bacon. Hopefully, Io would be awake soon, and he wouldn't have to eat breakfast alone.

"Would you like for me to cook that for you?" Nesa asked.

Jeremy couldn't help but chuckle. Nesa had been spying again.

"No, Nesa, I think I can handle some eggs and bacon," he said. He opened a cabinet door and pulled out a frying pan. "It can't be that hard."

"Would you like for me to fetch Io?"

"If she's awake, yes," Jeremy said. "Thank you, Nesa."

"Of course, sir," Nesa said.

He wondered what he would say to her when she came. Should he apologize? Certainly, she would not dwell on what had happened. He would start off with a simple 'good morning,' he supposed, and go from there.

He heard Io's door squeak open. She was awake.

He inhaled and got his words together.

He exhaled and waited for her to appear in the doorway.

Nesa

The Townhouse

Nesa waited until Jeremy and Io had begun to eat their breakfast before she sent the message to David. If she knew David as well as she thought she did, he would drop everything he was doing and come straight to the townhouse if he thought that Io was at all ready to be shipped off to the Core. Her message had been very vague. *Come quickly. We need to talk.* She hadn't meant for it to be vague on purpose, and she supposed she would have hell to pay later for it, but Jeremy had seemed pretty sure of himself, and perhaps Io would not be forced into the Core after all.

Nesa didn't want her to be miserable, she just wanted her to be gone. She did not like this wallowing Jeremy that Io had created. She much preferred the man who could not care less about those around him. The Jeremy who was out for himself. The Jeremy who, in his own way, needed Nesa. She had no use for this Jeremy. She supposed she was just jealous, as any girl in her situation would be. She would get over it as soon as Io was no longer in the picture.

She watched them eat in silence. The only words spoken had been 'good morning,' and sickening small talk. She wondered what they really wanted to say, but decided she probably did not want to know.

"Could I get you two anything?" she finally asked, breaking their uncomfortable silence.

"No, thank you," Io said, lifting her fork to her mouth.

"I'm fine," Jeremy answered, taking a sip of his orange juice.

This certainly was not going well, but it kind of made Nesa feel a little bit happy. The more awkward the two of them became, the more reason there would be for Io to leave.

Io would probably have to leave soon anyway, however, once David got the message from Jeremy. If she did not want to live a life serving the Core, her best option was to hide out in the city until she could make it to one of the outer cities, or perhaps one of the main cities, far away from Neo Victoria. Nesa wished her well, she really did.

The quicker she leaves, the better off she'll be, she told herself.

It wasn't like Nesa really had a conscience anyway—just an artificial sense of morality. She checked the message. David had not yet read it, but when he did, everything would be set into motion, and before the day was over, maybe Io would be gone.

"If you need me, call for me," Nesa told them. She clicked the camera off and welcomed the darkness that surrounded her. It would not be long.

She needed only to wait just a little while longer.

Graggöry
The Palace

"We're bombing the inner city," Lysithea said, her lips set in a solemn line across her perfect face. "I don't want to, but—"

"Lys," Graggöry interrupted. "I know you want to save everyone, but that's just not how this works."

She sighed and turned her gaze out the window. "I just didn't want to compromise the inner city. I thought perhaps the families from the outskirts could seek shelter here."

"I'm sure if there was any other way, David would—"

"David is an idiot," Lysithea said. "He would do nothing differently. I'm beginning to think he likes all this death and destruction. Honestly, Graggöry, how can you stick up for him? He's treated you so horribly recently."

"I suppose you're right," Graggöry said, "but I haven't really been that reliable, myself."

He leaned back in his chair and sighed through his teeth. What a mess he had gotten them into this time. He glanced to Lysithea. She looked so pale, so visibly shaken by all of it. He had done this to her. Never should he have asked her to kill those angels, but all he was good for was destroying things—he had destroyed all the innocence that had once resided in her.

"Lys, I'm sorry," he said, suddenly. "This is entirely my fault."

"Don't take so much credit," Lysithea said, turning her gaze away from the window to glance his way. "The world has been broken for much longer than this."

"You're right," Graggöry said.

"Of course, I'm right," Lysithea laughed. "I'm always right."

She didn't seem so sure of herself. He smiled. If he could not count on anything else in life, he could count on her. She was a miracle. He was lucky to have met her, and to have known her. Yet, he could not help but think of how much better off she would have been without him. It was too late to push her away now, however. She was in this just as much as he was.

"I'll send out a message on the NESAs," he told her. "Everyone who can, will be evacuated. As for the rest, Neo Victoria will honor them after this war is over."

"All those poor, poor people," Lysithea sighed. "All this blood, and for nothing."

"Ah, but it is for something," Graggöry said. "These small sacrifices are for the better good, Lys. You'll see."

Lysithea stood from the chair and straightened her blouse and skirt. She ran a hand through her blonde curls and gave one more fleeting glance to the window. "I don't know."

"You'll see," Graggöry said. "Neo Victoria will be victorious, as always."

"Neo Victoria is not the only thing I am worried about," Lysithea said. She looked over to him, crossing her arms in front of her chest. "There is actually something else that I'd like to talk to you about."

"I've to get these messages out, Lys," Graggöry said. "To save lives."

Lysithea looked terribly disappointed but nodded, biting her bottom lip.

"Tell me when this is over," Graggöry said. "Whatever it is, don't worry about it now."

Her face contorted into a grimace, but she nodded again. "All right."

"Go back to your post for now," he told her. "Go save your people."

"Right away, sir," Lysithea said, as she left.

Lysithea

The Palace

Lysithea closed Graggöry's office doors behind her, and stood in front of them for a moment, composing herself. *Go save your people.* Her people were dead, all of them. She bit her bottom lip and let out a slow, steady breath. All that was left now, were the poor fools, sitting ducks as they were, trapped inside Neo Victoria—a city that might not even exist twenty-four hours from now.

She pushed away from the doors and made her way down the hall to her office. If she didn't get back out on the frontlines, there was no telling what David would do. As much as Graggöry had placed his faith in the man, Lysithea could not trust him as far as she could throw him. David never cared for anything but himself, but somehow Graggöry was blind to it. It was plain to see that David was up to something, she just wasn't sure what exactly that was.

There was also the fact that every time she tried to tell Graggöry the truth about herself, he turned her down in some cunning way. It was almost like he knew what she was going to tell him, and he didn't want to hear it. Of course, he didn't want to hear it. The truth would probably destroy him and their relationship and any hope she had left in her heart.

Having even a sliver of hope was foolish. Hope would give her nothing but pain in the end. She frowned and opened the door to her office. She walked to her desk and shuffled around some papers that were atop it, not finding what she was looking for. Mumbling under her breath, she turned from her desk and marched back out the door, into the hall. She might as well get back out there before David had the chance to destroy everything entirely. There was a chance people could be saved—but who was she kidding? She couldn't even save herself.

Lucie
Hell

Graggöry was so close to finally breaking. Lucie watched him through her mirror portal and smiled. He was beginning to spend less and less time with Lysithea, merely because he was so close to killing her. The girl even wanted to tell him the truth—she was, indeed, the last angel. That would be the last straw, Lucifer was sure. It wouldn't be long now—but it wasn't soon enough. As long as Lysithea lived, there was a chance that Lucie's plan would fail. It was almost a shame that Lysithea had to die, though. Lucie admired her for what she did—killing off her entire clan just for love.

It was a classic tragedy. It was simply delightful—and now it ate away at the girl. If Graggöry didn't kill her, perhaps she would just slip into madness and kill herself. Lucie clapped her hands together, pleased. Soon it would all be over, and Lucie would finally be back where she belonged—in charge of everything. God could spend a couple millennia in Hell, just to see what he had put her through.

It pleased her to think about that future, but it was a fragile future, a future that could still be taken from her. If Graggöry wasn't going to kill the girl, and soon, she would have to ask David to do it. It would probably please him to kill her. She knew how much he disliked the girl. It could be a gift of sorts, for him—killing Lysithea.

"I'll go see him tonight," she told herself, closing the mirror portal. "We'll have a nice little chat about things."

Very soon, everything would fall into place. It was only a matter of time.

Jeremy
The Townhouse

"Well, is she ready, then?" David asked, pushing past the door and into the foyer of the townhouse. He knocked the ash from his hat and shoulders, glancing to Jeremy, ever expectantly.

"No," Jeremy said. "There's actually something I need to talk to you about."

"You haven't had a change of heart, now, have you?" David laughed, making his way up the stairs. When Jeremy didn't answer, he paused at the office door and glanced back at his brother, who was making his way up the stairs, an odd look on his face. "Oh, Jeremy, don't tell me you've changed your mind."

Jeremy ushered him the rest of the way into the office.

"Have a seat, David," he said through gritted teeth. "We're going to have a proper discussion about this."

"There isn't much to discuss," David said. "You gave her up the moment you brought her to the townhouse, Jeremy. It's already been done. The Core already knows something is up."

"Yes, but you could fix that," Jeremy said. "I can make them a weapon just as good as Io, if not better—I was wrong, David. She's still flawed."

"Bullshit," David growled. He stood behind the chair in front of Jeremy's desk, his fingers curling into the fabric on top, as his anger was proving to get the better of him. "You made a commitment, Jeremy. You wanted back in the Core. I did this for *you*, and now you're asking me to risk my job? What about the plan? Have you forgotten that?"

Before Jeremy could say anything, Io appeared at the door. "Could I bring the two of you anything?"

"Bring our guest some tea, would you?" Jeremy said, keeping his gaze steady on David. He watched him until Io was down the hall and halfway down the stairs, before looking away. "I'm asking you to have some compassion."

231

"Compassion?" David asked. He clenched his jaw. "What has gotten into you, little brother? Don't you want back in the Core?"

"Not at the expense of Io's freedom," Jeremy said. "The Core will make her do horrible things, David—you know it, and I know it… and those things will ruin her."

"Listen to you," David said, laughing. "You sound like a love-struck fool!"

Jeremy didn't say anything.

"Oh the gods," David said. "You are a love-struck fool."

"And what's wrong with that?" Jeremy coolly replied. "Haven't you ever loved something, David? Or is love beneath you?"

David took his hat off and ran a hand through his hair, looking up at the ceiling. He seemed to be calculating what to say, when Io returned with a cup of tea. Jeremy took it from her, urging her to go.

"You did this to him, didn't you, girl?" David finally asked, turning to Io. "You put these silly ideas in his head."

"I don't know what you're talking about, sir," Io said.

"Io, sweetheart, go wait downstairs," Jeremy said.

Io looked from Jeremy to David and back at him again, her face a little too pale. She was smart. She knew what was going on, and Jeremy knew it. "Please, Io."

Io gave him a desperate, pleading glance before nodding and walking back out of the room. Jeremy chewed on his bottom lip and looked back to his brother.

This was definitely going quite horribly.

"David, have a heart," Jeremy said. "She's just a girl."

"So? You knew that when you pulled her from that field. It didn't matter then, it shouldn't matter now," David said.

Jeremy offered him the cup of tea, but David shooed his hand away and paced to the far side of the room, sighing. "I can't talk my way out of this one, Jeremy. I can't protect you from the Core. I have to take the girl."

"Trial me for treason, but don't take Io," Jeremy said. "She shouldn't have to pay for what I've done—I won't say I regret taking her from Spiritus Vallem, but it was not fair of me to thrust this life upon her, David. She's good and pure and innocent, and you're asking me to give her to people who would have her kill anyone they deemed undesirable."

"Yes, how dare I ask you to go through with something that, may I remind you, was your idea. Not mine," David snidely replied. "You're the one who wanted back into the Core."

"I know what I wanted!" Jeremy shouted, then a little quieter, "I know what I wanted before, but I've changed my mind."

"I'm sorry, but it's too late," David said. "You've run out of time, and I can't keep stalling for you. We're going through with this, whether you like it or not, and in the end you'll thank me. Don't let silly, useless feelings mess this up for you, Jeremy. You could be a hero—Io will win this war for us, and you know she can do it."

Jeremy inwardly groaned and walked to the chair, sitting down. He rubbed his temple and looked over to David. There was no getting through to him. David had never loved anything in his whole life—he would never understand. He also liked to break things—so arguing that Io was pure and innocent and genuinely a nice person, would get him nowhere. It would only make David want to break her more. This certainly was a mess. Nesa had tried to warn him, he supposed, but he had thought that perhaps this time his brother would listen to him. He had wanted to believe that David had a heart.

"David, don't do this," Jeremy pleaded. "I'll make a new weapon to win the war."

"No, Jeremy," David said. "It's too late. We need Io and we need her now."

"I haven't even trained her properly," Jeremy said. "She's completely useless to you."

"She's a smart girl," David said, "I'm sure she will catch on quickly."

"David," Jeremy said, looking back up at him in a desperate attempt to change his mind. "Please. Please do this one thing for me."

"*This one thing*? When have I ever not done something for you, Jeremy? I've been getting your ass out of trouble for twenty-four years, and *this* is how you want to repay me?"

"I love her!" Jeremy said, at last. "I *love* her, David."

"Then, I'm sorry for your luck, brother," David said, "but I'm taking her. You'll thank me for it, later. You'll see."

"David—"

"The only thing love will get you in this world is killed. We *cannot* afford to fall in love, Jeremy. I pity you for not knowing this."

"Give me a day," Jeremy said, his face set in a stony grimace. "Give me today, and she'll be ready for you."

From out in the hallway there was a crash, followed by the thud of feet stomping down the stairs. A door slammed somewhere downstairs. Jeremy caught his breath.

"Sir," Nesa said, over the speaker. "We have a problem."

"What is it, Nesa?" David asked, frowning. He glanced toward the doorway and then back at Jeremy, his lips set in a line across his gaunt face. He looked greatly displeased. Jeremy let his breath out slowly.

"Io has… left, sir," Nesa said.

David briefly closed his eyes before looking down at Jeremy. "You have until the end of the day to find her, Jeremy. I'll be coming for her, whether she's ready or not."

Jeremy nodded, but remained silent, his mind racing. He stood from the chair and walked to the door, gesturing for David to leave first.

"Don't send the Core after her, David," Jeremy said. "Please. I'll find her myself. I'll deliver her to you."

"The end of the day, Jeremy. Find her," David reiterated before stomping down the stairs and rushing out the front door.

Jeremy stood on the top of the stairwell, watching the door for a long time before turning back to the office. He grabbed his coat from his chair and pushed it on before heading back down the stairs.

"I'm going to find her, Nesa," Jeremy said.

"Well, you don't need to look very far, sir," Nesa said.

"What do you mean?" he asked as he reached the front door.

"I mean, she never left, sir," Nesa said. "She's hiding."

He stepped away from the door and glanced around the foyer. "Where?"

"Under the stairs, sir," Nesa replied. "I lied, hoping David would go away."

"Thank you," Jeremy said. "I owe you one, Nesa."

"Of course, sir."

Io

The Townhouse

Io sat in the dark, listening to Jeremy and Nesa talk, thinking that perhaps she should have really run out the door and never looked back. But she supposed there was a chance that Jeremy had only been saying those things to David in the end, because David was not going to listen. Deep down she knew that Jeremy was on her side, but there was a part of her that knew a part of him still wanted back in the Core—and she was unsure of whether she could trust that part of him or not. Yet, he had told David that he loved her. She leaned her head back against the wall and closed her eyes, taking a deep breath. What could they possibly do now? She had no choice but to go with David. If she didn't, there was no telling what they would do to Jeremy.

"Io?" came Jeremy's voice through the door, followed by a gentle rasp. "Won't you come out now? He's gone."

"I'm not hiding from him," Io said, opening her eyes to look at the thin line of light coming in the closet from under the door. "I'm hiding from you."

"You don't really think I'm going to hand you over to David, do you?" Jeremy asked. Io pictured the hurt that was probably flickering in his dark amber eyes. She frowned and bit her bottom lip, not answering him.

"Io, I could never send you away with that man," Jeremy said. "You don't belong in the Core, and I know that now."

"All right, I'll come out," Io said, scuttling to the door. She opened the door, squinting her eyes as the sunlight flooded in, and crawled out of the storage closet. When she was all the way out, Jeremy reached out to pull her into a hug. She blinked, wrapping her arms lightly around him. He hugged her tighter, before letting go and stepping away.

"Right," he said, not saying anything about it. "Now that you're out, we have to hurry. We don't have much time."

"Hurry with what?" Io asked. "What are we doing?"

"You're leaving," Jeremy said, very matter-of-factly, glancing toward the back door.

"Leaving? But I—"

"You have to leave now, or he will take you, Io," Jeremy said. He looked her right in the eyes, his face serious, yet expressionless all at the same time. "Do you understand?"

"But... what about you?" Io asked, feeling all of the sudden frightened. "Jeremy, if I'm not here, and they come back for me, they'll kill you."

"I know," Jeremy said. He grabbed her wrist and tugged her along, up the stairs. "Just don't worry about me, though, Io—you have to save yourself."

"Why?"

They were in her room now, and Jeremy had tossed a bag onto her bed and was beginning to fill it with clothes. Io gathered up her quilt and stuffed it down into the bag, watching Jeremy as a sort of numbness overtook her.

"I want you to live, Io," Jeremy said. He zipped up the bag and helped Io with her new coat, the one he had been saving for her. "If I die, the world won't lose much... but you're something really special, Io. You could save them."

Though he seemed so adamant that she could actually save the people of this world, Io was filled with too much doubt—she had not been able to save her people, or herself, and now she was not going to be able to save Jeremy, either.

"Jeremy, that's not true. If you die—"

"No one will miss me," Jeremy said, the faint ghost of a smile tugging at his lips.

"I would," Io said, "and besides, there's no one left to miss me, either."

"I would," Jeremy said.

They watched each other in silence for a moment, and Io thought of how lonely she would be without him.

"There has to be another way," Io said. "You should come with me."

"Everybody in the Core knows who I am," Jeremy said, shaking his head. "No one knows you except for me and David. You'll be able to hide in the city until you can get elsewhere. It would do you no good if I were with you."

"Jeremy, I don't even know how to work this," Io said, waving her arm in front of him. "You've never told me how."

"I know, and I'm sorry," Jeremy said. He handed her the bag so she could slip the strap around her shoulder. "You'll have to figure it out on your own."

Outside, a loud boom rattled the townhouse. Jeremy marched over to the window, glancing out for a moment before shaking his head and turning back to Io. "They're bombing the city."

Io fidgeted, trying to slow her thoughts, and marched over to look out the window. She watched as a wall of smoke plumed over houses down the street.

"Jeremy—what will I do? Where will I go? I'm scared. I can't go out there alone."

"You can, and you will," Jeremy said, taking her hand again. He led her back out of the room and down the stairs, tugging her to the kitchen door. "You're strong and brave. You'll figure it out, sweetheart, and you'll be okay. I promise."

He opened the door and peered outside, glancing along the length of the alley. Io watched him and wondered what she had to say to make him change his mind and go with her. David and the Core would kill Jeremy when they came back later, and she was not here. She blinked back her tears and took a deep breath.

"Jeremy, come with me," she begged. "Please."

"I can't," Jeremy said, turning his back to the open door. "You have to go alone."

"Nesa, tell Jeremy to come with me," Io tried, glancing to the speaker above the kitchen doorway.

"Sir, perhaps you should—"

"No!" Jeremy said. "No, I will not go with you, Io, okay? You've got to do this for me. You can hate me, or feel however you want to about it, but you have to go so I know you'll be okay. I can't do what I have to do, if I'm worried about you."

Io flinched. "What do you have to do?"

Jeremy ran a hand through his hair and looked over her shoulder at the front door. "Don't worry about it."

"I am worried about it, Jer. I'm worried about you."

Jeremy considered this for a moment. He looked as if he might falter but shook his head and stepped out of the doorway, ushering Io toward the alleyway. "You need to go. Now."

"Jeremy," Io whimpered.

"You're a stubborn girl, you'll make it out there. Just promise me, Io, that no matter what happens, you will not turn back."

"Please don't make me do this."

"Io, just promise me."

All she could do was nod.

"Go," Jeremy said. "Now, while it's still safe."

She turned and stepped out of the door and took a deep breath, the cold freezing her lungs. Before she could muster up the courage to turn and face him again, she heard the click of the door behind her. Turning, she banged on it once. And then again.

"Jer, please open the door. I need you," she pleaded, pounding on the cold wood, as realization struck her. He didn't answer. "Jeremy, please. I… I love you, too." No answer.

She pushed away from the door.

"Okay, then, I guess," she said, turning her back to the townhouse. She looked down the alley, both ways, and bit her bottom lip. Perhaps, the best idea would be to leave the city entirely, though she had no idea what sort of things awaited anyone outside of Neo Victoria's walls.

She let out a sigh and dug a scarf from her bag, wrapping it around her neck. She wondered if she would make it anywhere before the cold ended her. It was highly unlikely she could survive these temperatures for long. She started down the street with little faith and a heavy heart.

She had lost her home and her family and her people and now she had lost the townhouse and Nesa and Jeremy and the comfort she had felt there.

Maybe, she thought, *I am meant to lose everything in the end.*

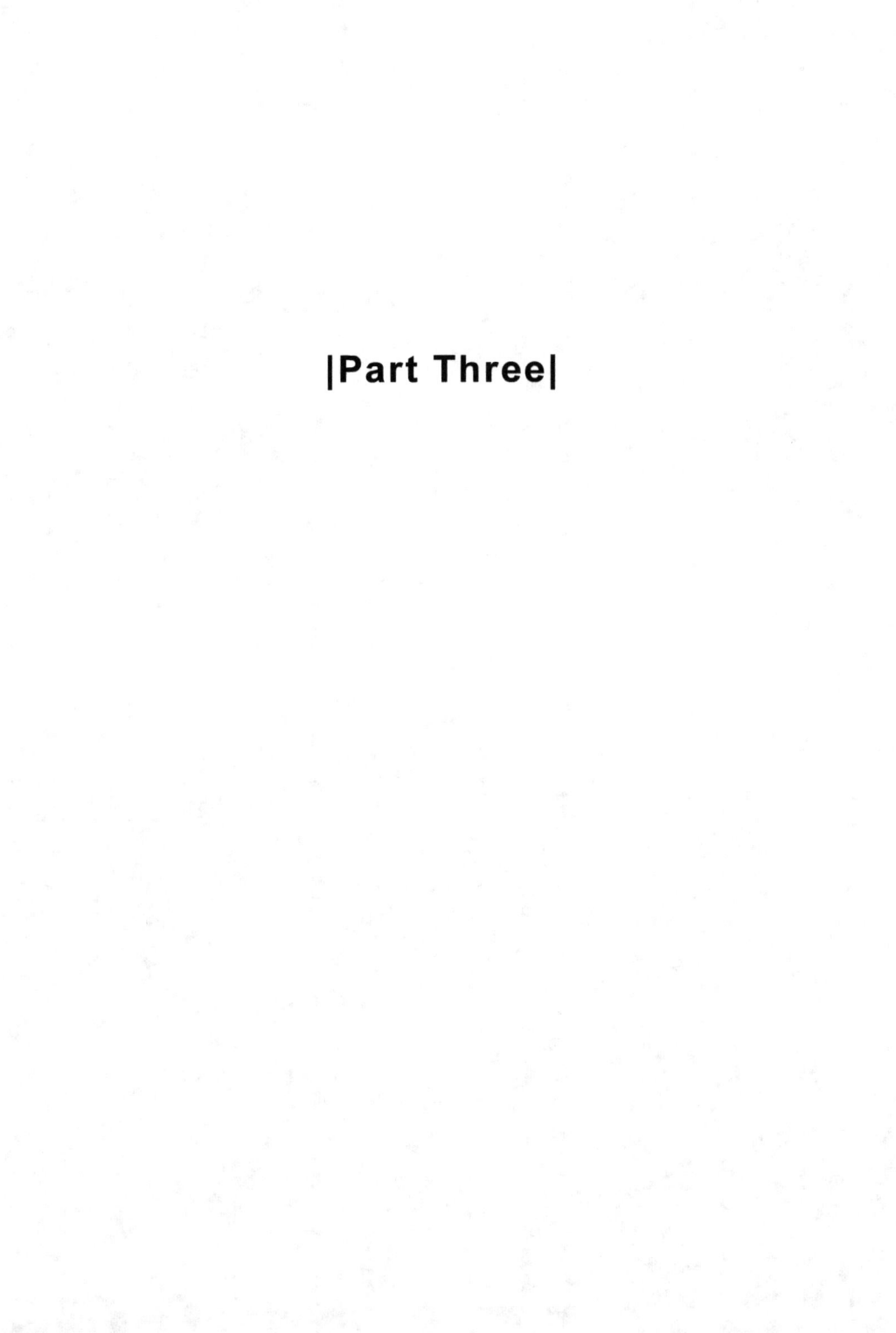

|Part Three|

David

The Palace

David marched up the mucky steps of the capitol, absolutely fuming. Of course, he should have seen this entire situation coming. After all, Jeremy had always been secretly too soft for the Core. Jeremy was almost too kind to a fault, and perhaps David should have known better than to have let him pick a girl to do the experiment on—had they found a suitable young man, this wouldn't have happened. David sighed and opened the large oaken doors that led into The Palace, pausing in the doorway for a moment as he considered what to do next.

Jeremy had asked him to not send the Core, but David had a sinking suspicion that Jeremy wouldn't hand Io over as easily as he tried to make it seem. If David knew one thing about his brother, he knew when Jeremy was telling a lie. Though Jeremy had thought years ago that he'd mastered the art of lying, David had always been able to see right through Jeremy's deception. He laughed to himself as he strode down the hallway and to his office. Of course, he would have to have his men go out and look for the girl; however, most of his men were out on the frontlines. This was not the most ideal time for his plan to go south, but he would deal with it like he always did. This wasn't the first time Jeremy had screwed things up.

He stepped into his office and closed the door behind him, before moving to his desk and digging through the papers there. Once he found what he was looking for—a picture from Spiritus Vallem of Io—he strode out of his office and down the hall, in search of Lysithea. Luckily enough, her office door was open and the light was on, so he stepped into the doorway and leaned against the door jam, crossing his arms, the paper still in his hand.

Lysithea was busy, shuffling through papers on her own desk, so enthralled in what she was doing that she did not notice him. He cleared his throat, but she continued to shuffle through the papers, not looking up.

"Lysithea," David called.

Lysithea looked up from what she was doing and eyed the paper in his hand. "What is it? I'm a little busy. Can it wait?"

"Actually, no," David said, rolling his eyes. He stepped away from the door and walked up to the desk, setting the picture down on it with a smack. "Jeremy's done something terrible, and I need your help."

"Jeremy, your brother? What did he do this time?" Lysithea asked, looking up at him. She glanced down at the picture on her desk, and David could have sworn she went ten shades paler than normal. She swallowed and took a deep breath. "What is this?"

"This is Io. She came from Spiritus Vallem," David said. "Jeremy thought that if he could make that experiment that got him kicked out of the Core work, that they would reinstate him. He took this girl from the valley and by some unknown miracle, didn't kill her—but now she's a weapon and she's been set loose in the city."

"A weapon?" Lysithea asked.

"Yeah, it's a long story and we don't have time."

"What exactly did he do to her?" Lysithea asked, glancing back up at him. There was a look in her eyes that he almost registered as fear, but he could not be entirely sure. "Is she dangerous?"

"Yes," David said. "She's extremely dangerous. Jeremy created a weapon, and set her loose in the streets of Neo Victoria—she's probably scared and frightened, and that will only make her more of a danger to herself and to others."

"You want me to go find her?" Lysithea assumed.

"My men are all out on the frontlines, fighting this war," David said. He ran a hand through his hair and let out a sigh. "I need you to help me find her."

"I'm also kind of busy with this war," Lysithea said, starting to shuffle through her papers again. "Find someone else to help you."

"Lys, please," David said. "I'm asking you as a friend. Please help me. I know you love this city, and you want the people safe and sound. We can't have this girl—this weapon—lurking around the streets, threatening the already threatened safety of our people."

She sighed. "All right."

He smiled. "Her name is Io. Her left arm and right leg are both robotic. She can contort them into weapons. Be careful. She really is dangerous."

"I can handle it," Lysithea said. "Don't worry. I'll get some of my men and women together, and we'll find her."

"Okay, thank you, Lys. I owe you one," David said. He turned to leave, leaving the picture of Io on Lysithea's desk.

"But David, what about Jeremy?"

242

"I'll take care of it, don't worry," David said, pausing in the doorway for a moment. "He won't get away with it."

"All right," Lysithea said, wearily.

"Don't worry," David reiterated, and then he left.

He marched back to his office, pausing briefly in front of Graggöry's door, pondering whether or not to tell him, before sauntering on to his own office. Lysithea would probably tell him soon enough, and he didn't really need Graggöry breathing down his neck for now. He would take care of everything, without Graggöry getting in the way. For now, he would go back to his office and devise a plan as to how to deal with Jeremy. He had known all along that Jeremy would take the fall for this plan, but perhaps he could save Jeremy the pains of a trial by doing the right thing and ending him. It was the only thing he could do for his brother. He would make it quick and painless.

Perhaps he had known it would come down to this all along, but none of it would matter once David was in charge. Thanks to Jeremy's sacrifice, Neo Victoria—the whole of Neo Erta—would be a better place. Jeremy could die, knowing that he had done something good for others.

However, David supposed he could also spare Jeremy. If everything else went according to plan, David would be in total power, and he could pardon Jeremy for everything that he'd done against the government. Perhaps, he would do that. It all depended on what Jeremy did next, he supposed.

Everything actually depended on what Io did next.

He sat down behind his desk and rested his head in his hands. What a mess this had become. If only Jeremy had stayed the course, there wouldn't be a problem. Out of everything that could have happened, David had never considered Jeremy falling in love. How insipid that was—there was no time for love in this world, though he supposed he couldn't blame Jeremy; after all, David was slightly enamored by Lucie. It was bound to happen eventually; this was just really horrible timing.

He glanced out the window, taking a long breath and letting it out slowly. Next he would have to tell Lucie—and Lucie would not be pleased with him. Perhaps, if he found Io quickly, and she came without a fight, he could prolong having to tell Lucie anything at all. That was a battle he was not yet ready to have, but he was sure he could talk his way back into Lucie's good graces.

"David?" came a voice from the doorway.

David glanced up, rubbing the stubble on his chin. Lysithea was peering through the open doorway at him. "Yes?"

"Who else have you told about this girl?"

"Just you," David said.

"Don't tell Graggöry, okay?" Lysithea asked.

"Why?"

"Just don't tell him," Lysithea said.

"All right," David said. "She's all yours."

"Thank you," she said. "Oh, and David?"

"Hmm?"

"If she attacks me or my men, I won't hesitate to shoot," she said.

"All right," David said. "Whatever you have to do, Lys."

"All right," Lysithea said. "I'll be going to find her now."

"Good luck," David said.

He watched as Lysithea turned from the door and went along her way down the hallway. Hopefully it wouldn't come down to Io having to be shot—she was his only hope, he couldn't afford to let her die. He needed this plan to work. It was the only way to save Neo Erta.

Lysithea
The Palace

Lysithea stood on the front steps of the capitol, staring down at the picture David had left on her desk in disbelief. If what he said was true, Io, her little sister, was still alive somewhere out in Neo Victoria, and there was no telling what horrors she'd lived through after Spiritus Vallem, being an experiment, and most likely a prisoner in Jeremy's home. Lysithea did not know much about Jeremy, she had only met him a couple times in passing at the palace, but she did know from what Graggöry had said that he was cruel and lacked caring for his experiment subjects.

"Jesus, Io," she hissed through her teeth, crumpling up the paper and stuffing it into her coat pocket. She glanced out over the streets. People were headed to the far side of the city, leaving their homes behind in search of shelter from the bombs that the Core had begun to drop. She shielded her eyes and looked up at the sky. The ash was still falling, as it had and as it would for years to come.

What would she do when she found Io? Could she turn her back over to the Core, knowing what the Core would do to her? Her stomach churned, an uneasy feeling creeping up her spine. She bit her bottom lip, thinking. Maybe she could let her get away. Maybe that was the right thing to do. Perhaps, she would just have to see what happened when she found her—and she would find her, she had no doubt in her mind about that. She *had* to find her, before David could, or before Graggöry found out about it.

Graggöry.

She would have to tell him the truth, and right away.

Even if he turned her away again, she would have to stand her ground. Graggöry needed to know. He deserved to know. She would tell him as soon as she found Io. She would have to.

Sighing, she turned her gaze toward the two men and the woman who were patiently waiting for her command. They were all in their slick black Core uniforms, and looked lethal.

"Hobbs, Williams, Jeffers," she called to them, stepping down the steps, two at a time. "Let's go."

"Yes, ma'am," they said in unison as they followed after her.

"If you see her, don't shoot," Lysithea told them. "I want to ask her some questions and we'll see if she'll come quietly, got it?"

"Yes, ma'am," they said again.

Lysithea rolled her eyes as they walked down the street (it annoyed her that people would follow her aimlessly just because she was higher ranked), in the direction that people were leaving from. They would go check out the streets around Jeremy's house first. She could be anywhere by now, but at least they had a place they could start.

"All right, be vigilant," Lysithea said.

Secretly, a part of her hoped that they would not find Io.

A part of her hoped it was all just a lie.

But hope had died in the last few days, along with the illusion that anywhere in Neo Victoria was safe.

She watched the faces of people as they passed by, waiting to see Io's familiar, ever-knowing face, but praying desperately that she had somehow made it out of the city. She tugged her coat close around her. Everything felt a little bit colder today.

Io

Neo Victoria

Io hastily walked down an alley, deciding to keep off the main stretch of street. The longer she kept herself hidden, the better off she would probably be. Deciding to take a break and think things over, she leaned back against the damp red brick of one of a duplex, taking a deep breath. She had decided many blocks back that being outside wasn't as exciting as she had once thought it would be. She missed the warm feel of sunlight on her skin. She missed the fresh air and the smell of pine and freshly blossomed flowers. Frowning she leaned her head against the brick, closing her eyes. Ash fell on her face and melted against her skin. She would never see the sun or smell those flowers again.

That life—that world—was gone.

She kicked her foot forward in the slush that had puddled at her feet, glancing back down at it. What was she going to do? Where was she going to go? And what good were her arm or leg when she didn't even know what they were meant to do—when she didn't even know what she was capable of? She glanced toward the mouth of the alley, blowing out a cloud of steam, like smoke. What had Jeremy been thinking?

She flinched as a pang gripped her heart. As soon as David realized Jeremy wasn't delivering her to him, or the Core, he would go after him. She had no doubt of that. Jeremy could end up imprisoned, or worse... dead. She shook her head. There wasn't time to be sitting around moping about what could happen—he had sent her away; he obviously knew what he was doing. She took a slow breath, trying to steady her heartbeat. Jeremy was smart, so surely he would figure something out. What she needed to worry about was herself and how she was going to, against all odds, make it out of the city and actually survive.

There wasn't much of a chance, she knew. The likelihood of this working was slim to none, but if there was one thing her mother had taught her, it was to hold on to hope. She pushed away from the wall and headed back out of the alley, pausing at the mouth to look both ways. She hadn't seen very many people in a couple of blocks, which she assumed was because she was headed in the wrong direction; however, the path of least resistance was heading straight for the ruined part of the city. True, there was a higher chance of running into a member of the Core, but unless someone was really looking at her, she decided she didn't really stick out much from the crowds of people she had seen earlier. Her skeletal hand was mostly hidden beneath her coat and the black leggings Nesa had set out for her covered her leg. The one thing that really gave her away were her eyes.

Just act cool if you see someone, she told herself, stepping out of the mouth of the alley and into the open street. *Look down and act like you know what you're doing.*

It couldn't be too hard to pretend to be absolutely normal. She laughed to herself as she followed the sidewalk down the street, pausing for brief moments to stare into the windows of the little shops she was passing. She supposed that Neo Victoria had been a lovely place to live, up until the bombs had begun to drop. She probably would have enjoyed living here—in another life. She put her hands in her pockets and continued on, watching the tips of her boots as she walked. Everything was eerily quiet, save for the booming from the bombs as the continued to ravage the city. *They're getting close to the townhouse*, she thought, glancing over her shoulder.

Perhaps, it wouldn't be destroyed. She wondered if this would have happened anyway, had she not left. Jeremy would have had to evacuate… and where would that leave her? Before his change of heart, he probably would have evacuated and taken her straight to the Core; however, now they probably would have stayed and died in the townhouse. At least then they would have been together. She frowned. What did it matter that they weren't together? She would have never known him had the valley not been attacked. She was being silly to nurture these notions that she loved him.

"Stupid girl," she said to herself, rounding a street corning.

"You there, halt!" someone called, and Io stopped in her tracks. She lifted her gaze to the faces of four individuals, dressed in sleek black and red uniforms. Obviously, they were members of the Core. She swallowed and took a step back, steadying herself. She looked everywhere but at them, trying to route an escape. But the only way out was to run right past them—and she didn't think she was brave enough to attempt that.

"Do you have any form of identification on you, miss?" one asked.

She shook her head.

"Your name, then," a second, very familiar voice said.

Io looked up into the face of the women who was speaking to her, only to catch her breath. Though she had not seen her sister in five years, there was no mistaking that Lysithea was standing before her now. An odd sense of relief, mixed with daunting confusion, flooded through Io. Her sister was alive. She wasn't completely alone, yet, if Lys was alive and clearly a member of the Core, that meant—the prophecy had been right. Dread shot through her. Lysithea had killed the angels, and the look in her eyes told Io that if needed, she would kill Io as well.

"The Lady General Lysithea asked for your name, girl," the other woman barked. "Tell us, or we will take action."

Io kept silent and continued to stare at Lysithea in disbelief.

"It's obviously the girl we're looking for," one of the men said. "Look there, at her hand... and those eyes, they're completely unnatural."

Lysithea raised her pistol. "Your name."

"You know my name," Io finally said. "You know it's me."

Lysithea swallowed and aimed her pistol a little higher. Her expression was unreadable. Io shivered. Though all their lives, their mother had groomed them to believe that Lysithea was a killer, never did Io actually think that Lysithea would ever hurt her.

"I'm not going with you willingly," Io added, taking a step back.

"Io—" Lysithea started but stopped herself.

Io lifted her hand, flexing her mechanical fingers. "I suppose your only other option is to kill me."

"She's brave," the other man said, staring at her skeptically. "I'll give her that."

"Come with us, Io," Lysithea said, calmly. Io thought it sounded a little desperate. Perhaps, Lysithea didn't want to kill her after all.

"No," Io said.

She took a step toward them.

"I know what they'll do to me if I go with you, and I would rather die."

The others lifted their pistols, all aimed at Io.

"At ease," Lysithea ordered them. "The only one who will shoot will be me."

They lowered their weapons.

Io glanced behind them, at the open road and the inviting mouths of the alleys that lined the street. Her only option was to get to one of them before Lysithea had time to shoot her. She looked back at Lysithea.

She wished it didn't have to be this way. Even if she was mad at Lysithea, she still loved her. She would give anything to run into her arms. They were all each other had left.

"I'm not coming with you."

Lysithea pulled the hammer back. "Come with us, Io. Please. It doesn't have to be this way. You don't have to die."

"Maybe I want to," Io said, hoping her sister wouldn't call her bluff, though she didn't have much to live for anymore anyway.

Io took a deep breath and a step back. *Just run.*

"Shoot me," she told her sister. "You would be doing me a favor."

She watched as Lysithea gave her one last, desperate, pleading look, before pulling her trigger.

Jeremy

The Townhouse

Jeremy had stood behind the closed door for a long time after Io had left, his palm pressed to the cool wood, slightly in disbelief at what she had said. Now, he was hurriedly flipping through the programs on the holographic screen of his master computer, downloading them all to a memory chip.

"Nesa," Jeremy said, glancing up at the little camera above the study door.

"Yes, sir?" The little light on the camera turned red.

"I'm downloading you onto this chip now," he said. "If something happens, I just wanted to thank you for being... well, for being a friend. You've gone above and beyond any other NESA system in this city, and I wanted to thank you for that."

"What are you going to do, Jeremy?"

Jeremy shrugged his shoulders, but a sly smile tugged at his lips.

"Jeremy—"

"I'm going to burn it down," Jeremy said.

"The townhouse, sir?"

"Yes," he said, and then added, "Don't worry, though. I'll make sure you're safe and sound in this chip and deactivated. You'll not have to witness it."

"But where will you go?"

"They'll kill me anywhere I go," Jeremy replied. "I don't know what I'll do after that—but I can't let them have any of the blueprints in the townhouse. On the chip, I have all the programs for Io—just in case. If the Core should get the chip..."

He didn't finish. Instead, he stood from the desk and walked to the window, looking out at the ash filled alley, and the blinking neon sign. He would miss the townhouse, the way he missed his mother and father—this was all he had left of them.

"If the Core gets this chip, I fear for the world," Jeremy finished. He turned back to his desk and looked down at the screen. "All right, Nesa. You've been downloaded. If this is the last time we speak—it has been an honor."

"An honor, sir," Nesa said. "Goodbye for now, old friend."

"Goodbye for now, old friend," he said, and hit the button to deactivate her.

He stood in silence, for a long while, looking down at the screen before peeling the chip out of the computer and placing it in the pocket of his flannel shirt.

Graggöry
The Palace

Graggöry wiped his mouth with the back of his hand, frowning as it only smeared the blood on his face. Stepping away from the slumped body of some nameless prostitute, barely propped against the wall, he looked out of the mouth of the alley, hoping no one had seen him. It had been many weeks since the last time he had fed off of Lysithea, and finally his body couldn't take it any longer—it needed to be sated.

But we want Lysithea's blood, a voice cooed. *Give us what we want.*

He could not afford to drink from Lysithea. If he did, he feared he would kill her. He eyed the body in the alley and frowned. He had killed this poor woman, though he hadn't really meant to. He turned from the body and made his way to fire escape that climbed up the side of the palace and stopped at his room. He climbed his way up the fire escape. It had never been this bad before—he desperately needed those cigarettes.

He climbed through the open window and walked into the bathroom to wash off the blood off, staring at himself in the mirror. He didn't like this version of himself. He didn't want to be this way.

Give us what we want, we've been waiting a long, long time.

"Oh, father, look how pitiful I have become," he said aloud. "I wanted to be someone you could be proud of, but I know I have failed."

His reflection stared back at him with large gray hopeless eyes.

He would lose the war and himself all in one fell swoop.

His only hope was Lysithea finding someone to make those cigarettes. He sighed. He wasn't so sure he could be saved anymore.

"I'm sorry, Lys," he said, looking away from his reflection. "I'll try harder next time."

We're still thirsty, Graggöry. Give us Lysithea's blood.

He shook his head as he walked out of the bathroom and into his closet, looking for a new set of clothes. He would not give into the blood lust.

You know you want her blood.

He changed his shirt, ignoring the voice.

Take it.

He took a deep breath and let it out slowly.

Give in.

He closed his eyes, feeling close to finally snapping. He would have to avoid Lysithea for a while—and she would not like it. He frowned. It was the only way to keep her safe, and he would do anything to make her safe.

"I'm not going to do it," he told the voices, but he wasn't so sure he could stop himself if the opportunity arose.

Pity... a voice snickered.

He groaned and made his way out of the room and down the hall to his office. There was so much to do, and he was running out of time. Something had to be done about the rebels and about the bombings. He frowned and made his way to his desk. Neo Victoria might not make it through the night, if they weren't careful.

What a mess.

Lysithea
Neo Victoria

Lysithea took a deep breath and looked straight ahead at Io, who was staring back at her with disbelief. She had just pulled the trigger, but purposely missed, just to show Io that she meant business. If Io didn't run and fast, she would have to haul her in to the Core, or she would shoot her dead right here in the street. Perhaps, that would be best for Io—what life would she have, being the property of the Core? Io was not a killer. Io was gentle and kind. Maybe that was just before, though. David's brother could have turned her into a monster.

Run, Io. Hurry up and run!

"Next time, I won't miss," Lysithea said. "Come with us, Io."

Run.

She hoped she could will it into existence. If she thought it long enough and hard enough, Io would somehow get it through her head and run away.

"I—" Io started, still watching her. "I can't."

Lysithea shot again, aimed close enough so that the bullet would whiz past Io's ear. Io darted this time, her eyes wide with horror. She sprinted past them, down the street, and disappeared into an alley. Before she could disappear though, Lysithea shot one more time, for good measure.

"Should we go after her, ma'am?" Hobbs asked.

"I'll go after her," Lysithea said, turning to them.

"By yourself?" Jeffers asked, glancing down the alley where Io had fled.

"Yes," Lysithea said. "She won't hurt me. It's a rather long story. I'll explain it to you later. For now, you three head back to the base and await further instructions. You should rest. We're on patrol tonight."

"Yes, ma'am," Williams said, lifting his hand from the grip of his pistol. "Jeffers, Hobbs, let's go. Are you sure you'll be all right by yourself?"

Lysithea nodded.

They bowed and started off down the road, leaving Lysithea behind. She watched them until they turned down another road before turning back toward the alley through which Io had escaped. She let out a sigh. What had gotten into Io? Did she truly have a death wish? Lys chewed on her bottom lip and started off after her sister. Io had headed straight into enemy territory. Lysithea had to find her before Io got into trouble with the wrong kind of people.

"Io!" she called out. "Io, come back!"

But it was of no use. She knew her sister would not come when called—especially not after Lysithea had taken those shots at her. She tightened the scarf around her neck and ventured down the alley, her hand resting on her pistol, just in case.

"Io!" she called again, and again, but Io never answered and there was no sign of her anywhere.

Io

Neo Victoria

All around her, buildings were in ruin. Beautiful Victorian homes had been reduced to nothing but rubble. She had stopped running, only to take in her surroundings. She dug her feet into a pile of glass, listening to it crunch beneath the weight of her boots. There was hardly a soul for miles—Io had passed one or two stray people some little ways back, but now it seemed as if she were the only one left in this part of Neo Victoria. In the distance, she could hear the muffled sound of her name being called.

It was ironic to Io that Lysithea had left so she wouldn't become the monster their mother talked of; yet, Lysithea had still turned against her people in the end. Had she really hated that life enough to kill the others? Io frowned. What would have driven Lysithea to do those things?

She took a deep breath. She could smell the buildings still smoldering. It brought back the memory of Spiritus Vallem, being swallowed by flames.

Io knew one thing for sure—that had not been the same girl that had left the valley five years ago. That Lysithea would have never killed a soul. Io shook her head. Perhaps, that Lysithea would have, if given the chance; after all, it had all been fated so.

Io chewed on her bottom lip. Lysithea's voice was getting closer. She started back down the street, looking for a structure that had not been entirely destroyed—somewhere she could hide from Lysithea. For Jeremy, she would try her best to not get caught again.

Io came upon an ancient cathedral, still standing amidst the rubble of the rest of the fallen world. She took a moment to admire it—the structure was so tall and magnificent. Io had never seen anything quite like it before. She imagined it would have looked prettier in Spiritus Vallem. Something so beautiful belonged there, where the sun could shine down on it, where it would be truly admired. She followed its long, cream columns up until the steeple collided with the dark, daunting sky.

She walked up to the closed gates, wrapping her fingers around the cold wrought iron. On the other side of the fence, nuns were tending to the lawn. She watched as they walked to and fro, from the main building, to the smaller ones, and back again. Somewhere, very close now, Lysithea's voice called out to her. She thought for a moment before calling out to the nuns.

"Excuse me," she said, loud enough so they could hear her, but not so loud as to give herself away to Lysithea. "I need help."

Two nuns glanced over to her, both of their gazes falling on her metal fingers, wrapped around the gate. They whispered to each other, and turned away, continuing on their way.

Io, only feeling slightly discouraged, frowned and rattled the gate. "Please! I need help, quickly!"

The other nuns continued to ignore her. She let out a sigh and unwrapped her hands from around the gate. "Please," she tried one last time.

Sanctuary, a clear voice said, from where she wasn't sure. *Ask for sanctuary.*

"Sanctuary!" she called, deciding it couldn't hurt to try. She glanced back through the rungs of the gate, before turning back to look behind her as Lysithea's voice seemed to be getting even closer. "I need sanctuary, quickly, please!"

"I apologize for the others," someone said from the other side. She peered back through the rungs, her gaze falling on the outline of an old man. "They saw your hand and thought you might be with the enemy. Though we've decided to stay with the cathedral, they're a little on edge about the war. I hope you'll understand."

The old man, whom Io decided must be a priest of some sort, and looked oddly familiar (though she couldn't quite put her finger on where she might have ever seen him before), opened the gate and stepped to the side, letting her pass. She entered the courtyard and looked around a bit nervously.

"I understand," she said to the priest. "I'll explain everything, but first I need to hide. Someone is looking for me, and I don't want to be found."

"Come right this way," the priest said, leading her down the sidewalk and to wide oaken doors with various scenes carved into the wood. She paused to admire it for a moment before hurrying inside the cathedral. "Come, sit and tell me your story, child."

She sat in a pew and shrugged off her coat, revealing her metal arm. "It's a long story, and you might not believe it."

"Try me," he said with a chuckle. He sat down beside her and leaned back against the pew.

"Well," Io said. She looked around the room, taking in the tall walls and wide, domed ceilings. "I don't know what exactly you believe, but I'm assuming you must believe in a god of some sort to have all of this."

"Yes, we believe in the true God," the priest said, tilting his head.

"Well," she said. "You might actually believe me then. You see... I come from a place outside of the city. It is... er... well it was a paradise."

"Spiritus Vallem," the priest said. "Yes, I have heard of it."

"Not many people have," Io said. "Many people don't even believe it existed."

"I believe it," the priest said. "I am very old, and have seen many things. I also have great faith that it is true—about the angels in that valley."

"Well," Io said, frowning a bit. "The angels are no longer in the valley. The Core killed them off. It was a massacre."

"I see," the priest said, frowning, though this didn't seem to surprise him any. "That's awful, but how do you know?"

"I was there," Io said, solemnly. "I saw it happen, and I almost didn't survive, myself."

"Then you must be..."

"I am an angel from Spiritus Vallem. I don't think many others are left."

"That explains your eyes," he said.

"Yes, my eyes seem to always give me away," Io said, remembering the day in the valley when Jeremy and David had found her. They had gone on and on about her eyes, and she hadn't understood why until now.

"Well, how are you here now? What happened?"

"I should have died in the valley with the rest of the angels, but a man found me and brought me to Neo Victoria, to turn me into this," she said, gesturing to her arm. "I'm probably really dangerous, but I don't even know. I had to leave him before I could fully understand any of it."

"Well, there must be a reason you did not die that day," the priest said.

"I know of no reason why I should have survived," Io replied.

"And the man? What happened to him?"

"He'll probably be dead before the sun sets," Io said, a grim feeling giving way to the numbness she had been feeling from the shock of it all. "He wanted to give me to the Core—he was going to use me as a way to get reinstated—but he changed his mind and sent me away."

"And you were running from?"

"My... sister," she hesitated. "My sister ran away from the valley five years ago and somehow got mixed up with the Core. She must have been sent to look for me, and when she found me, I—I taunted her, and she shot at me, twice."

"I see," the priest said again.

"You don't believe me, do you?" Io asked, frowning. She knew it all sounded far-fetched, but she had been rather hoping that he would believe her. "I'm not making this up, I promise."

"No, I believe you. I'm just listening. It seemed like you wanted to talk about it."

"Oh," Io said, nodding. "Yes, I wanted someone to listen. I need some advice."

"Advice about what?"

"What to do."

"What to do about what?"

Io gave him a quizzical glance and gestured all about her with her hands. "I need some advice on what to do next. I obviously can't spend the rest of my life hiding in here, though it is a lovely cathedral. I don't know whether to go back for Jeremy, even though he told me not to—or if I should do as he said and leave the city. I have absolutely no idea what I'm doing—I have never been outside of the valley; I don't know how any of this works. If I don't go back, Jeremy will probably die, but—"

"But?"

"I don't want Jeremy to die," she whispered, miserably. "He saved my life, I feel that it's only right for me to save his."

"Well then, it seems to me that you have found your answer," he said with a smile. "I think you know where you're meant to be."

Io considered this, chewing on her bottom lip again. "I suppose you're right."

She stood from the pew and grabbed her coat, slipping it on. She gave one last glance around the sanctuary before turning back to the priest. "Thank you for listening, and thank you for giving me a hiding place."

"It is what I'm here for," the priest said, "to listen."

"I've to go," Io said, glancing toward the door. "Hopefully my sister has given up and gone home—wherever that is."

The priest chuckled. "If she's still out there, you're welcome to come back, Io."

Io smiled as she made her way out of the cathedral and back onto the lawn. Avoiding what seemed like judging stares from the nuns, she made her way to the gate, peering out through the rungs of wrought iron to see if her sister was still out there looking. The coast appeared to be clear. She turned and gave a wave to the priest who had followed her out, before opening the gate and stepping back out into the desolate streets of Neo Victoria.

Hopefully, she could remember how to get back to the townhouse. She glanced up at the sky, which was already growing dim with twilight. She didn't have much time before David would show back up, looking for her.

Halfway down an alley she paused. How had the priest known her name? She shook the thought from her mind.

If she wanted to save Jeremy, she needed to hurry.

Father Baxley
Cathedral of Our Lady Victory

Father Baxley sat in the pew for a long while after Io left, praying for the youngest daughter of his dear friend. Abraxos would be pleased to know his children were alive, though it seemed they were all in grave danger here in the city. He wondered whether or not it had been a good idea to send Io off like that—she would be much safer in the sanctuary. He had seen in her eyes, however, a wild desire to save the young man she spoke of—a man he assumed to be that young scientist who had been discharged, Jeremy Lancaster. He had prayed for Jeremy many nights, having known his mother for quite many years. She had been a patron of the cathedral from a young age, and it had been a pure tragedy the day that she had been killed by those bombs out in the Wastelands.

He wondered if Io could save him. Though she had been clearly modified, she was still only a girl—surely she was no match for the Core. No one was.

He stood from the pew and looked out of the door, to the open courtyard outside. A bomb set off, rattling the cathedral. They would probably have to leave soon. He supposed he could get the others out and come back—he would not leave the cathedral, for good. There was no need to have the others in the direct line of danger, though.

He stepped out of the door and out into the falling ash, shielding his eyes.

"Be with her, old friend," he said to the spirit of Abraxos, glancing toward the gate. "She will need your guidance now more than ever."

Lysithea
The Palace

Lysithea strode up the front steps of The Palace, shivering both from the cold and the uneasiness of what was probably to come. She had to talk to Graggöry tonight, before something horrible happened to Io. The future seemed so unpredictable and incredibly frightening. There was no telling how Graggöry would react to the truth—she had been lying to him this whole time, he certainly had every right to be angry with her; however, now was not the time for everything to fall apart. They needed to stick together if there was any hope of any of them getting out of this war alive.

She had to save Io, and Neo Victoria, and somehow, Graggöry, even if after this, he never wanted to speak to her again. She frowned. That was the last thing they needed—division in the face of complete disaster. But she had to do this. She had to do it for herself and for Io and for him, because he deserved to know the truth. If he tried to turn her away tonight, she wouldn't go. This was important. This had to be done.

Lysithea took a deep breath and walked through the large oaken doors into the palace. No one was around—which struck her as odd. She paused in the foyer and looked around. There wasn't even a security guard. Perhaps Graggöry had evacuated the others, since the bombs were getting closer to the city's center with each passing moment.

She walked up the stairs, and down the hall to Graggöry's office. The door was slightly cracked so she pushed it open a little and peered in.

"Graggöry?" she called, looking around the dark room. For days this was how she found him, hiding in the dark. She frowned and pushed the door open enough so she could see him. Again, he was sitting at his desk with his head in his hands. "Graggöry, we need to talk."

"Not now," Graggöry said. "I want to be alone."

"No," Lysithea said, stepping in and closing the door behind her. She flipped on the light switch. "We need to talk. Right now."

Graggöry looked up, squinting his eyes as the light found him. He ran a hand through his hair and sat back in his chair, eyeing her. "This better be important."

"There's something I have to tell you," Lysithea said, evenly. She took a deep breath and let it out through her teeth. "I've been lying to you."

Graggöry blinked, his lips twitching downward into a frown. "What, exactly, have you lied about?"

"You know how... how I told you the angels were all dead?"

"Yes."

"Well, that was only partially true. All the angels aren't dead," Lysithea said. She closed her eyes and took a deep breath, trying to find the courage to finish what she wanted to say. "All the angels aren't dead, and I'm one of them."

Graggöry frowned, but did not look surprised. "Go on."

"I'm one of them, and... and I saw my sister today."

"Your sister?"

She couldn't tell if this was going well. Graggöry's face gave nothing away.

"My sister, Io. Jeremy—David's brother—took her from the valley the day of the massacre and turned her into some sort of weapon. Do you remember that weapon proposal he turned in to the Core? It must be something to do with Io."

"Io," Graggöry said, with calm precision. "You have a sister."

"Yes," Lysithea said. An uneasy feeling swept over her. She bit her bottom lip.

"You're an angel," he said.

"Yes."

"You killed your family, your people?"

"Yes," she said, her whisper barely audible.

"Why would you do that?"

Lysithea blinked, tears slipping down her face now. "I... I did it for you."

"Lys, that's a horrible reason to do something like that," Graggöry said. "You should have said something. If I had known, I would never have asked you to do that."

"I was too scared to tell you the truth," Lysithea said, stifling a sob. "I didn't want you to hate me."

"So, lying to me was really the best option?"

She looked at him, the glamour gone from her lavender eyes. "I..."

"Were you ever going to tell me?" he asked. He set his hands down on the desk, watching her. "Or were you going to keep living a lie?"

"I would have told you, I was just—"

"Waiting for the right time? Scared of me, perhaps?"

"You're angry..."

"You think so?"

"I'm sorry," Lysithea said. She nervously grabbed her arm, curling her fingers into her coat's thick sleeve. "I wanted to tell you. I should have told you."

"You should have," he said. "Tell me, Lysithea. What else have you been lying about?"

"I haven't lied about anything else," she squeaked. "I want to help you. I love you. I want to be with you."

"Yet you lied to me? About something substantially important, at that."

"Please forgive me," she begged. "I need your help. We have to find my sister."

"Sounds like you ought to get going then," Graggöry said.

"Please," she said. "Please, Graggöry."

"I think you should go now," was all he said in return. "Go. Leave me be."

Lysithea stood there, watching him for a moment, letting the silence settle around her. What had she done? What would she do now? When he did not look back up at her, she took a shaky breath and turned, opening the door and slipping out into the hall. She closed the door behind her and stood in front of it for a long time.

What had been done was done. She needed to figure out how to find her sister.

She was out of time.

Graggöry
The Palace

Graggöry shut the lights back off and sat in the dark, the darkness comfortably cocooning him. His blood was boiling. He took a deep breath to try to steady the rapid beating of his heart.

Well, you shouldn't be so surprised, a voice snickered. *We told you what she was.*

He growled, slamming his fist down onto the desk. "Silence."

Don't be angry with us, the voice chided. *We did not lie to you.*

You should have killed her while you had the chance, another voice said. *She was so weak and defenseless. It would have been perfect.*

Angry as he might be, he did not want to kill Lysithea. In fact, he had sent her away to make sure that that would not be how all of this ended. He needed some time to compose himself, to let the anger die down a little. He would not have Lysithea's blood on his hands. Though she had lied, he still loved her. That would not change just because she was really an angel; however, it hurt him that she had felt that she could not tell him.

"Oh… Lys," he sighed, glancing toward the window. She would be out there, in the cold, searching for her sister amidst the bombs and rebels ravaging the city. He should be out there with her; however, there was something he needed to do first.

He tapped open his computer's screen, scrolling through the main NESA's security folder. There had to be something from David in there, somewhere, and he would find it and get to the bottom of all of this, once and for all.

He tapped open a file, and pressed the play button, listening to the transmission.

"David, my darling, things aren't going so well," a very familiar voice said. He had definitely heard that voice before… in his head. He turned up the volume and continued to listen. "Perhaps, you'll just have to kill them both for me."

266

So David had been up to something. Graggöry frowned. Lysithea had been right—David was definitely not a friend. He sighed and scrolled through some more files, playing a few more clips, just to verify that he'd heard that voice before. There was no mistaking it—that was the voice he heard the most in his mind.

He let out a sigh and closed the computer. He needed to get to the bottom of this—but how? He ran a hand through his hair and rested his arms on his desk, his chin in his palms. Betrayed in one day, by the people closest to him. He closed his eyes. What could he do with any of this? What could be done about it?

Perhaps, he needed to forgive Lysithea and ask for her help. No, that was something he definitely could not do. She was not safe, not with his blood lust, not with his anger, and definitely not with the voices. He pushed away from the desk and started for the door. He would find David and get to the bottom of this, right now. He strode out of the room and into the hall, looking around, half expecting to see Lysithea waiting there. When she wasn't, he let out a sigh of relief and continued down the hall.

He made it to David's office. The door was open, and David was inside, fumbling around with something on his desk. Graggöry cleared his throat. David, looking a bit startled, lifted his hands from the desk and looked up at the doorway.

"I need to talk to you," Graggöry said, leaning against the door jam. "It's rather important."

"I'm a little busy at the moment," David said. "We have a situation on our hands."

"I've been made aware of that," Graggöry said. "However, there seems to be a situation involving you, as well. Would you care to explain?"

"Explain what?"

"Late night chats with a woman in your office, perhaps?" Graggöry pressed.

"You must mean Lucie. She's my girlfriend," David said. He stepped back from the desk and stuffed his hands into his coat pockets. "I hardly have any time away from here, so she comes to visit me."

Graggöry only half believed this. He tilted his head, pondering on whether or not he should go more into detail about their midnight chats. "I see."

"I can explain everything to you later, but I've really got to go take care of something," David said. "I don't know what you've heard, but it can all be explained."

"When you get back, I expect you to come talk to me," Graggöry said.

Oh now he's a liar, too, a different voice cackled. *Everyone lies to poor Graggöry.*

He frowned.

"I promise, I will come clear this up," David said. He stepped around Graggöry and out into the hall, placing his beret back onto his head. "I shouldn't be long."

Graggöry watched him go, disbelief settling in the pit of his stomach. He had known this man for the better half of fourteen years, and never once had he ever expected him to lie straight to his face. People were full of surprises today.

He waited until David was out of sight before turning and entering the office. Perhaps, he could find something damning in here. Trying to be quick about it, he shuffled through the papers on David's desk, uncovering a black notebook. Thinking that there must be something interesting in there, Graggöry picked it up and flipped through the pages.

Convince Jeremy to finish his experiment.

He flipped a little further.

Present Io to the Core and figure out what to do with Jeremy later.

Well, Graggöry thought, *that's certainly cold.*

He closed the notebook and decided to take it back to his own office. He stepped around the desk and made his way back into the hallway before heading back to his office. Tossing the notebook onto his desk, he sat back down and opened his computer again. He would scan the pages of the notebook into the computer and put the notebook back where he found it before David had the chance to get back and find it missing.

Graggöry knew he was walking on a fine line. If David was really plotting his demise, he ought to be more careful about this; however, he supposed he wasn't afraid of David, and if David wanted to try to end him, he would gladly accept the challenge to stay alive, and if it came down to it, kill David instead. There was also this Lucie he would have to take care of—she must know something of the voices in his head, because hers was clearly one of them.

He sighed. Tonight, it seemed he was losing everything.

Io and Jeremy
The Townhouse

After deactivating Nesa, Jeremy had begun to douse the townhouse in gasoline. His blueprints, his plans, his childhood, and his memories—he would set them all aflame. Everything would be reduced to smoke and ruble and the Core would not be able to take anything from him.

Looking around the foyer one last time, Jeremy pulled the matchbook from his vest pocket and lit a match. He tossed it to the floor and watched as the flame took, and spread slowly up the stairs.

"Goodbye," he said to the townhouse before turning to leave. He walked out the back door and closed it behind him. He could already hear the flames crackling as they devoured years and years of memories. He supposed it was for the best—he couldn't leave everything to David, who cared nothing about memories and only of himself.

He turned to watch the house burn. Feeling both a little relieved and a little sorrowful. The townhouse had served him well, but he supposed that before the night was through, bombs would have taken it anyway. He took a step back and turned to leave, stopping in place when his eyes fell on Io, who was standing at the mouth of the alley.

"Jeremy," Io said, a smile spreading across her face. "You're okay."

"What are you doing here, Io? I told you to run," Jeremy asked, his voice low and steady, not giving away the anger that was growing inside of him. "I told you to not turn back, no matter what."

"I know what you told me," Io said, "but I couldn't leave you here to die." Io glanced to the townhouse and frowned. "You're burning it down?"

"Don't change the subject, Io," Jeremy said. "You shouldn't have come back."

"I'm sorry," Io said, "but I couldn't leave you behind in good conscience."

Jeremy opened his mouth to say something but shut it and shook his head, marching over to Io. He took her hand and tugged her forward, turning to lead her out of the alley. "We have to hurry. We've got to find somewhere to hide."

"There's a cathedral, the only one I've seen in Neo Victoria today, down passed where the bombs have already fallen. I sought shelter there earlier today, and the priest told me that if I needed to, I could come back. They'll let us hide in there," Io said, being tugged along behind him.

"A cathedral, huh?" Jeremy said. "Clever girl."

They were almost to the opposite mouth of the alley when someone behind them cleared their throat.

"I don't suppose you're trying to run away," David said, a frown tugging at his lips. "I wouldn't advise it, if that's the case."

Io and Jeremy turned to face him, and Io let go of Jeremy's hand and shrugged off her coat, her metallic arm shimmering in the dying daylight.

"Well, I certainly am not going with you," Io said, when Jeremy stayed silent.

David laughed, motioning for his men to come join him in the mouth of the alley. There were five of them, in total. Io still had no idea how to work her arm, but she had a few ideas to try if things got a little dicey.

"What a brave girl, you've got there, Jeremy," David said. "Such spunk. She'll do you proud in the Core."

"I'm not going to the Core," Io said. "Did you not hear me? I'm not going with you, and neither is Jeremy, for that matter."

David snapped his fingers and his men lifted their pistols.

"I don't think you've much of a choice, little girl," David said, his own hand resting on the grip of his pistol. "There are five of us, and only two of you. And Jeremy certainly does not have a weapon."

"I'm a weapon," Io coolly replied.

"Ah, yes, that you are," David said. "But do you know how to work any of that? Last I checked, Jeremy said you weren't ready."

"I—"

"You should stand down and come with us without a fuss," David said. "It's the best thing for you to do, if you want to keep Jeremy alive."

Io gave a sideways glance to Jeremy and chewed on her bottom lip. Of course she wanted to keep Jeremy alive, but she also knew that David was lying. Jeremy would go down regardless of if she went with them peacefully or not.

"I think I'll take my chances," Io finally said.

"Io, he's right," Jeremy said, so quietly that Io almost hadn't heard him. "You don't know what you're doing. Stand down."

Io turned to look at him. "You too, huh?"

Jeremy gave her a sad smile.

"Well, I'm not standing down," Io said with an annoyed sigh. "If they kill us, they kill us, but I'm going to fight."

"All that spunk doesn't change the fact that you still don't have a clue of what you're doing," David said. He lifted his pistol, aimed for Jeremy.

"Try me," Io said.

David pulled his hammer back.

"Prepare to fire," he said to his men.

"Io, think really hard about what you want your arm or leg to turn into," Jeremy said, suddenly. "They react to your thoughts."

"Oh, so you're giving her a little lesson, now, are you?" David asked, turning the gun on Io. "You think that's going to save either of you?"

"Ignore him, and think *really hard*, Io," Jeremy continued.

"Nothing's happening, Jer," Io said, a bit panicked.

David chuckled and glanced over his shoulder at his men. "Don't shoot to kill."

"Jer, *it's still not working,*" Io cried.

"On one boys. Three…" David said, and began to count down while he watched Io frantically waving her arms. "…and one."

Io heard the click of the pistols, and panicking even more, jumped in front of Jeremy. To her surprise, the metal on her arm burst into tiny pieces and reconfigured in front of them into a shield. The bullets hit the shield one by one, but nothing touched Io or Jeremy. Io bit her bottom lip, thinking, when all of the sudden, the metal on her leg burst through the flimsy fabric of her leggings and formed, what she assumed was some kind of gun. She had only ever seen her father's hunting rifle before today, but this gun looked a little beefier than her father's rifle and definitely beefier than the guns David and his men had. She picked it up, careful to keep the shield in front of them. The men began to fire again, and Io gave a fleeting glance to Jeremy before jumping out from behind the shield to shoot.

She had never shot a gun before. If she hadn't been holding it with both her hands, she feared it might have kicked so hard that it would have hit her in the head, and then she would be no help to Jeremy at all.

Io had also never killed someone before, but now as adrenaline coursed through her veins, she knew she was going to have to kill these men if they had any chance of making it out alive. She aimed the gun and shot again, this time, taking one of them out with a yelp. He fell to the ground; clutching his chest, he looked up at her for a fleeting second before collapsing, face down in the street. His gun slid on the slick street and stopped at her feet. *How lucky*, she thought. She kicked the gun to Jeremy.

"Well, look at you," David said with a snide smirk. "A natural born killer."

271

Io did not want to kill, but she also did not want to be killed. She said a prayer in her head for the fallen man, and another for Jeremy to make it out of this alive, even if she should fail.

"I told you I'm not going with you," Io said.

The remaining men lifted their guns, aiming them at Io.

"Don't shoot her," David said. "She's too valuable, we need her alive."

David raised his gun and shot at the shield. Jeremy, who was peering over the top, holding the gun, jumped back and fired a shot off. The man next to Jeremy fell dead on the street. Io glanced back at Jeremy, who was staring wide-eyed at the dead man.

Obviously, Jeremy hadn't wanted to kill anyone either.

"Well, well," David said, staring at Jeremy with a look of surprise. "I would have never taken you to be a killer, but here we are. I'm kind of proud of you."

"Oh shut up," Io said. The gun in her hand shifted into something entirely different, and when she tried to aim and pull the trigger, something horrifying happened. The gun went off and David fell to the ground, clutching his arm.

"What the hell," David cursed, looking down at what used to be a solid arm. He looked back up at Io before turning his attention to his other men.

"Rogers," he said, very calmly. "Go radio in back up."

One of them nodded, and turned to leave. Jeremy pulled the hammer back on his pistol and aimed for the man.

"Let him leave," Io said, eying the remaining two men. "There won't be anything left here but bodies, anyway."

Jeremy gave her a skeptical look, a little shocked that something so sinister had come out of her mouth. David laughed and lifted his gun in his other hand, shooting. Pain seared through Io as the bullet hit her hand. The gun, too heavy for Io to hold it in just one hand, fell to the ground, skidding over to David. Before Io had time to think, the remaining officer lifted his gun, aimed for Io.

"I don't think so," Jeremy said, and shot the other man.

Io couldn't tell if David was completely pleased or completely pissed. He grabbed Io's gun and stood up, and before Io could process anything, he was upon her, the weapon drawn back and then all at once smacking down against her skull. She let out a cry as she fell to her knees, surrounded by bright color, a shrill scream in her head.

"Jeremy, run!" she cried out as he hit her again. She took a sharp breath and tried to steady herself to stop the world from spinning, but it was all in vain. The weapon and the shield disintegrated, but the metal did not go back to Io's body, instead it fell, many tiny pieces, into the street. Without his weapon, David wrapped his working hand around her throat and squeezed as hard as he could.

"What a pity, you have to die," David said through his teeth.

Io reached out to try and push him away, but the world was spinning too quickly, and she was running out of air. She gave one last, blurred glance at Jeremy, before giving into the darkness that was now surrounding her.

Jeremy watched in horror as Io's body became limp beneath David. David let her throat go and fell back, reaching for his pistol. He aimed it at Jeremy.

Jeremy lifted his pistol and aimed back at David.

"I didn't think it would end this way," David said. "I didn't really think I was going to have to kill my own brother."

"Likewise," Jeremy said.

"You won't kill me," David said. "You're too weak."

Jeremy pulled the hammer back.

"I would be doing you a favor, killing you," David continued. "The Core will have you executed anyway. This way will be less painful. It's almost a little romantic, both of you ending here in this alley."

"I knew you were cold," Jeremy said, "but never, in a million years, had I would have thought you were this evil."

"A pity you're just realizing this now," David said. "Drop your weapon, Jeremy."

Jeremy shook his head.

"Drop. Your. Weapon."

"You killed her, and now I'm going to kill you," Jeremy said. "It should have been done long ago. You should have died that day in the square."

"Who's the cold one now?" David asked, pulling his pistol's hammer back.

A shot rang out in the alley.

Chrezabel
Spiritus Vallem

[Before]

Lysithea has left the valley. Chrezabel stands in the kitchen, looking out the window at the freshly fallen snow outside.

"She left because of you," Abraxos says, "because of the ideas you've put in our daughters' heads."

"Leaving will not change the outcome," Chrezabel says. "She knows this. You know this."

"There is no outcome to change—these things you see are not true, Chreza," Abraxos says. "They're only nightmares you've put in your own head."

Chrezabel turns from the window to look at her husband. "You know that that isn't true. You know what I see is what is to come. It's happened before. It will happen again."

"Then what would you have me do? Go and find her?"

"We need to leave the valley before it is too late," Chrezabel says. She takes a deep breath and lets it out slowly, leaning back against the kitchen island. "If we stay here, we're nothing but sitting ducks."

"You know we can't leave," he says. "This is our home."

"Leaving won't change the outcome, anyway," Chrezabel says. She frowns. "Io and Lysithea must choose."

"Choose what?"

"Which path they will take," Chrezabel replies. "There's a verse, from the old, forgotten book that says something like, 'Enter through the narrow gate; for the gate is wide and the road is easy that leads to destruction, and there are many who take it. For the gate is narrow and the road is hard that leads to life, and there are few who find it.'"

"Your point?" he asks, slightly annoyed.

"The prophecy speaks of two angels, the savior and the destroyer. Io and Lysithea must choose which one they want to be on their own. We cannot help them choose. I have seen the outcome of both ways. I know how this will end."

"It won't matter," Abraxos says. "We'll all be dead, anyway, according to you."

Chrezabel pities him. Perhaps, if he had known the truth, this would not have been the life he had chosen.

"I would have chosen this life a hundred times if that meant I could be with you in the end," Chrezabel says. "I did not mean to put ideas in our daughters' heads. I only meant to guide them to make the right choice. Against all hope, I did want to think things could be changed—I wanted thing to end differently."

"I know," he says. "I'm sorry."

Chrezabel looks out the window one last time before stepping away from the kitchen island and making her way into the foyer.

"I'm sorry, too," she says, and disappears into the next room.

Io

Somewhere

Everything is bright—too bright.

Io squints her eyes and looks around. Fallen buildings lay on either side of the road, similar to what she has seen in Neo Victoria. She begins to walk down the road, to where, she does not know. Up ahead, a beautiful gate stands, blocking the rest of the roadway. She smiles sadly. This must be the end.

She must be dead.

Jeremy
Neo Victoria

Jeremy stared at David's lifeless body for a long time. He ought to feel something, but instead, he was completely numb. David was dead, and he had killed him. He took a deep breath and held it in, pondering on what to do next. He needed to get out of the alley, needed to find somewhere to hide. The Core would no doubt be looking for him now that he'd killed such a high-ranking officer. He swallowed the bile that had crept up from his stomach, and glanced to Io.

Io was sprawled out, on her back, her eyes half closed, half opened. She most certainly looked dead. He walked to her, dropping to her side as he took her wrist to feel for a pulse. He felt nothing. David had killed her. He looked back to the house, which was too far-gone to save now—wild flames hungrily engulfed it. The heat was almost too unbearable, but he continued to kneel next to Io. He had no way to save her. The last of the life serum was trapped, melting in the flames.

He couldn't just leave her in the alley to be taken by the Core and studied like some dead animal. He picked her up, cradling her in his arms, and carried her to the mouth of the alley.

Where would he go? What would he do with her?

There's a cathedral, Io had said. He would take her there. Perhaps, they would have some place to bury her. He carried her down the empty streets, past the fallen homes, and to the gates of the cathedral.

Before he could call out, an old priest, who gave him a once over, his eyes pausing on Io, greeted him.

"Oh dear," he said, opening the gate. "Please, come in young man."

Jeremy carried her through the opening, taking in the cathedral. It was massive and beautiful, and suddenly he knew why Io wanted to be there.

"You must be Jeremy," the priest said. "She told me about you."

"Yes, I'm Jeremy," Jeremy replied. "What did Io say about me?"

"Ah, Io," the priest said. He smiled sadly. "Is she gone?"

Jeremy nodded, saying nothing more.

"Come, bring her this way—we'll set her in the sanctuary until the morning."

Jeremy followed him into the sanctuary and lay her on the floor before the alter. When he didn't say anything, the priest said, "Do you believe in miracles, Jeremy?"

Jeremy considered this, but shook his head. "No."

"Do you not believe that Io was a miracle?"

Jeremy thought this over and realized it was true. "I suppose you're right."

"Have faith," the priest said. "Miracles do happen."

"Unfortunately, I think her miracles have run out," Jeremy said. He looked down at her, fighting his sadness. "I think this is the end."

"That it might be," the priest said.

Jeremy turned away from her and looked down the rows of pews.

"I have a room for you," the priest said. "I prepared it for if Io came back."

"Thank you," Jeremy said. "I appreciate it."

"You may stay however long you need," the priest said. "We will arrange for someone to… bury Io in the morning. For now, try not to worry about it."

Jeremy nodded. He wondered about David, dead, out in the street behind the townhouse, which was probably nothing more than smoldering ash now. What would be done about him? He followed the priest to the room and thanked him, before closing the door. On the bedside table sat a lamp and what he assumed must be a very old bible. He walked to the bed and sat down, taking the bible in his hand. It had been a very long time since he had seen one of these—his mother had been very religious, but he had not. He flipped it open and skimmed through the pages. He supposed that the words gave hope and comfort to some, but he feared it did nothing for him. Lying down, he opened the bible to a page and started to read. He had nothing better to do, and he didn't really want to sleep anyway. Perhaps, if he gave it a try, he could find something comforting between the books covers.

He read on through the night.

Crosbie and Jynx
Imogen Square

Crosbie and Jynx stood in the snow, in front of the fountain in the middle of the square. Jynx was bent over the fountain, staring down at the twinkling stores' lights in the murky water. Crosbie brought his hands up to his mouth, blowing on them to keep them warm. He glanced over to Jynx, who turned her head to look up at him.

"Do you think this is the closest we're going to get to seeing the stars?" Jynx asked, gesturing to lights' reflection in the fountain. "Do you think the ash will ever stop falling?"

"I don't know," Crosbie said, looking up at the sky. "Maybe someday."

Jynx looked up at the sky too, scrunching her nose. "I hope we're alive to see it."

"It hasn't stopped for at least 50 years," Crosbie said. "It's been falling since before our grandparents came above ground."

"I know," she said, "but I like to think it won't last forever."

They stood like that, looking up at the sky.

"Aside from the ash, you know, I really wish things could be like this all the time," Jynx said.

"Like what?"

"Happy, I guess," Jynx said. "Everything has been looking up lately, right?"

"Mhmm."

"Do you think Max is back home yet?" Jynx asked, pushing away from the fountain and standing back up. She stretched her arms above her head and let out a content sigh. "Should we go home and see?"

Crosbie glanced at the watch on his wrist and made a face. "I guess he should be back by now, and it is my turn to make dinner. I guess we can go back if you're done looking at the lights."

"I just wanted to see the square, one more time... just in case."

"I know," Crosbie said. "That's why I brought you."

She smiled. "Thank you. You're the best little brother."

He smiled back at her. "Let's go home, Jynx. Maybe tomorrow we can go see the ducks."

"The ducks!" Jynx exclaimed. "I love the ducks!"

Crosbie chuckled and started down the sidewalk. Jynx scampered after him, humming to herself. For once, Crosbie agreed with Jynx on something—he wished things could be like this all the time. He knew, however, that the world they lived in was cruel, and any happiness they felt now was fleeting.

David

Somewhere

He has been here before, in a world between worlds. The darkness blankets him and everything around him. He closes his eyes and sighs. This must really be the end, and he's been sentenced to an eternity of nothingness.

"David, *my darling*, open your eyes," Lucie says.

David reluctantly opens his eyes and looks up into Lucie's pale, round face.

"You've got a lot of explaining to do, and not a lot of time to do it," Lucie murmurs. "Would you care to tell me about this angel of yours?"

"I made a mistake," David says.

"Yes, *my darling*, a mistake that has cost you your life, it would seem," Lucie says, her perfect lips tugging downward into a frown. "It's a shame, too. I really liked you."

"I can't die," David groans. "I'm so close. You have to send me back again."

"Why would I do that?" Lucie asks, tucking a strand of her chocolate curls behind an ear. "You double-crossed me."

"I didn't mean to," David says. "I was trying to help."

"You knew I needed those angels dead," Lucie says. "I told you so."

"I know," David says, "but she was only going to live long enough to help me get rid of Graggöry, and then I was going to end her, I swear."

"A whole lot of good she did you," Lucie laughs. "Talk about plans backfiring."

"Lucie, forgive me," David says. "I can fix this."

"How can you? You're dead, my darling. Absolutely dead," Lucie says.

"You can bring me back, just like before."

"You're rather mangled," Lucie points out. "You're missing... crucial pieces."

"I have Jeremy's plans," David says. "In my office, on my desk, in a notebook. There are blueprints and instructions. You can have them turn me into a cyborg, like Io—the angel—and I can end her for you."

"And General Lysithea," Lucie says. "She's one, too."

"I suppose if you bring me back, I'll kill her too."

"Or you'll cross me for a second time," Lucie says. She lifts her hand, curling her fingers as she looks down at her nails. "I can't have that."

David tries to sit up, but he's weighed down by something he cannot see. "Dammit, Lucie, I'm telling you I'll fix it."

"I don't know," Lucie says. She drops her hand and looks down at him.

"Please, Lucie," he says. "I can fix this."

"I'll let you live, if you convince me."

"And how should I go about doing that?" David asks.

"Do you love me?"

"What does that have to do with anything?"

Lucie frowns. "Oh, so you don't love me, then?"

"I do," David groans. "I love you, and I'm sorry."

"I'm not convinced," Lucie says. "Try harder."

"I've loved you since the first moment I saw you," David says.

"Hmm," Lucie mutters. "I suppose, if you *promise* you'll kill them all—that girl, and the general, and Graggöry—I will forgive you, and give you another chance."

"I'll do it," David says. "I'll do anything you want."

"You've said that before," Lucie reminds him.

"I mean it this time," David says. "Please believe me."

"I always did have a thing for liars," Lucie says. She reaches her hand out to him. "Come, let's go. We've not much time, my darling, we have to hurry."

He reaches up, realizing he can move again, and takes her hand.

She pulls him up and tugs him along with her deeper into the darkness.

Io

Somewhere

Io walks down the long, narrow road, toward the beautiful, towering gates. The closer she thinks she gets, the further away the gates become. She frowns and pauses, looking at her surroundings once more. Everything is in ruin, and there is no sign of anyone else—she is completely alone here. She looks back to the gates, and knows that her family is there, behind them. She wants more than anything to pass through to the other side. She would do anything to be with her family again.

"You cannot go there," a voice says from behind her.

She turns to face an elderly man, cloaked in white. Their eyes meet, and she shivers. His irises are blue and green and brown and gold and lavender—every color she can imagine—and they look as though they have seen an eternity. He smiles at her, and nods, like he knows what she's thinking.

"Why?" she asks, at last. "Why can't I go?"

The man shakes his ancient head and looks toward the gates.

"It is not your time," he says. "You must go back."

She thinks of the world she has left behind, of how cruel and dark and cold it is. Beyond the gate, she knows there is a paradise waiting, something more beautiful than even her beloved Spiritus Vallem. She lifts her hand over her heart, clutching at her white robe. There is a longing there, deep in her soul.

"I don't want to go back," she says. "I want to be with them."

"I know," he tells her, looking back to her. He smiles. "I know what it means to miss someone. I know your heartache."

"Then let me go through," she pleads. "Let me go to Paradise."

"I cannot," he says. "You must go back."

"There's nothing left there," she says, thinking of her last moments. Jeremy was probably dead. Her sister was a traitor. David had won.

"You're wrong," he says, like he's read her mind again. "Your story is not over, yet, my child. There are people who still need you, people you can still save, if you are brave enough."

"I'm not brave," Io says. "I'm tired and I want to be with my family."

"You are very brave, Io," he says.

"I want to be with my family," she says again.

"I'm sorry," he says. "You can't be with them."

"When?" she asks.

"You know I cannot say."

She lets out a sigh and turns her gaze away from the gate. She chews on her bottom lip thinking. Perhaps, if she goes back, things can be mended.

"Do you think I can save them?" she asks.

"Some of them, yes," he tells her.

She considers this.

"I will go back," she finally tells him. "I will finish what's been started."

"I knew you would," he says with a smile. He motions to the way she's come. "Go back, Io."

Io nods, giving the gates one more fleeting glance before looking back to him.

"But Lord," she asks, realization dawning on her, "how will I know what to do next?"

"You will know," God says. "You're a clever girl."

She nods and turns from him, starting back down the road.

Lysithea
Neo Victoria

Lysithea walked down the sidewalk, kicking at clumps of ashen mush with every step. She shoved her hands in the pockets of her jacket, wishing she had brought a thicker coat with her. Thinking back to the last place she saw Io, she paused and turned around. She had to hurry. After she had heard the news about David, she feared the worst for her sister. Every member of the Core was looking for her now, and they weren't planning on taking her in alive.

"Io, where are you?" she whispered to the cold, steam slipping from her lips and dissipating into the air. "Come out, come out, wherever you are…"

She cut through an alley, and paused at the mouth, looking both ways down the desolate street. This would have been easier with Graggöry's help. She sighed and shook her head—he'd probably never speak to her again. She was a little peeved about it. True, she had lied to him about something rather important, but she had also obediently served him for the past five years—she had even killed for him. Did that really mean nothing? She frowned ad started down the street, watching her reflection in the windows of the abandoned homes that lined it.

"Io!" she called out and listened to her voice echo down the street, answered by nothing but the sound of the wind. "Io, please!"

Maybe Io was already dead and all of this searching was completely pointless. A part of her hoped it was true—that maybe she had died and she wouldn't have to suffer with the rest of them when the whole city fell to the rebels. There was still the part of her, however, that hoped beyond hope that Io was safe, that perhaps she had gotten out of the city alive, and she could start a new life somewhere else—somewhere far from Neo Victoria. News of her existence surely hadn't made it past the city's walls. Outside of Neo Victoria Io would be safe.

Maybe she should give up her search and go back to the palace, in a last ditch effort to get back in Graggöry's good graces. They were evacuating the capitol district already. If she knew Graggöry, he would still be in the palace, waiting to be taken by a rebel or a bomb. She could save him, if she hurried.

She cut back through a different alley, heading back in the direction she came. Somewhere in the center of the city, a bomb went off. The rebels had made it far enough into Neo Victoria that they would probably overthrow Graggöry and take the city by morning. She looked up into the dark, starless sky, and prayed to whoever was listening. In the morning, Neo Victoria would be nothing more than a fallen sanctuary, a graveyard of devastated homes, and a cage to a now fallen people. Sunrise was only an hour away. There wasn't much hope left for them.

"Please," she whispered to the dark street. "Please save my city."

She knew in her heart that the city would fall. It was her punishment. She never should have agreed to kill the angels in Spiritus Vallem. She should have told Graggöry the truth.

Another bomb went off, somewhere much closer to her now.

She tried to ignore the pang in her heart as she kept on toward The Palace. She tried to hold on to the last of her faith, but there wasn't much of it left. The city would fall. It was much too late.

Jeremy
Cathedral of Our Lady Victory

Jeremy opened his eyes to dim sunlight that flooded over him from the window next to the bed. He turned onto his side and stared out at the ashen snow. He hadn't slept very well, and only a little, and felt groggy, almost hung-over. He had been hoping beyond hope that yesterday's events had only been a dream, that Io and David weren't dead—that everything could still be saved, but when he had opened his eyes to see he was still in the church, all his hope had dissipated. He let out a slow breath and turned to stare at the ceiling. He supposed he should go see Io, but a part of him would rather stay in bed and not think about it.

This was entirely his fault, he had realized. Had he not been so ambitious, had he just succumbed to the fact that he was no longer in the Core, if he had just found something different to do—Io might still be alive.

No, he reminded himself, *the angels would have been killed either way.*

Io would have still died.

He let out a slow breath. Last night, he had decided there must be a god, and this god was cruel and cold and unforgiving. But there must be something greater than himself; something that sent him Io, something that gave him a glimpse of hope and took it from him all at once.

He turned his head to the closed door, pondering what he was going to next. They would have to bury Io. He frowned. If she had just stayed away, she would probably still be alive right now; but his Io was loyal and courageous and strong—definitely not afraid of David or the Core. Not even afraid of death. Despite everything, he smiled. He would never forget what Io had taught him yesterday.

He probably didn't have long to remember—the Core would find him and kill him soon enough. He frowned and sat up, pushing his legs off the bed. He sat there for a moment before reaching for his gun on the nightstand. He slipped it into his coat pocket as he stood up and made his way to the door.

No one was in the hallway as he made his way back to the sanctuary, which struck him as odd, but he shook off the feeling and continued on his way. He wasn't quite sure what he would do when he saw Io. He had so much to say to her, yet he knew she wasn't there anymore to hear it. Walking into the sanctuary, he stared down at his feet, not quite knowing if he was ready to see her. He walked along the narrow path between the pews and paused at the end, finally bringing himself to look up.

He blinked.

There was no body lying before the alter. Io was gone. He looked around, a little perplexed. What had happened to her? He frowned and scratched his head, turning to walk out of the sanctuary. Where had everyone gone? He bit his bottom lip and walked back into the sanctuary, a sinking feeling growing in the pit of his stomach. Perhaps, they had fled the cathedral, and perhaps they took Io, to scrap her metal and her organs.

Surely, not, he thought, sitting down on the first row of pews. He rested his head in his hands, his arms resting on his knees. *They wouldn't just take her, would they?*

Perhaps, they buried her and fled during the night, or the rebels had come and taken them somewhere—but wouldn't he have noticed that during the night. His confusion slowly turned into anger. He would never know what happened to her. He closed his eyes and let out a sigh. This was probably his punishment for everything he was going to put Io through, before he had changed his mind. His newfound god continued to become crueler by the second.

What was he supposed to do? He considered his options: hide out in the cathedral until he could come up with a stable, solid plan, or take his chances trying to get out of the city. He started trying to talk himself into leaving the city, when a noise behind him caught his attention. He reached into his pocket, wrapping his hand around the grip of the pistol.

"Jeremy?" said an oddly familiar voice.

He went rigid.

That voice belonged to Io, but that was completely impossible.

"Jeremy?" she asked again.

He considered his options. Either Io was really back from the dead—which he supposed wasn't completely far-fetched, or David had outsmarted him and had the Core scientists make a clone, just in case something had gone wrong with the real Io. He pondered what to do.

When he heard the ruffling of fabric as she began to walk down the aisle toward him, he jumped up, spinning around and drawing his pistol. He aimed it at her. This imposter certainly looked like Io, down to ever last detail, including her broken limbs.

"Stay right there," he said, his voice quiet. "Don't come any closer."

Io stared at him, wide-eyed. She lifted her hands up. "Okay, don't shoot."

He tried to see her eyes—to see if they were different—but the light coming through the open double doors behind her made it impossible. If she was a clone, and he had semi-talked his way into believing this, she was a pretty good one. He took a step toward her, the gun aimed at her chest.

"What did you do with Io?" he calmly asked. "Where is her body?"

"I'm right here, Jer," she said, tilting her head. "I'm me. This is my body."

"You're very convincing," Jeremy admitted, but kept his weapon drawn. "But Io is dead. I watched her die. I carried her dead body in my arms."

"I did die, but I've come back from the dead," Io said. She ran her flesh hand through her hair, moving it out of her face. "Look, I don't even have any weapons—my body is broken. Put your gun down."

"How do I know you're not a clone, sent from the Core to collect me?"

"I don't know," Io said. She bit her bottom lip. "Ask me something only the real Io would know."

"Okay," he said. He mulled over what to ask her.

"Well?" Io asked after a moment, shifting her weight uneasily from side to side. She crossed her arms in front of her chest. "Are you going to ask me something?"

"What did Io say to me through the door yesterday afternoon, before everything happened?" Jeremy asked.

"That's easy," Io said, perking up. "I said that I needed you and that I loved you, too. You didn't answer me, though, so I wasn't sure you heard me."

"I heard you," he said, lowering his weapon.

"Well, now that that's over and you're not going to shoot me, do you think I could maybe get a hug?" she asked, laughing. "I did just come back from the dead, you know. I'm a little traumatized."

Jeremy smiled and stuffed the gun back into his coat pocket before walking the rest of the way to where Io was standing. "I suppose you can have one hug."

Io threw her arms around him, burying her face into his neck.

"I'm so happy to see you, Jer. I thought you were dead."

"No, I'm very much alive," Jeremy said, wrapping an arm around her. "Completely unscathed, as you can see."

"And David?" Io asked.

Jeremy frowned. He did not really want to think of his brother. "He's dead."

"Oh," Io said. She squeezed him tighter. "I'm sorry. I know he was your friend."

"Yes, something like that," Jeremy said.

Io unwrapped herself from him, and looked around. "Where is everyone?"

"I suppose they left during the night," he said. "They were gone when I woke."

"Should we look for them?" Io asked. "What if—"

"I think we should leave the city," Jeremy said. "The chances of getting out without being caught are slim to none, but it's worth trying. We can't stay in this cathedral forever."

Io frowned and tilted her head. "I can't leave the city."

Jeremy blinked and gave Io a quizzical look. Why ever would she want to stay in a place where everyone wanted her dead? "What do you mean you can't leave the city?"

"My sister is here," Io said.

Jeremy raised an eyebrow. "You have a sister, and she's here?"

"Yes," Io said. "She left the valley five years ago. Her name is Lysithea."

"General Lysithea?" Jeremy asked. "Graggöry's girl?"

"I don't know who Graggöry is," Io said, "but yes, Lysithea is a general in the Core. I ran into her yesterday and she shot at me twice."

"And you want to go find her? Someone who clearly wants you dead?"

"I don't think she really wants me dead," Io said. "She missed both times, I think she was just shooting at me for show."

"Well, for your sake, I hope you're right," Jeremy said. He ran a hand through his hair and looked out the double doors, to where the sun, as dim as it may be, was trying to shine through the windows. "So, what's the plan?"

"You're going to go with me?" Io asked.

"I'm certainly not letting you go alone," Jeremy said, looking down at her.

"Where does Lysithea stay?" Io asked.

"With President Graggöry," Jeremy answered. "In The Palace."

"Good, we can start there," she said. She turned for the door. "Let's hurry."

"You want to go into the heart of enemy territory?"

"If you don't want to come with me, you can stay here, and I'll come back for you when I'm finished," Io said, a smirk tugging at her lips. "I didn't take you for a coward."

"I'm not a coward," Jeremy said, and it sounded convincing enough, though he wasn't sure whom he was trying to convince. "If you want to go to The Palace, I'll get you there."

He motioned for the door, starting down the aisle. Io followed behind him.

"What are you going to do once you find your sister?" Jeremy asked as they walked out of the front doors of the cathedral.

"Ask her to come with us," Io replied.

"And if she doesn't want to?"

Io frowned, glancing up at him. "I don't know."

"Well," Jeremy said, opening the gate for her. "I suppose it's worth a try."

Io nodded, and stepped out onto the sidewalk, turning back to wait for him. He closed the gate behind him and reached out to take her hand. Tugging her along, he started down the sidewalk. This was completely crazy, but he would do it or die trying, because that's what Io was going to do.

Lucie

A Core Laboratory

"It's done, miss," a man with a long face and pointed nose said from the doorway of the operating room. He pushes his small, round spectacles up the ridge of his nose. "He should be waking up soon, if you would like to come see him."

Lucie looks up. She sets the book she is reading down with a snap. She sets it down and stands up, straightening the bottom of her dress with her hands. "That didn't take long."

"Thanks to the detailed direction he left, miss, he didn't have any problems fixing him up—of course, until we can do something about it, his face won't be entirely reconstructed. I'm afraid he looks rather frightening, this way."

Lucie walked into the room, pausing at the doorway in front of the man. She bit her bottom lip as she stood on her tiptoes to peer down over David from a distance. His face looked like a metallic skull, no longer the devilishly handsome face from before. She would have to make his brother pay for that.

"And what of his thoughts?" Lucie asked, glancing from David back to the scientist. "Will he be himself, or—is he someone new entirely?"

"Thanks to a little invention his brother made," the man said, seeming to hesitate when he brought up Jeremy. "We were able to download all his brain functions, his thoughts, his feelings, et cetera, onto a chip that we installed in his new 'brain.' Though, there could be some glitches, he should be as good as knew, and still himself, miss, don't worry."

She let out a sigh of relief. "Well that's certainly good to know."

The man nodded, and walked back over to where David lay on the operating table, making a few minor adjustments before David had the chance to wake up. Lucie walked over to him and reached out to stroke David's metallic cheek.

"My poor, poor darling," Lucie said. "We'll get our revenge, don't you worry."

The man gave a sideways glance at her. She smiled.

"Listen, darling," she said to the man. "Could you perhaps bring in your team? The surgeon and the metal worker and the sorcerer? I would like to thank you all, personally."

"Certainly, miss. I will call for them."

The scientist left the room for a moment and came back with the rest of them. After they filed into the room, Lucie walked to the door and closed it, locking it as she turned around to face them.

"Gentlemen, I would like to thank you," she said, facing them. She smiled. "You did an excellent job with my darling David, but unfortunately, this is the end of the line for you."

She flexed her fingers, her fingernails growing out into sharp blade-like claws.

"I'm sorry," she said as her disguise slipped away, revealing her true self to them, "but I have to kill you all now."

The men stared at her in horror, before one reached out to grab a scalpel. She chuckled. That certainly was not going to save him. She took a step toward them and willed the lights to turn out, before tearing them to pieces, one by one. When she was done, she turned the lights back on and slipped back into her disguise. She couldn't bear to let David see her in her true form. The shame she felt was almost too much.

Turning her attention back to the table, she licked the blood from her hands. On the table, David let out a sigh, and turned his body, opening his haunting, robotic eyes. She smiled down at him and hurried to his side, un-strapping his arms, one flesh, the other metal, from the table.

"David, my darling," she said. "I'm glad you're awake."

"I feel... different," he said, looking down at his hands.

"You look different," Lucie pointed out. "You have some metal on your lovely face, and your eyes are... well, they're not really your eyes, but... I did what I could to save you."

"Thank you," David said. He sat up, his metallic face twisting into a grimace. "Well, the pain is certainly not normal, but I suppose it will subside with time."

"You did just come out of an operation," Lucie said. "It's going to take some time to recover."

"Time is not on our side," David said. "We have to hurry. The sooner we end those fools, the better."

"I agree," Lucie said, "but don't you want to rest?"

"I can rest after they're all dead," David said. He swung his legs off the table and slid off, standing before Lucie. "I'm going to right my wrongs, and then the both of us shall get what we want."

293

"Oh, how lovely," Lucie chirped, clapping her hands together as they left the room.

Crosbie and Jynx
The Metal Shop

Crosbie peered down into the dark metal shop, frowning.

"He's not here," he said to Jynx, who was busy turning circles in the kitchen.

"Well, where could he be?" Jynx asked, coming to a halt. She wobbled over to him, peering into the dark room. "He should have been home hours ago."

"I don't know," Crosbie said, "but I don't like it."

Jynx frowned and leaned against the door jam, still looking down into the dark. "Should we go after him? This isn't like Max."

"Maybe he's still at the palace," Crosbie said. "Maybe he got held up there."

"He would have called," Jynx said. She took a deep breath to keep herself from panicking. "Have you sent him a message?"

"I did hours ago," Crosbie said. "There was no reply."

"Maybe something didn't go right with the job," Jynx said. "Maybe he's just really busy trying to fix something."

"It was a simple job, I don't think that's the case," Crosbie said. "But maybe."

Jynx sighed. She pushed away from the door jam and walked into the kitchen, nervously pushing in all the chairs at the table.

"Okay," Crosbie said after a moment. "Let's go look for him."

"Really?" Jynx asked, perking up. "At the capitol?"

"Yeah," he said. "We'll start there."

"I've never been to The Palace before," Jynx said. "I bet it's wonderful."

"It's really not anything special," Crosbie said.

"Oh," Jynx said, a bit disappointed.

"We'll have to be careful," Crosbie said. "All the districts from here to the capitol have been evacuated… there could be rebels or bombs or—"

"Maybe we shouldn't go," Jynx said, crossing her arms in front of her chest.

"Ah, don't chicken out on me now, Jynx," Crosbie said, a smirk tugging at his lips. "We'll be okay."

Jynx looked from him to the door and back to him again. "Okay. I'll go."

Crosbie grabbed his coat of the back of his chair at the table and shrugged it on. He picked up Jynx's coat and tossed it to her. She slipped her arms into it, and he chuckled at how delicate she looked.

"Man, if the enemy does catch us, you're a goner, sister," he laughed.

"Thanks," Jynx said, rolling her eyes. "Let's just hope the enemy doesn't catch us."

"Right," Crosbie chuckled. "Come on, let's go find dad."

"Right," Jynx said, and followed him out the door.

Graggöry
The Palace

The last of the city was being evacuated, but to where the evacuees were going, he had no earthly idea. The outer cities had fallen to the rebels, weeks ago. He had decided before the sun had made its way into the sky, that he would stay and watch the city fall. Either the rebels would kill him, or David—somehow miraculously back from the dead—would. It didn't matter to him at this point. He was going crazy and he had nothing to live for. He had failed everyone.

How many people would he have to let down before he died?

He let out a breath, his shoulders slumping.

Since he had kicked Lysithea out, the voices had subsided. Had he ever been hearing them to begin with? Did all of these crazy thoughts to kill Lysithea stem from his own fear of failing? He couldn't know. Instead, he sat in eerie silence, waiting to die. He deserved it, for what he had done. He deserved worse than death, really. He leaned back in his chair.

He supposed he ought to be proud of himself. He'd kept his composure pretty well the last few weeks without the help of any magic. He hadn't killed Lysithea.

He frowned.

He wondered if Lysithea had found her sister, and if they had made it out of the city. Every member of the Core wanted her sister dead. They would blindly follow David until the end, and it seemed as though the end was nearing. He closed his eyes, when suddenly his office doors creaked open. He kept his eyes closed, not really caring if it was David come to kill him.

"Graggöry? It's me," Lysithea said, walking into the room. "I know I'm the last person you want to see, but… I've come to apologize."

He opened an eye to look at her. Sure enough, there was Lysithea, standing in front of his desk, her face dirty from the ash, her hair disheveled from the wind. She was watching him with concerned lavender eyes. He supposed her eyes were beautiful. She was beautiful. He smiled. Maybe he was imagining this. Maybe Death had come to him in the form of his angel.

"I'm sorry," she said, shifting her weight from side to side as she grabbed at her arm, nervously. "I know I lied to you about being an angel, but I promise I didn't lie about anything else."

"I know," he finally said. "I'm sorry. I was angry."

"I know you're angry with me," Lysithea said. "I'm angry with myself."

Graggöry gave her a sad smile and glanced behind her shoulder at the dim lit hallway. "I suppose you didn't find your sister?"

"No," she said. "I stopped looking and came back to get you."

"To get me?" he asked.

"Yes, everyone is evacuating. I know you, though, Graggöry. I knew you would be here, waiting."

He chuckled.

"Your death wish is not funny," Lysithea said, shaking her head.

"You were right, by the way," Graggöry said, "about David."

"What about him?" she asked.

"He was plotting to murder us," Graggöry said, leaning his head back against the chair. "He was talking to someone who... who sounded like a voice in my head. I haven't quite figured it out yet, but I should have listened to you."

"He was your friend," she said. "I understand why you didn't want to believe me."

He nodded his head and let out a sigh.

"We should probably get out of here," she said. "Before David finds us."

"I ought to stay," Graggöry said. "I ought to face all this."

"Don't be crazy, love," Lysithea said, a frown threatening her lips. "Come with me. Let's leave together."

He considered this. Perhaps, he could go with her. They could figure this out together. He would like that. He wanted to be with her. It might be too dangerous though. He could still kill her.

"Please," she said. "You're the only thing I have left in this world. My sister is probably dead. My family is gone. Let me save you."

It pained him to see her this distraught.

"All right," he said, sighing. He pushed his chair away from his desk, standing. He gave one quick glance around the office before walking around the desk. He reached out and placed the palm of his hand onto her cheek. "If we, for one reason or another, don't make it out of this alive, Lys... I failed at everything I've tried to do, I have probably failed you the most, but... you are the greatest thing that has happened in my life, and I love you."

She blinked, leaning her head into his touch. "I could say the same thing."

He leaned down and kissed her forehead. "Let's go, love."

"All right," she said. She glanced out the window at the snow, before grabbing his hand. Together they walked out of the room and into the hallway. Somewhere close by a bomb exploded and rattled the palace. She gripped his hand tighter. He squeezed her fingers, trying to reassure her that they would be okay. He looked down the hall and supposed he was ready for whatever happened next.

Io

The Capitol

Io followed Jeremy down an alleyway somewhere in the capitol district, keeping a close eye out for anyone dressed in Core attire. There were hardly any people left. All the buildings they passed were empty. The bombs had not yet reached this far into the city, but they were getting closer by the minute. Every so often, another went off, and rattled the buildings that lined the street.

"How much further?" Io asked, tugging on Jeremy's hand. He peered around the corner of the mouth of the alley, and then looked back down at her.

"The Palace is just right over there," he said, gesturing to a large while marble building. "It looks like the Core has already evacuated, I haven't seen anyone in a long time."

Io looked at the palace and then started down the street before Jeremy tugged her back into the alley.

"You can't just go walking out there like that," Jeremy said. "Just because we can't see them, doesn't mean they aren't there. We've got to be careful."

He led her out of the alley and to the other side of the street. She watched as he peered around the next corner before tugging her along with him. "Come on, we'll go through the back."

"Do you think they're still in there?"

"Maybe," he said. They ran to the other side of the big open square in front of The Palace, seeking shelter in the narrow alley beside it. Io pressed up against the marble, taking a deep breath. They had made it. She smiled and closed her eyes, tilting her head up to the sky. She let her breath out with a sigh, opening her eyes to glance at Jeremy.

"Come on," he said. "The door is over here."

Io nodded and followed him down the alley. They stopped in front of the door, and Io reached out, wrapping her fingers around the knob. She glanced at Jeremy who nodded, his hand wrapped around the gun in his coat pocket, just in case, she guessed.

She yanked on the door, tugging it open just as someone pushed it open. Jeremy drew his gun, his intake of air making a faint hiss in the silence.

Io jumped back, letting go of the door, a little surprised squeak escaping her lips.

"Hands up," Jeremy barked, motioning for the two figures in the doorway to step out into the alley.

"Io!" one of the cried. "Oh, Io, you're alive!"

Jeremy looked to Io, and then to the woman in the doorway and back to Io. Io, who was clutching her chest, glanced up to them, a slow smile spreading across her face.

"Sister!" she exclaimed. She rushed forward and threw herself on Lysithea, clutching her. "Oh, Lysithea!"

Jeremy dropped his hand down to his side, slipping the pistol back into his pocket. Io pulled away from Lysithea and held her at arm's length, looking her over. She looked well, only a little ruffled.

"What are you doing out here?" Lysithea asked her. "The Core is looking all over for you, Io… they'll kill you if they find you."

"I came to find you," Io said. She glanced to the man standing at Lysithea's side before looking back at her sister. She dropped her hands down to her sides and took a step back. "What are you doing?"

"We're escaping," Lysithea said. "David is looking for us. He's trying to take power. He wants to kill Graggöry and overtake the city."

Io gave her a skeptical look before turning to Jeremy.

Jeremy had gone pale.

Jeremy
The Capitol

He stared at General Lysithea in disbelief. There was no way David could possibly be alive. Jeremy had him shot him point blank in the head. No one could come back from that.

Lysithea must have seen the look he was giving her, because she turned to him, a hesitant, sympathetic look spreading across her face. She chewed on her bottom lip, the same way Io did when she was thinking about something.

"David is dead," he said, to clarify. "I would know."

"Yes," the man, President Graggöry said. "You would know."

Lysithea gave Graggöry a disapproving glance before turning to Jeremy. "He was dead… but apparently he had your blueprints in his office. The Core scientists brought him back to life and reconstructed his body, using those blueprints."

"How could he have had any of my blueprints?" Jeremy asked. He pointed to his pocket. "I have them all right here, and I destroyed my home so he wouldn't get them."

This whole story was completely impossible. There was no way he could have gotten any of the blueprints… unless he had memorized them. *That bastard*, Jeremy thought, silently cursing his brother.

"That's not the point," Lysithea said. She frowned. "The point is, he's somehow miraculously survived your fatal gunshot wound to his head, he's been turned into some sort of killing machine, and now he's not going to stop coming after us until we're all dead."

"I see," Jeremy said through his teeth. He looked to Io, who was looking at Lysithea with a peculiar expression painted on her face. He had to get Io out of the city at all costs. There was no way he was going to let David kill her twice. "Then we should go."

"Where will we go?" Lysithea asked.

"Clearly, we need to leave the city," Graggöry replied. "That's our best bet."

"No," Io said.

They all turned to face her. She ran her hand through the length of her messy onyx curls.

"We can't leave the city," Io said. "We should stay and fight."

"Neo Victoria has fallen," Graggöry said. "There's nothing left to fight for."

"No, we don't need to fight for Neo Victoria," Io said. "We can worry about the city later. Our priority right now should be coming up with a plan to defeat David. If we run away, David will get what he wants, right?"

"Io, that's completely crazy," Jeremy said. "We can't just take on some super weapon."

"I'm a super weapon, remember?" Io asked, rolling her eyes. "I can do anything he can do."

"Correction: you could do anything he can do, but now your arm and leg are completely useless," Jeremy said.

Lysithea looked Io over. "Can't we fix her?"

"We don't have a blacksmith, nor a trained sorcerer," Jeremy said. "I have all the blueprints, but they're completely useless without those two things."

A noise at the mouth of the alley caused them all to turn, Jeremy and Lysithea grabbing their weapons.

At the end of the alley, two heads were peering back at them.

"Jer," Crosbie said. "I think we can help you."

"Guys!" Jeremy said, almost falling to his knees.

"Who are they?" Lysithea asked, her gun still trained on Crosbie.

"Put your gun down," Jeremy said. "These two are my friends!"

"I'm Crosbie, the blacksmith's son—I can fix her limbs," Crosbie said, reaching out a hand to Lysithea.

"And I'm his sister, Jynx," Jynx said, and snapped her fingers. A flame formed. "I know how to power them."

Crosbie

The Capitol

"I can't believe we found you!" Crosbie said.

"What are you two doing here, anyway?" Jeremy asked. "The city's evacuated."

"We came to look for Max," Jynx said. She leapt for Jeremy, wrapping her arms around him as tightly as she could. "I've missed you so, Jer! You were away for a long time."

Jeremy hugged Jynx but pulled away after a moment.

"What happened to Max?" he asked Crosbie.

Crosbie glanced at the others and shook his head. "I think David got him."

"He hasn't contacted us since he came here," Jynx said.

President Graggöry and Jeremy exchanged glances.

"Well, let us help each other then," Jeremy said. He took a step to the side and gestured to the others in the group. "This is Io. I'm so glad you finally get to meet her."

"Didn't know anything 'bout her," Crosbie said, and reached for her hand. She was really pretty, even though she looked like a mess. "Pleasure to meet you, Miss Io."

Io took his hand and smiled, "The pleasure's all mine."

"This is Lysithea," Jeremy said, shooing Crosbie's hand away from Io's. "She's Io's sister, and also—"

"You're President Graggöry's girlfriend," Crosbie said. "Nice to meet you."

"It's nice to meet you too," Lysithea said.

Jynx was fidgeting beside Crosbie.

"I think we ought to get back home," Jynx said, "before we're found."

"Good point," Crosbie said. He turned to Jeremy and gave him a smile. "Well, Jer, let's get Io back to my place, and we can fix her up. What do you say?"

"Sounds like a plan," Jeremy said.

"This way, guys," Crosbie said, taking Jynx's hand.

They made their way out of the alley and back to the shop.

David
The Palace

"They couldn't have gone far, and they must be shielding themselves with magic, because I can't find them myself," Lucie said, her voice laced with annoyance. "But don't fret, my darling. We'll find them soon."

"Neo Victoria is a large city," David said, as he slid his hand across the holographic screen in Graggöry's office. He was looking at maps of the city. "We just have to keep looking."

"What will you do when you find the girl?" Lucie asked. "She's the only one who can probably stop you."

"If she isn't dead, she's broken," David said. "I saw it. She fell apart in the alley behind Jeremy's house, when I thought I killed her."

"How lovely," Lucie said. "It should be easy to kill the others, then."

"Of course," David said. He closed the computer screen and walked to the window, looking out at the desolate street. "We'll search for them in the morning."

"All right," she said. "I'll be going for now, then, my darling."

"Goodnight, then," David said from the window.

"Goodnight," Lucie chirped, as she stepped through her portal.

David frowned. Where could they all have gone, and was Io even with them? He was so sure he had killed her. Shrugging, he stepped away from the window and made his way to the open door. It didn't matter if she was still alive or not—tomorrow he would find them and kill every last one of them, and after that, he would save Neo Victoria and run the Core the way it should have been running all along.

He stepped out into the hall and made his way toward his room.

It would certainly be simple enough to do, and he would finally get what he wanted. Tomorrow, everything would fall into place. He only needed patience, just for tonight.

Io

The Metal Shop

Io sat patiently on the long worktable inside of Crosbie's father's shop, watching as Jeremy and Crosbie carefully fitted her new arm onto her body. They had been busy for most of the night, Crosbie building her leg, and Jeremy searching his blue prints in hopes of upgrading her, so she wouldn't fall apart again.

"I think we'll be fine, even if it does fall apart again," Jeremy said as he idly twisted a screwdriver with one hand, the other being used to flip through blueprints on the blue shimmering screen to his side. "We'll have Jynx with us, and if it falls apart, she can use her magic to fix it."

"I don't know how good I am at magic," Jynx said. "I can easily do it when I'm taking my time, but who knows how I will perform under pressure."

"You'll be fine," Io said with a smile. "I have faith in you."

"Yeah, Jynx, you're amazing," Jeremy said.

"You ought to listen to Io," Lysithea said from the doorway. "She's a Seer. I bet she already knows how this is all going to end."

Jynx turned to Io, eyes wide. "Do you know?"

"I've only had one vision about this," Io said. She looks to her sister and frowns. "It's hard to say how this will turn out for sure. It is possible to change fate."

"How?" Jynx asked. "I thought fate was a fixed sort of thing."

"No," Io said, smiling. "Sometimes peoples' paths are changed."

"I see," Jynx said. "Hopefully fate is in our favor."

Io closed her eyes and smiled.

Jeremy stopped fiddling with her arm. She opened her eyes turned her gaze to him, only to realize he was staring right at her.

"You don't have to do this, Io," he said, frowning. "It's dangerous and idiotic and—"

307

"The only way we are going to defeat him, is if I stand up and fight," Io said, reaching out to fluff up his hair. "It's the right thing to do. I was sent back to make things right, and I intend to do so."

"You sure are brave," Crosbie said as he finished screwing on her new leg.

"Or she has a death wish," Graggöry said from the kitchen.

"I've conquered death, twice," Io laughed. "What more is there to be afraid of?"

"Well if we can't talk you out of it, I suppose we'll stand with you," Lysithea said, pushing away from the door jam and walking down into the workshop. "You never cease to amaze me, little sister."

Io smiled, feeling brave but also feeling a little uneasy. There was no way to know for sure if she could actually defeat David unless she tried, but that miniscule chance of failure was eating her up inside. These people were counting on her—the fate of Neo Victoria, of perhaps even the world—was in her hands.

"We should rest," Io finally said, yawning. "We have a long day ahead of us tomorrow."

"You're right," Jeremy said. "This is enough for tonight. We'll do a system check in the morning and decide what to do from there."

Io slipped off the table and stretched her arms over her head. "Everything will look better after a good night's sleep."

Crosbie lead them all back up the stairs and out of the workshop. They laid blankets down on the floor and found as many pillows as they could. He apologized for not having enough beds, but Io assured him it was all right.

"This is perfect," Io said, reassuringly.

They all settled down for the night and drifted off into uneasy sleep.

Bright sunlight is shimmering in through the open window of the cottage. Io lounges on a pillow, her arms resting on the window seal, her head pressed against her palms. It is so peaceful here, in the valley—here in her dreams. Fabric rustles behind her, but she keeps still, looking out the window at the wildflowers that are fluttering in the wind.

"Sissy," Kale says, his voice just as bright as the room. "I miss you."

She pulls away from the window and turns toward her little brother, a soft, sad smile stretching her lips. "I miss you, too."

He comes to sit down in front of her, taking her hand with his tiny one. He looks at her with a very knowing glance—his lips stretched into a serious, perplexed smile.

"It won't be very long now," he says to her.

She doesn't know what he means. "Very long until what?"

"What momma is always talking about," Kale says. "It's almost time."
Her little brother is very wise for being so small.
"Yes," she says. "It's almost time."
"I love you," Kale says. "No matter what happens, I want you to be strong."
Those were her words to him. She smiles. "I will be, I promise."
He smiles, and just as it began, the dream ends.

Io and Jeremy
The Metal Shop

Jeremy opened his eyes and turned his head, so he could see the window on the kitchen door. The sun had barely just come up. He looked over at Io, who was still sound asleep and frowned. Today was the day—and he was not exactly looking forward to it. He had hoped that somebody would have tried to talk her out of it by now, but no one had. In fact, they all seemed content with letting Io risk her life to save their own. He sighed and closed his eyes, lifting a hand to rub his temple.

When he opened his eyes again, Io was staring back at him, still groggy from sleep. She smiled, and he smiled back. She sat up, yawning.

"Jer," she whispered. "Let's go in the other room and talk."

He nodded and pushed away the covers, before standing and helping her up. They walked to the workshop door, and Jeremy opened it for her. She stepped down into the dark room, flipping on the light switch as she walked down the stairs.

"What do you want to talk about?" Jeremy asked, closing the door behind him.

He followed Io to the table and helped her up to sit on it. She swung her legs back and forth as she leaned back, her arms stretched out behind her to help hold her up. He wondered if she was cold; after all, she was wearing the pair of pajama shorts Jynx had let her borrow for while they had worked on her leg yesterday.

"Lysithea told me something yesterday that I didn't know," Io said.

For a moment, Jeremy's heart sunk. If it had come out of Lysithea's mouth about him, it was probably something bad. He took a step toward her and nervously ran a hand through his mussed hair.

"What was that?" he asked, biting his bottom lip.

She gave him a sort of sympathetic look. "He's your brother."

"Oh," Jeremy said, a little relieved. "Yeah."

"I didn't know," Io said. "I thought you were just—you killed your brother."

"Well, I don't know if you've heard," Jeremy said, teasing her a little because he didn't care much for the look on her face, "but he's marvelously back from the dead."

"Don't be silly," Io laughed, shaking her head. "I'm trying to be serious here."

"I'm sorry," Jeremy said. "Please, carry on."

"I just wanted to tell you that… that I know it must be hard," Io said, "and that I'm terribly sorry that you had to do that."

"Don't fret about it, much, love," Jeremy said. "It was a long time coming."

Io's lips curved from a frown into one of the most beautiful smiles he had ever seen. "You called me love this time."

"I did?" Jeremy asked. He bit the inside of his cheek. "Oh, so I did."

"Say it again."

"What?"

"You know what."

"Love?"

"Yes," she laughed.

He reached out to cup her face in his hands. "Love."

She laughed a little but then her face became solemn.

"Jeremy, if things don't go the way we're hoping—"

He lifted a finger to her lips. "Things will go splendidly. You're absolutely amazing, Io."

"It's just that—"

"You were brought back for a reason, love," he said, he ruffled her hair and then dropped his hands to his side. "You've got this. Besides, you'll also have me and Lysithea and Jynx. Lysithea and I have weapons, and Jynx has her magic. It's going to be okay."

He wasn't sure if he was trying to convince her, or himself. He still felt uneasy about the whole matter, but he knew in his heart that this was the way things had to be. Io had been sent back from the dead to help protect everyone from the evils of a world ruled by David. Though he would miss his brother, he supposed it was better to put David out of his misery before it was absolutely too late. Things had already happened that could not be undone.

"Jeremy?" Io asked, bringing him out of his train of thought.

He looked down at her and smiled, reaching out to move a strand of her hair behind her ear.

"Io, I love you," he said. "I'm not going to let anything else happen to you."

"I know," she said, and smiled. "I love you, too."

They watched each other for a long time in silence, before Io looked back to the door. She tilted her head, her hair falling into her face.

"You know; your friends are pretty great. Do you think we ought to wake them up? We do need a game plan," Io said, glancing back at Jeremy.

"Yes they are, and I suppose we ought to," he said. He started for the door. "You wait here. I'll go fetch the others."

"All right," Io said. "I'll be waiting."

She leaned back, watching him go.

A new, almost giddy type of nervousness settled over her.

Lysithea
The Metal Shop

Lysithea walked down the steps that lead to the metal shop, clutching her mug of coffee and trying to not spill it as she went. She walked over to the table and took a sip of the coffee before smiling at Io. Io smiled back. She hadn't seen Io in five years and, not surprisingly, she had changed quite a bit—they both had, she had to admit. Lysithea was not the same, frightened, eighteen-year-old girl that had left the valley on that winter's night when Io had asked her to stay.

"It's been a long time," Lysithea said.

"Yes," Io replied, kicking her legs to and fro. "I had thought I would never see you again, Lys."

Likewise, Lysithea thought, but did not say it. She had thought Io was dead, like the others—and it was her fault that had all died in a bloody, now unnecessary massacre. She took another sip of her coffee, wishing she knew how to apologize to Io. She supposed things would have come to this, regardless of if she had killed the angels or not—but at least the world had a fighting chance before. Now they had Io, and slim chances of making a significant difference. She hoped for the best outcome, watching her sister. Now that she had found her again, she didn't want Io to die at the hands of that power-hungry fool.

"Today is the big day, huh?" Lysithea asked, as Graggöry and Crosbie made their way down the stairs.

"Yes, but I'm ready," Io said. "I know in my heart this is the right thing to do."

"I hope your bravery doesn't get you killed," Graggöry said, coming up to stand beside Lysithea. "David is a cruel, unforgiving bastard, and he's cunning, too. More importantly than that, he's come back from the dead as a highly equipped killing machine, with a vengeance, which makes him an angry god."

"David is no god," Io said. "He can be killed, and I will kill him."

Lysithea continued to watch Io. Before, Io would never have talked about killing someone, at least not as off handedly as she did now. It was almost frightening.

Jynx and Jeremy joined them, Jeremy jumping up to sit beside Io on the worktable. Lysithea watched them, tilting her head. How interesting it was that things had turned out this way. She silently apologized to Jeremy for assuming the worst about him. She had thought that he had tormented her sister, making her into a, dare she say, monster, and the whole while forcing her to bend to his will. Clearly, it wasn't like that. In fact, it seemed they actually cared for each other.

"So what is the plan?" Jynx asked, pulling Lysithea from her thoughts.

"I think we should call him out somewhere," Io said. "He's looking for us, so we should pick a place and send him a message over the NESA to meet us wherever we choose."

"You *are* crazy," Graggöry laughed. "Forget the element of surprise, all-together. Just call him out, like you're going to have a playground fight after school!"

"You know he's got the whole Core under his control now, right?" Lysithea said. "We can probably beat David, but not the entire Core."

"Well," Io said with a smile, "I'm prepared. I don't need the element of surprise, and as for the Core, we'll defeat David and put Graggöry back in charge. Simple as that."

"All right," Lysithea said. "We'll call him out, but to where?"

"Imogen Square," Jeremy said.

"Why specifically there?" Lysithea asked, as she leaned again the table.

"That's where he should have died," Jeremy said. "He should have died the day those rioters blew up the square."

"Third time's the charm," Graggöry said, crossing his arms in front of his chest. "If Io can actually do this—perhaps this time we'll be lucky, and he'll not come back from the dead."

"We can use our NESA to send him a message," Crosbie said. "First, let's make sure Io is working."

"Make something, Io," Jeremy said, giving her arm a once over. "Anything."

Io looked as though she was thinking for a moment before the metal on her arm burst into the pieces, reconfiguring into a pistol.

"Looks like it's working, then," Jeremy said.

"Good deal," Jynx said. She laughed. "Glad to know I did it right."

Lysithea shook her head. "Come on, Graggöry. Let's go send him a message."

"The rest of us will get ready," Io said.

They all walked up the stairs.

David
The Palace

If a fight is what you're looking for, look no further, the message read. How cheeky Graggöry was being. *Meet me in Imogen Square at noon.*

He looked at his watch. He only had a few minutes, but what did that matter? There were no Core officers left in the city to go with him. He would have to face Graggöry, and perhaps Lysithea, alone.

"Lucie," he said, turning to where Lucie lay draped across the chair by the window. They were in Graggöry's office again. "They've called me out."

"How delightful," Lucie said, clapping her hands together. "What fun we'll have."

David rolled his eyes as he walked around the desk. He pulled up the computer screen and scrolled through the map of the city until he came to Imogen Square.

"I suppose so," David answered her.

He still needed to find Jeremy, and perhaps Io, if she somehow had survived. There was no telling where in the city he was hiding.

"We'll go take care of this problem first," David said to Lucie. "And then we'll find my brother and take care of him."

"I do hope we find them," Lucie said. "I want to watch them suffer."

"Don't worry," he said. "We'll find them."

Lucie sat up and stretched her arms over her head.

"Come, let's go," David said, and they left the room to head to the square.

Crosbie
Neo Victoria

Crosbie followed his newfound comrades down alleyways and roads as they made their way toward the square. Though he had his doubts, he felt mostly confident that Io could save them. She would follow through on their promise to avenge his father. He felt a sinking feeling in the pit of his stomach, and frowned.

His father was most likely dead.

He looked to Jynx who was busy following Io. Now she was all he had left. If things went south during this fight, he would make sure he pulled her to safety. He would give his life for Jynx. She had become more than just a clone of his sister—she was his sister now. He clutched his father's gun in his hand.

They came upon the square but kept to the alley. Jeremy peered around the corner at the mouth, and motioned for them to follow.

In the square stood a man, whose face was completely metal: a cyborg, just like Io. Standing next to him was a woman dressed in a dress the color of freshly spilled blood. They were talking to each other, the woman throwing her head back and laughing.

The group made their way into the square, their weapons ready.

"Well, well, well," the man called from across the way. "All of you made it. What a lovely surprise."

"David," Jeremy said. "This doesn't have to be the end."

"Oh, but doesn't it?" David said. "I know you've come to kill me."

David turned his attention to Crosbie and Jynx.

"And who might you be?" he asked.

Crosbie, who had been nervously chewing on the inside of his cheek, stood up a little straighter and said, "I'm Crosbie, and you killed my father."

David let out a chuckle. "Three reckless adults, two stupid kids, and a cyborg angel. How charming. Too bad you'll all be dying."

Crosbie lifted his gun. "Not if you die first."

317

David lifted his arm; the end of it had turned into a barrel. "I don't think you want to do that, kid."

To Crosbie's right, Jynx mutter an enchantment, and a thin veil of magic settled in front of them. She had made a shield.

"Oh, a magician," David said. "How lovely of you all to have brought entertainment."

Io stepped up beside Jeremy.

"David," she said. "This is the end."

"Hello, Io," David said. "It's nice to see you again."

Io let out a snarl. "I would say the same, but it's not true."

David took a step back and aimed the tip of his arm to Io.

Io

Imogen Square

Io's heart was racing. She took a deep breath trying to stay calm and steady. She didn't have the luxury to give into her fear now. *I'm strong and courageous*, she told herself. *I can change fate. I can defeat David.*

"I've come to kill you," Io said.

"Lovely," David said. "It's very cute how you think you can."

Io stepped forward and lifted her arm, the metal bursting apart to form a gun.

David kept his aim steady. "Perhaps, you should say your goodbyes. I'll give you a few moments."

"Io—" Jeremy said, suddenly stepping up beside her. "Look this way."

She turned her head toward Jeremy, keeping an eye on David. "Hmm?"

Jeremy took her face into his free hand and leaned forward, planting a kiss on her lips. He pulled away, dropping his hand back to his side. "Sorry, I had to do that. You know, just in case I die."

Io struggled to keep her cool, smiling as she turned her gaze fully back to David. "You're not going to die, Jer," she said.

"How touching," the woman said, stepping up beside David. "Don't you think so, my darling?"

David snickered, "Touching, my dear Lucie, however, tragic."

"It's a shame you lovely people have to die," Lucie said. "You're all very entertaining."

David aimed for Jeremy. "Now that you've gotten your last words in, brother, I believe it is time for us to say goodbye."

Before Jeremy had the chance to say something snide back, a shot rang out in the square. Io had no time to conjure up a shield with the metal on her leg. She looked to Jeremy in horror, as rather large bullet sped toward them.

To her left, Jynx stepped forward and mumbled something, conjuring a shield in front of Jeremy. Io sighed with relief and kept her gun aimed at David. She pulled the trigger, another shot ringing out across the square.

The bullet clanked off the hard metal of David's robotic arm, not doing any damage.

"You're going to have to try harder than that," David said, laughing. He aimed his gun for her, and shot off a few rounds. Io had made a shield and blocked the bullets, her wings suddenly protruding from her back. They glistened in the light. She lifted off the ground.

"David," Io said, after a moment, when he aimed his gun toward Crosbie and Jynx. "I'm your enemy, not them. Fight me, leave the others out of it."

"I would gladly fight you," David said. "I just wanted to watch you suffer first."

The metal configured into a bigger pistol, and Io shot it off at him from the sky, a laser bullet streaming out from the tip and making its way toward David. It hit his shoulder and melted a hole through the metal.

"Oh would you look at that," David said to Lucie. "I've made her angry."

He shot another round at her, the bullets hardly puncturing her shield.

"Why don't you come out from behind that thing and actually fight me? I didn't take you for a coward, Io."

Io sighed and the shield disintegrated, forming another, smaller gun. She reached out and grabbed it, aiming it at Lucie. "If you want it this way, then okay."

"That's a good girl," David said, another gun forming. He took it with his free hand and aimed it Jeremy. "On the count of three? One, two—"

"Three!" Io shouted, pulling her triggers.

A bullet hit her arm, another bouncing off of Jeremy's shield.

Lucie stumbled back, clutching her chest. "You shot me. David—that bitch just shot me."

David glanced to Lucie and then back to Io.

"I didn't think you had that in you," David said. "I'm truly amazed."

"You're trying to hurt my family," Io said, her wings lifting her even higher. "So I'm going to hurt yours, too."

Lucie pulled her hand away from her chest and looked at the crimson blood that coated it. She let out a cry and looked over to David. "Well? Stop playing with her and just finish this already!"

David sighed and rolled his robotic eyes. "Yes, dear. Whatever you say."

He opened fire at Io, who quickly dodged the bullets and opened fire on him. Jeremy, Lysithea, and Crosbie opened fire as well, their bullets hitting David and ricocheting off his arm and his head.

Io wondered if there was any way to actually kill him. If she could hit his heart, perhaps, they would have a chance. She lifted her gun and tried to aim as she continued to dodge his bullets in the air.

"Shoot his chest," Io called out to the others. "That's the only way we can wound him."

She shot her laser gun at him once more, the bullet melting a hole through his metallic skull. She supposed there wasn't any brain left in there—only wires and machines, keeping his body alive.

He cursed and stumbled back, before catching himself. The gun on his robotic arm disappeared and he lifted a hand to his head, feeling at the hole she had left there. He let out a snarl, and shot at her again, this time, the bullet sliced through her good shoulder. She flinched and bit her bottom lip as the pain coursed through her. Catching her breath, she counted in her head, trying to think of anything other than the pain. She lowered herself to the ground.

"Io!" Jeremy said and started for her. She motioned for him to stay where he was and lifted her gun back up, fighting the pain.

"Goodbye, David," she said through a grimace, and shot her weapon.

David stumbled back and fell to the ground, groaning in pain. Lucie looked down at him, and then to Io, who aimed her gun toward her. She stepped back and shook her head.

"No, I'm not going to die today," Lucie said, as a portal appeared behind her. She looked once at David and frowned. "Goodbye, my darling. I've not much use for you if you die and don't finish these horrible people off."

David cursed under his breath and lifted his gun to her. "You're not very useful either," he said, and pulled his trigger.

Io watched Lucie stumble back before catching herself. She lifted her hand to the new hole in her chest. Her crimson eyes flickered black and she hissed, stepping toward the portal.

"You shot me, you worthless bastard!" Lucie cried. "And to think I ever might have loved you!"

Io aimed Lucie's way and squeezed her hand on the trigger. She shot again, and the bullet skimmed the skin on Lucie's neck. Lucie cried out and stumbled toward the portal.

"I'll be back for you," she hissed at Io. "I'll be back for all of you."

She staggered to the portal and entered it, and before Io could get off another shot, the portal closed. Lucie had disappeared behind the veil.

"Damn," hissed Io, before she launched herself into the air again, hovering over where David lay on the ground. Her guns fused together to make one big one, and she aimed it at his chest.

David barked out a pained laugh and lifted his gun with what little strength he had left. "On the count of three."

"One," Io said, inching a little closer.

"Two," David said, his face twisting into a grimace.

"Three—"

Three shots echoed off the buildings around the square.

Graggöry
Imogen Square

Graggöry saw it coming, even before the bullet had left the barrel. He looked from David, to Lysithea, who was standing directly in the line of fire. He leapt forward, pushing Lysithea out of the way just as a sharp pain pierced through his chest.

"Graggöry!" Lysithea cried out, stumbling to the ground.

He blinked and let out a slow breath. He coughed, and blood speckled his hand. His chest burned. He fell to his knees, clutching the hole.

"Graggöry!" Lysithea cried again and scrambled over to his side. She looked down at the hole in his chest, her eyes wide and mortified as the blood spread across his shirt and vest.

"Lys," he said, struggling to speak. "It's okay. You're okay."

"But you're not!" she cried, clinging to him. "You're hurt."

"I'm fine, love," he said, though he knew he was not.

He looked to Io, who was staring back at them in horror. She glanced back to David and muttered something that he could not hear before one last shot rang out. David's body fell limp in the grass.

"She did it," he gasped, the blood choking him. "She really did it."

"Yeah," Lysithea said, stroking his cheek. "She saved us."

Pain surged through his body, causing him to double over. Lys let out a soft cry and continued to clutch him.

"I need to lie down," Graggöry said.

"Of course," Lysithea said. She helped him down onto the grass.

He coughed again, more blood splattering from his mouth.

"Lys," he said, very softly. "You're the greatest thing that ever happened to me."

"You said that," Lysithea said, wiping a tear from her eye.

"I know," he said. "I just wanted you to know, just in case..."

"You aren't dying," Lysithea whimpered.

Graggöry closed his eyes, shaking his head. He tried to breathe, but his lung was filling up with blood too quickly. He began to choke on his own blood.

"Graggöry," Lysithea said, clutching his arm.

He couldn't answer her. He couldn't breathe.

"Graggöry!" she cried, but he shook his head.

His world began to spin as he struggled to breathe. He reached up and took her hand, clutching it until everything began to fade, and he slipped into the peaceful dark.

Lysithea

Imogen Square

"No, no, no, no, no," Lysithea murmured over and over as she rocked Graggöry in her arms. "No, no, no, Graggöry, no…"

Jynx crouched down beside them, looking to Lysithea before her eyes fell onto Graggöry.

"Maybe I can help him," she said after a moment. "I can use my magic until we can get him help, Lys."

Lysithea looked up at Jynx through the tears in her eyes and smiled. "Please."

"I've never done this before, so I have no idea if it will work," Jynx said. "But I can try."

Lysithea watched her and nodded her head, numbly. "Anything is better than nothing."

Jynx placed her hand on Graggöry's chest and muttered a few words that Lys did not recognize. Graggöry's body emanated a purple glow.

"I'm using the magic to fix him," Jynx explained.

"To fix him?" Lysithea asked.

"Yes, to fix the hole in his lung," Jynx said. "I think it's working."

They sat like that for a few moments, but Graggöry never moved. Jynx pulled her hand from him, wiping the blood off on her jeans.

"This is all I could do," Jynx said. "It's up to him now."

"Thank you," Lysithea said. She leaned forward and hugged Jynx. "Thank you so much."

"Of course," Jynx said. "I don't know if it will work, but… I like the two of you. I don't want him to die."

Lysithea smiled and let Jynx go before she scooped Graggöry up, laying his head in her lap.

"You'll be okay, love," she whispered to him. "You're going to be okay."

Graggöry stayed unconscious, but she continued to stroke his hair and coo at him. She hoped beyond hope that Jynx had fixed him, and that he would live—though she did not deserve a miracle. She looked down at his gaunt face and smiled.

Maybe we all deserved another chance, she thought.

She looked up from Graggöry, noticing that everyone had gone completely quiet. She turned her gaze to where David lay in the grass, her eyes going wide with horror.

Io

Imogen Square

Io stared down at David's blood-spattered body and took a deep breath. Her weapons dissipated, and her hand fell to her stomach, where blood was gushing forth from the giant wound David had inflicted on her.

She took a shaky breath and turned to look at Jeremy, who was looking at her in pure horror. He stood there for a moment, staring, before rushing over to her. She collapsed to her knees beside David, her wings disappearing, and let out a groan. Pain surged through her body and blurred her vision. She fought the urge to pass out.

Maybe this was how she would end. She could finally be at peace. She could finally be with her family. God would not have to send her back. She had completed her task. She had saved Neo Victoria. She had saved the world from David.

Jeremy scooped her into his arms, and held her, rocking her as he murmured to her that she had done it, and that she would be okay, and that he loved her.

"I know," she whispered, her face contorting into a grimace

"It's going to be okay," he said.

"I'm tired," Io whispered. "I'm very tired."

"Don't close your eyes," he said. "Stay with me."

She shook her head, and lifted a bloodied hand to his face. "I've got to rest now."

"No," Jeremy said, tilting his head to her touch. "You've got to stay conscious."

"I... can't..."

"Io," Jeremy said. He stopped rocking her, looking down at her, his eyes wide and full of a terror she had never seen before.

"I'm sorry," she whispered.

"Io," he said again, a little more frantically.

"I love you," she muttered.

"I know," he said. "I know, but don't leave me."
She gave him a smile before closing her eyes.
A bright warm light was waiting for her.
I'm sorry, she thought, as she stepped through it.

Jynx

Imogen Square

"Jeremy," Jynx said, kneeling down beside David and Io's bodies. She reached out to touch Io, but Jeremy drew her back, away from Jynx's touch.

"I can help," she said, her voice just a whisper. "I can help her."

Jeremy set Io's body down in the grass and looked to Jynx.

Jeremy didn't notice David's robotic hand as it inched toward Io, latching onto Io's metal fingers.

"All right," he said, looking to Jynx. "Fix her."

She placed her hand over the hole in Io's stomach, grimacing at the warm blood as it coated her palm. She muttered her enchantment and Io's body glowed a dim purple.

Io's body came back together, the pieces slowly fitting back into place. The hole in her stomach closed, and the scratches on her face and arm began to disappear.

Jynx held her hand there, until the hole was gone.

"That's all I can do," she told Jeremy. "Until we can get help."

"Okay," Jeremy said.

He scooped Io up into his arms again and gently rocked her.

Jynx watched him, an unfamiliar feeling pitting itself inside of her. It was obvious to her that Jeremy loved this girl. What did that mean for her? She frowned.

"It will be okay," she told Jeremy. "I promise; it will be okay."

"Thank you, Jynx," Jeremy whispered, but never looked away from Io's lifeless body.

Crosbie
Imogen Square

Crosbie watched Jeremy and Io, and then Lysithea and Graggöry, before turning to his sister, who was wiping the blood from her hands.

"What will we do now?" he asked Lysithea. "Where will we go?"

"I don't know," Lysithea said. "We need to find help."

"Do you have anyone you can call?" Jeremy asked.

"Yes," Lysithea said. "I still have people who will be loyal to me, even if the rest of the Core has fallen."

"Send them a message," Jeremy said. "Tell them we need help."

Lysithea opened the screen on her watch and typed out a message.

"They're coming," Lysithea said, after a moment. "My officers are going to come help us."

"Where will we go from here?" Crosbie said. "We need medical supplies. We need a doctor."

"We'll figure it out," Lysithea said. "Someone can go for supplies and help."

Crosbie looked back to Jynx. They had successfully taken David down— Max was avenged. He supposed that he and Jynx didn't need to stay with the others anymore. They could go home if they wanted. They could evacuate the city with the others.

"We couldn't have done this without you," Lysithea said to him, like she had read his mind. "You're welcome to come with us."

"But where will we go?" he asked. "There isn't anywhere safe."

Jeremy
Imogen Square

Jeremy looked from Io to Crosbie, who was giving them a skeptical look. He sighed and scooped Io up into his arms. He carried her away from David and set her in the grass by Graggöry.

He thought for a moment, about what they could do, about where they could go. He looked to Io and then he looked up at the sky, shielding his eyes from the ash as it fell. He took a deep breath. They would have to chase the rebels out and reclaim their city somehow. They couldn't just let all of Neo Victoria fall to ruin. He supposed he would bring that up to them later, after they had gotten some rest and Graggöry and Io were better. There was still hope—things could be changed. That's what Io had said—fate wasn't fixed.

"We'll go to the cathedral," Jeremy finally said. He moved Io's hair from her face and looked back up at the others. "Until we can figure something else out, we'll go to Io's sanctuary."

They all nodded in silent agreement.

Lucie
Hell

Lucifer stood over David's hunched body, her claws digging into her palms as she looked down at him, a bit disappointed and a bit angry. She tugged on the chain that was wrapped around his neck.

"You shot me," she growled. "You actually tried to kill me."

"Forgive me, Lucie," he chokes. "I didn't mean—"

"No, no," Lucifer said. "It's 'Lucifer' now, not 'Lucie,' and you can't talk your way out of this one. Not this time."

She dragged the chain forward, walking along the dim lit hallway. He stumbled and crawled after her, tugging on the chain as it choked him.

"You could have had it all," Lucifer said, coming to a halt at the end of the hallway. "You could have been my king, and yet… you betrayed me. Twice, even."

"I didn't mean—"

"But now, instead of enjoying your eternity in Hell, I have to make you suffer, just like the rest of them."

"Lucie—"

"I think I'll put you in the pit," she spat, yanking him forward. "Come along, pet, let me show you something splendidly horrible."

He crawled over the hot coals following after her, groaning.

Lucifer laughed, her cackle echoing down the hallway and into the dark.

Io

Spiritus Vallem

The sun shimmers in through the windows, warming Io's face. She stands at the window, looking outside. How fitting that this is where she had ended up when her soul had left her body.

It's over, she thinks to herself with a smile. *I've done it.*

Behind her, fabric rustles. Someone is standing in the doorway. She doesn't take her eyes away from the window, looking out over the vivid yellow flowers that are blooming in the fields.

It's over, she thinks again. *I can rest. I can stay here.*

In the window she sees her mother's reflection. She smiles, glad that her mother has come to greet her. She turns from the window.

"I was wrong," Chrezabel whispers, standing in the doorway. She looks to Io, a defeated, hollow look in her lavender eyes.

Io looks back to her, in horror.

"Io," she whispers. "I was wrong."

End.